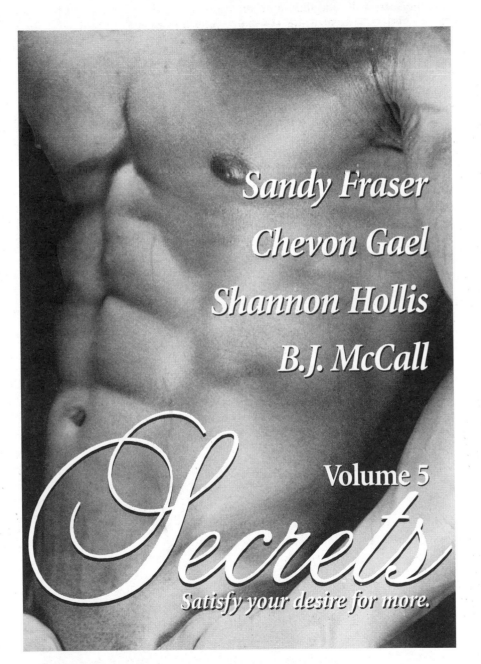

Sandy Fraser

Chevon Gael

Shannon Hollis

B.J. McCall

Volume 5

Secrets

Satisfy your desire for more.

SECRETS Volume 5
This is an original publication of Red Sage Publishing and each individual story herein has never before appeared in print. These stories are a collection of fiction and any similarity to actual persons or events is purely coincidental.

Red Sage Publishing, Inc.
P.O. Box 4844
Seminole, FL 33775
727-391-3847
www.redsagepub.com

SECRETS Volume 5
A Red Sage Publising book
All Rights Reserved/December 1999
Second Printing, 2001; Third Printing, 2002; Fourth Printing, 2003
Copyright © 1999–2003 by Red Sage Publishing, Inc.

ISBN 0-9648942-5-4

Printed in the U.S.A.

Cover design, layout and book typesetting by:

Quill & Mouse Studios, Inc.
2165 Sunnydale Boulevard, Suite E
Clearwater, FL 33765
www.quillandmouse.com

Contents

Alias Smith
and Jones

❧⟡❧

by B.J. McCall

To My Reader:
A chance meeting. A handsome executive. Anything is possible.

Chapter 1

Smith Wilding scanned the crowded airport bar. Thanks to a sudden snow-storm, his morning flight to New Orleans had been delayed. Odds were he'd be stuck for the rest of the afternoon, perhaps the night. His gaze caught and held on a shapely pair of nylon-clad legs. Ever-so-slowly he assessed the woman sitting alone at one of several tables lining the floor-to-ceiling windows. The runways were barely discernable, and the woman's attention remained on the swirling snow. Her conservative gray suit and simple hairstyle told him she, like the hordes of business-class travelers mingling around the gates and concourse, had been caught off-guard by the fierce storm.

Thankfully all the barstools and tables were occupied. Every single seat, except one. Focusing his gaze on the woman's long legs, he headed for the empty chair which just happened to be the molded plastic seat at her table.

"Excuse me," he began. "I could use a drink. Do you mind?"

She gave him a brief nod, then turned her attention back to the storm. Although her face wasn't knock-down gorgeous, something about her intrigued him. Per-haps her eyes. Large, slightly tilted, dark brown and seductive. Bedroom eyes.

"It looks like we have a bit of a wait," she said, without looking at him.

He'd barely taken his seat when a barmaid hustled over. He noted the empty glasses on the table, ordered a martini for himself and another white wine.

"How'd you do that?" she asked, swiveling around in her chair. Her knee bumped into his. "I had to wait so long, I ordered two. That waitress hasn't been within ten feet in the last hour."

"Should I call her back?"

After a long assessing stare, she grinned. "No, I have a feeling she'll be around. Come here often?"

"Only when there's a blizzard."

She pushed aside the two wineglasses. "Lucky me."

"I'm Smith —"

The grin disappeared. "Sure you are. I guess that makes me Jones." Abruptly she turned her attention back to the falling snow.

Surprised by her rudeness, Smith considered returning to the first-class lounge and the complaining gaggle of elderly couples who'd driven him to the public bar. "Would you rather I left?"

Those big brown eyes locked with his just as the waitress delivered their drinks. While the girl took her time removing the empty glasses and crumpled cocktail napkins, Smith enjoyed the amused expression on his new companion's face. The fine lines about her eyes told him she had recently slipped into her thirties. She wore little make-up, giving her a fresh, no-nonsense look he liked. Her mouth bordered on seductive, but her stubborn chin guaranteed she wasn't easily impressed or conquered.

Swinging her long legs around, her skirt slid several delightful inches up her thighs before she stood. "You stay put... Smith. I need to brave the line at the ladies room."

Sexy and bossy.

As she turned and marched through the crowd, Smith decided legs like hers made up for bad manners and assertiveness training. Briefcases and garment bags were pulled out of her path by admiring men in three-piece suits. Executive management written all over her, she acknowledged their efforts with a slight nod rather than a smile.

Retrieving his cell phone from his brief case, Smith called his friend at the airport management office. Verifying the worsening storm would close down the airport for hours, he disconnected and called a nearby hotel. Since his grandfather's corporation had recently acquired the hotel chain, obtaining the best suite took less than a minute. Looking around the bar, he felt sorry for the mass of travelers, the majority of whom would spend the night on the uncomfortable chairs and floors of O'Hare International.

But not him, and hopefully not the bossy number in the gray suit.

A few minutes later, overcoats, briefcases and carry-on luggage parted like the Red Sea as she returned. Tall, with legs that never ended.

Smith wanted to see every fabulous inch of her.

His grandfather would be perturbed by his delay, but Smith had about as much control over the weather as he had of his imagination. Just the thought of those long legs wrapped around his waist made him welcome the tempest slamming the Chicago area.

Meredith Collier knew that look. She'd seen it before. On *Smith* it wasn't blatantly horny, just casually sexy. Sexy as hell if the truth be told. That waitress was nobody's fool. She'd spotted the knock-out build beneath his expensive tailored suit, and the Rolex complimenting his manicured, but masculine, hands. Never mind his mesmerizing, green-flecked, hazel eyes and classy looks that literally shouted good breeding. While everyone else looked tired and rumpled, each mahogany-colored hair on his head lay perfectly in place.

Smith was no chump decked out in a good suit.

She'd been interested, a little, until he tried that old trick. When he'd introduced himself as Smith she'd looked for the telltale imprint of a wedding ring. Seeing none, she classified him as engaged. Only a fool would let a guy as attractive as Smith run around without a ring.

When women ruled the world, and that day would come, marital status would be planted in a chip. She smiled at the thought of simply scanning a prospective lover. She'd like to scan Smith.

At least he was good for fast waitress service and holding her chair for a much needed visit to the ladies room.

Thanking him as she slid into the molded plastic seat, she turned her attention once more to the snow.

"You must not be from Chicago."

"Why's that?" she asked without looking at him.

"When you grow up around here, you lose that look of wonder by the time you're eight."

"It doesn't snow in San Francisco."

"Lucky you. What's your business in Chicago?"

She liked his voice. "Training conference."

"What do you train?"

Hearing the smile in his question, she swallowed the quip on her tongue and glanced at him. "Bank employees. Everything from how to answer the phone to regulatory requirements."

"Sounds interesting."

"No it doesn't." She turned and leveled a *don't fuck with me* look across the table. "What do you want, Smith?"

"Your undivided attention would be a good start."

Meredith picked up her wine. She knew she should keep her attention on the swirling snow and ignore this handsome stranger, but she couldn't resist his challenge. As his interested gaze slid over her face, the thousand facets of color in his eyes changed. Colors ranging from green to gray to light brown. All of a sudden she felt warm. She leaned forward. Her lips parted. His hand moved. Heart suddenly pounding, she anticipated his fingertips caressing her cheek and skating across her lower lip. That old tingle began.

"A good start? Is there more?" She missed being touched, missed the feel of a man's arms. How long had it been? A while. Months since her fiancé had confessed his infidelity then crushed her with the revelation that he'd wanted to marry someone else.

Smith's eyes gleamed in anticipation, as if it were a given she'd soon be in his arms, his bed.

To hell with men. She leaned back in her chair and stared at the snow.

An odd silence stretched between them. She thought about apologizing then dismissed the idea. She owed Smith nothing.

"Would you like a cup of coffee?"

She nodded. He barely lifted his hand and the waitress was at their table asking in her breathy voice what she could do for him.

Turning from the snow, Meredith met his gaze. It was damn hard to ignore him. "I'm sorry. It's been a long day."

"And a longer night. All incoming flights have been diverted to other airports until morning."

"And every hotel is booked by now."

"Not necessarily."

"What's up your sleeve, Smith?'

"I can get you a room —"

"Your room, right?"

"Your own room, but I'd like you to have dinner with me."

"What else?"

"That's up to you, Jones."

"You're good."

He said nothing, but his silence told her he hadn't missed the double meaning of her words. He probably was very good.

When the waitress reappeared with two cups of coffee, Meredith considered

Smith's offer. As soon as the waitress walked away, she asked, "You don't own the hotel do you?"

"Not exactly."

She picked up her cup. The coffee smelled fresh. She wondered if the waitress had made a new pot just for this man. "How exactly?"

"My grandparents are the major stockholders."

"My own room? My own key?"

Smith nodded, but the delicious grin on his face made her suspicious. She sipped her coffee. "Just dinner? In the dining room?"

He lifted his cup and eyed her through the rising steam. "If you insist, but my suite has a dining room. You can watch the snow."

"Why me? I'd think our waitress would jump at the chance."

"Perhaps, but I like a challenge."

As he sipped his coffee, she wondered if he kissed as good as he looked. "Tired of sweet young things falling at your feet?"

He looked straight into her eyes. "You excite me, Jones. I'd like to spend the evening with you."

"The *evening*?"

"What happens after dinner is entirely up to you."

Meredith knew exactly what she wanted for dessert, but it wasn't her style to gush. "I'm supposed to be flattered?"

"Just offering an alternative to sleeping in a chair."

"What... what makes you think I'm interested?"

"If you weren't, you would have told me to get lost by now. And your voice wouldn't have softened and your eyes —"

"My voice did not change," Meredith said despite the fact she knew it had. This entire episode shrieked *fantasy*. Trapped in a blinding snowstorm with a sexy stranger. No commitments. No heartache. Just pleasure.

"What do I have to do to convince you? Shall we exchange ID's?"

"No," she blurted out.

His eyes narrowed. "You don't have a husband do you?"

She shook her head.

"Shall we start again. I'm —"

"No names." Meredith leaned forward and crooked her finger. A half-smile curled his lips as he matched her stance, his face mere inches from hers. Deliberately, she dropped her voice into a husky whisper. "I like the mystery."

He did the same. "Don't tell me I just walked into some wild female fantasy?"

"It's a possibility."

"Shall we go?"

"You'll never get a cab."

He glanced at his Rolex. "A car is picking us up in fifteen minutes."

As soon as he stood, the waitress hustled over. He handed the girl a fifty and told her to keep the change. Beneath the warmth of his gaze, Meredith rose. When she picked up her coat, he plucked it out of her hand and held it for her.

He shouldered her garment bag, then picked up his briefcase and coat. Facing her, he smiled. A smile so genuine, she matched his easy stride out of the bar and down the length of the concourse.

Once inside the car and sitting beside *Smith*, Meredith reconsidered her decision. It was foolish to go to a hotel with a stranger. He could be a sexual deviant or worse.

Despite her usually cautious nature, Meredith trusted Smith. Maybe it was just his direct approach or the way he looked at her with snowflakes dusting his eyelashes, but for once she wanted to act out one of her fantasies.

Then she'd fly home and forget all about him.

At least he's first class, she thought as the bellhop opened the door to a spectacular suite far larger than most homes. Her modest two-bedroom, one-bath house would almost fit into the living room. She glanced at the dining area. Her home would fit with several feet to spare. Crackling flames drew her to the fireplace. She crossed the marble foyer and the carpeted area between two plush sofas, down two steps into a conversation pit complete with thick carpet and soft pillows, to the circular fireplace. She turned and faced her host. The logs were fake, but she welcomed the heat licking her cold legs.

Smith directed the bellhop to deposit her items in a room to her left while he opened a pair of double doors to her right. Good to his word, she had her own room. Did he suspect she had absolutely no intention of sleeping in it?

After tipping the bellhop at the door, Smith removed his suit jacket, laid it across the back of one sofa and strolled toward her. "May I?"

Meredith turned toward the fire. Another kind of delicious heat struck her body as he slipped her coat off her shoulders. The image of him undressing her flooded her mind. Heat coiled low in her belly.

"Jones?"

He stepped close behind her. So close she could feel the warmth of his body. His hand settled on her upper arm. His breath feathered the ribbon of skin between her hair and her collar. "You must be chilled to the bone. If you'd like a hot bath...."

As she turned to face him, her arm brushed his chest. The brief contact made her want to touch the rest of him. Instead, she nodded.

He began to step away, then paused. Her coat slid to the carpet as he grasped her waist and tugged her close. His mouth closed over hers and she welcomed the sweet warmth of his lips, relished the pressure of his body against hers. Her senses sparked. Needing, seeking the contact, she clung to him.

He broke the kiss and buried his face in her hair. "I've been wanting to do that since I first laid eyes on you."

When he pulled away, Meredith stifled a moan.

"Your bath?" Placing his hand on the small of her back he led her into the bedroom. Her pulse leaped at the muted watercolor hanging on the wall above the king-size bed. Two figures, locked in embrace, their legs entwined. Forcing her gaze from the painting, she skirted the bed and joined Smith at the bathroom door. A large round tub, big enough for two, was built into one corner and a glass shower stall stood beside it. Double sinks beneath a row of lights above the mirror. Several white rugs covered the marble floors.

"Satisfied?"

Not yet. "The room is beautiful. A definite improvement over the airport waiting area."

"Take your time."

As he closed the double doors, Meredith wished he'd kissed her again, acted on the consuming rush of desire flowing between them. Although she and *Smith* didn't know a thing about each other, she felt he wanted something special, something more than a few impassioned minutes.

Meredith definitely wanted more. She wanted to be touched, caressed, pampered.

Eager to be with Smith, she stripped off her clothes, and stepped in the shower. Welcoming the hot fingers of the spray on her breasts, belly and thighs, she thought of his hands, his lips, caressing, touching, easing the ache inside her. She cupped her breasts, kneading them in anticipation, relishing the surge of raw desire.

She definitely needed Smith.

Smith opened a bottle of champagne, his thoughts lingering on Jones's response to his kiss. Even now he could feel the sweet pressure of her firm breasts, her inviting mouth. She'd been an exquisite temptation, but Smith had learned long ago that quick, heated exchanges were only a momentary relief. He preferred the sated feeling after a long night of lovemaking, savored the complete exploration of a sensual partner. These days only a fool would jump into bed with every willing female. Unlike the waitress, Jones was cautious. She'd choose her lovers carefully. And after she'd taken what she wanted, she'd kiss them goodbye and never look back.

But she'd leave you satisfied.

How the hell he knew that, he wasn't sure. But he had good instincts and he'd learned long ago to follow them. He wasn't going to regret a night in Jones's arms.

He wondered what she liked. Would she cry out when she came? Would she want him to go down on her? Smith intended to explore, in detail, every pink fold until she was wet, until he tasted her heat. The thought alone made him hard.

When he heard her bedroom door open several minutes later, Smith turned. A soft, dove gray sweater and short black skirt hugged her curves. As she approached, his gaze lingered on the smile teasing the corners of her full mouth, then slid to the gentle sway of her breasts. His breath caught at the sexy motion of her thighs brushing one another as she slowly placed one long leg before the other. His gaze slid lower, hugging the tempting curves of her knees, her calves, lingering at the sight of her bare feet. The image of her naked slammed into him. He looked into her exotic eyes and hoped she'd walk right into his arms and demand he please her now, on the rug, before the fire.

Instead she took the glass of champagne from his hand and sipped. She glanced at his obvious erection, licked her red lips. "I'd like to watch the snow."

Smith strolled over to a hidden panel, opened the small door and punched a series of buttons. The lights dimmed, and to the left of the fireplace, automatic drapes silently slid apart. Outside snow swirled before the floor-to-ceiling, double-paned glass.

She stood, a delicate silhouette before the immense window, waiting, making his blood thunder.

Meredith sighed when his arm wrapped about her middle. Without speaking he stood behind her. She offered him a sip of champagne. Together they finished the glass.

His breath caressed her cheek, his lips brushed her neck. At the touch of his tongue to her skin, the crystal flute slipped from her fingers. In a heartbeat she was in his arms, her breasts crushed to his chest, his lips pressed to hers.

Rocking, one against the other, they strained against the cloth barriers separating them. He clutched at her short skirt, bunching the soft material between his fingers until her buttocks were exposed. Like firebrands, his fingers slid beneath the narrow ribbon of her thong panties. She gasped, breaking their ardent kiss, as his warm fingers slid forward tantalizing the skin along the strip of black lace, down the crease of her thigh, between her legs.

Smith was amazed how tightly she held his fingers. How wet she was. Stretched to the limit, his erection throbbed painfully. He needed her wetness.

Slowly he eased his fingers from her tight sheath and touched her partially open mouth. He nearly came when she suckled gently on his fingers. Blood pounding in his veins, he unzipped her skirt and slipped it over her hips, then slowly removed her sweater. Except for the scraps of black lace barely covering her breasts and thatch of curls, her skin gleamed, soft and delicate.

Her breath labored as much as his own. She unclasped her bra, and her reflection caught his eye. An image, provocative and bordering on the perverse, popped into his head. Long-legged with high, firm breasts, flat belly and slim hips, Jones had the build to make it work.

Taking her about the waist, he turned Jones toward the glass. As he tore off his clothes, he focused on the lacy thong between her buttocks and grinned. Grasping her breasts from behind, he watched her face as he fondled her breasts. As her nipples peaked beneath his fingertips, her lips parted. Their gazes locked and held as she leaned against him. Her expression, daring and wanton, shot pure lust to the tip of his penis. When she shifted her legs in readiness, he released her breasts, then retrieved a foil packet from his pants.

Condom in place, he slid his hard cock beneath her slim buttocks. Splaying his hand over her belly, he lifted her slightly and guided the tip of his penis under the thong and between her slick folds. Then he leaned forward pushing her flush against the glass.

Trapped between his hard body and the smooth window, between fire and ice, Meredith's breath caught as he eased his length deeper inside her. Their position demanded his control. His exquisite progress heightening her awareness of his size, his length, her tightness. Each movement gentle, yet intense. Each slow thrust pressed her sex, her nipples firmly to the glass, forming a triangle of sensation. He rotated his hips, each measured penetration searing her clit to the glass, bringing forth a unique friction, a cool burn.

Driving her wild.

Hot skin. Cold glass. Testing the boundaries of sensation.

His feverish skin sealed to hers, making her aware of his straining muscles, his strength. His breath came in hot gasps, grazing her neck, inciting a thousand fiery ripples to race along her skin. He stroked the sides of her breasts; she moaned and strained against the slick glass. Aching for release, she cried out. Her drenched sex burned, the sweet pressure increasing as his slow, intense thrusts edged her closer to climax. He nipped her shoulder, then laved his own sweat from her skin, the slow, sensual strokes sending her over the edge.

Chapter 2

"That was...,"

"Amazing?" Smith asked through labored breaths.

"That too," Meredith admitted, breathing rather heavily herself.

He took a tentative step back. Free of the glass, she splayed her hands against the window and leaned her torso forward. Beyond the window, the heavy curtain of snow created a surreal mirror. It was if the world had gone white and nothing existed but this room. This moment. This man.

She looked at Smith's shadowed reflection, savored the strained ecstasy on his face as he pushed his solid erection deeper within her. Secured about the waist by his strong fingers and thumbs, Meredith slid her hands lower, balancing her weight against the glass, inviting his penetration. His strokes, slow and shallow at first, soon turned to deep, pleasing thrusts.

She needed him. At this moment, she needed him more than anything else.

The need, mutual, almost desperate, dampened their skin with moist heat. Her knees trembled from the sheer force of their mating. Together they peaked, his eager thrusts and her taking of them stilling into one amazing moment of shared bliss.

He held her until they both regained their senses, then stepped back, forcing their flushed bodies to separate. Needing the warmth of his arms, Meredith turned.

He pulled her tight and held her.

He was all muscle. Hard and masculine. Her breasts, her belly, even her thighs felt pliant and warm. She hugged him, crushing her breasts flat against his chest and burying her face in the hollow of his neck.

Afterglow. She hadn't believed it existed until now.

A bell chimed softly, breaking the spell. Smith grasped her hand and headed toward his bedroom. The front door opened as he pulled her inside and shut the door. Once again she was crushed to his sweat-dampened chest. "I ordered dinner," he said, sliding his hand through her hair. "How about a quick shower, a meal, then something delicious for dessert?"

Once inside his bathroom, Smith opened the shower door. Meredith slipped out of her thong and stepped inside the generously proportioned stall. Adjusting the temperature, she stood beneath the spray. The hot water pummeled her belly and thighs. Her heart, her womb still thrummed from Smith's lovemaking.

She turned. He stepped into the stall. His gaze studied her every curve and hollow, reminding her of a boy before a candy store. But Smith was no boy. His wide shoulders, flat stomach and muscled legs, every masculine inch of him, perfection.

Without speaking he pulled her to him and kissed her. For several minutes they stood beneath the spray, content in one another's embrace, exploring each other with their lips and tongues as if this was their first kiss, so gentle and sweet they could be fully dressed standing in a public place.

When the kiss ended, Smith continued to hold her. "I like you, Jones."

"I like you, Smith. I like you a lot."

His hands slid from her back, then he reached around her to turn off the water. His gaze fastened on her breasts, and her nipples contracted beneath his sensual stare.

He reached out and grazed each taut peak with his forefinger. "I like your nipples," he said in a slightly husky voice. "They're big and inviting."

Although his words pleased her, Meredith sensed Smith didn't expect a thank you or an exchange of compliments. He guided her out of the stall, then grabbed two towels and handed her one.

She dried off quickly, then slipped into a white terry cloth robe provided by the hotel. As she tied the sash, she glanced at Smith. He stood before the mirror, a towel draped about his trim waist, fingercombing his short hair.

When he walked up behind her, their gazes met in the mirror. His smile was sexy. Like her, she knew he was thinking of how they'd watched each other's reflections in the window as they'd made love. He leaned to his right and flipped a switch. A bank of heat lamps bathed the bathroom in a golden glow.

Smith turned Jones around, took her by the waist and set her bottom down on the marble counter. She wrapped her legs around his waist and her arms about his neck. He kissed her. Her lips moved beneath his, hungry and demanding. She was making him hard again. Her demands dissolved into soft touches of tongue and lips. "What's for dinner?"

"I'll check." Reluctantly he pulled away from her embrace. When her sultry gaze slid to his erection, obvious beneath the damp towel, his cock jerked.

As he walked out of the bathroom, Smith thought about the hours until morning. Despite the fact he'd just had the best orgasm he could remember, he wanted her. If any woman could keep him going all night, Jones could.

Smith opened the bedroom door, glanced about to make sure the hotel staff had set the table and left, then strolled into the dining area. He lifted a silver plate cover. A small billow of steam assured him their dinners were still hot. Smiling he replaced the cover. Did Jones realize she was dessert? Still grinning, he headed back to the bedroom, dropped the damp towel and retrieved a robe from the closet.

He pulled the sash tight as he entered the bathroom. Before him Jones lay across the marble counter, robe open, with knees bent and feet wide apart. She glowed, golden and alluring, marvelous and naked, beneath the lamps.

Mesmerized he stared at the enticing slit between her legs. Shades of rose and pink, soft and inviting, lay nestled in a dark thatch of curls. Sensual and sexy, she was obviously comfortable with her nudity.

Who was she, really?

Come morning, Smith intended to end the mystery. After all, San Francisco was only a plane ride away.

Meredith propped herself on her elbows and looked through her legs at Smith. She knew he'd been staring at her crotch. She'd sensed his slow perusal while she bathed beneath the hot lamps. Unfortunately he'd wrapped a thick robe about himself making it impossible for her to judge his physical reaction. He certainly looked sexy. The casual interest he'd displayed at the airport was long gone....

Pushing herself up to a sitting position, she swung her legs around and slid off the marble counter. Wrapped snugly in her robe, she walked up to Smith, kissed him briefly, then headed for the dining room.

Meredith licked her lips. The food was delicious, the thin-sliced beef cooked to perfection, but her interest focused on the man sitting across from her. His hands moved with grace and deliberation. Masculine hands with deft, pleasing fingers. She shifted in her chair and crossed her legs. When Smith lifted his gaze, she laid down her fork and reached for her wineglass.

His hand closed over hers. Exquisite sensations ran along her arm as his thumb caressed her palm. Meredith's heart pounded. Smith had a way of touching her, looking at her. She recalled how he'd held her after his provocative style of lovemaking. His kisses, ranging from lusty plundering to sweet exploration, were soul satisfying. He made her feel wanted, appreciated, utterly desirable. Candle-light and romance danced in his eyes.

This is how love is suppose to feel. Tender and aching. Quiet and raging.

But Smith didn't love her. He'd only been blessed with the ability to make her want to pretend for a few, short, potent hours.

Later, as they lay naked in each other's arms before the fireplace, Smith asked, "You're not... is there anyone?"

Although he'd spoken softly, the quiet enchantment had been broken. Thinking briefly of her ex-fiancé, Meredith pulled away.

"Don't." Smith reached out and took her hand. "I'd like to know your heart isn't elsewhere."

The firelight played on Smith's handsome face, obscuring his eyes. Part of her wanted to embrace his words, but logic told her, come morning, she'd just be a memory. A one-night stand with a stranger. A diversion from the storm. In six months, would he even remember her at all?

"There's no one waiting for me," she answered truthfully.

He rose to his knees and leaned forward, pushing her down on the padded bench surrounding the fireplace. "That's going to change."

She bit back words of protest as his mouth covered her breast and suckled her tender nipple. She grasped his torso with her thighs, urging him on. They'd made love after dinner and despite two glorious orgasms, she wanted him again. Wanted him so much. Too much.

His lips grazed her belly, sending tremors of delight along her skin. She arched her hips, and moaned when his mouth rested against her already pulsing center.

Honeyed and hot, Smith tasted her desire. She bucked wildly, thrusting her sex against his mouth. He flicked his tongue over her clit until it budded and Jones raised her hips high, demanding release. Closing his lips over her, he suckled, drawing on her needy clit. She tensed beneath his lips, her legs trembled as she came.

Smith eased his tongue between her quivering folds to taste the hot nectar of her climax.

Her thighs relaxed and Smith lapped one last time at her sweetness before she lowered her hips. She'd made him hard again. So hard all he could think about was being inside her, bringing her to climax again. But this time he wanted to watch her. He needed to see her face as she came.

Smith groaned as Jones straddled his thighs and accepted his sheathed length. Her gaze locked with his as she moved her hips in a wanton display of grace and desire. Riding astride, she took him, drawing him inside her, over and over, making him forget she'd brought him to a heart-stopping climax followed by near exhaustion a short hour or two earlier.

But this time the fire built slowly, fueled by her supple undulations. The provocative sway of her breasts, tipped with large, dusky nipples held him spellbound, kept him hard.

"Is there someone waiting for you?"

Her whispered question came from left field, hitting his sexually saturated brain like a hard blow to the temple. He hesitated. Let her words penetrate.

"No," he gasped as he regained his rhythm. "No one is waiting."

Already caught in his special fire, Meredith accepted, reveled in his passionate thrusts. When his lips closed over her breast and drew lustily at her nipple, she denied the sharp pain his hesitant answer had driven into her heart, acknowledged only her physical need of him.

Increasing the tempo of her hips, she rode him, challenged him to match her hunger. Thrusting her fingers into his hair, she pulled back his head, then kissed him.

A forceful kiss, devoid of love, savage and lust-filled.

She dug her fingers into his shoulders, driving her nails into his skin as she forced the hard length of him, deeper, pounding her sex against his.

He slapped her buttocks. The light stinging impact of his hands drove her wild.

From somewhere inside her womb, her climax wrenched itself free. Unlike anything she'd experienced before, Meredith welcomed its intensity, wresting every morsel of gratification from her flesh.

Finally she stilled.

Smith's chest heaved beneath her hands. Her own breath puffed in harsh gasps.

"Christ, I thought you were going to pull it off."

"You didn't like it?"

"I loved it. For a moment there, I thought I was having a damn heart attack. My chest still hurts."

"Next time I'll be gentle," she teased.

"Next time you're liable to kill me," he said, then quirked an eyebrow. "But I'll die happy."

Hours later, Meredith quietly left the hotel. Smith slept soundly in his bed, unaware the quickly moving storm had passed over Chicago and now pummeled the southeast. As her plane broke through the cloud cover over O'Hare, Meredith closed her eyes and wished she'd had the courage to leave her phone number. But as she'd looked at her sleeping lover, common sense had prevailed. The hesitancy in his answer had spoken volumes. She didn't need to deal with an unfaithful man. Once was enough.

No way in hell would she be the other woman.

Meredith steeled her heart. Smith had been a fantasy. A night of pleasure. No one fell in love with a one-night-stand.

Smith raced along the concourse, dodging travel-weary passengers and various pieces of luggage. He still couldn't believe she'd gone. Not after a night like that! He'd called the terminal for her flight gate number, dressed and headed straight for the airport. As he reached the gate, the digital lights behind the airline counter scrambled and a new flight number and destination appeared. Frustrated, Smith walked to the window. Jones's flight was already on the tarmac.

Didn't the damned woman realize he was more than a convenient layover? Hadn't his lovemaking convinced her he wanted her in his life?

Despite the crowd of people filling up the gate area, Smith leaned his forehead against the glass and wondered if he could obtain the passenger list from his buddy in airport management. But what if Jones didn't wish to be found? What if she was married? Or engaged?

Pulling away from the glass, Smith shook his head at the empty airplane bay. Deep inside he believed Jones had been truthful. She had no husband, no lover. She just didn't want him.

That was the hell of it. He wanted her and she was gone without so much as a goodbye.

Even if he had the passenger list, how many names would he have to chase down? The hell with the passenger list, he knew what she did for a living. How many banks could there be in San Francisco? Not enough to deter him. And when he found her... what then?

One thing was certain, he would accept the directorship on the board of West Coast Bank his grandmother had offered. As the bank's major stockholder, she was ready to step down and enjoy retirement. At seventy-five it was about time. And Smith needed a respite from his grandfather's escalating attempts at matchmaking.

Besides, West Coast's headquarters were in San Francisco and so was Jones.

Chapter 3

Meredith stared out her office window. Far below heavy rain pounded the narrow streets of San Francisco's Financial District. She touched the cold glass, with an odd sense of longing, of something missing. A feeling she couldn't ignore or deny. Strange after so many weeks to still hunger for Smith, still ache for his special touch. She'd expected to file him away, a wonderful memory, nothing more. Instead, she felt an intense sense of loss, as if she'd left part of herself abandoned, lost in that Chicago storm.

Her heart?

She slapped her open hand against the glass in sheer frustration. Smith wasn't going to appear like a knight in shining armor and tell her he loved her. Undoubtedly, her one-night-stand had returned to his wife or girlfriend. What had she expected when she'd asked him if anyone waited for him?

No one is waiting for me. She'd wanted to hear the words, but she'd known the moment he'd hesitated before he said them, he would lie. And he had. It was the nature of men. Smith was no different.

Better they'd separated as strangers.

At the familiar sound of Jim Murphy's voice, Meredith turned from the window and greeted the President and CEO of West Coast Bank. Jim stood at her open door, his pleasant bespectacled face beaming at her.

"There's someone I'd like you to meet," Jim said, as he stepped inside her modest office.

Meredith, used to Jim bringing around anyone from bank executives to neighbors, was about to speak, but when she saw Smith standing just outside her office the words caught in her throat. In a heartbeat she took in his polished good looks, the way his broad shoulders filled her doorway. Every hair in place, his gray suit, crisp white shirt and burgundy-patterned tie gave him a conservative look from head to toe. Except Meredith knew beneath those executive's clothes, Smith wasn't the least bit conservative. A vision of him, muscles straining, skin damp with sweat, caught in the throes of lovemaking, filled her heart.

His eyes narrowed. Meredith could swear he looked more angry than surprised, while she felt…. She couldn't move. Her lips were frozen. Her fingers twitched, and her heart thudded against her ribs. What on earth was he doing here? How had he found her? Had he been looking or was this some awful twist of fate?

"Meredith's in charge of training. Considering our recent merger with Great Pacific, we've kept her pretty busy," Jim began. He glanced at her. "Is something wrong?"

Meredith's brain refused to connect with her lips and tongue. She shook her head.

"Good to see you again, Miss Jones," Smith said, taking a step toward her and holding out his hand as if they'd never shared that passionate night. "Smith Wilding. We met in Chicago about two months ago. We shared… a table. It is Miss Jones?"

Smith? His name is Smith? Oh God, he wasn't lying. "Meredith Collier," she finally managed.

"Collier." He said the word slowly as if memorizing it. "My mistake. I could have sworn the name was Jones. Sorry, I'm usually very good with names."

"Smith's our new director," Jim offered. "For the next few months he'll be familiarizing himself with our operation."

I screwed a director. As if he'd read her mind, Smith gave her a priceless grin. She couldn't have heard Jim correctly. "Director?"

"Mrs. Wilding has decided to retire. Smith will be taking her place on the board. I have to tell you," Jim said, turning to Smith. "I'll miss your grandmother."

Wilding? Wilding! The bank's major stockholder Wilding? Oh my God.

Wondering why the corporate gods hated her, Meredith forced a smile and a grip on her tangled emotions.

"My grandmother loves this city and West Coast is her pride and joy," Smith said. Meredith resented his poise and ease. As if the two of them had shared nothing more than a table. "Once I've settled in the family apartment, I'm sure she'll visit."

Apartment? "You're moving to San Francisco?"

Before Smith could answer, Jim Murphy's secretary interrupted the conversation. When Jim excused himself to take a phone call, Smith's gaze focused on her, pinning her to the spot. "If Miss Collier doesn't mind, I'll wait for you here."

After Jim had hurried out of room, followed by his secretary, Smith asked, "Does my moving to San Francisco bother you, Jones?"

Unsure of the play of emotions on her face, Smith waited. Murphy had introduced him to over a dozen employees. His foolish heart banging against his ribcage, he'd followed Jim from office to office. Meredith Collier, he'd repeated the name dozens of times thinking of Jones, the woman he knew so intimately. The woman he loved. After dozens of calls pretending to be an attendee of the Chicago conference looking for a fellow trainer whose name he'd forgotten, Smith had found her right in his own backyard. He'd thought about calling, but he wanted to see her face, needed to see her reaction.

She'd plagued his thoughts, his dreams. The moment he'd stepped into her office, he'd wanted to sweep her into his arms just to assure himself she was real. Then he'd wanted to shake her and ask why the hell she'd walked out on him. Instead, he'd managed to keep his emotions in check and explain the dumbfounded look on her face. Obviously she hadn't expected to see him again.

Cold steel right to the heart.

He'd been fooling himself. In his dreams he'd seen Jones rushing into his arms. But Meredith Collier hadn't moved a muscle. Not so much as a polite smile.

"Smith. You didn't just want a one night stand?"

"It's not my habit to disappear at dawn."

"It seemed less complicated that way."

"For whom?" Smith waited, but she didn't answer. Except for the hairstyle, and the business suit, Meredith Collier looked nothing like the assured woman he'd met in Chicago. His sudden intrusion into her real life obviously made her uncomfortable. Even her breath came in ragged little puffs. Was Jones just some fantasy, a personality she assumed while having assignations with strangers? The thought he was merely one of many slammed into his ego with the force of a good left hook.

Could he have read her so wrong? So damn wrong he'd changed his whole life on an illusion?

"No one here knows... I haven't told anyone about... about you. I don't intend to."

There, she'd let him off the hook. They could pretend they'd had a momentary chance meeting in an airport bar. Maybe for him that was exactly what it was.

His lips twitched, a half smile teased the corners of his mouth, but his eyes held no laughter. He stepped forward, his stride eating the short distance between them. Then he touched her. His thumb traced the line of her jaw, his fingers slid along the contour of her neck as his warm palm came to rest against the telltale pulse drumming in her throat. "Just our dirty little secret, right, Jones?"

"If I'd known who you were —"

"You didn't want to know." His voice had dropped to a husky whisper bringing forth all sorts of memories. Wild, wanton memories. "When I was inside you, loving you, you still didn't want to know."

Her pulse leaped. Blood pounded in her veins, throbbing eagerly against his palm as their gazes locked, then heated. How many times in Chicago had he looked at her like this; wanting, demanding, challenging her to climax once again? Her lips parted as his fingers slid into her hair. All she could think of was being in his arms, feeling him inside her again.

Jim Murphy's hearty laughter, booming from the hallway, dropped an invisible curtain between them. A rush of cool air touched her skin as his hand dropped away. She barely heard his polite goodbye as he walked out of her office.

Until recently, Meredith had loved coming to work. Over the years she'd adopted a routine of purchasing a morning coffee before joining her co-workers for the slow elevator ride to the fifth floor offices. Now, she nodded politely as Smith joined the group crowding the elevator. His hazel eyes barely made contact with hers as he divided his attention equally among the bank's employees, especially the females. He treated her as if they were passing acquaintances, easily dismissing the events in Chicago. How long had it been? How many weeks since....

Only nine weeks. Nine torturous weeks.

If only it had been a table they shared that night, and not a hotel room, she wouldn't be having such annoying dreams. Images of Smith came in the night, reminding, teasing her. Even now her breasts tingled.

She sipped her latte. No more decaf since Smith had shown his handsome face at West Coast. Last night she'd tossed and turned until the sheets and blankets were twisted and tangled. If only he'd kissed her that day in her office. Surely, her memory of the night in his arms was all out of proportion to reality. Over the weeks she'd built it up, made the fantasy more special than the reality. If he'd kissed her, the spell would have been broken and she'd be free of this night fever, free of the erotic images and thoughts. She couldn't concentrate on the job. She couldn't sleep.

Somehow she had to rid herself of Smith. Dismiss this fascinating male. Forget his touch, his voice. Deny her own physical reactions.

As she stepped into the elevator Meredith knew the corporate gods had chosen to punish her. Smith's spicy cologne filled her nostrils. When she turned to face the doors, he stood in front of her. Unsmiling, but polite. She hated the way he said Miss Collier he might as well have said *Miss Liar*. The effect was the same.

A flippant remark came to her lips, but the presence of co-workers restrained her tongue until he turned and blocked her view. When several employees crammed into the already crowded elevator, Meredith moved into the corner. Smith followed.

When he deliberately wedged her into a small triangle of space, Meredith reached up and cupped one firm buttock. What possessed her, she didn't know. But once she touched him, she couldn't stop. Beneath her exploring fingers, the muscles of his buns and thighs tensed. Her actions were foolish and risky. If anyone noticed.... But everyone's attention was focused on the senior accountant and the joke he was telling.

As the elevator stopped on the third floor, she pinched Smith, hard. When several employees exited, Smith shifted along with the remaining riders, but didn't so much as glance in her direction. At the fifth floor, everyone stepped out, except for Smith. Before Meredith could follow her co-workers, Smith placed his finger on the open door button.

"I requested a tour of several of our branch offices. Jim suggested you as my guide. I'll pick you up at ten."

After what she'd just done, how could she spend the day with him? She'd pinched a director on the ass! What had gotten into her? Meredith backed out of the elevator. "I have several reports —"

"The reports can wait. I can't."

As the doors slid together, Smith winked. For several heartbeats, Meredith stared at the closed doors, then hurried to her office. What couldn't he wait for?

She pushed aside the thought that he wanted her. What had happened in Chicago couldn't happen here. That night they'd been just a man and a woman caught in a storm. No identities, no job titles, no connection other than a short-term physical bond. Now, everything had changed.

Smith practically owned the bank. While she held a position and title she'd worked damn hard for, there were several rungs left on West Coast's corporate ladder. With a remark from him, her career could climb or plummet. Meredith swore as the buttons on her telephone lit up. No man, not even a rich, powerful and too-handsome-for-his-own-good one would derail her from her long-term objectives by a short detour in his bed.

Even if he was extraordinary between the sheets.

"It's going to rain."

Undeterred by her sharp demeanor, Smith gave her a calm, but determined look. She wasn't going to avoid or ignore him. Not today. "I have a coat and umbrella in the car."

When she stalked past him without a word, he held back a smile. Bossy Miss Jones was back. Didn't she realize how much he loved a challenge, how hard it had been to wait for her to react after that first day?

He'd come so close to kissing her that day in her office. And she'd wanted him to kiss her. In that short moment he knew she'd yearned for him as much as he ached for her. When he'd touched her, he'd felt her pulse leap. And her eyes. He'd seen that look before. He needed to see it again.

He should have asked her to dinner, while her blood still smoldered. Instead, he'd relished his foolish revenge, and let her cool off. Then she'd avoided him. He'd waited, hoped for a sign of desire, a welcoming signal. Something to tell him she needed him. Instead, she ignored him. Days turned into two weeks.

When his nightsweats had became unbearable, and his revenge unrewarded, he'd arranged to get her away from the bank where she couldn't dismiss him. Then she'd touched him, fondled him, deliberately drove him wild in a situation where he was unable to respond. But he'd gotten the message loud and clear.

She still wanted him.

He'd even welcomed her taunting pinch.

What a charmer. Meredith leaned against the headrest. She was tired. Tired of tellers, service representatives, and branch managers oohing and ahhing over Smith. Not for one second would she admit that jealousy had anything to do with her discomfort. How could she be jealous?

"How far to the Golden Gate?"

"About five miles," she answered without looking at him. She glanced at her wristwatch. "Once we cross the bridge, it will only take us about half-an-hour to return to the office."

"We're not going back. I want to see the ocean and feel something besides cement beneath my feet."

What did he have in mind? An image of Smith, his shirt, wet, clinging to his chest and arms, pulling her down to join him on a rainsoaked beach, filled her thoughts. Meredith blinked, banishing the image. The intimacy of sitting beside him within the vehicle, so close she could inhale his scent, must be getting to her. "We'll be late."

"No one expects us."

"People will talk."

"About what?"

"It's still raining." Knowing her excuses were exactly that, excuses, Meredith peeked at Smith. He was smiling. An all-knowing smile that told her he knew she wanted to avoid being alone with him.

"What's the matter, Jones? I thought you liked my company. Or is your attention limited to a few lusty hours?"

"Things have changed."

"I've noticed."

"I don't sleep with my bosses."

"I'm not your boss."

"I don't sleep with bank executives, co-workers, women, animals or married or entangled men!"

"You got me there."

But how? Did he mean executives or married? It was on the tip of her tongue to ask, but what difference did it make? He was still a director. Once you screwed around with the men at the top, you were tagged forever. No one lived down the reputation, no matter how good they were at the job.

When Smith took the last freeway exit before the Golden Gate, a perplexed

Meredith sat silent as the vehicle climbed the winding road toward the Marin headlands. On a good-weather day, winds blustered and whipped one's clothes, but no one sane would brave the grass-covered cliffs towering over the confluence of the Pacific Ocean and the San Francisco Bay during a stormy day.

Only a man crazy enough to take her, up against a plate glass window during a snowstorm.

Staring at the windshield, Meredith recalled the sensations she'd felt, pressed between Smith's muscled body and the glass. Again she experienced the heat, the sweet burn of ecstasy. Suddenly, deep inside she felt molten, liquid, game for any excursion Smith had in mind.

She glanced at him. A delicious light flickered in his eyes. "I hope you like the rain… as much as you like the snow."

His words, the timbre of his voice told her he intended to have her, to take her in the wind and rain and make her his once more. He braked the car at the termination of a dead-end road, shut off the engine and opened his door.

The wind whipped his hair as he stepped out of the vehicle and removed his raincoat, tie and suit jacket. The light rain spattered his face and shirt as he tossed his tie and jacket into the back seat. Leaning inside the car, he retrieved his raincoat, and brushed his lips to hers. Warm and inviting.

The fleeting touch held her breathless, expectant as he draped his coat over his shoulders and circled the car. He opened her door. When he held out his hand, she had her moment to refuse, to deny. But the moment passed and her hand slipped into his.

Pulling her into his arms, he backed her against the car, and pressed his chest, groin and thighs to hers. He drew his coat around them in a protective cocoon. Seduced by his heat, his strength, and commanding lips, Meredith forgot the wind and rain in the storm of Smith's kiss.

Wild and eager, their lips and tongues warred, each seeking consummation of simmering desire held in check far too long. Need beyond anything Meredith had thought possible consumed her. She held Smith about the waist, hugging him, demanding his heat, wanting his love.

And he wanted her. His rock hard erection pressed against her belly. His hips flexed, urging her legs apart. He wanted her to feel him.

Meredith welcomed his hands beneath her wool skirt, his eager exploration of her thighs and hips. Needing to reacquaint herself with the feel of his skin and the sculpted definition of his torso, Meredith grasped the tails of his shirt and pulled. Just as she touched the bare skin of his back, skimmed her fingers over his powerful lats, his fingers slid beneath the confines of her panty hose. Her flesh trembled as he cupped her buttocks and began an impatient massage.

He tore his lips from hers. Rainsoaked hair plastered to skull and forehead, he looked as he had when they'd stood in the shower that night in Chicago. But now his gaze held a questioning intensity, an edge. The air between them electrified. His hazel eyes burned with desire beneath spiked lashes. "I've missed you. There hasn't been a day I haven't thought of you. A night I haven't dreamed of you."

His words shot pleasure through her middle. He hadn't forgotten her. He'd thought about her, wanted her, missed her. As much as she missed him? His fingers pressed into the curve of her buttocks. She licked a raindrop from her upper lip. "You couldn't have told me inside the car?"

He pulled at her panty hose, baring her backside. "There's something about you and storms that get to me."

"We'll catch cold."

He slid his hand between her legs, bringing every nerve ending alive with the touch of his fingers. "You won't be cold, Jones."

She gasped as he touched her, teased her humming flesh, then slipped one finger inside. He was right, she wasn't the least bit cold. In fact, she felt hot. So hot and tight and wet, she might explode. His touch excited her needy flesh, making her welcome the cold rivulets running down her forehead, trickling along her neck.

Thrusting her hips against his hand, Meredith sought release. She moaned as he kissed the rain from her face, her neck. His heated breath chased away the cold as whispered murmurs of longing, burning need, touched her soul, set the impassioned pace of his hand, his fingers. Her moan rose into a cry as the tempo of his penetration increased. For countless nights, she'd wanted this man, needed his touch. Despite the rain and cold, she wanted to strip off her clothes and make love in the thick, wet grass alongside the deserted road.

Her climax came in sharp, urgent waves, leaving her breathless and wanting more.

"Come home with me. Let me love you. Tonight, all night." Smith felt the desperation in his voice. He couldn't recall ever begging a woman for sex. But this request wasn't about sex, it was about wanting and needing for the first time in his life. If she refused....

"I need you, Meredith," he admitted.

Her eyes were closed. Her lips slightly parted. He was a fool to break the moment, to give her the chance to cool off. She was here, hot and ready for him. He wanted her, but he wanted more than an eager climax and a friendly parting.

When her fingers brushed his erection, his breath caught.

She fumbled with his zipper, then reached inside his pants and freed his throbbing penis. "Can't wait. Now."

He dug in his pants pocket for the foil packet he'd brought in expectant preparation. Thank God.

Pushing her eager hand aside, he sheathed his throbbing erection, then lifted her against the car. When he encountered the nylon barrier, he nearly lost it. He yanked her panty hose down to her ankles, knocked off her shoe and tore the restricting fabric from her foot.

He grasped her naked buttocks, positioning her to receive him. Sliding easily into her hot, moist passage, he penetrated swift and wonderfully deep. And nearly came.

Her legs snaked around his hips, holding him firmly, demanding his vitality. Barely aware of the now pouring rain, Smith thrust his hips, driving his length over and over, willing her pleasure, needing her love, wanting her climax.

The fingernails digging into his back, the intense clamping around his cock, and the satisfied moan coming deep from her throat told him she'd peaked. Weeks of unfulfilled desires rushed upon them like a tidal wave.

He couldn't get enough of her.

Even as he broke a sweat, his shoulders and back unbelievably drenched, he remained deep inside her. He'd waited so long. An eternity.

With eyes still closed, he sought out her lips, kissing her gently, savoring their joining.

How he loved the feel of her.

The sound of an approaching vehicle snapped him back to reality. Had he completely lost his mind? They were screwing their brains out in broad daylight. He pulled out and pushed Jones's bare legs from around his waist. When he stepped back, he discovered his raincoat lying on the asphalt beneath his feet. As he scrambled to retrieve the drenched coat, he swore. Jones laughed as she hopped around trying to place a wet leg into her sodden panty hose. Finally, wisely, given the ever-increasing sound of the closing vehicle, she gave up and discarded the mangled nylons, stepped into her lost shoe and pulled her raincoat tight about her waist.

Shuddering in the cold wind, he pulled his raincoat over his wet shirt. Again he caught a muffled laugh as Jones opted for the car. As the passenger door slammed shut, he secured the belt of his coat. When he turned to face the vehicle, Smith's heart leaped. A four-wheeler bearing a national park insignia pulled close and braked.

Smith, knowing he looked thoroughly disheveled, stepped forward as the driver's window lowered silently. A young, clean-shaven park officer eyed him suspiciously. "Is everything okay, Sir?"

Smith reached up and pushed his wet hair off his forehead. "We got caught in a cloudburst. Should have taken the umbrella. But the view is worth a little wind and rain."

"Getting a little late," the officer remarked as he leaned forward.

Smith glanced over his shoulder. Sexy Miss Jones had once again disappeared. Prim Miss Collier, her wet hair miraculously styled back from her face, her lips an inviting pink from freshly applied lipstick, had stuck her head out the open window to smile warmly at the officer.

After a quick thank you to the park official, Smith groaned aloud with relief as the vehicle turned around and retreated down the road. Thank God he wasn't required to present his identification. He hadn't zipped his pants, much less removed the now uncomfortable condom. No wonder Jones had been laughing.

He spotted a trash can several yards away and began walking. When he heard his name, he turned. Jones was pointing to the ground where her pantyhose lay in a tangled pile. How had the park officer missed those?

After retrieving the wet nylons, Smith again headed toward the battered bin chained to a post. Muffled laughter followed his steps.

"It wasn't monogrammed?" Meredith asked, barely suppressing a giggle. She couldn't resist teasing him. He'd looked so damned embarrassed when she'd pointed out the pantyhose.

He tossed his wet coat in the backseat. "What?"

"The handkerchief you tossed."

"You're enjoying this." He turned to face her. "How would it have looked if we had gotten arrested for lewd and lascivious acts in public?"

"Is that a misdemeanor or a felony?"

"Must I remind you that it was *your* underwear I just tossed."

Meredith shifted in the seat letting him know she was more than aware she was bare beneath her skirt. His gaze dropped to her knees and his hand followed. Cold fingers dipped between her thighs sending powerful messages along her already sensitive flesh.

Although she knew they should rush back to the city and part ways forever, her flesh was indeed weak. And he knew it. His eyes danced as he leaned toward her. She gasped as his fingertips skimmed her damp curls, then teased her pulsing center. Unsated, their lips met, joined in a lusty mating.

"Come home with me," he whispered against her mouth. Her hips lifted, begging silently for more. "Let me do this right."

His invitation brought forth heated images. An evening in his arms. Another night of magic and passion.

"I want you. Naked. I want to touch your breasts, feel you against me."

Angled awkwardly, Smith pressed her back into the soft leather seat. His hips were moving, his body arching with each probe of hand, fingers and tongue. Meredith strained against his hand.

Wrenching back, Smith abruptly stopped. She opened her eyes and looked into his. His jaw was clenched. His breathing rapid.

"My house. Your house. A hotel. Anywhere, but in this damn car."

"What are we doing?"

"What we've both wanted to do since that first day in your office. It's been a lifetime since Chicago. At least for me it has."

"I can't have an affair with you, with a director."

"You already have." His hand caressed her center as if to remind her of the situation. She clamped her knees together in protest of the liberties she'd allowed, then scowled at him. His hand remained.

"I want a decision, Miss Collier."

"This is crazy. If we're discovered...."

He pushed his fingers deeper. "Where?"

"I think I should go home." Despite her reasonable words she wanted his hand right where it was. She wanted him. If they were at her house right now, she'd be tearing off her clothes, and his. Could she regain her senses during the short drive home?

"Your house." Slowly, he removed his hand causing her thighs to tremble as his fingers slid along her bare skin. "You don't have girlie stuff all over your bed do you?"

"Girlie stuff?"

"Stuffed animals, pillows, lace and bows."

Meredith thought about her flower-pattern comforter and buckled her seatbelt. "A ruffle here and there."

He brushed her lips briefly then started the car. "Any dogs or cats?"

"One cat. Fat and docile."

Smith turned the car around, then drove toward the freeway. "Does it sleep on the bed?"

"*It* is a male. Oliver sleeps on the bed."

"Not tonight."

"Great, another one that hates cats." Meredith realized her mistake as soon as he hit the brakes.

"Another one?"

Smith's hazel eyes narrowed. His knuckles stood out, stretched tight and white, around the wheel.

"Most men don't like cats."

"I like cats. I just don't like competition. Feline or otherwise."

He let the statement hang. She was tempted to let him think she had another lover, but there had been enough deception in their short, but intense relationship.

"I was engaged until last summer. He hated Oliver."

His hands relaxed. "No lovers since?"

"No."

"Have you seen him since the breakup?"

"No."

A smile teased the corners of Smith's face as he lifted his foot from the brake. The car eased forward, and he pressed on the gas. He felt as if a heavy burden had been lifted off his shoulders.

"No one until that night in Chicago?"

"No! No one else has —"

He wanted her to go on. He needed her to admit she cared about him. He had to know he wasn't just another guy, that he hadn't been wrong about her. "Has what?"

"Has fucked me senseless? Is that what you want to hear?"

His heart rate jumped. "Do I fuck you senseless, Jones?" he asked as he joined the flow of traffic heading south over the Golden Gate.

She was silent until they'd crossed the bridge. "You know you do," she whispered.

"Want me to do it again?"

She turned toward him and curled her legs up, forcing her short skirt high. "What do you think?"

He asked for directions to her home and switched lanes to follow the 19th Avenue signs. He drove for a while wondering what kind of fool would let her get away. Smith couldn't imagine a better sex partner. Jones hadn't lost any of her fire. He'd been ready to come in his pants again within minutes of a great climax. Lord, she made his blood run hot. He still had a hint of a hard-on as he accelerated onto the southbound freeway. At least he'd relaxed from the utterly painful stage to pleasant anticipation.

He couldn't wait to see her naked. Just thinking about her breasts, feeling her taut nipple in his mouth caused his cock to stretch. It was damn hard to concentrate on the traffic when she gave him new directions through the narrow streets of Pacifica. After he shut off the engine, he glanced at the small, but attractive house, one of many crowded on the high cliffs overlooking the ocean.

His steps were eager as they rushed to the front door.

She turned the lock. "I'm sure there's some rule against this."

A thick heavy mist had replaced the rain. Smith shivered. He wanted to strip off his wet clothes and get naked. "Against what?"

She stepped inside, and turned to face him. "Fucking me senseless. I'm sure there's a paragraph in the employee handbook."

"I've very good at breaking the rules," he said, daring her to send him away, praying that she wouldn't. When she stepped back to let him enter, he released a breath he hadn't realized he'd been holding.

Chapter 4

Meredith waited, near breathless as Smith's gaze was drawn to the focal point of the living room, a large window offering a panoramic ocean view. Would the expanse of glass remind him of Chicago? What would he think of the glass solarium and spa right off the master bedroom? How many fog-shrouded nights had she relaxed in the hot tub and thought of him, wanted him with her?

Thick clouds and heavy mist obscured the familiar, but still awesome view of the white-capped Pacific and rugged coastline. The last grayish light of dusk outlined the bookcase, tables, lamps and chairs, leaving one ghostly pool upon the white loveseat facing the window. Meredith reached for the lamp, but changed her mind as Smith brushed past her. The dimness reminded her of another room, another stormy night.

Familiar anticipation flared. Although they'd come together, her passion still simmered. How could it cool when his very presence held her spellbound, made her blood run hot?

At work, she could push aside her thoughts for short periods, force herself to briefly forget he was now a part of her day-to-day existence, if not part of her life. But today, after hours in close proximity, she'd been unable to reason, unable to resist.

He hadn't seduced her. She'd wanted him, needed him. Knowing she had nothing to gain and everything to lose, including her heart, she'd offered herself, willingly and passionately.

Even now she should send him packing. That might have been possible had he not walked into her home, and stood before the window. Had he not just spoken her nickname. Had not the yearning in his husky whisper been as urgent as her own.

Meredith glanced up. Silhouetted against the window, Smith waited for her. Once again the flames of passion licked her breasts and heated her center. Flames hot and wanting. As fiery, as exciting as the first time she'd been in his arms. Meredith moved toward him, dropping her damp coat heedlessly on the pale carpet. The rain had stopped, leaving a heavy mist, reminiscent of swirling snow, dancing beyond the glass.

Smith's eyes glowed. His deep breath, audible. Another reminder of another window, another night. A heat, wrought from countless dreams, from memory, coiled between her legs.

"This glass isn't as sturdy."

He shucked off his wet coat. "I'll be gentle."

She reached for buttons of his shirt. "I don't want you to be gentle. Not yet. I want it like it was."

His sodden, dress shirt dropped to the berber carpet, followed quickly by her wool skirt, her shoes. Her need flamed as he stripped off his wet clothes. Naked and splendid he reached for her. She welcomed his hands beneath her sweater, eagerly anticipating his touch as he worked the front clasp of her bra.

When he gathered her close, Meredith gasped. His nipples were hard beads beneath her palms, his skin icy. "You're freezing."

"I'm fine."

She took his hand and led him through her darkened bedroom. As she opened the siding door, Meredith flipped on a series of light switches.

Concealed lights outlined the hot tub, peaked through lush palms and ferns, reflected off the tile floor. Muted golds, lush greens, the air as soft and warm as a humid, summer night. A touch of paradise surrounded by misted glass. Her place to relax, to dream.

Circling the tub, she bent to remove the cover. He rushed to assist her. Across the intimate expanse Smith stood, his gaze, naked and passionate, caught in the pool's dancing light.

One night. It was all she would allow herself.

In two strides his arm snaked about her middle. He twisted his hand in her hair. One night.

She moaned, already mourning his loss, knowing the emptiness that awaited her nights. His thumbs raked her nipples, bringing an ache, familiar, yet new.

He climbed into the tub and held out his hands. "You have no idea how many nights...."

Meredith's heated breath stilled in her chest. Had he too tossed and turned, ached in the darkness? She stepped into his waiting arms. Together they sank into the water's inviting warmth.

His lips brushed hers, once, then once again. Gentle touches, brief and intoxicating, a portent of things to come. His wet skin slid against hers, the water a silky lubricant as her breasts brushed his chest, their legs touched, entwined.

He cupped her face with his hands. His arms tensed beneath her palms. He held her, his gaze locked with hers. Slowly his thumb traced a path along her cheek, across her lower lip.

"You're as beautiful as I remember. More beautiful." She could hear the desire in his voice, and trembled. She wanted to believe him. And she would, at least for tonight.

Her eyes drifted closed and their lips met, wanton and seeking. The water lapped about them as their bodies tangled and sank deeper into the warmth. His hands clutched her neck, her shoulders, the length of her back, then grasped her buttocks. Lifting her against him, Smith slid onto the smooth fiberglass bench. Settling her on his lap, he licked the moisture from her breast. His mouth, hot and wet, covered her nipple, anchored her to his desire.

Although they'd touched, loved before, the impact of Smith's loving made Meredith gasp, struggle to breath. Her mound skimmed his arousal. Her thighs clutched his hips. Heat fused as he held her in his arms, the mere contact of their flesh binding them, making them one.

Gently he built an unbearable heat, too wonderful to believe, so exquisite she couldn't speak. She could only feel, absorb, need.

Arching her back, Meredith thrust her sex to his and offered herself completely, letting him know that this night was his.

Smith felt her surrender. He knew the exact moment she'd given herself physically, lowered every sexual and sensual barrier to him. But would she ever surrender her heart?

He felt the pounding of her blood, the heavy thrum of her heart beneath her breast. She shuddered when he released her swollen nipple. Grasping her slippery thighs, he urged her to her knees. Trailing kisses along the pliant flesh of her belly, Smith paused to tease the indentation of her navel.

Wrapping his arms about her middle, he pressed his face to her belly. His heart pounded in his chest. He shuddered. Did she have any idea what she did to him? How she turned him inside out?

Lifting her out of water, he twisted, seating her on the wide rim of the tub, then knelt before her. His fingers skimmed the inside of her thighs, back and forth, until she opened, trembled from his needy caress.

Slowly, lovingly, he brushed her sex with his breath, understanding the fingernails digging into his shoulders were as much an expression of her intense pleasure as were the muted demands catching in her throat.

The touch of his tongue came softly, a reverent survey of each fold, crevice, exposing the hidden bud of her pleasure. Touching, caressing, she urged and guided him until the storm of sensation she wrought grew so intense Smith thought his heart would give out.

He relished the feel of her trembling flesh, the wild thrust of her sex against his mouth, and the sweet agony of her climax. He wanted to love her, satisfy her. He wanted to be the one she longed for, the only one she wanted.

She'd made his own pleasure secondary. That had never happened before.

An exultant cry tore from her throat, her eager thrusts shuddered to stillness. He laved her trembling flesh until her gasps eased, then mingled with soft, contented sighs.

He rose and his breath caught at the satisfied look on her face. Deliciously sated.

Nothing was more important than pleasing her. He wanted to bring her to climax, over and over, feel her quiver beneath his tongue, his lips, his urgent thrusts.

Smith's fingers trailed along her damp thigh, the curve of her hip, to the roundness of her breast. He filled his hand with her softness. Her nipple peaked in answer to his caress.

When her eyes fluttered open, an ache, new and overpowering, swelled his chest with a fierce urgency, his voice with a husky timbre. "I love your breasts."

Aching with love, his need to express his love pressed hard against her soft mound.

His lips captured hers, their tongues touched, mated, and in that moment they became one. His grasp on her breast tightened.

If only he could hold her heart so easily.

The ache intensified. His heart threatened to burst. Needing to speak, to express all the strange, intense feelings Jones evoked, he tore his lips from hers. "I love everything about you."

But did she love him?

Her lips grazed his neck, the soft, moist touch of her tongue teasing him beyond belief. He waited for her response. Waited for the words he desperately needed to hear. She didn't speak. She held him tight, her knees clasped about his middle, her sex open and exposed. He welcomed the exquisite strain she wrought, accepted what she was willing to give. For now.

He gasped, each breath a pleasure, as she rained a volley of tender kisses and tantalizing nips over his chest, across his belly. He groaned. He wanted, needed her. Intended to love her till she moaned in utter contentment.

She slid off the rim, and backed him across the pool. Willing to please her in any way conceivable, Smith complied with her gentle prodding. A provocative gleam came into her eyes as he sat on the rim of the tub and she knelt between his thighs. When she licked her lips, his erection jumped in lusty anticipation.

As she took him in her mouth, he groaned. Low and guttural, almost an animal growl. She was teaching him all over again how good it felt to be a man. How it felt to be loved.

Closing his eyes, he savored the sweep of her wet hair against his belly, the brush of her soft breasts to his thighs, and the lusty pressure of her tongue, lips and teeth, enticing his strained flesh.

He'd never felt so good. He never wanted it to end.

And if Smith had his way, it never would.

"Did you love him?"

Smith's question forced Meredith's tired brain to function. She didn't want to think of the past. Cradled in Smith's arms, she wanted to enjoy the spa's soothing jets pummeling her fatigued muscles and not think at all. Thinking would only remind her of what she was about to lose. She wanted to ignore her heart. "What difference does it make?"

"Did you love him?" His voice was soft, but insistent.

Love? She wasn't sure how to define the word. "A year ago I would have said yes. Now, I'm not sure."

"Why?"

Meredith wished he'd stop asking questions. "I don't know why."

"What's changed?"

I met you. She lifted her head from his shoulder. The solarium was filled with steam, giving the room a misty, dreamlike quality. Soft forms, no defined edges, except for Smith's eyes , Smith's questions. "Maybe I got a little smarter, a little less trusting."

"He screwed around?"

She hoped Smith didn't want details. He wasn't getting them. Moving away, she managed an answer. "Yeah."

He caught her about the waist and pulled her against his chest. He snaked a leg over her thigh, trapping her against him. "I don't screw around."

"Remind me again what happened in Chicago. Tell me again no one was waiting for you."

She waited for him to rush to his own defense. Reassure her. He remained silent. This was a conversation for the breakfast table making it convenient to separate, not one for soft lights, warm water, and entwined bodies. "She's willing to share? Or, perhaps she forgives a periodic lapse when you're gone?"

"There is no she."

"It doesn't matter since there is no us."

She felt his muscles tense, his arms tighten about her. "What we have is special."

"What we have is great sex."

"That's your definition of what we have?" His voice touched her. A husky whisper of disbelief.

"Tell me I'm the only woman you've ever picked up at an airport."

"I won't lie to you. Ever."

Did she want to know? His eyes told her he would be truthful, brutally truthful.

"Am I the only one?"

"The only one that mattered."

Was she the one? An odd pain sliced through her heart. She'd heard his husky declaration. But men could say anything when their dicks were hard.

"We're lovers. We're not in love." She'd tossed down the gauntlet. He didn't look away.

"Speak for yourself, Jones. I'm crazy about you. You know I am."

Then why don't you say I love you? Say it now. Why only lusty whispers in the heat of the moment?

"You don't believe me, do you?"

Then tell me you love me. Tell me over and over again. Tell me you want this forever.

"We have something —"

"There has to be more!" Avoiding Smith's intense gaze, Meredith looked away. She could still hear the heartbreaking news of last summer. She knew good sex wasn't enough to sustain a relationship, yet she'd hoped for more. Great sex should be an expression of the love two people shared. But she'd been wrong.

She couldn't be wrong again. She'd been loved for the sex, for being a sensual partner, but that wasn't enough then and it wasn't enough now. She wanted more than a couple of passionate nights a week. She wanted every day, every night. She wanted what Smith wasn't offering, his love, his devotion, forever. "Great sex doesn't last," she said, looking him right in the eye. "Most of our conversations have been when we're naked."

His hand slid along her spine, dipping at the small of her back, then up over her hip. "I like you naked."

"Take sex out of the equation and what do we have?

"This isn't just about sex."

"Isn't it?"

"I love you, Meredith. I just don't know how the hell to convince you."

Meredith's heart skipped a beat. She wanted to tell Smith she loved him, but those words came so easily to men. Mistaking passion for love, she'd worn a diamond on her finger for months. Was she making the same mistake with Smith? "Love is long-term, we've only got tonight."

His eyes narrowed. "Tonight?"

This time when she pulled away, he let her go. She climbed out of the spa, grabbed a towel from a narrow, wooden table, and secured it over her breasts. "I can't afford a long-term affair with you. I'm up for a promotion, and I won't have it said that I screwed my way into it."

"I don't have control over those decisions and you know it."

"You have influence. If I get the job everyone will attribute it to you and the Wilder name."

"Office romances happen every day."

"If a man screws around, he's lucky. If he gets a promotion out of it, he's smart. But reverse the situation and what do you have? An office slut who's willing to spread her legs to get ahead."

"It's the nineties. Things have changed."

"Tell that to Alice Lester!"

His lips thinned. He didn't understand. Why should he? In his position he didn't have to compete for promotions, hope for raises. He'd been at the top of the game for years.

"Who is Alice Lester?"

She hadn't meant to expose her friend, but maybe Smith needed a lesson in reality.

"She had an affair with —" Meredith caught herself. "With an executive. Her promotion to marketing coordinator was attributed to the hard work she'd done in his bed rather than her contributions to several successful ad campaigns. Even after the affair was long over, the whispers continued. Whenever she received a raise, recognition, or won a promotion, people speculated. *Who had she fucked for this one?*"

"You can't live your life in fear of a few petty minds."

"You're a man. The same rules don't apply. You can't possibly understand."

He stood. As he stepped out of the tub, steam rose from his shoulders and chest. For a split second, she wondered if she was making a mistake by letting him go.

"No one knows about us."

She shook her head dismissing her foolish thoughts. "No one's going to know."

A bead of water slid down his chest toward his belly. Meredith's gaze followed the droplet's slow progress. Resisting the urge to stop it with the tip of her tongue, she turned away. "There is no *us*."

He grasped her shoulders, briefly, then removed the towel. Hugging her from behind, he cupped her breasts. "Tell me that when I'm inside you. Tell me that when you shudder beneath me."

He caressed her breasts, her belly, her sex. The pressure of his erection to her buttocks, emphasized his words. "You shouldn't listen to your small brain," she quipped.

"What do you want from me?"

Everything. "Nothing."

He pushed his finger inside her. His lips skimmed her shoulder, along her neck, his tongue slid inside her ear. "Nothing at all?"

When his thumb flicked over her clit, her protest died in her throat.

"You're wet, Jones. You're wet for me."

He picked her up and sat her down on the edge of the wooden table. Pushing her knees apart, he stepped forward and thrust his hands into her hair. Molding his fingers about her scalp he tilted her head back, forcing her to look at him.

"Was it ever like this before?"

Strained with passion, his voice touched her heart. She should lie, let him think he was just another sexual encounter, but the intensity of his feelings revealed by the heat of his breath, the rapid rise of his chest, the anticipation in his eyes, and the tremor in his hands drew the truth. "Never."

His shoulders sagged with relief. The pressure of his fingers relaxed. "I had to know."

"Why?"

He smoothed back her hair. His stroke, tender, affectionate. "You walked out on me in Chicago."

"Isn't that the way it was supposed to work? No good-byes. No awkward parting."

"If it had been someone else... but something happened. Something I never expected."

"No one's ever walked out on you before?"

"No one I wanted."

"If I had stayed?"

"We would have had this conversation weeks ago." He touched his lips to hers. "You have no idea how much I want you."

"You've had me."

He leaned forward, pressing her back until she lay upon the table. "Not as much as I need."

She welcomed his mouth on her breast, the eager tugging on her nipple. Clutching his arms, Meredith arched against him, thrusting her mound to his belly. His biceps flexed beneath her hands as one hand grasped her buttocks, holding her to him. Slowly, she moved beneath him, guided by a primal rhythm, a burning need to join, to mate, to become one.

When he slipped her legs over his shoulders, she whispered his name, almost said she loved him. The urge to speak her heart tempered by his words. He'd spoken of love, but he hadn't promised forever. He leaned over her, pressing the tip of his penis to her heat. Despite her doubts, she wanted him, and positioned her hips to receive him.

Swearing under his breath, Smith pulled back. "My pants are —"

"You want your pants?"

Smith groaned. "I'm a little too naked."

"You may be naked...." She let the rest of the sentence hang and licked her upper lip. "In my bedroom. Top drawer, next to the bed."

He straightened and touched his fingertip to her lips. "But the *moment* has passed."

Her legs slid from his shoulders. She poked at his erection with her toe. "I'll still want you."

"But you won't tell me you love me, will you?"

"I wasn't going to tell you."

He smiled, an easy, confident, very sexy smile. "Yes, you were. Next time, I'm taping a condom to my ass."

As he walked toward her bedroom, she sat upright to gain a better view of his backside. He had great buns. "That I've got to see."

When he didn't return right away, Meredith, thinking she'd been mistaken about where she'd placed the condoms, entered the bedroom. Smith sat on the bed, running his hand along the top rail of her brass headboard. When he glanced over his shoulder at her, his eyes held a lusty sparkle that revealed he'd already thought of more than a couple of uses for the railing.

"I want to make love in your bed."

"Tired?"

Reaching out he snagged her about the waist and pulled her onto the bed. "Of you? Never."

He wanted to love her, here in her bed, fill himself with her scent, immerse himself in the place where she dreamed. Would she dream of him tomorrow? Had she ever?

He needed the memory of loving her here. He loved the silky feel of her, her scent, everything about her. Especially the appetite she had for him.

Lifting her, he slid beneath her supple thighs, tasted the heady sweetness of her lust. She moaned and grasped the brass railing. He thrust his tongue inside her, teasing, tasting, letting her set the tempo, wanting nothing more than the privilege to please her. Her sex moved, fluid and graceful, performing an erotic dance above him. When she shuddered, he almost shared her climax. Her satisfaction rippled through him, making him painfully aware of how much he needed her.

She sat back, resting her weight momentarily on his belly. Grabbing the rail, Smith pulled himself up. He reached out, searching frantically for the foil packet he'd left on the bedside table. The moment her mouth covered him, he was on the verge, caught in the magic of her lips, the enchantment of her tongue.

Clinging to the rail, like a man hanging onto a lifeline, Smith fought the storm of his own climax. He loved this fine edge, hovering between bliss and fulfillment. The latter always heightened by the intensity of riding the edge. And no one pushed him harder than Jones.

When she grasped his balls, his breath caught hard in his throat, cutting off his air supply. Her pull on his sac was measured, intense, but gentle. His heart threatened to jump out of his chest. She'd taken him to the brink, almost tasting the little death, then pulled him back to earth. Tugging lightly, she offered a tiny ration of relief, a respite from the wildness she'd wrought. Her breath, soft and hot, skimmed his pulsing flesh.

Smith was thankful when she snatched the crumpled foil packet from his fist. Understanding he was ready to burst, barely in control, she sat across his thighs and sheathed him quickly. Still the movement of her hands had him wanting to come. He groaned when she lowered herself slowly, taking each inch of him, flexing, squeezing, enveloping him with her tight, wet sex.

He cupped her breasts, filling his hands with her softness, making her cry out when he rolled her beaded nipples between his fingertips. Her sex flexed, pulled him over the edge and into a place he'd never been before. Into heaven.

He wanted to love her, fuck her, then love her again.

Exhausted, Meredith lay on Smith's chest. Her legs felt like noodles, warm, limp and utterly delicious. Threading his fingers through her hair, his thumb caught her under the chin, then tilted her face toward his. She pushed herself forward, scrapping her tender nipples across his chest, to touch her lips to his.

His lips were gentle, tasting, feeling, taking nothing, making no demands. His touch delicate and warm, his arms solid. This was what she loved about Smith, his ability to need a simple kiss, his wanting to hold her once the passion storm had passed. She liked to lie in his arms, cuddling and kissing, knowing just moments before he'd been thrusting like a bull, seeking climax, tapping every primal urge in both of them.

He touched his lips to her cheek, her temple, her forehead, the tip of her nose. His eyes, warm and glowing, gazed into hers.

Could this be it? The real thing? Sex with Smith was a whole new experience. The quiet moments, the sweet kisses a refreshing change.

"I love you. You make me feel complete, fulfilled. You're in my dreams. I can't stop thinking about you." Smith's voice was soft, his poignant words touched her heart. She closed her eyes to experience the unfamiliar surge swelling her chest, making her heart suddenly too large for her ribcage.

"You're fantastic in bed!"

The pain came fast, piercing the euphoric bubble, crashing her back to reality. Her head dropped to his chest, pressing her forehead to his warm skin. She could feel his heart drumming.

"What's wrong?"

"Nothing," she managed, despite the sudden clogging of her throat. "Nothing at all."

He caught her chin with his hand, forcing her head up. "I meant that as a compliment."

She forced back her tears and faced him. "Thank you."

He scrambled to a sitting position and took hold of her arms. His eyes darted over her face, searching her eyes. "I love you. What will it take to convince you?"

Meredith swallowed the lump in her throat. "I don't want love." *Not the kind which only requires a few hours in bed.*

"What the hell *do* you want?"

Hiding the pain clawing at her foolish heart, Meredith steeled herself. "Like you said, it's been awhile since Chicago. I needed —"

"You think this is just about — that I'm—" His chest heaved. Anger raged in his eyes. "Damn you, Jones."

She pulled away, wanting to shower and wash his heady scent from her skin. He yanked her back, crushing her to him. "If this is about fucking, then I want to fuck."

She glanced down at his limp cock, thinking he couldn't possibly rouse himself again. Smiling, she looked up at him.

Smith hated to be challenged, and Jones was telling him he didn't have it in him. True, she'd wrung him dry and made him want to wallow in satisfaction till morning, but he'd be damned if she'd reject his sincerity and throw his love back in his face.

"Come morning is it over between us?"

When Meredith nodded, Smith hated her. But only for a split second and only because he finally understood what head-over-heels-in-love meant. His plan had backfired. He'd thought a night in his arms would have her declaring her love, demanding his, but all Jones wanted was a temporary lover.

Despite her callous words, Smith wasn't convinced she felt nothing for him. Couldn't believe her sighs, her cries, the catches in her throat weren't from the heart. When they came together, they loved with a passion too hot to burn out. Smith wasn't about to give up.

"Sleep with me. Tomorrow you can say goodbye."

Chapter 5

Terrible day for an interview. Meredith fastened the top button of her red jacket. Usually her power suit gave her confidence, but no matter how hard she tried, her well-applied makeup and forced smile couldn't make her look or feel upbeat.

Why hadn't Smith stopped her? So what if she'd decided to end their relationship, if two passion-filled nights could even be called as much, the least he could have done was protest. But he hadn't. Not when she'd slipped from his arms a short hour ago. Not when she'd showered, waiting hopefully for him to join her beneath the stinging spray. No, he'd waited, silently, in her bed while she'd done her makeup and hair, then watched as she dressed.

She caught his movement in the mirror as he rose from her bed. Unable to resist the allure of his strong body, she turned. Slowly her gaze slid over the strength of his legs, the thrust of his genitals, his taut belly and up to the width of his shoulders. She noticed the dark shadow of his beard, the set of his mouth, then dared to confront the challenge in his eyes. He stared at her, waiting. She couldn't say it. *I want you, but I want all of you. Not just that glorious body. I want the rest of your life.*

"Shower's all yours." Even to her own ears, she sounded lame. "I'll make coffee."

He turned and walked into the bathroom. Just before he closed the door she imagined him with a condom taped to one of his buns and smiled. But her smile died quickly. If Smith ever taped his cheek, he wouldn't be doing it for her.

A short twenty minutes later as she reached for the door handle to leave for work, Smith finally spoke. "The table in the solarium, what's it for?"

He stood close, so near she could touch his chest, his freshly shaved jaw or fondle him if she took the notion. She folded her hand into a tight fist. "It's a bathing table."

"Sun bathing?"

"That too." His eyes danced with devilish curiosity. Meredith couldn't resist tempting him. "It was designed for bathing... someone else."

She certainly had his attention. His nostrils flared and his chest expanded from a slow intake of air. "Tell me."

She shouldn't do this. She should hold her tongue, ignore the husky plea in his voice, suppress the resulting heat flooding her middle, and reject the sudden thumping of her heart.

"You lay naked on the table," she said, her voice barely above a whisper. "I fill a wooden bucket with warm water, then dip a special sponge in the water, lather it slowly with scented soap. Perhaps I'll choose sandlewood. Perhaps spice. Then I wash you. I begin with your feet. I'm very thorough. I stroke your calves. I dip the sponge again and rub your thighs. I have hours to accomplish my task."

"Are you naked?"

Deliberately she kept her voice sensually soft, her words slow. "Yes. I bend and dip the sponge again. I continue my quest. I wash your buttocks, soaping the curve of your hips, the crease at your thighs, taking my time. I slip the wet sponge between your cheeks, working the soap, back and forth. My sponge skims your balls, then I touch them, hold them, caress them. Finally, I move to your back, washing, massaging your tight muscles. Relaxing you. Soothing you." Meredith moved closer, her words, the image of Smith naked, his skin and muscles rippling beneath the sponge making her hot.

Smith raised his hand. His fingertip touched her neck at the throb of her heartbeat. "What happens next?" he asked, his voice raspy.

"I take the sponge and soap my breasts and belly. The soap runs down between my legs."

Smith spread his fingers and wrapped them about her neck, forcing her face up, her lips inches from his. "And?"

"I massage your back with my breasts, slowly, back-and-forth I rub against you using the soap and water as a slick lubricant. My nipples are hard. So hard, they scrap along your skin while my belly strokes your buttocks and thighs."

His thumb raked her jaw. "You're lying on me. You press your mound tight against me. My thigh is between your legs."

"You've heard this story before."

"Don't say goodbye."

"Why couldn't you have been a salesman, anything but —"

"And if I were a salesman, would you be bringing me home tonight? Would I be stretched out on that table?"

"I want that promotion. I worked my ass off for it. I won't have it said I didn't earn it — an affair isn't a good idea right now."

"Is that what we have?"

"We're lovers. Strangers who have connected for momentary satisfaction."

"We're hardly strangers. I know every inch —"

"You know what turns me on. You know the sensual me, nothing more."

"Some couples are married for years and don't understand each other the way we do."

"It's not enough. One of these mornings you'll wake up and the novelty will have worn off."

"You're wrong." Smith grabbed the door handle and strode outside to the car. There was no eye contact when he yanked the passenger door wide.

After a silent drive into the city, Smith pulled over to an unloading zone near the bank. Her hand shaking with doubt, Meredith reached for the handle. Smith leaned over and opened the door. "Good luck on your interview."

She was surprised he knew. "You're not coming in?"

He shook his head, pulled back and wrapped his hands about the wheel. As she placed her feet upon the sidewalk, Meredith tensed, wanting and not wanting him to stop her. When he did nothing, she whispered, "Goodbye."

"How's the new digs, Assistant Vice President?"

Meredith glanced up from the file drawer she'd been reorganizing and smiled at the man responsible for her promotion. Her new office was almost double the size of her old one down the hall. She hadn't made it to the executive floor, but that was the next goal on her career agenda. "I like it. Thanks, Jim."

"Thank Norm. He selected you as his assistant. He wants to retire in two years. All the man can talk about is that sailboat."

"Don't worry. I'll be ready," Meredith assured him. Vice President, head of Retail Banking would soon be within her grasp, so why didn't it feel wonderful? She'd worked hard for this position, knowing it would lead to the executive level. She'd earned her new title, deserved this promotion, but the victory seemed hollow.

Hollow and empty because the one person she wanted to celebrate with had jumped on a plane to New Orleans over three weeks ago. She'd gotten what she wanted, her new job, her corporate title, and Smith out of her life.

Meredith's phone rang. The caller was Jim's secretary. "Mrs. Wilder's arrived for the board meeting," Meredith said, conveying the secretary's message as she replaced the receiver. How strange Smith had disappeared without a word and his grandmother was in town for the monthly meeting. "What happened to Mr. Wilder? I thought he'd taken her position on the board."

"Smith changed his mind. He tendered his resignation and Lydia is here to resume her seat. Seems Smith's changed his mind about a lot of things lately. Has the whole family upset." Jim glanced at his watch as he headed for the door.

A dozen questions popped into Meredith's mind, but Jim waved and left her office. Why had Smith resigned? Would she ever see him again? Questions she reminded herself she had no right to ask. Smith was gone and his personal life was none of her concern.

The duties of her new position combined with the transition of her old ones to a new employee overwhelmed her Friday. When the receptionist buzzed her about a delivery, Meredith's confusion increased when a dozen red roses in a lead crystal vase were placed on the edge of her desk. With a quick "have a good day", the delivery girl scurried out of the office. Meredith glanced at the new plant sitting atop her file cabinet, and discounted her mother as the sender. Her heart pounded as she plucked the card nestled among the roses.

"Congratulations, Jones."

Meredith leaned over and inhaled the fragrance of the nearest rosebud. Anyone, even the nosy receptionist, reading the note would assume the sender was someone called Jones. For the rest of the day, Meredith caught herself staring at the roses and thinking about Smith.

Later that evening she found a card in her mail. Her heart pounded wildly when she opened the envelope to see a picture of a red rose, dewdrops beaded on the soft petals. Inside, the writing was bold, the message simple.

"Meet me for lunch, Saturday noon, at Captain's Table. I'll wait for you. Smith."

The letter bore a local postmark. He must be back in San Francisco. She wondered why he hadn't chosen to visit her at the bank or show up on her doorstep.

Most of all she wondered why he wanted to see her. Why he'd chosen a local place near her home for their rendezvous rather than a restaurant in the city?

When she walked into the Captain's Table the following day, Smith was waiting. Despite his snug-fitting jeans and navy sweater he looked out of place, too classy for the seaside cafe with its faded curtains, scarred tables and vinyl-covered booths. His loafers too polished for the scratched linoleum floor. As usual his hair lay perfectly in place.

"The roses were beautiful, thanks." She extended her hand instead of throwing herself into his arms the way she ached to do. Three weeks had been a lifetime. Her erotic dreams had returned. Now that he'd shared her bed and her spa, the memories were far too potent. Any place she looked in her home brought forth a tide of sensual images. Smith naked. His muscles bunched and straining. His face etched with passion as they came together.

He grinned at her as if reading her thoughts, then leaned down and pressed his lips briefly to her cheek. "Not as beautiful as you."

"Why are you here?" she asked taking a seat in the nearest booth. "I thought you decided to quit banking?"

He sat opposite. "I don't want to talk about work."

"What do you want to talk about?"

"You. How good you look. How much we missed each other."

"Did we?"

"Don't even try. I see it in your eyes. You're as horny as I am."

"If you believed that, why didn't you knock on my door?"

He leaned forward, his gaze intent. "I love you, Meredith," he said, his husky voice sending shivers running down her spine. "I want to make love to you until I'm exhausted, but today isn't about that."

His voice, his words triggered a heat in her middle. A simmering heat she'd tried to deny since laying eyes on him. "So what is today about?"

"We're having a date."

"Aren't we beyond the date stage?"

"We're starting over again. We're going to do all the things dating couples usually do."

"Usually do?"

"Hang out. Get to know each other. I hope you like fish and chips?"

He smiled, quite pleased with himself. She nodded, wondering how he'd chosen one of her favorite spots. Despite the rundown interior of the restaurant, the fish and chips were the best in the Bay Area. He reached out, his fingers barely touching her hand. Another set of shivers danced along her spine. Part of her loved the idea of a date, the romance of the seaside, but if Meredith had her way, she'd take him home, strip him naked and make love until the sun came up. In foggy Pacifica that might not happen until noon. "And after lunch?"

"We walk on the beach. We hold hands, we talk."

Maybe he'd lost his mind in the last three weeks. "Hold hands?"

He leaned back in the booth and picked up a menu. "Yeah, hold hands. Shall we order?"

Smith kept his word. They walked along the beach, talking and holding hands. No matter how many simmering looks she gave him, he managed to steel himself and ask another question, broach a new subject, but he did allow himself to wrap his arm around her shoulders or waist. Several hours later, they stood by her car.

"We could go home and watch the sunset." She wasn't ready to let him go. She didn't want to go home alone. The memories of Smith were far too potent, too intense to dismiss. Images forever seared into her memory.

He leaned against her car and pulled her close. "You'd end up on my lap again, and tomorrow morning you'd hate me again."

"I don't hate you."

"You're not a morning person?" he quipped. "Is that why you push me away?"

"I have my promotion. You're not a director. Problem solved."

He shook his head. "I don't want an affair. I don't want to make love all night and sneak out in the morning."

"I don't want that either."

"Don't you? Are you going to tell anyone about us? Your friends? Your co-workers? Or do I remain your secret lover?"

He'd read her right. She had no intention of telling anyone about him. The last thing she wanted was to be the subject of office gossip. "I don't talk about my personal life."

"Fine. We date until you're ready."

"Ready?"

"Ready to commit to me." His voice was firm, filled with challenge.

Was he ready to be part of her life? "Commit to you? Your life, your goals, the very air you breathe? Been there. Done that. No way."

His eyes searched hers, probing her defenses. "How about our life, our goals?"

My God, could he be serious? "I didn't mean that —"

"You don't have to defend yourself. I won't hurt you."

"I'm not —"

"Since day one, you've shielded part of yourself from me. Give *us* a chance."

"We've only spent a couple of nights together," she said, feeling the need to remind him.

"Don't push me away. We've shared a lot more than a couple of nights."

A flippant remark hovered on the tip of her tongue. He cocked his head and wagged a finger at her. "Don't you dare tell me it was just sex. If this was just about sex, I'd have knocked on your door last night."

"You thought about it?"

"I thought about it, and so did you. Tell me, Jones, how've you been sleeping lately? Do you like being alone? I don't."

"I've been busy." She couldn't tell him how much she missed him. How badly she wanted him.

"What do you dream about?"

Should she tell him about her dreams? Taunt him with the erotic images plaguing her nights. "I don't recall."

"I dream about you. I dream about unbuttoning that red suit. About stretching out on that table and being bathed. Most of all I dream about being inside you."

"Then come home with me."

He pulled her close. Even through the thick material of her jeans, Meredith felt his erection.

"Not yet," he whispered, loving the feel of her tight against him. *Not until you tell me you love me.*

Her lips curled into a sexy pout. Just looking at her made him hard. When he'd decided to court her, to earn her love and trust, he knew it would be difficult to resist her and keep his libido under control. This was just the beginning, and already he was in pain.

"How about Monterey or Carmel? The weather should be great tomorrow."

She pushed away from him, breaking the sensual contact. "You're serious about this dating thing?"

"You can bet your bank account on it." He reached over and opened the driver's door. "Time to say goodnight, Miss Collier."

Once she was settled behind the wheel, he caressed her cheek. "See you tomorrow."

The following Friday as Meredith ambled into her office, she wondered what surprise would arrive today. After a glorious Sunday afternoon, Smith had taken her home, given her a chaste kiss at her doorstep and said goodnight. Monday the gifts had begun to arrive. She'd received a selection of truffles, on Tuesday a music box, Wednesday brought balloons, and yesterday a bottle of champagne. What would Smith dream up for Friday?

She wished he'd give himself. That's what she really wanted, the intimacy, the closeness of lying naked in his arms, but Smith was determined to romance her. Despite her growing frustration, she was enjoying herself and they *were* getting to know each other. They both had been raised in the same faith and had attended parochial schools. Their stories of school had them both in stitches. Their outlook on life and politics was almost identical. They were bonding. Bonding in a whole new way that had nothing to do with sex.

But in the background, beneath the laughter, the easy conversation, desire simmered. The touch of Smith's hand, an unguarded look. Meredith felt his heat, his passion. All the more delicious because he'd forbidden the sensual. Smith's chaste kisses and gentle wooing showed a resolve, a stubborn streak Meredith admired. One she was determined to break.

When she returned from lunch, a stuffed cat, resembling her Oliver, sat upon her desk. A card tied round its neck. *Dinner at Ernie's. Cocktails at six? Meet me in the bar.*

Meredith patted the cat's head. *And bedtime at nine.*

Smith took her hand and escorted her to the car. Around them the city lights glowed like a million stars, even the street lamps sparkled. All evening he'd been a perfect date. The food and wine were delicious. Only one thing was missing. Dessert. Champagne and chocolate-dipped strawberries were in her fridge. A couple nights ago she'd dreamed of feeding him strawberries in bed, letting him lick champagne off her breasts.

"Come to lunch tomorrow, and meet my grandmother," he said, breaking into her passion-laded thoughts.

"I've met her," Meredith responded automatically.

"Not as a bank employee, but as my —"

"Does she know about us? About Chicago?"

"She knows how I feel, that I love you."

Meredith's breath caught. Her throat felt frozen. "You told her you loved me?"

"When I changed my mind about the directorship, I had to explain." He'd wanted to wait until he had a ring on Meredith's finger, but he'd done so many things his grandmother had termed "out-of-character" recently, he'd confessed. It had felt good to share his feelings. He couldn't recall ever opening himself up so completely, except when he was with Meredith or speaking of Meredith. She'd broken him open, his mind, his heart, his soul and taken him to the extreme, to ecstasy. When he'd come back to earth, he'd realized he belonged to her. Exclusively.

Exclusive hadn't been part of his vocabulary, as far as women were concerned, ever. His grandmother had looked shocked.

As shocked as Meredith looked now.

"What are you saying?"

Smith wanted to tell her everything; how he'd upset his family when he decided to live in San Francisco, how he'd been willing to spend days, weeks, whatever it took to find her. Why his work, his family had become secondary to her. Instead he waited, hoping she'd put into words the questions he knew were spinning in her head.

"Giving up the directorship couldn't have anything to do with me?"

"Why not? You made the rules."

She shook her head. Her dark hair swirled about her cheek. "What rules?"

"You couldn't have an affair with a director, and you didn't want me, us, to interfere with your promotion in any way. I gave you what you wanted."

"But what about what you want?"

"I want you. I love you." He leaned down and brushed her lips with his. "One of these days you'll believe me."

He was pleased, but not surprised when she thrust herself against him and wrapped her arms about his neck. Her innate sensuality had kept him spellbound from the beginning. He loved sex, and he needed a woman in his life who not only appreciated his drive, but enhanced it. Meredith not only met his needs, she challenged them. But she was far more than just a bedpartner. He now had a friend, a companion, and hopefully a wife. Unable to resist, he wrapped his arms around her and kissed her.

Her lips were soft, and tempting. Her hands slipped beneath his jacket, around to his back. She caressed, teased and cupped his buns, pressing herself tight against him. He understood she was trying to seduce him, and he loved every minute of her effort. He was hard and she was very pleased with herself. Several minutes later they were both breathless, hungry for each other. When she fondled him, Smith knew he had hit his limit of control. "Time to say goodnight."

Dropping his hands to his side, he pushed his weight from the door, forcing her to step back. He had to let her go, allow her time to think, to consider his words. If she told him she loved him, he didn't want it to be in bed. When she agreed to be his wife, she couldn't be naked.

She had to be dressed, her mind unclouded by sex. She must never regret her decision. He opened her car door and pressed a piece of paper in her hand. "The address, and my private phone number. Call me anytime."

"While you're in bed?"

"Consider it your personal nine hundred number."

As she drove out of the parking lot, Smith wondered what time she'd call. If he wasn't careful, he'd be proposing with his dick in his hand.

Chapter 6

Meredith picked up the phone a couple of times, then set it aside. She had every intention of calling Smith and having phone sex, she'd even thought of several steamy scenarios, but his invitation to lunch with his grandmother had taken her by surprise. All the way home she'd thought about his declaration of love. The dating, the gifts, his determination to forego sex convinced her Smith was serious. But meeting his grandmother added a whole new dimension to their relationship. An official dimension. Was she ready to declare herself, to commit?

She and Smith had begun as passing lovers, but that had changed the moment he'd walked into her office. She'd been his prey from the beginning, but hadn't seen it until now.

Meredith rolled onto her side and picked up the phone. She liked being chased, and Smith was sure to make getting caught a sexy adventure. Did she want to remain caught?

Yes! The word turned over and over. Her answer would be yes. Yes, she loved him. Yes, she wanted him forever. If he didn't ask her to marry him, she'd kill him.

Meredith giggled as she punched in his number. The phone barely rang. He'd been waiting.

"Are you naked?"

"What took you so long? I'm hard already."

His words formed a delicious image. She wiggled her bare bottom against the sheet. "I've been thinking about you, about us."

"You belong to me, Jones. You have since Chicago. I claimed you that night."

"Do you belong to me?"

"When I breathe, it's your scent. When I ache, it's for you. When I dream, it's of you."

"With a line like that, how did you ever remain single?"

"I hadn't met you."

"You're good," Meredith teased. "But I told you that in Chicago, at the airport."

Smith chuckled. "I remember. We're good, Jones. We're good together."

Meredith waited for the question, telling her just how good he thought they were together.

"Make love to me, Jones. With your feelings. With your words. Tell me how you feel, how much you want me. Make me come."

Swallowing her momentary disappointment, Meredith closed her eyes and let the images emerge. "You're naked, standing before me, your desire blatant, pulsing. A feast for my eyes. I lick my lips in anticipation, but I'd rather lick you.

Just the thought of my tongue, my mouth, my lips on you, makes me hot." Sighing, Meredith ran her hand over her heated flesh, over her breasts, her belly, pausing between her legs. "I'm forced to rub my thighs together, to ease the pressure."

"Are you touching yourself?"

"Yes, but I need more."

"What do you want?"

"You. I want to feel you in my mouth."

"Take me," Smith coaxed, his voice thick with desire. "Make me come."

"I kneel before you. My hands clutch your thighs. Your muscles tense beneath my fingers. My nails dig into your flesh."

"I've never been so hard. It hurts. It's wonderful."

"I take your straining flesh in my mouth, back and forth, moistening your skin, easing your pain. Over and over. My tongue presses you and I can feel your blood pounding, vessels pumping against my mouth, filling you, making you hard as steel."

"Your mouth is wet and hot. You feel incredible."

"I am hot. You make me wet," Meredith admitted, her own fingers easing the intense pressure between her legs. "I take you deeper, I want all of you. My lips caress you, squeeze you, my mouth tugs and pulls. I'm too excited to be gentle. Too hot to be a lady. I fondle you, you're tight and full. The pleasure builds, you ache for release. I wrap my hand around you, my eager fingers kneading your needy flesh, increasing the tempo. I touch you, I lick you. My mouth throbs with pleasure. I'm so wet. Faster, hotter, until you're swollen, ready."

The only sound Meredith heard was Smith's ragged breathing, her own gasps of pleasure.

"My God, I haven't done that in years."

A smile wrought from satisfaction curled her lips. "Did you come?"

"By my own hand, alone in my bed."

"You weren't alone."

"I'm glad. I was feeling selfish."

Meredith wadded the sheet between her legs. Despite her climax, she still throbbed. "The next call is yours."

"I can't wait."

"You could come to me," she coaxed, knowing the relief was momentary. "Sleep with me."

"I still don't know how you feel, what I mean to you."

"You're everything. My pleasure. My —"

"Lover? I want to be your heart, your husband. Think about it. I'll see you tomorrow."

The phone line went dead. Meredith stared at the receiver in disbelief. Had Smith proposed?

Meredith smoothed back her hair, then rang the doorbell at the tenth floor apartment. She'd chosen her gray wool suit and pink silk shell. A strand of pearls and matching earrings complimented her outfit. If Smith decided to get down on his knee, she'd be ready.

Smith's grandmother, dressed in white wool and pearls, gave her a quick, but thorough appraisal, then welcomed her. Lydia Wilding looked sweet and endearing, maybe a tad little-old-ladyish, but Meredith remembered Jim had told her that behind that white hair and genteel, Louisiana demeanor was a shrewd businesswoman. Even Lydia's eyes, penetrating, hazel, accented with flecks of green, reminded her of Smith.

Despite the expanse of glass providing a breathtaking view of the city, the dining room was intimate and inviting. The gleaming table, an elegant blend of fine china, sparkling crystal, polished silver, and linen napkins complimented the arrangement of pink roses in the center.

And Smith, dressed in a dove-gray suit, completely at ease in the midst of this refined opulence as he'd been at the Captain's Table with paper plates and plastic forks.

Over poached salmon, the conversation was sprinkled with the proper amount of the getting-to-know-you small talk and inquiries about Meredith's duties at the bank. After lunch, tea was served in the living room. When Smith left the room to answer a phone call, Lydia smiled at Meredith. "How nice, we have a few moments alone."

Wondering if Lydia had arranged the call, Meredith returned the smile. For the moment the small talk was through. Mrs. Wilding had something to say.

"I had to meet you," Lydia began, then paused. Instead of responding to the stretch of silence, Meredith waited. "Since you've come into my grandson's life, he's been doing the most unpredictable things."

"Things?"

"We've raise him like a son. His father was our oldest. Our only son. We're concerned."

"What things?"

"He reneged on an agreement with his grandfather, and practically within the same breath announced his decision to move to San Francisco."

"I thought he moved here to assume your chair on the board."

"He did. I made that request two years ago. Four months ago he decided to accept then changed his mind again. Because of you."

"Are you sure?"

"You've had quite an impact on Smith. You've even put the *M* word into his vocabulary."

Marriage? Was Smith thinking of marriage? He had used the word commitment. Needing clarification, Meredith asked, "The *M* word?"

Lydia smiled. "Monogamy, dear."

Her cheeks suddenly hot, and her heart thumping hard against her chest, Meredith hoped her shock hadn't been written all over her face. Since marriage and monogamy were synonymous in her mind, she'd been unprepared for Lydia's choice of *M* words. Should she be complimented, or was Lydia merely warning her?

Meredith picked up her cup of tea. The china cup clattered loudly against the saucer. "You were so astounded, you had to meet me?"

Lydia's eyes narrowed. Meredith had wanted this woman to like her, wanted her approval, but Lydia Wilding seemed more curious than seriously considering a possible new family member. In a heartbeat Meredith knew monogamy alone was unacceptable. She wanted it all, and she wasn't about to settle for an affair, even a long-term one. Feminist ideals be damned. She wanted his name, his commitment legally. She wanted more than a promise of fidelity. Smith had said she belonged to him. Well, if he belonged to her, she wanted it on paper. But what did Lydia want?

"Smith is all we have. We, his grandfather and I, want him to be happy."

Meredith set her tea aside. She'd heard the unspoken *but* at the end of Lydia's sentence. Her soft southern accent belied the importance of the conversation.

"You don't really like tea, do you, dear?"

"No, right now I'd like a —"

"Sherry?"

"Sounds perfect." It didn't, a dry martini would have been perfect.

Smith strolled back into the room. "Fix us all a drink," Lydia ordered with sweet, but absolute authority. "Meredith would like a martini, and so would I."

Waiting until Smith was across the room with his back turned, Meredith challenged Lydia. "Why do I bother you, Mrs. Wilding? Maybe it would be good for him to be monogamous for awhile."

"What are you two whispering about?"

"Nothing," they both answered, simultaneously reaching for the glasses in his hands.

Meredith noted the quirk of Smith's left eyebrow as he sat next to her on the sofa. "What have you been doing, Grandmama? Meredith is full of questions, I can see it in her eyes."

"I told her I wanted to meet her."

"And?" Smith asked, without glancing at his grandmother.

"I told her you've been peculiar lately."

"I'm in love," he said, in a matter-of-fact tone. "Isn't that explanation enough?"

"What was the agreement with your grandfather?"

Lydia reached out and placed her hand on Smith's arm. "Let me explain. Otherwise I fear she won't believe you."

Smith focused his attention on his grandmother. "What makes you think she'll believe you? The idea is so outdated, I don't believe it myself."

"I'll decide what I believe. Go on, Mrs. Wilding."

Smith relaxed back into the sofa. Meredith sipped at her drink as Lydia began.

"My husband wanted Smith to settle down, raise children. Since he's shown no inclination to do so, my husband told him if he wasn't married by age forty, an old Wilding tradition of bride selection would be revived."

"The night I agreed, Grandpapa and I had had a few drinks."

Lydia glanced at Smith. "Not a few, dear. Lucius had opened a second bottle of Southern Comfort. If Smith didn't find a suitable female by his fortieth birthday, he had to marry the bride of my husband's choice."

"You'd let your grandfather select your wife?"

"The practice was quite common in the last century," Lydia interjected.

"I'd forgotten until he reminded me last Christmas," Smith explained. "It had become a point of honor, a gentlemen's agreement if you will. I was on my way home to meet *my grandfather's choice* when the snowstorm closed O'Hare. I couldn't go through with it, I reneged."

The expression on Smith's face told her his decision had plagued him. "What did you tell him?"

"Lucius had planned an engagement party," Lydia explained. "The whole family had been invited. He'd chosen a distant Wilding cousin. He was positive once Smith met her —"

Met her?

Smith ignored his grandmother along with her question. His gaze locked with hers. "I told him I had met the woman I wanted to marry."

"But how could you tell him that? You didn't even know my name. No one falls in love in one night," Meredith blurted out. "Or was I a convenient excuse to get out of a difficult situation?"

Smith's eyes narrowed. His mouth thinned into a straight line. Meredith glanced at Lydia whose mouth had dropped open in a most unladylike fashion.

Lydia picked up her drink and stood. "I think I should leave. I'm sure I have a phone call to make."

"You weren't an excuse," Smith said as Lydia disappeared down a hallway. "I told them the truth, I just didn't offer any details."

"It was a fluke we ran into each other. You couldn't have planned on finding me."

"It was no fluke. You told me you worked for a bank and you'd been in Chicago for a training conference. It was a matter of time."

"I didn't tell you what bank."

"If you had I wouldn't have had to wait two months."

"So you flew out here and started calling banks? I don't believe it. Do you know how many banks there are in San Francisco?"

"Actually I do. I called most of them before I had the sense to call my own."

"You expect me to believe within one night, you fell in love, decided to cancel *your* wedding, and move to San Francisco to find me?"

"Actual wedding plans hadn't been made."

"And if you hadn't met me?"

"I'd given my word."

"You were going through with it?"

"I had just turned forty. My grandfather was relentless. A wife, children to carry on the Wilding name sounded reasonable."

Disgusted, Meredith jumped to her feet and stalked over to a large plate glass window overlooking the bay. The sun had just broken through the low clouds and sailboats skimmed across the glimmering water. She touched the thick glass with her fingertip.

"So I was your excuse? Surely by now your grandfather has given up on this silly notion of picking out your bride."

"I didn't need you as an excuse." He stood directly behind her. His voice low and sexy. "As for coming to San Francisco, that was because of you. Otherwise, if I wanted to remain single, the family holdings are nationwide. I had my choice — Chicago, New York, Atlanta... I may have disappointed my grandfather, but he wasn't about to relieve me of my corporate responsibilities."

Meredith glanced at his reflection in the window. "I don't know what to believe."

Smith placed his hand over hers, pinning her palm against the glass. "If you believe anything, believe I love you. Only you. Maybe it's not supposed to happen in one night, but it did."

He stood behind her, watching her reflection in the glass as he'd done that night in Chicago. She'd fallen in love that night, and it had scared her. Her feelings for him had been far too intense to deal with rationally the next morning.

"All my life I've avoided a commitment." Smith said. "Not this time. We are different. We connected. Even after weeks apart — I thought you felt it, too."

"Last night, on the phone, was that a proposal?"

Smith touched his lips to her hair. "I'd planned it differently, but I meant it."

The memory of what they'd been doing came to mind. "It was different all right."

"I could do it again."

"It wouldn't be the same."

Smith grasped her about the waist and turned her to face him. "What are you saying, Jones?"

"I love you."

"And?"

"I'll marry you, anytime, anywhere, under any circumstances."

"How about here as soon as we get a license?"

Meredith glanced at the well-appointed living room. "You'll want to live here?"

Smith shook his head slowly. The green flecks in his eyes sparkled and his lips curled in a sexy grin. "The bathing facilities are inadequate, but some night when the fog is thick as snow, we can borrow the place."

"You'll want me to sign a pre-nuptial?" Meredith asked outright. She'd rather know now, than have some Wilding lawyer slap an inch-thick agreement on her desk tomorrow with the expectation she'd willingly sign on the dotted line.

"Pre-nups are advance divorce agreements. Divorce isn't an option I'll consider. You have my word."

"A gentlemen's agreement, then," Meredith teased, relieved that Smith had placed no conditions on their marriage, but love. "Shall we drink on it? Perhaps a glass of Southern Comfort?"

"For my bride, Dom Perignon."

About the Author:

Sandy Fraser lived in Southern California, but recently passed away. Published in book-length women's fiction, she loved the opportunity to push the sensuality envelope and to tell the forbidden in Secrets.

Strictly Business

by Shannon Hollis

To my reader:
In this high-speed, high-tech world, sometimes you just
have to stop and let love catch up to you...

Chapter 1

Elizabeth Forrester closed her office door and fell into a chair before her knees gave out.

Settled.

One hundred thousand dollars, but it was still less than they would have had to pay in court. She leaned her forehead on a stack of evidence, the laser-printed type blurring in front of her eyes. She had every e-mail message in the stack practically memorized. The chronicle of a seduction, from the first innocent messages to the latest three-page document that detailed a middle-aged man's sexual fantasies with a twenty-four-year-old woman.

Online sex on the company network. Elizabeth groaned. Every keystroke sitting right there on the system backup tapes for the lawyers to extract. How could a man so smart be that dumb? The woman had used him as skillfully as any craftsman used a tool. It was enough to make her grind her teeth. Giving one hundred thousand dollars to Malinda Burke offended every principle Elizabeth possessed. But the thought of sitting in court beside the shaking husk of what had once been a senior Director offended her even more.

What she wouldn't give for a cool glass of wine.

But it was only three in the afternoon. She had to make an employee retention pitch in half an hour, and then interview two people for the compensation manager's position. She pushed the thought of the wine away. As Director of Human Resources, one of her responsibilities was to make sure a lawsuit like this wouldn't happen again. She called up her freshly written policy on her computer screen — the fruit of the last four months of hell.

"Stratton Hill management realizes that healthy relationships among its employees are key to their quality of life. However, personal relationships must remain within the best interests of the business. In order to encourage focus and productivity, management requests that employees adhere to the following principles: (1) Relationships between persons in the same management chain are discouraged. In particular, a romantic relationship between a manager and his/her employee is prohibited due to the risk of favoritism and conflict of interest. (2) If the behavior of two employees disrupts or causes discomfort to their co-workers, disciplinary action may follow. Should the employees require three warnings, transfer or termination may result. Thank you for your understanding and compliance."

She tapped the "send" key and the policy went out over the system to every Stratton Hill employee in the country. God help them if they didn't comply. She wasn't going through this ever again.

Her administrator, Jenny, poked her head in the door. "Are you OK, Elizabeth?"

Elizabeth pulled <u>Burke v. Stratton Hill</u> together and locked the files in one of the cabinets against the wall. "I am now. I just sent you-know-what out over the wire. Be prepared for the deluge."

Jenny braced her shoulders and shook her curly hair back — the soldier before the final charge. "I've been taking self-defense classes."

Elizabeth laughed. "That's what I like about you — you're so proactive. Can you give me some pointers?"

"Nope, just a reminder." She relaxed back into informality. "You've got a meeting with Garrett Hill in ten minutes. About the technician theft problem in the Canadian office."

"Right." One problem down. Another to go. They'd just got the retention situation in Portland under control, and now the brightest minds in the Vancouver office were being lured *en masse* over to AlphaTech Computers, their biggest competitor. Elizabeth wished AlphaTech would quit opening offices in cities where Stratton Hill had already hired the best development techs the industry had to offer.

She took a deep mental breath and looked on the bright side: she was going to spend a whole hour in a strategy meeting with Garrett Hill, the most beautiful man in Silicon Valley. Taking her presentation folder and laptop from Jenny, Elizabeth headed down the hallway to the executive offices. You'd never catch her complaining about the time she spent listening to that voice, or watching Garrett's sexy backside as he pointed out profit margins on the wall screen. Sitting next to him, she had to resist the temptation to reach out and touch his thick, dark hair as it curled on the back of his neck.

She put the images out of her mind as she slipped into the conference room. Thinking about Garrett Hill was crazy, after the afternoon she'd just spent. Her heart and her body might crave him, but her head had to keep her own strict policy in mind. He was the Chief Technical Officer of the company, and one level above her in the management chain. No matter how strong the urge, hell would freeze over before she'd let her deepest, most secret fantasies see the light of day. Not only would she lose all credibility in the insular world of human resources for breaking her own policy, she'd lose her job.

But there was no harm in looking. No harm in enjoying his company.

She was fourth on the agenda, and presented her key employee retention proposal with as much presence of mind as if Garrett weren't sitting two chairs away, watching her intently out of darkly lashed blue eyes. She tried not to play to him, but every time she turned to explain a concept, his gaze would flick up and meet hers. The presentation material had his interest, anyway. It certainly couldn't be her sober, dark blue suit with the skirt only her grandmother could call short. Little did he know, she thought as she finished the proposal and sat down, that under the suit jacket and jewel-necked silk blouse, her nipples had tightened in an involuntary response. If she couldn't have his hands on her, at least she could capture his gaze.

He waited for her as she gathered her materials at the conclusion of the meeting. "What was the verdict?" he asked. She glanced toward the open door. The entire workforce probably had their ears to the walls of the conference room. But Garrett was a senior executive, and the former boss of the departed victim. It was her responsibility to tell him first before submitting a formal report.

"Settled," she said quietly. He stood close, his attention absolute. She could smell a faint whiff of his cologne, and resolutely blocked it out.

"How much?"

"One hundred K."

"My God." He turned away, one hand on his hip, the other rubbing his face. "She could make a living at this."

"I hope not. Her attorney does, of course." She couldn't keep the bitterness out of her tone.

"It hurts."

"I know. But dragging us all through court would hurt even more."

He nodded, and turned back to her again, his eyes somber. "Nice job. Thanks for sticking with it. I know this has been your whole life for the past couple of months."

"Not quite my whole life." She smiled, and was rewarded with an answering smile. She pushed her response to the warmth of his praise back down to a professional level. "I try to keep my perspective on this job. If I let it take over at the risk of my personal life, it will consume me."

"That's right. You're at the helm of the Quality of Life program." He changed the subject. "So let's talk some more about the problems in Vancouver."

She nodded. "Looks like we have some work to do if we want to stay ahead of AlphaTech. The salary structures in Canada are very different, but I'm not sure it's salary alone. I know a motivation consultant out of Seattle who might help."

"Whoa," he said, sitting sideways on the conference table. "Hold on a minute. I was thinking about another approach to the problem. Sit down and let's think about this."

It was no wonder Garrett Hill had been written up in *Fortune* as one of the most influential executives in the Valley. He made her feel as if her input was the single most important thing he would hear all day. When you talked with Garrett, even something as trivial as a good morning in the hallway, you knew you had his attention.

This was one of the sexiest things about him.

Elizabeth didn't want to sit in one of the low conference chairs. His masculinity was potent enough without the domination of physical space. She edged the chair out of the way, dropped her laptop and folder on the seat, and leaned against the table a cautious few feet away.

"What did you have in mind?" she asked.

"A personal visit." His gaze held hers, and she lifted a dark eyebrow, prompting him to continue. "There's a feeling of disconnection out there, of being cut off from what's going on at Corporate headquarters. A little bit of visibility, some one-on-one conversations, and some plain humanity would go a long way to bring them back to the fold."

She nodded. "I think so, too." With a smile, she added, "And it's a little more friendly than a motivation consultant, I suppose."

He smiled in return, and her concentration narrowed on his mouth. What wouldn't she give for just one kiss from that mouth, with its Duchovnyan lower lip and sculpted outline...

"So I'd like you to go with me," he said, jerking her out of her five-second fantasy.

Travel with you? Spend hours on an airplane beside you? Hotel rooms?

She clamped down hard on the first rush of instinctive self-doubt. She'd never survive the trip without making an utter fool of herself.

But he was looking at her expectantly, waiting for an answer to what was, for him, probably just another unwelcome business trip to solve a problem that shouldn't have occurred in the first place. She pulled her professionalism around her, a guise as sober as her navy blue suit.

"Sure," she said. "When do we leave?"

Garrett folded himself into the first class aisle seat next to Elizabeth and tried to find a comfortable position. Alaska Airlines only thought these seats were bigger. Men who were six foot two knew better.

His daughter Jessie's good-bye still sounded in his memory. "Be good to yourself, daddy," she had said. "Don't worry about me. I'll have that bug fixed before you get back."

He smiled. If she could write that software fix for her science project before he returned Wednesday morning, he'd hire her himself. His thirteen-year-old genius. They were quite a team.

"I brought along some ideas," Elizabeth said, bending to slide her laptop under the seat. "My market analyst says that —"

"Elizabeth," he said solemnly, the smile still curving his lips, "for the duration of this flight I don't want to hear a word about retention or market analyses or even lawsuits. I want to have a drink and relax and talk about something completely trivial and unrelated to work." He touched her arm. "Okay?"

She froze, gazing at him with those wide gray eyes that reminded him of winter rain, and looked down at his fingers.

He removed them. "Got it?"

"Got it." Her voice sounded muted. He hoped he hadn't offended her. She took her job so seriously.

As the plane headed north for Vancouver, he accepted a Scotch from the flight attendant and risked a glance to his right. Elizabeth was looking out the window at the Sierras below. Her dark hair waved away from her face, swept into a roll at the back of her head. He'd never seen it any other way. Well, once. At the summer picnic she'd pulled it back into a French braid, but that hardly counted. At that same picnic she'd worn denim shorts that had knocked his socks off. Her legs were sensational, long and slender, with firm thighs and delicate ankles. He'd never seen that much of them since, and he wanted to.

In the six months since she'd joined Stratton Hill he'd found himself wanting more of Elizabeth Forrester in every way. He knew about her professional background, but nothing about her personal life except that she did a lot of volunteer work. He knew her marital status, but nothing about the people or things or places she cared about. He'd seen glimpses of her body, but other than that brief contact moments ago, had never touched her. What he did know was that when she walked into a room, people smiled. Her joy in life was catching, her caring involvement with people, sincere. He wanted her to share some of that joy and care. With him.

It was frustrating and challenging at the same time. And now with this Malinda Burke harassment thing, the possibility of satisfying his desire and his primitive craving for Elizabeth's warmth was more remote than ever.

At least they'd accomplished something together. She'd proven him right in his strategy to humanize the firm. Too many of the software engineers spent long hours cooped up in their offices, sweating over microcode in order to make Stratton Hill number one in its market. He admitted he had once been the worst offender. From their first interview, he'd known Elizabeth Forrester could take on the job — human resources and public affairs — and make the company's work atmosphere so appealing that people would compete to hire on with them. And she had. The fact that she was single and gorgeous and made his adrenaline pump every time he passed her in the hall had nothing to do with her success.

For the flight she had put on black slacks and a black angora turtleneck. Not much of an improvement on her business suits, unless you noticed the details. And he was a detail man. The slacks outlined a smooth pair of hips and a waist curved to fit a man's resting hand. She had a hell of a walk, too, a sort of graceful sway that drew his attention to her backside and kept it there all the way down the jetway to the plane.

She sighed, her breasts lifting and falling, and settled into her seat. He swallowed and glanced away, afraid she would notice the direction of his gaze. That thin angora sweater had been designed for only one thing. He imagined how the angora would feel under his palms. Thank God she hid under wool or linen jackets in the office. He'd never get any work done otherwise.

Garrett spent an entirely enjoyable few minutes speculating on the kind of bra she might be wearing. Not the wired, push-up kind. Those curves were anything but artificial. And no padding. Her nipples poked at the soft angora just enough to be utterly distracting every time he glanced over. Big nipples. He loved big nipples. They were so sensitive and erotic. Suckable. He shifted in his seat as the blood rushed to his groin, filling him, making him stiff.

Jesus. Think about something else.

Women's nipples were supposed to subside. Then why didn't Elizabeth's? Why were they still hard, poking through her bra, through her sweater, making him crazy?

She was turned on. That was it.

So what was she thinking about, there with her head tipped back against the seat, eyes closed? What was making her nipples tight and delicious and too damn visible for a public place? The guy across the aisle thought Garrett hadn't noticed him sneaking peeks at Elizabeth's breasts. She was with *him*, dammit.

"Penny for your thoughts?" he blurted abruptly, and then wished he could just get blown out the nearest window. What a stupid thing to say. He didn't want to know, anyway. She was probably thinking about the latest man in her life and the fact that because of him, Garrett Hill, she wasn't going to see him for three days.

Good.

Elizabeth smiled. "I was just thinking about Vancouver. I used to spend my summer vacations there. My aunt and uncle had a couple of acres out in White Rock and my brother and I would come for a month every year."

The first personal information she'd ever given him, and it had to be a fib. Summer vacations did not make a woman's nipples hard. He was right. She was thinking about her boyfriend, and that annoyed him no end.

"You know the area? Great. You can drive the rental car." He tipped his head back and stared at the door into the cockpit. He would not look at her breasts any more. Let that horny jerk across the aisle have the pleasure.

For all the good it was going to do either of them.

Elizabeth dropped her suitcase on the floor in the hotel room and sank down on the bed.

She'd done it.

She'd actually managed to spend two hours on a plane beside Garrett Hill without climbing into his lap and begging him to make love to her. She was going to have to buy a padded bra — or tape herself down. This was ridiculous. She was glad he was a cranky traveler. If he'd been charming and attentive, the way he was in the office, she would never have been able to sustain what little control she had.

Oh, Lord, she had to keep control. Her career depended on it.

Elizabeth began to unpack. One black skirt, with three silk blouses and coordinated jackets. One black dress for Tuesday night's management dinner. And one pair of grey leggings and a comfortable grey sweater to watch *The X-Files* in. Her favorite show would start in half an hour, giving her enough time to change, press tomorrow's blouse with her travel iron, and take the pins out of her hair.

At five minutes to nine, she settled in the middle of the bed and zapped the television on with the remote control.

Someone knocked at the door.

She crossed the room and looked out into the hallway. There was no one there. Frowning, she locked the door. When the knock came again, she realized there was a discreet door on the far side of the room, next to the bureau.

Adjoining rooms.

Great. As if this weren't difficult enough. Why hadn't she paid attention when the clerk had handed them their room keys?

"Elizabeth?" Garrett called softly, his voice muffled.

"Be right there."

A combination of anticipation and dismay spritzed into her bloodstream as she opened the door. What did he want? In her dreams he would flatten her against the wall and kiss her into a frenzy. In reality he probably wanted to go over the retention strategy one more time with a captive listener.

She opened the door, and her breath caught in her throat.

He leaned easily on the jamb, his arms crossed. The top three buttons on his shirt were open, enough to show the dusting of black hair on his chest, and his tie hung down either side of the open placket.

Don't do this to me, she thought, dazed. *It isn't fair that you look this good.*

He looked her over slowly. "Your hair's down," he said in a soft tone of surprise, as though he thought she might wear business attire to bed.

"I'm watching TV," she said.

His boyish grin made her bones melt. "*The X-Files?*"

She nodded, smiling sheepishly as though he'd caught her with her hand in the cookie jar.

"I saw the previews last week. You know what they say. You don't want to watch it alone."

"Is that an offer to protect me from paranormal activity?"

He opened his mouth as if to say something, then changed his mind. "I'm a fan too. Can I join you?"

Not dressed like that, you can't. "Sure." She stepped back and he closed her side of the twin doors behind him, leaving his side open.

As the show's teaser scene came on, he settled against the bed's headboard with a couple of pillows behind his back, while she sat, cross-legged, on the end. When the opening theme began, she looked over her shoulder.

"I'm glad you're here. This has to be a ten on the Chris Carter Creep-Out Scale."

"Does that bother you?"

"I like the UFO and psychic ones. No blood."

"I'll protect you."

"Ha. I'll remind you of that at three in the morning, when I can't sleep." The minute she said the words, she heard the double entendre and wished she could bite them back.

His eyes crinkled with a slow smile, his lashes dropping over a glance that acknowledged her slip as clearly as if he'd said so. And that he liked it.

Mortified, she turned back to the television, hugging her knees protectively against her breasts. She was going to have to watch her mouth. It was bad enough that she was sitting on a hotel bed with the Chief Technology Officer. Clumsily veiled come-ons only made it worse. He was going to think she was so desperate that she'd break her own policy to get a chance at him. He could sue for harassment, whether he had invited himself into her room or not.

She got through the rest of the hour by concentrating on the show. The episode made her blood run cold, but it kept her from falling into forbidden fantasy about the man on the bed behind her.

She shut the television off at ten o'clock and got up. "I'm glad I didn't set my VCR to tape that one."

"I told you. It's a mistake to watch that show alone." He swung his legs off the bed and pulled his tie off. "So. Are we ready for tomorrow?"

"Yes, sir. Presentation, budget, encouraging words. All here."

"Elizabeth." His voice was low, a bass caress. Oh God, that voice. It was enough to crumble her resolutions and make her throw her ethics out the window.

"What?" she whispered, her throat dry. He stood two feet away, rolling his tie up in a neat engineer's coil.

"Don't call me 'sir'."

She tried to turn it into a joke. "But you're the veep. We all have to call you 'sir'."

"No, you don't. We're co-workers. We're here to get the job done." He moved over to the door. "Join me for a drink? I've got some wine in the minibar."

She wrestled temptation to the ground. "No, thanks," she whispered. "I need to go over my notes one more time, and then I need some sleep."

"Call me, won't you?"

She looked up at him, confused. He stood so close, she could almost smell the warm, rumpled cotton of his shirt mixed with his utterly distracting cologne. "Call you?"

"When you wake up at three in the morning."

"I …" She floundered, trying to come up with a snappy retort that would break this intimate spell, but the images were too much for her.

With a smile, he slipped through the adjoining doors. Thank God. She shut hers behind him, locking it more to keep herself out of his room than to keep him out of hers.

She leaned on the door, her heart thudding in her chest. Her knees wobbled. With a featherlike brush of her fingers, she touched her nipples through the grey tunic sweater. A fiery trail of desire arrowed from the two sensitive points down to the soft, damp place between her legs, triggering the scent of her own desire.

He couldn't possibly know the effect his unconscious flirtation had on her. That was just his way. He used that softly persuasive tone on practically all the female staff, and it never failed to work. He wasn't responsible for her body's reactions. She was. And she had to keep them under control.

But that didn't stop her from taking the pillows he had been leaning on and sleeping on them, her face pressed into the warm, scented hollow where his head had been.

Chapter 2

Monday morning, when Garrett came to collect her, Elizabeth opened the door in stocking feet as she shrugged into her suit jacket.

"Hi, I'm almost ready."

"Take your time." He stood just inside the door, wearing a navy suit that made his eyes a deeper shade of blue, and brought out the smooth planes of cheekbone and jaw.

She dragged her gaze off him and retreated to the end of the bed. Shoes. She needed shoes. As she slid one foot into a high-heeled pump, his gaze traveled down her legs to her stocking-clad foot and rested there as she slipped it into the second pump.

She was acutely aware of his attention as she picked up purse and briefcase. Slowly, his gaze moved up her legs, past her conservative skirt, paused for a moment on her blouse, and stopped on her face.

"Shall we go?" he said, and held the door for her.

She felt breathless, as if he'd physically run his hands the length of her body.

Off limits. Don't even think about him that way, she told herself fiercely as the elevator dropped six floors and deposited them in the lobby. *He appreciates women. He's nice enough to pretend he appreciates you. But you work for him, and even if you didn't, he's not the kind of man who will make you happy.* His heart belonged to Stratton Hill, and he had a reputation for working longer hours than anyone she knew. Any woman who loved him would always have to take second place to his driving desire for success. She straightened her back. Her mother had taken second place to IBM for thirty years. It wasn't going to happen to Elizabeth. She wanted success, too, but not at the cost of a life outside the workplace. She had attained many of her goals—the respect of her peers, a directorship at a Fortune 500 firm, a reputation as a role model for young women. She was working on the last goal—a rewarding relationship with a loving man. Fantasies about Garrett Hill were fine in their place. But he was not the man who could give her what she needed in the long term.

The Vancouver office had arranged to have them picked up at eight thirty, and from then on it was one appointment after another. While Garrett met with the management team, Elizabeth met individually with the engineers, gathering data and formulating her own opinions about what direction they should take to retain the talent in the area. Her path crossed Garrett's several times during the course of the day. Each time he managed to exchange a smiling look or crack a whispered joke in passing that, despite her determination not to let him affect her, lifted her spirits and made her warm inside. He had the gift of making her feel as though they were partners, up here to accomplish something that mattered.

After lunch she heard his name in a hushed conversation outside the conference room door, where she was beginning her trip report on the laptop.

"Have you ever seen Garrett Hill before?" a woman's voice asked.

"No," a second woman replied. "But I recognized his voice. He looks even more gorgeous than he sounds."

"I'll say. Who's that he's with?"

"The HR director from head office."

"Do you think they're…?"

"For Pete's sake, Elise. You're going to get yourself in trouble one of these days. Didn't you read that policy in your e-mail? She's the one who wrote it."

Elizabeth froze in her chair, her notes forgotten. She felt cold, guilty — as if she'd been caught in the wrong. But no one could possibly know her internal struggles about Garrett Hill. Her behavior towards him was always professional and cordial. Particularly today. Those women were just speculating. It sounded as if it were a hobby.

But it made her realize how very thin was the line between fantasy and reality. The thought of the employees speculating about her ethics when she was trying so hard to live up to them chilled her. She had to be more careful than ever about hiding her feelings.

Accordingly, she opted for room service that evening, forcing herself to ignore the puzzled hurt in Garrett's eyes when she declined his dinner invitation. A little distance would be good for her. Keep her out of the danger zone.

But that didn't help to control the leap in her senses when she heard the quiet knock on the adjoining door at nine-thirty. She was dressed in nothing but a flowered silk slip that the Victoria's Secret catalog had assured her was a nightgown, with a matching short robe over it.

As she went reluctantly to the door, she wished she'd put on her sweater and leggings. This was no outfit to keep resolutions in.

Cautiously, she opened the door. Garrett stood in the opening, one hand kneading his shoulder, his face creased with lines of pain. "Garrett, what's the matter?" she asked, her voice filled with concern.

Frowning, he took in her silk dressing gown and the smooth length of bare leg it revealed, then looked away. "Do you have any aspirin?" he asked.

"No, I don't. Sorry. Did you pull a muscle or something?"

"I probably slept the wrong way last night. It's been hurting all day."

"You looked like you were in pain this afternoon, during the last meeting. Can I do something to help?" She hated to see that drawn look on his face. The thought of anything hurting him hurt her, too.

"Do you know how to give a back rub?" he asked, cocking one eye at her hopefully.

"The best. Come in and lie down." She led him over to the neatly made bed. He sank onto his back, grimacing as the movement tweaked his shoulder. "You need to lie on your stomach," she instructed gently.

Holding her gaze, he reached out with one hand to hook her gently behind the knee. Her entire leg suddenly became extra sensitive, as though his hand had passed over it from thigh to ankle. Thank God she'd shaved, she thought, and was instantly ashamed of herself. She had no business enjoying his caress. It was practically illegal.

His expression grew still and absorbed, as though his whole being was focused on experiencing the touch of her skin. He tugged again. "Come here."

She resisted. "No. On your stomach."

"Shirt on or off?"

She swallowed. "On. This is strictly business, Mr. Hill."

"But it hurts."

"I can get to where it hurts through your shirt."

"None of the professionals do it that way." He lay on the bed, holding her gaze. One at a time, he unfastened his shirt buttons, then slowly pulled the tails out of his waistband. The muscles of his chest flexed as he rolled briefly to one side, then the other, pulling the shirt out from under him.

Elizabeth knew her jaw had come unhinged, but she was powerless to control her face as her employer bared his body for her. Rumpled white cotton contrasted briefly against the dark mat of curly hair on his chest as he rolled to the center of the bed. He wadded up the shirt and shoved it under his chin to align his neck and shoulder muscles.

And oh, were they nicely aligned. There was something about the male back that had always excited Elizabeth. She took a moment to drink in the sight of all that sculpted muscle covered in smooth, tanned skin, and then at last, she knelt on the mattress beside him and gently laid both hands on his shoulders.

His muscles were warm and hard beneath her palms. She kneaded firmly, working her way down to the knot between his spine and his right shoulder blade. "Here's your problem," she murmured. "Relax and I'll work it out." She went after the knots in his muscles mercilessly until he was soft and pliant under her probing fingers. The pleasure of touching him, the smooth texture of his skin against her palms, enveloped her in a sensuous haze. With each passing moment her firm resolutions paled until her ethics seemed only a smoke screen between her and what she really wanted. He made small sounds as she worked over him, sounds she could imagine him making as he loved a woman. Her breasts, confined only by two thin layers of silk, began to ache as her nipples responded to her thoughts.

Stop it, she implored her body. She felt the secret place between her legs moistening and swelling. *Stop, before you lose it*!

She finished with a brisk karate chopping motion up and down his back with the blades of her hands, and sat back.

"That felt so good," he said as he rolled over slowly, his voice husky and slurred. "Why don't we run away together?"

His eyes were half shut with relaxation and pleasure as he regarded her. Reaching up, he crossed both hands behind his head. She saw his gaze drop and intensify, and realized two things at once.

The first was that the wrapped front of her dressing gown had loosened with her efforts, and her cleavage was exposed in its fragile covering of flowered silk. The second was that, under his pleated charcoal trousers, Garrett Hill was as aroused as she.

With a muffled indrawn breath, Elizabeth slid off the bed and turned away, pulling her dressing gown together and tightening the sash.

"If you're all right now, Garrett, you'd better go," she said in as calm a voice as she could muster. "We have another back-to-back day tomorrow, and the dinner will probably run late, too."

"What are you wearing, Elizabeth?" His voice was low, husky.

"I brought a black dress."

"No, I meant under that little silk robe."

Desire slammed through her and heat washed into her cheeks. *A snappy response, quick! Turn this into a joke and divert him!* The trouble was, she couldn't think of a single thing to say except the truth. And the truth would only make things worse.

As she struggled with her own silence, Garrett added, "I bet I know. I just saw a little silk nightie with nothing underneath. Am I right?"

"Garrett," she managed in a whisper, still with her back to him, "this is a highly inappropriate conversation. Please go back to your own room."

He didn't move. She could see him in the mirror, stretched out on her bed with his hands behind his head, all that chest exposed, that rampant male sexuality mocking her. Available yet not available. *He's your senior exec*, she told herself firmly. *Remember that. And while you're at it, remember dad and what he did to you and mom. Remember second place!*

"Elizabeth, we're not in the boardroom any more," he said. Her back burned where he watched her.

She closed her eyes briefly, trying to muster moral strength from somewhere within. "Garrett—"

Closing her eyes was her second mistake. Not making him leave was her first.

He came up off the bed behind her. She dragged in a breath as he reached around her and gently pulled loose the tie of her dressing gown. Her chest felt as if it would burst as he brushed the dressing gown off her shoulders and she stood in front of him clad only in the nightie, with its spaghetti straps holding up the silk. Should she run for the bathroom with its sturdy lock, or stay here and tough it out? Poised for flight, the indecision made her quiver.

"I've thought about this in the boardroom often enough," he whispered, his breath fanning her ear. The only part of his body that touched her was his erection, brushing her backside gently, teasing.

Fire burst inside her at the husky hunger that made its own music in his voice. The moment of anticipation hung breathlessly between them. Resistance. She had to resist. "You are off limits," she whispered as firmly as she could manage.

"And why is that?"

She took a deep breath, and her breasts swelled against the silk that covered them. He stood so close she could feel the heat of his body suddenly increase.

"You're my employer," she whispered.

"I'm not. You report to Alan Stratton. Your policy…" He placed his fingertips on her waist, bracketing it, and she jumped. "…applies to people…" Lightly, he touched her ribs. "…in the same management chain." His fingers slid over the silk, inching upward. "Not to us. You're so beautiful," he whispered against her ear. His breath made her shiver. Slowly, he tongued her earlobe, tracing a wet, erotic trail on the thin, sensitive skin. "I've wanted you since I first saw you. Watched your skirt ride up in Alan's staff meeting when you crossed your legs. Wished you'd take your suit jacket off and let your hair down. Wished you'd look at me just once with that smile in your eyes, as if I were a man, not a title." His fingertips rested just below her breasts. "And here you are, in a silky little nothing that shows and hides everything all at once. But I haven't seen your smile yet, and I want to."

"Please don't," she said in a ragged whisper, her eyes half shut in response to the seduction of his voice and his hands. "It isn't fair."

He made a gravelly sound in his throat, and she shuddered. "You aren't fair, either. You drive me crazy. You've got gorgeous breasts, Elizabeth. I want to sit behind you and touch them during presentations. Suck your nipples. Make you respond to me the way I respond to you."

She was going to die of desire. "Garrett, we—" she began, but with a touch as light as the silk that covered her, he brushed her nipples. "We can't... oh..."

Fire danced from his fingertips, lanced through her breasts and down into the wet, soft place between her legs that wept for him. He snugged his erection into the cleft of her buttocks, pulling her against him. She arched away, driving her breasts into his waiting hands. He groaned and cupped them, squeezing them, dragging his hands over the thin silk so her nipples abraded his palms.

She couldn't allow herself such pleasure. "Garrett, don't!" she protested in agony, whirling and pushing against his chest.

For answer, one arm slid around her waist, pulling her against him, and he bent his head and kissed her. *I've wanted his mouth for so long*, she thought as she gave up the feeble struggle and drowned in the delight of it, parting her lips, taking his tongue as it teased hers. His other hand cupped her breast, fingers sliding over the silk, feathering the nipple with his thumb. She wrapped both arms around his neck, pressing her mound against his rigid erection, as he stroked his tongue with hers, silently telling her what he wanted.

He pulled her backwards onto the bed and she fell on top of him.

"God," he gasped. "You're practically falling out of this. I want to look at you. Let me, Elizabeth. Please."

He was begging her. Garrett Hill, co-founder of Stratton Hill, was begging for pleasure only she could give him. The voice that turned her on in conference calls was husky with need, just as she'd imagined it. The mouth she adored lay against her throat, saying the words she craved.

"I can't," she cried. "This isn't right." She tried to roll away but he caught her and with both hands on her wrists, pinned her down. He threw one trouser-clad leg over both her bare ones and buried his face between her breasts.

"Yes, it is," he said, the words muffled against her skin. "Nothing's ever been so right." He transferred both wrists to one hand and grasped the hem of her nightie, pulling the slippery fabric up and over her head.

Then he was still.

He gazed at her body, his breath rough in his throat. She knew she should struggle, pull her wrists out of his grasp, even roll over and conceal her body in the rumpled bedspread. But she couldn't. That spellbound gaze was what she had secretly desired for months.

"Why do you hide under those dark suits?" he asked in a wondering tone. "You're beautiful. So beautiful." His voice faded to a whisper and he lowered his head.

Elizabeth cried out as his warm, sleek tongue dove into her cleavage, licking, tracing her curves reverently. He laved her breasts in wet, concentric circles, working toward her nipples, until Elizabeth was writhing and moaning with anticipation.

"Gorgeous nipples," he murmured against her skin. "On the plane... I could see them right through your sweater. What were you thinking about?"

"You," she said on a sigh, arching her back, pressing her left nipple toward his mouth with insistent, desperate movements.

"Me!" He lifted his chin, eyes wide, and she nearly cried out in frustration. "Please, Garrett," she begged.

"For that you get what you want, darling girl," he said, and lowered his head to suckle her. She moaned and lost herself in the pleasure as her sensitive nipples responded to the short, feathery strokes of his tongue, then teasing nibbles and bites.

He released her wrists and cupped her with both hands, lifting her breasts until her cleavage was high and convex. "I want you to wear a strapless black velvet dress tomorrow night," he whispered. "One that pushes you up and out, like this."

"You do?" she asked weakly. The dress she'd brought was modest at neck and hem. Long-sleeved. Professional. The thought of displaying that much of her body to the world was frightening.

He sat up, his hands never leaving her skin, and pulled her into his lap. She straddled him, gasping, her hands on his shoulders.

"Then in the elevator I can pull the cups down and lick you, like this." He demonstrated, his mouth closing around her nipple, the areola dimpling under his circling tongue. "When the doors open again, there we'll be, prim and proper as can be. No one but you and I will know that your skin is wet underneath."

Oh God, that voice and the pictures he made with it could seduce her as easily as his body. Her thighs clutched his narrow waist, the fabric of his trousers abrading her soft skin. She wanted to feel his skin against her legs. She wanted to peel his zipper down and reveal his erection. He lifted his face, his eyelids half closed, his lips swollen from loving her, and the last breath of her resistance faded. She bracketed that beloved face with both hands and took his mouth with hers, rubbing her breasts against his chest in slow, sinuous movements as she imprisoned his tongue between her lips and stroked it.

He moaned and reached for his fly. She lifted up long enough for him to divest himself of his trousers, and took control herself, peeling his shorts off, drawing them down the length of legs honed by hours of running and working out. His penis sprang out of its imprisonment, swollen and beaded with impatient liquid at the tip.

"Look what you do to me," he murmured, reaching for her again. "Sit in my lap. Imagine we're in the office. What are you wearing?"

She settled her swollen, slick mons against the length of his shaft, her thighs tight against his waist. "Mmmmm," she murmured as he squeezed her breasts gently together and sucked both nipples at once. "A very conservative, high-necked blouse." He made a sound of protest. "And a pleated skirt with thigh-high stockings and no panties."

"No conservative blouses allowed," he said firmly, cupping her with both hands and kissing her throat. He moved his hips, stroking his length through her wetness. "I want you to wear the kind with the pleats that crosses over the front. Like your green one." He buried his face in her cleavage, lifting his hips and grinding his penis between their bodies. She arched and stroked him in response. "Sometimes in meetings your blouse gapes open and lets me see your black lace bra. You should wear it more often. It's cut so low it barely hides your nipples." His words, breathed against her skin, made her feel swollen. Heavy. Her body was close to bursting with desire. "Some days you move suddenly and your areolas peek out... on those days I never get a single damn thing accomplished. I just sit in my office and dream about doing this."

"Garrett..." she moaned as he sucked hard on her aching nipples, drawing her flesh in as if he wanted to make her part of himself.

"What, sweet girl?"

"Please."

"Please what? Tell me what you want."

"I want you inside me."

He lay back and pulled her with him. "Are you ready for me?"

She groaned. "I've been ready since we left the Valley." And for months before that, she added silently.

"Ride me, Elizabeth," he whispered, smiling up into her eyes. A smile of such warmth and passion she could hardly believe it was for her. "I want to see your face when you come. And I want to look at your beautiful breasts when I do."

Her gaze holding his, she stroked his tumescence slowly with her body, not allowing him to enter her but moistening it with her juices, leaning forward now and again to taste his mouth. He took himself in one hand and stroked her clitoris with the head. She moaned.

"Lean forward, baby," he whispered. "Let me suck you at the same time."

He suckled, pulling at her nipples hungrily, stroking her clitoris with the swollen tip of his penis. It was like being licked in both places at once. She gasped and shuddered, the pleasure coalescing in an explosion deep within. She cried out his name as he arched and pulled her onto his thick, rigid cock, sliding up into her as the last of her orgasm rippled around his urgent flesh. He filled her, stroking hard, his hips lifting and bucking, causing her breasts to quiver. He gripped her hips and stabbed upward, making her cry out as her body clasped him again and again.

With a rough cry of fulfillment, he exploded inside her, his strokes turning into shudders at the answering quivers in her body. Still sheathed inside her as tightly as a sword in a wet, slippery scabbard, he wrapped both arms around her and drew her down to lie on his chest, where their hearts beat frantically together until she couldn't tell where hers left off and his began.

Chapter 3

Garrett heard Elizabeth's alarm clock go off through the open adjoining door as he knotted his tie. She made a soft, heartbroken sound when she realized she was alone in the bed, and he moved quickly to the door to reassure her he hadn't left her.

Leaning on her elbows, her hands gripping the edge of the mattress, she looked up with parted lips. They were too swollen, too delectable for him to resist. He knelt beside the bed and took her chin in his palm.

"Time to get up," he whispered, and tasted her lips, stroking her lower lip with his tongue. She groaned, reaching for him. "No, no, sweetheart. Time to go to work." He cupped her breasts in both hands. He was ready for her again. She was so soft and pliant and desirable, all tousled from his lovemaking.

What a night. What a woman.

"Don't want to work," she murmured against his mouth. "I want to make love with you."

"You will. All day. Come on, into the shower with you."

She swung those sensational legs over the side of the bed and stood up slowly, rubbing her body sinuously against his trousers and crisp white shirt. "Come with me?" she suggested, her eyelids heavy with desire. The sweet scent of sex on her skin rose hot between them. She pouted, her lower lip glistening, waiting for a kiss.

Lord above. This was the buttoned-down Elizabeth Forrester, this sensuous woman with the body of a goddess and a mouth made for sin? He had wanted to claim some of the warm attention she showered on people for himself, but he'd never dreamed of anything like this.

"No," he said, taking her by the shoulders and aiming her into the bathroom. "I'm dressed. Go shower. And then I want to watch you dress."

She was showered and dried in fifteen minutes. "So," she said, standing by the closet door, "what should I wear?" Her challenging glance over one naked shoulder nearly undid him, but he stayed where he was, savoring the pleasure of looking at her round backside and the luscious profile of her left breast from his seat on the edge of her bed.

"Tell me you wear stockings, not pantyhose," he said, his voice husky.

"Yes, I do."

"Put them on."

Her back to him, she pulled a pair of black bikini underpants from her suitcase and shimmied into them. Then she sat on the bed and pulled on a pair of thigh-high black stockings with lacy tops. Slipping her feet into black high-heeled pumps, she slowly strolled around the corner of the bed and stood in front of him.

He suddenly felt as if his shirt were a size too small.

"All right so far, boss?" she asked, reaching out to touch his cheek with one fingertip.

"Oh, yeah," he gritted.

She smiled. "Good." She reached into her suitcase and pulled out her bra, and he stopped her.

"No. No bra."

"No bra? Are you serious? I have to wear a bra."

"No." The pleasure of the day to come was almost more than he could stand, and it showed in his voice. "I want to look at your nipples through your blouse all day. I want the branch manager to suspect you've got nothing on underneath, but not really know. I want to fondle you when no one's looking, maybe even taste you. Go on. Put your blouse on now."

Her gaze clung to his and her lips had parted. She was breathing faster, and when she slipped the emerald green silk blouse on, crossing the surplice front and buttoning it at the waist, her breasts lifted and fell in a way that confirmed his fantasies had been accurate.

"Ah, Elizabeth," he breathed. The silk clung lovingly, the pleats stretching apart over her curves. The lamplight glistened in the silky-smooth valley of her cleavage. "Yes." He got up and touched her nipples with his fingertips, stroking them in tiny circles. "Nothing between me and you, between you and everyone's eyes, but this thin little bit of silk. We can make love all day simply by looking at each other. Don't you think that's erotic?"

"I think it's crazy," she whispered. "I can't possibly…"

He slipped a hand inside the V created by the two pleated halves, lifting one breast as though his hand were the cup of a bra, and her voice faded on an indrawn breath. The silk glimmered as it slipped over his knuckles.

"Yes, you can. Now, your skirt."

Frustration fought with uncertainty as she tossed her hair back and pulled away. Her black skirt hugged her hips and fell just to the point at the top of her calves which emphasized the sculpted curve. Then she moved into the bathroom to put up her hair.

Garrett leaned on the door frame, watching as she lifted her arms, twisting her chocolate-dark mane into the neat French roll. Her back arched.

"Mmmmm." His appreciation rasped deep in his throat. He waited until her hair was in place, then moved behind her and filled his hands with her flesh wrapped in warm emerald silk.

"No," she said impertinently, twisting out from under his touch and walking over to the closet for her jacket. "If delayed gratification is what you want, Garrett, that's exactly what you're going to get." She shot him a challenging look from under thick lashes. "Look only. No touch."

"We'll see about that."

She kept her jacket on through breakfast and the first two meetings of the day. But as she walked down the hall beside him on their way to the conference room, where they were scheduled to watch a multimedia presentation developed by the sales group, he was amply rewarded. The lights of the hallway glinted off the glossy jacquard surface of her blouse, highlighting her delicious double bounce as she walked.

He nodded to the people seated around the conference table, shaking hands with the sales team. The lights went down, and Elizabeth shrugged out of her jacket. As the presentation opened, he glanced to his right. He had chosen seats in the back of the room on purpose. He disliked sitting in the front of a theater, and besides, he wanted the attention of all the other men in the room firmly focused away from him and Elizabeth.

He could just make out her profile next to him, dimly lit by the colors playing on the screen. She was building barriers between them again this morning, despite the way they had made love last night, despite the way she had joined him in playing out his fantasy today. There had to be a way to break through that resistance and make her see that he was hers ... and had been from the first. He craved her. Not just physically—although making love with Elizabeth was the best he had ever known—but in his heart, in that deepest part of him that had been empty and crying out for solace since Juliet had left him years before.

He was hers. And she would be his or he'd die trying.

Slowly, he slid one hand under her arm and touched her nipple. She drew in a startled breath, and her nipple hardened instantly under the silk. He traced its shape with feathery strokes. He had never met a woman whose nipples were so sensitive and at the same time so lush and erotic. And the shape of her breasts seemed to satisfy some aesthetic need within him — they were big, yet so firm and erect and round, ripe for a man's hands and mouth. It was obvious they were a source of enormous sexual pleasure for her when he touched them... a pleasure he loved to give her.

Slowly, he reached into the V of her neckline and cupped her left breast, marveling that his hand could hardly contain it. But he couldn't enjoy it long; someone at the front of the room shifted and turned his head, and Garrett sat back.

Under the table, where it was utterly dark, he ran a hand up Elizabeth's thigh, past the smooth nylon of her stocking to the skin exposed above it. She sat back in her chair and drew one foot up under her, opening her legs. He took the invitation immediately, absorbing the secret softness of her inner thigh against his fingers. Her skirt whispered against the back of his hand as he touched the damp crotch of her panties.

She shivered, echoing his own excitement. Desire pooled in his groin, heavy and pulsing. His sex thickened, stretching the fabric of his briefs.

He slipped a finger inside the band of her bikini panties, sliding down into her curly thatch. Above the table, his other hand cupped his chin thoughtfully, one elbow on the arm of the chair, as he stared at the screen. The presentation had ten minutes to go and he hadn't absorbed a kilobyte.

He found her clitoris and stroked. Her lips parted as she tried to control her breathing. As his finger slid over the creamy-slick nubbin, she bit her lower lip. Garrett drew the pleasure out, stroking on both sides, then underneath the wet little pearl of her pleasure. With every uneven breath, her breasts thrust against the confining blouse but he couldn't touch them as she came, no matter how much he wanted to. He felt a rush of wet heat and her back went rigid as her lips clamped shut on a cry. He stroked her twice more, luxuriously, making her shudder, before he slid his hand slowly from her body.

She pulled her skirt down and crossed her legs. Profile turned toward the screen, she remained still and collected until the lights came up.

The juices of her orgasm dried on his fingers as the general manager got up and began to speak. Garrett leaned his chin on his hand, his fingers resting on his upper lip, breathing deeply. The scent of Elizabeth. Rich with her own special tang.

As the meeting concluded, he dragged his mind off the woman next to him, and stood up to make a recommendation to the group. The plan he'd formulated with Elizabeth and the general manager, Brady Grant, a young man of about thirty-four whose affability and keen business sense made him one of the rising stars at Stratton Hill, was unanimously agreed to, and the meeting broke up with handshakes and smiles all around.

Garrett saw Brady shake hands with Elizabeth, his grip so enthusiastic that her breasts jiggled before she was finally able to extract her hand. Brady placed himself between her and the small crowd near the projection screen as he asked her something in low, earnest tones.

Garrett moved in beside them, his briefcase in one hand. "Ms. Forrester, may I have a moment with you?"

"Certainly." With a sinuous movement of escape, she walked to the far side of the conference table, put on her jacket, and began to slide several file folders into her own briefcase.

Garrett smiled at Brady. The man was a huge asset to Stratton Hill, even if his timing was lousy. He'd been one of the first to take Elizabeth's Quality of Life strategies and implement them in the Vancouver office. "Thanks for the great presentation, Brady," he said. "I appreciate all the work your people put into it. I'll see you this evening at dinner, all right?"

"Yes. You're welcome, Garrett. I was asking Ms. Forrester if she — er — if the two of you would like to join me for lunch? There's a little place around the corner that serves great hot and sour soup, and I promised Ms. Forrester I'd take her there if she ever got up to see us."

So he was asking her out to lunch, was he? No doubt so he could ogle her over steamed rice and get a little steamed up himself.

"You two know each other?" Garrett asked, still smiling.

"She was my first call when this tech theft thing first came up. We've been talking off and on for several months over the new programs, too."

Elizabeth smiled at Brady, and his eyes seemed to glaze over. "If we hadn't come soon, I'd have had to put a separate line on my phone just for your calls."

"Right. Elizabeth." His tongue lingered on the syllables of her name, and Garrett lost his patience.

"I appreciate the offer, but we have a lunch meeting scheduled with an outside consultant. I was hoping to take a few minutes now to brief Ms. Forrester on what I want them to accomplish during the next quarter. If you'll excuse us?"

Brady nodded and gave a halfhearted smile, clearly disappointed. He backed out of the room and Garrett closed the door softly.

Pushing the thumb lock in firmly, he turned to Elizabeth. "Months of phone calls? E*liz*abeth?" He drawled her name, exaggerating Brady's pronunciation.

"An outside con*sul*tant?" she riposted in the same tone, sitting on the edge of the conference table. "First I've heard."

"Me too," Garrett said unrepentantly. "But I saved you from becoming the object of Brady's fantasies over lunch." His slow, hot gaze perused her, and he stripped her jacket off, tossing it on a chair. She leaned back on her hands, and his lips parted as the pleats in the front of her blouse spread. "The man is smitten. He didn't take his eyes off you once." He stepped closer, and touched the fragile fabric over one nipple. "Neither did anyone else. Including me."

"That's what you wanted, wasn't it?" She stood and wrapped her arms around his neck, crushing her breasts against his chest. Their firm heaviness inflamed him, and he stiffened again, pressing against her pelvic bones. "The only one I want looking at me is you," she whispered, her breath soft against his mouth. He dipped his head and licked her lower lip, sucking it into a kiss.

"You owe me for saving you," he murmured gruffly. He slipped a hand into her blouse and fondled her breast, pushing it up and shaping deep, curved cleavage. He kissed her throat and moved down, pushing her blouse aside and licking the exposed areola with wet, swirling motions. "I bet Brady wants to do this. He thought he was hiding it, but I could tell." He suckled her nipple fiercely, and she moaned. He felt her hands close on his cock, and he shuddered. "Yeah. You owe me." She stroked him through the fabric of his trousers, her fingers tight on him, as urgent as he.

She unbuckled his narrow leather dress belt and the button at the top of his fly. His cock leaped and bucked against the backs of her fingers as she eased his zipper down.

"Mmmm," she murmured, plunging both hands into his briefs. Her arms squeezed her breasts together, and the sight combined with her hands on him nearly made him lose control.

She sank slowly to her knees and he reached behind him for the back of a chair. "Elizabeth —" he said, his voice a rough whisper in his throat. "God —"

She pulled his briefs down and devoured him whole. His body convulsed as her luscious lips surrounded his cock, her tongue swirling around the base of the head, where he was most sensitive. She sucked on him the way he sucked her nipples, pulling him in and making his knees go weak.

He pushed her blouse off her shoulders but the storm of pleasure blotted out the ability to do more. It was an effort to drag air into his lungs. Her lashes spread on her cheekbones like dark fans, closed in pleasure and concentration. Her pulsing tongue and the suction was going to pull the soul out of him, was going to make him burst, was going to —

He made a sound that could have been a shout but was strangled by the need for secrecy into a hoarse whisper, and he exploded into her loving mouth.

Chapter 4

Never in her life had Elizabeth lived through a day like this one. Nothing in her past relationships had prepared her for the sheer sensual pleasure and raw enjoyment of sex shared with Garrett Hill. In the ladies' room, Elizabeth took a wet paper towel into the stall with her. The scent of her own juices, she was sure, acted like a magnet to horny men — general managers and salesmen in particular.

She had never exposed her body like this before, never known the secret sense of power that a woman could exercise over men. Garrett was teaching her the potential of her own sensuality —and the fact that he was enjoying it to the full made it no less valuable a lesson.

She washed her hands and ran a comb through her hair, catching the few stray strands that had come unmoored when she had gone down on her knees to him. The memory of his swollen flesh in her mouth, of the sounds of surrender and passion she could tease from him, made desire ripple through her body.

It was time to stop fooling herself. This powerful emotion, this desire — face it, this impossible love she'd been denying for months — was more intense because deep in her heart, she knew it couldn't last past the end of this trip. She bit her lip and pushed away the thought. She wanted to think about the sweetness of the moment, about these few days of loving Garrett, not the price she would eventually pay.

After he'd collapsed into one of the conference room chairs, he'd drawn her into his lap and rested his forehead on her collarbone. His uneven breathing had slowed against the upper slope of her breast. The few intense moments of silence and closeness they shared were like nothing she had ever experienced before. His hair was soft under her fingers as she'd stroked him with a feathery touch. His body, so hard and warm and strong, had curled around hers in an embrace so sweet she was still flushed with warmth.

Maybe that was what drew her to him so strongly. Not his charisma and authority, although no one in the Valley could deny that. Several women had pursued him on the basis of that alone, if office gossip could be believed. No, she'd sensed a vulnerability within him — a yearning in his eyes she'd seen when he thought no one was observing him. That yearning called to the deepest part of her nature, the part that wanted to share and console and heal.

She loved him. There was no escaping it — and no sharing it, either. Not as long as either of them worked at Stratton Hill. She loved him. But she loved her self-respect and the fulfillment her career brought as well.

Elizabeth straightened her jacket and smoothed both hands down the front of her skirt. There. At least she was presentable again, her gaze level, the flush in her cheeks receding. Only two more meetings, and she and Garrett could return to the hotel. She wasn't ready yet to let the fantasy end.

Fortunately for her ability to concentrate, both meetings were with the human resources generalists stationed in the Vancouver office. Garrett would be in a different wing of the building with a focus group of technicians. She had no doubt that his enthusiasm and sheer love of the business would be catching. If AlphaTech called tomorrow, no matter how attractive their offers, they'd be fresh out of luck.

At five o'clock she commandeered the conference room to steal a few moments of quiet to enter more notes into her trip report. As she pulled the pad out of her briefcase, a folded piece of paper fluttered to the floor. Frowning, she picked it up. It was the white grid paper the engineers used, not the yellow legal pads she wrote on.

She opened the paper. The words were written in block capitals in dark blue ink.

"Harken, Jezebel, flaunting the charms of thy flesh to tempt the souls of men. Harken lest thou be damned to hellfire forever, to tongues of flame which will lick your body and consume it. Woman was made to submit to man, not to tempt him past bearing to thoughts of sin. Vengeance is mine, saith the Lord! Your soul can still be saved if you submit to His power. You must strip yourself naked of all worldly lusts and go down upon your knees before him. You must take the rod of his punishment between your lips and accept his power as it fills you. You must submit. Only in doing this can you be saved."

Somebody saw us, was Elizabeth's first panicked thought. Her stomach clenched as she did a quick scan of the conference room. Though it had exterior windows, they were fifteen floors up. There was only one door to the hallway, and no interior windows at all.

Common sense returned. She crumpled the note and tossed it in her briefcase. Stratton Hill was harboring a nut, that was all. A religious nut who couldn't handle the guilt of his own sexual fantasies and had to level the blame at the woman starring in them. In this case, herself. Well, Garrett had told her that the imaginations of Brady and the salesman were probably running wild. She hadn't expected it to get this wild, though. Writing the note had probably been as close as the nut would come to an orgasm.

She had to remember her professionalism and call a halt to Garrett's erotic suggestions from now on. She glanced at the crumpled ball of paper. Should she show it to him? No. It was an unwelcome reminder of her own guilt, and she didn't want anything to spoil the fantasy bubble they were living in. Reality would bite soon enough. Garrett would probably initiate a manhunt and then all hell would break loose. The nut case could be any one of fifty or sixty people on the floor, and was probably harmless. She dismissed him from her mind.

Back at the hotel, Elizabeth knocked on Garrett's door. After a moment he opened it, a marbled paper shopping bag in one hand. Slipping his free arm around her waist, he kissed her with a sensuous thoroughness that left her mindless and gasping. Lord above, his mouth was going to be her undoing.

"What's in the bag?" she asked, when she could think clearly enough to string words together.

He lifted a dark eyebrow and walked over to the bed. "I meant it, you know," he said. Reaching into the bag, he pulled out a length of black velvet.

"Meant wh— oh, my God, Garrett. You didn't."

He looked pleased and feral at the same time, laugh lines crinkling at the corners of his eyes. "Oh, but I did. This hotel has a great shop downstairs. *Veni, vidi*, Visa."

He held out a strapless dress.

"Where the hell is the rest of it?" she demanded breathlessly. "Garrett, I couldn't possibly wear that to a business dinner."

"We'll talk about that later. Come on. Try it on for me."

So much for calling a halt to his erotic suggestions. With a resigned sigh that only half disguised her dismay, she reached back and unzipped her skirt. Stepping out of it, she unbuttoned her blouse, every cell aware that Garrett's eyes were locked on her. She pulled the blouse open slowly, feeling the whisper of silk as each pleat resisted and then surrendered. The blouse slid liquidly down her arms and she dropped it on top of the skirt.

"Looking at you is almost as much pleasure as touching you," Garrett whispered. "Let me touch you."

"No," she whispered back. "We're getting dressed for dinner."

He held out the velvet dress and she stepped into it carefully. She shimmied the soft fabric over her hips and leaned forward to fit her breasts into the boned cups of the bodice. She reached behind, her back arching, and sang the zipper up its track.

"Dear God," Garrett breathed.

The dress nipped in her waist and snugged over her bottom, leaving a smooth length of leg below. The rich texture of the velvet made her skin look as delicate and translucent as fine porcelain, and made her eyes and lips look even more sultry. The boned cups supported her breasts, pushing them up and out in classic round curves, a magnet for the eye.

Garrett ran his skillful, long-fingered hands over her hips, up her ribs, and cupped her velvet-covered breasts as he watched her in the mirror. "You don't need any jewelry. A pair of earrings at most." Slowly, he stroked her bare curves with his fingertips. "Does it turn you on when men look at you?"

She tried to concentrate on answering him while the pleasure rippled along her skin. "I don't know. I've never dressed this way in my life," she sighed. Other men's responses didn't matter. Only Garrett's. "It turns me on when *you* look at me. And touch me like this."

"Why do you hide this beauty under those dark suits?"

"Beauty isn't professional."

"I wouldn't say that." He kissed her shoulder. "But I must admit, it was your brains and your success that got my attention at first." He turned her to face him. They shared a look that contained the memory of their first interview, and the mutual respect in their interactions since.

"Nobody at Stratton Hill even knows I *have* a body," Elizabeth said firmly.

"Except me," Garrett whispered. "I know how luscious your nipples are, how erotic you smell after making love. I know the sensitive spot behind your knees that you like me to lick. I find it incredibly sexy that your breasts are so sensitive, and that looking at them across the dinner table will be like touching them in public. I like being the only one who knows." He kissed her, his tongue sliding against hers, hot and languid. "You're a fantasy come true."

The heat of desire in his voice and eyes kindled her responses into a blaze. He nuzzled her bare shoulder, tasting her skin, his kisses slow, as though it mattered to him that she experience the pleasure each movement brought. But his words struck a wistful chord in the part of her mind that still resisted him even when they were locked together in mind-bending love.

"I'm not a fantasy," she whispered, brushing one cheek against his hair as he bent to his pleasurable task. "I'm real. Our relationship — everything you just said — is the fantasy, Garrett."

His movements stilled and he lifted his head to look into her eyes. "What do you mean? Of course you're real. You're the most real, intense part of my life right now."

Right now. That's all it was. The hotter the flame, the briefer its life. The hurt splashed through her body and chilled her passion as effectively as a bucket of cold water. He could fit her in on a trip, where his working hours were limited, but what about later, when they returned home? Even if she could get around that damned policy, a relationship was next to impossible.

She stepped out of his arms and he straightened, puzzled.

"What's the matter? What is it?" With brisk, businesslike movements she unzipped the velvet dress and took it off, pulling her silk robe off its hanger and wrapping it around her. "Elizabeth, for God's sake, talk to me."

"I need to face the truth," Elizabeth said, trying to get the honest words out before she lost her courage. "Our... my feelings for you may be very strong, but they don't change reality. And the reality is that not only do we now have a policy against what we're doing, we have an extremely harassment-sensitive work force, thanks to Ms. Burke. You're the most visible person at Stratton Hill. I have a professional reputation. Add one to the other and it precludes any relationship between you and me, Garrett." She paused. She didn't dare look up into his eyes. "Also, I have strong feelings about what it takes to preserve my quality of life. Or I did," she finished miserably. "Until now."

"I told you before, that policy is for people in the same reporting structure. It doesn't apply to us since you work for Alan. It's nobody's damn business what I do with my private life, anyway. And what's this about the quality of your life? Look at me, sweetheart." He frowned as he struggled to make sense of her words. "You make it sound as if I'm having a negative effect on it."

Elizabeth laid both hands on his chest and spoke quietly. "Please don't mis-understand me. We've had an incredible two days, and I'll treasure them always. But I can't do this." He took a breath to speak, and she covered his mouth with a finger. "Let me finish. I care about you and I think you care about me. But everything else aside, our goals in life are too different. You live for Stratton Hill. I can't. I just don't see a future for us. Not the kind I'm looking for, anyway." Elizabeth's voice failed on the last words, and the tears choked off anything more she wanted to say.

Garrett tried to take her in his arms. "Elizabeth. Darling. I never thought I'd hear you say you care. I can't believe it. It's —"

"Garrett, didn't you hear any of what I just said?"

"Of course I did, but I'm focusing on the important part. We care about each other. That's what matters most."

For an engineer and a strategist, he could be surprisingly unrealistic. "But I'm looking for a future, Garrett. A meaningful future. And I don't think you can offer me that."

"What do you call a meaningful future?" His voice was too quiet.

She needed to explain this clearly, without sounding like a needy female. Her mother's behavior with her father flashed into her memory, and stiffened her resolve. "It's not as if I want white picket fences; I'm just not that kind of person. But I do want a home I can share with a man I love and respect. I want a partnership where the first priority is our life together. And some day I want children, which will make it even more important that our priorities are in the right order. Which would mean business in second place."

"Do you expect me to propose?" He was trying hard to understand. Elizabeth's heart squeezed with love and her own pain at having to deny them both what they desperately wanted.

"No, of course not. It's too soon to expect anything from each other."

He dropped her hands as if they burned him, and walked over to the window. "That's the most unkind thing anyone has ever said to me." His shoulders were rigid with hurt.

"Oh, God." For an expert in human resources, she was really making a mess of this. Where were all her communication skills when she needed them? "What I'm trying to say is that Stratton Hill isn't my entire life now, and won't be in the future." She crossed the room, and touched his shoulder blade with a gentle hand. "Garrett, my dad gave thirty years to IBM. I grew up without him. For God's sake, my mother took me to the father-daughter dance because he was tied up on a project and couldn't give me the time. I've learned the hard way how important it is to put relationships first."

He turned to her slowly. "And you think I wouldn't?"

"I know you wouldn't," she said, her voice husky with tears. "I've seen how you —"

Someone banged on his door in the adjoining room and they jumped, startled. Elizabeth twisted away from him and pushed him into his own room. If anyone from Stratton Hill caught him in her room in her present state of emotional and physical nakedness, they would both be hopelessly compromised.

"We're not done yet," Garrett promised as she tried to push the door shut against his shoulder. "Count on it."

She bumped the door shut with the weight of her body and flattened her back against it. "How can you defend what everyone sees every day?" she whispered into the empty silence.

Male voices murmured for a few moments on the other side of the door. When her telephone rang, she was concentrating so hard on distinguishing the voice of Garrett's visitor that she jumped again. *My nerves are shot*, she thought as she drew in a deep breath, trying to make her heart slow down. *This has got to stop.* She picked up the receiver. "Elizabeth Forrester."

"Hi, Elizabeth. It's Brady. I'm next door, using Mr. Hill's phone. I came to pick you both up and take you to the restaurant."

The restaurant. Right. She was supposed to face Garrett across a dinner table in front of an audience and pretend nothing had happened.

"How kind of you, Brady," she said, hoping her voice didn't sound as strained as she felt. "I'm just changing. I'll be ready in ten minutes if that's okay."

"That's fine. I'll be down in the lobby. I'm looking forward to seeing you... in a more relaxed atmosphere. It's probably been a stressful couple of days. You sound as if you could use a drink."

His voice was warm with concern and a kind of teasing friendliness. She could use some friendliness. Nice, uncomplicated, platonic friendliness.

"Thanks, Brady," she said, her voice sounding a little closer to normal. "I'll take you up on it. See you all in a few."

She hung up and turned to the bed, where the velvet dress lay twisted inside out. Innocuous. Only fabric. It had been constructed to bewitch and seduce, but it needed a woman inside it to make its designer's dream come true.

In a brief moment of weakness, she allowed herself to ask *what if*? What if Garrett shared her views? What if he and she were alone, without Stratton Hill, and with hope for the future? She could wear his gift to dinner, seduce him from across the table... could allow herself to be seduced by the hunger and appreciation in his eyes. Could look forward to the night — and the days — to come.

Elizabeth sighed. *What if* was a useless exercise. He would be a different man, and then she probably wouldn't be so attracted to him. His confidence, his success, his drive, the way he drew people to him—all these things made him what he was. She treasured that in him, even though she knew it meant her own unhappiness. Maybe she'd just imagined the vulnerability in his eyes in those unguarded moments. There was no room in this situation for happiness.

In the business world she had schooled herself to deal with reality, no matter how hard it was. And a woman faced reality in a high-necked, medium length, black georgette dress.

Chapter 5

The hurt in Garrett's eyes as she met him in the hallway was so painful she had to turn away. She had rejected his gift, had returned to her old look instead of the unbound, sexy one to which he had introduced her. It was like rejecting him a second time. She led the way out of the elevator into the lobby, her shoulders prickling with awareness of his gaze — and his disappointment. As Brady waved from the doorway, Garrett leaned over and whispered, "Stockings?"

"Pantyhose," she replied grimly. "Don't push me."

Even their banter was gone. She felt his emotional withdrawal from three feet away. He pulled his executive formality around him like a magician's cloak and they climbed into Brady's car, some kind of long, gas-guzzling classic she couldn't identify, which was running at the curb under the *porte cochère*. She slid into the wide front seat while Garrett fulminated in the back, and responded automatically to Brady's running commentary on the landmarks they passed. Anything to keep from turning around and feeding her weakness by gawking at Garrett. In his double-breasted charcoal suit and silk tie, freshly shaved and combed, he looked good enough to eat.

Bad choice of words, Liz, she chided herself as a bolt of desire zipped along her veins and made her shift restlessly in her seat.

"Your Caddy's in great shape, Brady," Garrett said in an effort to be sociable. "What year is it?"

"Fifty-nine," Brady said proudly. "My brothers and I have been restoring it for most of our lives. Do you drive a classic?"

"No. A Lexus. This kind of thing is fun, but it isn't my style."

Brady subsided, evidently believing he had been snubbed, then turned to Elizabeth a few moments later. "You told me not long ago that you're an *X-Files* fan," Brady said with a grin, unaware of the tension between his passengers. "You know it was filmed here, right?"

"I'd heard that, yes."

"Sometime when you're up here I'd be happy to take you on an *X-Files* tour of Vancouver. What a marketing pitch, eh? I'm surprised the Ministry of Tourism hasn't hit on it yet. We could also go to Lighthouse Park, where they filmed 'Darkness Falls.' And Stanley Park, of course. Did you know they made Siberia out of a parking lot for 'Tunguska'?"

"No, I didn't. That's fascinating." Any other time it would be. What if she and Garrett could get away and do something like that together?

What if. Stop it, Liz. It's pointless.

"I doubt Elizabeth will be able to get to Vancouver very often," Garrett pointed out in a voice devoid of expression. "I trust we won't be having employee retention crises on a regular basis."

"No, of course not," Brady assured him in the rear view mirror, then negotiated his way around a bus. "But the techs are pumped up now that they've met you. I'd recommend twice yearly visits. At least."

"I'll be happy to come," Garrett said. Elizabeth looked out the window at the Vancouver skyline and the mountains beyond.

"Oh. Great!" Brady recovered fast. "I think the connection with Corporate can only improve morale. But you know, Vancouver is also a great place for a vacation."

"I know," Elizabeth said absently.

"Elizabeth used to come here as a child," Garrett explained to Brady, staking out unspoken rights to her personal history.

"No kidding!" Brady said, a flush mounting his cheeks as he ran a hand through his reddish-brown hair. "So I'm just telling you what you already know."

"I know the area, that's all. I had no idea about all the *X-Files* stuff," Elizabeth said. She really had to be more approachable. Garrett was going to crush poor Brady if she didn't step in and lighten things up. "That tour you mentioned sounds like a lot of fun. No moonlighting as a guide for the tourists, though. We need you full time."

"Another career path bites the dust," Brady said, shaking his head with mock regret. "But at least you'll get a preview tonight. We're meeting my staff in the restaurant in Queen Elizabeth Park. That's where they filmed the graveyard scene in the pilot episode."

"I'm not eating dinner in a graveyard!" Garrett exclaimed.

"Relax, sir. This place is one of the classiest in town."

Under any other circumstances, Elizabeth would have been enchanted by the view from the restaurant. It sat on a hill, surrounded by parkland. The lights and towers of Vancouver glimmered in the late summer twilight as the sunset faded. The maitre d' led them to their table, where the three members of Brady's immediate staff were already seated. Over the past two days she had become acquainted with Marie D'Aoust, who ran the technical writing arm of the development organization, as well as the two men who were responsible for software development and the quality and test functions.

The note she'd found in her briefcase flickered briefly in her mind's eye. Were any of these people the author? She closed her eyes briefly. *Nice going, Liz. Of course not. You've been working with them in close quarters for two days. You have bigger problems right now than obscure religious nuts.*

Brady pulled out her chair for her, and then sat down next to her. Garrett shook hands with Marie and seated himself opposite Elizabeth. His gaze rested on her — somber, watchful and very, very sexy.

It was going to be a long dinner.

Elizabeth sipped her wine as Garrett asked Brady about the employment situation in Vancouver, and how it might affect their ability to attract talent in the area. The conversation stayed businesslike until after the entrées had been cleared and the dessert menu presented.

"I couldn't," Elizabeth protested to the waiter. "The prime rib was the best I ever tasted. Anything more would be too much."

"We could split the blackberry cheesecake," Marie suggested.

"I can't even do that. I'm full."

"I'll split some with you. My daughter and I do it all the time," Garrett said, turning the charm of his smile on Marie. To the waiter, he said, "The blackberry cheesecake, please. And two forks."

Helplessly, Elizabeth watched Marie, whom she knew from their coffee room conversations to be happily married and four months pregnant, melt and dissolve under that smile. *Jealousy is idiotic and immature*, she scolded herself, finishing off the last of her wine. *He turns that smile on everyone. You have no special rights to it.*

The waiter discreetly brought a second plate as well as two forks. *You do this with your daughter?* she thought. *When do you ever see her?*

The lights dimmed, and behind her she heard the sounds of a band tuning up. As they swung into 'In The Mood,' Elizabeth found herself dangerously close to tears. She wanted to dance. With Garrett. She wanted to wear her strapless velvet dress and spend the rest of the evening in his arms, his body brushing hers, held close to his white shirt, the heat of his skin penetrating the fabric under her hands. *Stop hurting yourself, Liz.*

For the Director of Human Resources, her choice in relationships sure was lousy. If she had any sense at all, she'd go for Brady Grant. She had to admit he was adorable. She'd never been partial to redheads, but he had nice eyes and an engaging grin. They had Vancouver and *The X-Files* in common, to start with. And Brady had one thing going for him that Garrett didn't.

He practiced what he preached. The programs they'd set up for the Vancouver office were successful because he backed them. This technician theft thing was a temporary aberration. For the most part, the employees here seemed to be happier and more fulfilled in their families and communities than those in many companies in their market. And all because Brady believed in what she was trying to do. If he had had kids, *he'd* have time for them.

The music pulled at her, making her shoulders sway and her foot tap.

"Do you like this one?" Brady asked. "These guys are pretty good. They play the clubs in town a lot. My brother knows the bass player."

"Love it. 'In The Mood' is one of my favorites."

"Would you like to dance?"

A sideways glance at Garrett's face was enough to decide her. The Rolling Stones were right. *You can't always get what you want.* "Sure."

Brady grabbed her hand and led her out onto the dance floor, where half a dozen couples twisted and swung energetically to the music. He was a good dancer, smooth and easy to follow. She hadn't danced in years, but felt the steps coming back, knew instinctively when to swing out to arms' length and when to whirl back in.

The song ended, and the band segued into Bob Seger's 'Old Time Rock and Roll.' Brady and Elizabeth jived like teenagers. Elizabeth let the music and the beat lift her away from her misery and the hopeless waste of her love on an unattainable man. She concentrated on the steps and on the male admiration in Brady's eyes, and maneuvered so that they were dancing on the side of the room closest to the band, with a crowd between her and Garrett.

Halfway through the third song Jim Wilson, the QA manager, tapped Brady on the shoulder. "Mind if I cut in, boss?"

Elizabeth smiled, and over Jim's shoulder saw that Eric Bouvier was dancing with Marie. Though she clasped Jim's hands and responded to his conversation as they swung together, she had no control over her feminine antennae, which were continuously scoping the room for Garrett. She and Marie traded partners and she was hardly aware of it. Where was he? Who was he dancing with? Why should she care, anyway?

"I'm going to pull rank on you, Eric."

Eric faded into the crowd as his Chief Technology Officer slid an arm around Elizabeth's waist and took her hand. The band picked that moment to slide into a slow, bluesy number that kicked her heart into panic mode.

She said the first thing that came into her head. "Pulling rank is bad for morale."

"It's an option I exercise once in a while. Why are you avoiding me?"

"I'm not. I'm fraternizing with the troops."

"Are you sure that's all you're doing? Brady Grant was practically glassy-eyed when he staggered back to the table."

"Stop it, Garrett."

"I didn't see much body contact during those fast numbers, but for a determined man — or woman — I suppose it's possible."

"There was no body contact. Not that it's any of your business. You and I have no claims on each other."

She should have known better than to challenge him like that. He pulled her an inch closer, not enough for any indiscretion to be observed by their co-workers, but enough for the tips of her breasts to brush his shirt front. "Only this," he murmured under the music. "And this." He changed direction, and his leg slid between hers, his thigh hard and uncompromising. His lashes dropped low over his eyes, and the glinting heat in them made her shiver. His gaze dropped to her mouth, and she realized with horror that her lips were parted for a kiss.

"Damn you," she whispered. He watched her lips move. Garrett could make simple speech into a sexual act just by the intensity of his focus. If she licked her lips now it would be as overt an invitation as removing her clothes.

"What for?" he responded. "For making you want me?"

"Yes."

"For making it plain that I want you? Even covered to the neck in this prim little outfit?"

"Yes. I look professional, and don't you deny it."

"You look unapproachable." He pulled her another inch closer, and she tried to resist until his breath brushed her ear. "You have such beautiful breasts it makes me hard just knowing they're under there, barely confined in that black bra," he whispered. "And when you're turned on, like you are now, the scent from between your legs mixes with your perfume."

A bolt of pure desire sizzled through her. His voice was so sexy, his body warm against hers as they moved to the slow beat of the music. She was drowning in him. Drowning in his seduction in front of the whole room.

"So why are you denying the magic between us?" he demanded softly. "We're lovers for two days and it's the best I've ever known — and suddenly I'm not good enough for you any more." His hand played on her back, a delicate sensation that traveled from lumbar curve to waist to shoulder. The pleasure of his touch made her want to weep at giving him up. "Help me understand, Elizabeth."

The tears rushed to clog her throat. Another few seconds and she was going to break down and make an even greater fool of herself. "It isn't what you've done, it's what you are, Garrett, don't you see? You're a good man, a successful leader. That's great in the work place. But at what cost to your home life? I lived it once. I'm not going to live it over again."

"You don't think my personal life is a success?"

The sense of loss seemed to harden into a ball in her chest, and her body chilled. "How can it be, Garrett?" she asked sadly. "You don't spend any time on it."

She pulled out of his arms and wove through the swaying crowd back to the table. Brady looked up, startled, as she appeared without her partner. Marie, who was sitting the dance out and sipping soda water, took in her white face and trembling lips, and got up. "Come on, Elizabeth. Time for a trip to the powder room."

"Thanks, Marie. I'm not feeling too well." Elizabeth was surprised at how normal her voice sounded. "I'm going to ask the maitre d' to call me a cab."

"I can take you back," Brady put in, jumping to his feet.

"You can't leave Garrett in the lurch, Brady. In Human Resources we call that a career-limiting move. But thanks for the offer."

She gathered up her purse and, head high, left the lights and the music behind.

Chapter 6

Elizabeth tossed her handbag in the direction of the bureau and fell face down on the bed, her body racked with the ache of loss. She wept all her pent-up tears into the bedspread, then stumbled into the bathroom to wash her face and blow her nose. Bracing her hands on both sides of the sink, she stared at the flushed, disheveled reflection in the mirror.

Get a grip, Forrester. You've had your cry, now hold your head up and get on with your life.

Turning away, she stripped off the georgette dress that had once seemed so stylish. She hung it in her garment bag and picked up the strapless velvet from the bed where she'd dropped it earlier.

Of course she had to return it.

She caressed the velvet, ran a finger inside the boned cups. Damn dress. It symbolized these two days somehow; sexy and forbidden and completely unrelated to real life. Where would she ever wear a dress like this, anyway? She didn't go to supper clubs or operas. When she wasn't working she was with friends, or her brother and the kids, or volunteering, or teaching other people her practical methods in organizational management. She had a *life*, for Pete's sake.

A life that didn't include fantasy men who bought dresses like this.

Oh, go on. Just once more.

She popped the clasp of her bra and tossed it on the bureau. She stepped into the dress and zipped it up, then stepped into her black high heels.

There.

A full-length mirror hung on the back of the bathroom door. She modeled in front of it, smoothing the dress down her hips with both hands, taking pleasure in eroticizing her own body. Garrett had taught her that much, at least. She'd spent so many years covering it up for the sake of professionalism that she'd forgotten anyone might want to look. Not that there had been many takers, but as long as there were men like Brady Grant out there, she had hope for the future. Getting ahead in business had taken a lot of her energy, though she'd learned to find a balance. She'd chosen HR on purpose as women seemed to rise faster there. *The caregiving arm of the business*, she thought. *That doesn't change*. But she was good at it.

She wished she were as good at intimate relationships.

With a sigh, she reached behind her for the zipper. If Garrett had left his adjoining door open, she could slip in and return his gift. She'd leave it on the bed, where he would see it when he came in. It would hurt him to find it there as much as it hurt her to give it back, but it was the only thing to do. The sooner they ended this, the better.

A discreet knock sounded at the door and she froze. "Who is it?"

Garrett? If he found her wearing the dress again, she'd be right back at square one and all of tonight's pain would have gone for nothing.

"It's Brady, Elizabeth. I need to talk to you."

Brady! What on earth could he want at this time of night? Had he left the dinner party early? What had happened to Garrett?

"I — I'm not feeling well, Brady." Reaching backward, she fumbled at the zipper.

"It will only take a minute. Please, Elizabeth. It's important."

She couldn't answer the door in this dress. Awkwardly, she pulled at the zipper, but it was stuck in its track.

"Elizabeth?" He knocked again.

Oh, for heaven's sake. She jerked the zipper back up, straightened the dress and yanked the door open.

Brady's jaw dropped an inch as he took her in from top to bottom. His mouth opened and closed for a second before words came out. "God almighty!"

"Come in, Brady," she said in a resigned tone, stepping aside to let him pass and closing the door behind him.

"Are — are you going out?" he asked, feeling for a chair and dropping into it. He rubbed his face and raised bemused eyes to hers.

At least he had the decency to look her in the face. "No."

"I thought you were sick. You looked pretty bad when you left and I was worried. But now you look — you look — " He paused and swallowed. "Great!"

"Thanks." This was the most ridiculous situation she'd ever been in. No explanation would make sense. And who said she owed him one, anyway? "What was it you wanted to see me about?" She tried to keep her tone professional, as if this were a formal visit to her office.

He dragged his gaze off her décolletage and made an obvious effort to remember why he was there. "I know it's none of my business, but you were so upset when you left that I felt I had to do something." He held up both hands as she opened her mouth to reply. "Now, I know you're going to say that I could have called, but I wanted to see you. To make sure you were all right."

"I'm fine."

"Can I ask what it was that upset you?"

"Nothing upset me, Brady. I was tired. Stressed out. I just needed some quiet time."

"We all need that. You know, I enjoy our talks on the phone. I feel a real connection with you. I had this image of you built up in my mind; someone young but motherly, somehow. Someone with lots of integrity who would always do the right thing. Someone incapable of cruelty or deceit."

Elizabeth resigned herself to listening to him empty his soul of whatever was bothering him. She sat down in the chair on the other side of the round writing table. "That's a lot to discern from phone conversations, isn't it? What is it that —"

"It is, but I think it's accurate. Except for one thing. You don't look... motherly."

To heck with emptying his soul. There was definitely something weird going on here. Something even stranger than her own behavior tonight. She had to find out what he wanted and get him out of here. "Brady, what —"

"You look sensational. Does anybody know you dress like this in private?" His voice took on a tone she knew all too well. A tone she hated. One that meant all her careful constructions of professionalism were about to be blotted out by sex.

"No, of course not. I mean, I don't usually dress like this."

"I like the way you dress. Discreet. Professional. I had no idea you looked like this undern…"

"Brady, this conversation is inappropriate. I think you should go before I have to register a complaint."

"A complaint? Just because a man gives you a compliment?"

"It's inappropriate between two managers of this company, even if we're in different branches of the organization."

"I'm not here as a manager, Elizabeth. I'm here as a man. I think the world of you; I have right from the beginning. I know you like me, too, and trust me, otherwise you wouldn't have let me in just now."

"I thought you had some kind of HR difficulty you wanted to discuss. If that's the case, then please tell me. If not, I'd like to get some rest." How much more diplomatic could she be?

"I have an HR difficulty, all right. I'm very, very attracted to the HR director."

"Brady…" she sighed in exasperation.

"Give me a chance, Elizabeth. Spend some time here with me. I think you're the most beautiful and — and ethical woman I've ever seen. And the sexiest, if you don't mind my saying so. The way you're dressed tonight… well, it's almost as if you walked out of a dream."

She was tired of being a dream and a fantasy. She was tired of providing an object for every man in creation to look at. It was going to stop right here.

"I appreciate your feelings, Brady, but I'm afraid I can't return them. I'd like to keep our relationship on a friendly business level, if you don't mind."

His appreciative male smile slowly faded to dismay. "I sure as hell do mind. What do you call friendly?"

"Something that's more appropriate. I believe —"

"How can you talk about appropriate when you're dressed like that? Who are you waiting for, anyway? Garrett Hill?"

She stood up abruptly, turning to show him the door before her face gave her away. "That was uncalled for. What does Garrett Hill have to do with this?"

Brady leaped from his chair and followed her, confronting her in the narrow space between the end of the bed and the bureau. "You have one dance with him and you come back to the table looking like you just lost your best friend. Then I come up here and find you parading around in a dress only a lover should see, in a room right next door to his. It looks pretty obvious to me."

"Then your vision isn't very good," she snapped. "Your logic is as warped as your ideas. Now, please leave my room and hope to God I don't decide to report you in the morning."

"Report me for what? Telling you my honest feelings?"

"Harassing me and casting aspersions on my character!"

"Your character isn't what I thought it was at all. You're a deceiver and a tease!"

"Out! Now!" She whirled for the door, but he caught her halfway there. The first cold surge of fear rolled in her stomach. One arm gripped her waist, the other was wrapped around her neck, her chin in the crook of his elbow. The fine wool of his suit jacket rubbed roughly against her skin.

Oh, God, tell me this isn't happening. Tell me this isn't Brady Grant, a man I trusted and liked! Why does nobody know how flawed and unpredictable he is?

"I'm not going anywhere," Brady whispered, breathing the words. "And you're not going to report me. I'll just tell them what a Jezebel you are, meeting me at the door dressed like a hooker, trying to seduce me." The arm locked around her waist loosened and one hand slid up to cup her left breast.

Jezebel? In a moment of horrified clarity, she knew who had written the note.

"You've brought me to this," he whispered, pressing his hips against her backside. "This is all your fault."

"What are you going to do?" Elizabeth whispered.

"Make you repent. Make you sorry you ever deceived me and led me on."

He gripped the tab of her zipper and yanked it past the spot where it had stuck. The bodice of her dress loosened and fell away. In a savage movement, he grabbed a handful of velvet and pulled it down. The dress fell in a puddle at their feet. He lifted her off the floor and kicked it away.

"Lord God," he prayed over her shoulder, and bit her neck in a paroxysm of ecstasy. He cupped one breast roughly, squeezing it as though he was testing it for ripeness, grinding his erection into her bikini panties in an unconscious parody of Garrett's passion only hours before. He clamped the other hand over her mouth, so that her scream was muffled into a high whine. Cold terror tore along her veins. *Garrett*, she prayed. *I'm so sorry. Please come. Please.* It was hopeless. His pride wouldn't let him try her door, even if he came back in time.

Brady stepped around in front of her, undoing his fly with one hand, grabbing her arm with the other and backing her into a corner of the room. "Don't scream," he snarled, flexing his fingers and making her gasp with pain. "My hands are strong. Your neck is small. It won't take much to shut you up."

His eyes devoured her, hot and filled with lust mixed with hatred, and she nodded, head moving jerkily, like a marionette's. She stood in front of him in black bikini panties, thigh-high stockings and black high heels. Undoubtedly every sexual fantasy he'd ever had. How could she make that work to her advantage? Every second she could distract him was a second where help might arrive.

Pretending modesty, she tried to cover her breasts with her hands.

"No!" he said, swatting her hands away. "I can look on sin unafraid."

"You sent me that note, didn't you?" she murmured, trying to look as if his male power overwhelmed her.

"Of course. Slut. You came to that meeting with no bra on just to tempt us all, didn't you?" He covered her breasts with both hands and squeezed. She whimpered with the pain. "You like that, do you? You wanted to tempt me. You wanted me to come to your room. That's why you put on that dress, isn't it?"

"Brady!" she gasped. "You don't need to hurt me."

"How else am I going to punish you, Jezebel?"

"You don't have to do that. We're friends, remember?"

He splayed a hand on her chest and pushed her down on the bed. "Friends!" he spat. "Don't tell me what to do! You don't deserve me or my friendship. You're just a cheap tease and you're going to get what you deserve."

Chapter 7

The evening he had planned so lovingly had backfired with a bang and gone downhill from there. What was the matter with him? Garrett groaned, running a hand through already disheveled hair and making absent circles on the tabletop with the base of his snifter of cognac. He was supposed to be one of the most brilliant and articulate businessmen in the Valley. Why, then, was he such a miserable failure at communicating with Elizabeth? What was it going to take to convince her how important to him she had become?

It was bad enough that she had walked out on him during the two minutes he had managed to claim her as a dance partner. He was unable to communicate his love with his body. His verbal skills were a dead loss. How was he going to succeed?

The answer came easily. The way he'd seen Elizabeth act when she had to get to the bottom of a problem. She tackled the thorniest issues with sensitivity, gentleness, and dogged persistence until she found a way to solve them. He could learn a lot from her. In more ways than one.

He pushed the snifter away and got up. A lesser man would have ordered another, but Garrett preferred to be clear-eyed and in control, even if his only task was to walk out of the hotel bar and get on the elevator.

You're in control, all right, his memory mocked. *Except when you're with Elizabeth. A helluva lot of control you show there.*

It was true. The only reason he was skulking in the bar after a concerned and strangely quiet Brady Grant had dropped him off was that he hadn't been ready to go to his room yet. He hadn't wanted to hear the subtle sounds of Elizabeth getting ready for bed, so close, yet so out of reach.

Maybe not so far out of reach, after all. She didn't know all there was to know about him, and he intended to rectify that… if she'd let him.

He sighed and glanced out the window as he wove past the empty tables in the bar. The bar looked out on the rear parking lot, which was brightly lit. He frowned and stepped over to the window. How many '59 Caddies could there be in this neighborhood on the same night? And why was it parked in the back, by the restaurant dumpsters?

Garrett recalled all the friendly little hints Brady had dropped all evening. Maybe Elizabeth had taken him up on them. Maybe he should just get out of her life. She'd run it very capably before he'd come along; he was sure she'd do the same afterward.

Sure. I will definitely do whatever she wants. After I find out whether Brady's in her room or not.

The elevator was too slow. He took the stairs two at a time, and let himself into his room. Dropping his key and jacket on the bed, he opened his adjoining door and stood still, his ear against her door, trying to calm his breathing.

Brady was definitely in there, all right. Garrett heard the murmur of their voices, and pain sluiced through him. The pain of total rejection, of being supplanted by someone less worthy of her even than himself. Garrett bowed his head and was reaching blindly behind him to close the door when he heard Brady's voice suddenly intensify in volume.

"...and you're going to get what you deserve!"

Garrett's blood seemed to congeal in his veins as he heard Elizabeth scream. "No! Help! Someone h..." The word was cut off by the sound of an open palm hitting flesh.

"Quiet, Jezebel! I warned you!"

Fear for Elizabeth and a killing rage blazed up in Garrett. There was no door handle on his side, no way to get into her room save one. He backed up and with all the speed and strength he could muster, slammed his body into the door. Unbolted, it gave, and he burst into Elizabeth's room like a runaway freight. His momentum carried him over to the bed, where he tackled Brady with such force that the other man slid off the other side, Garrett on top of him.

Weeping with terror, Elizabeth leaped off the bed and ran into Garrett's room to call hotel security, her voice shaking so much she could hardly get the words out.

Once he saw that Elizabeth was unhurt, Garrett turned his full attention to making sure Brady would never assault a woman again. Brady might be younger, but he was no match for a man of Garrett's size and strength — a man who was protecting his woman. With a final blow, Garrett laid him out on the carpet and jumped up, panting.

There was no sound from his room. He crossed the carpet, and as he did so Elizabeth peered out around the jamb as if it had taken an act of courage to see which of them was still standing.

Their eyes met in one unforgettable moment of perfect clarity and understanding.

Elizabeth burst into tears and ran into his arms.

Garrett retained the presence of mind to bundle Elizabeth into his bathrobe moments before hotel security showed up at the door. The police arrived shortly afterward and took Brady away, shouting recriminations and threats of lawsuits as he was manhandled down the hall to the elevator. When Elizabeth and Garrett had given their statements and were left alone at last, Garrett led her gently into his room.

"I don't know about you, but I'll feel safer if you're in the same room with me tonight. I can call Housekeeping and they'll bring me a rollaway so that —"

"Garrett." Elizabeth laid a finger on his lips. "You don't have to. I can sleep in my own room. It's over. I'll be perfectly safe."

He tried to keep the flicker of pain from showing in his face, but from the way Elizabeth bit her lip, he could tell she had seen it. "Safe from me?" he asked bitterly. "Or just from any crazy who walks into your room?"

"Please don't," she whispered, turning away and hugging herself around the middle. "Not after what we've just been through." She began to shiver, and his heart broke.

"I'm sorry," he said. His throat closed on the words. He put his arms around her and simply held her, rubbing her back, until the tremors subsided. "You've had a horrible shock and I'm a cretin to make it worse for you."

"Stop bad-mouthing the man I love," she said, muffled, into his blood-speckled shirt front.

"What was that?" Hope leaped in his chest.

"Nothing."

"Tell me."

She shook her head and tried to pull away. "I'm sorry. It was a mistake. I say stupid things when I fall apart."

"Do you love me, Elizabeth?"

She drew in a breath and paused. His whole life passed before his eyes.

"Of course," she said, and the blood surged into her cheeks. She bit her lip. "Pointless as it is."

"Stop that. You give meaning to my whole life, do you know that?"

He'd thought to bring a smile to the lips he adored. It didn't happen. "I can't do that," she said against his chest. "Only you make your life meaningful, and you choose to do it by devoting yourself to Stratton Hill. There won't be anything left over for me or anyone else. That's why giving my heart to you is pointless."

The cold started at his fingertips and crept up his arms. "Don't tell me this, Elizabeth."

"Don't tell you the truth? You're consumed by the industry, Garrett, and in a business sense that's a good thing. But I've seen the hours you work. I've driven by at night, and the lights are on in your office. Your car is the only one in the lot. I know you have a daughter and it frightens me. If you can't spare any time for her, what would you be able to give me?"

The cold had reached his heart now as he realized the depth of her conviction. Gentleness and persistence, he reminded himself. There was a solution. He could not lose hope or control now.

He kept his voice pitched low. "My daughter's name is Jessie. She's thirteen. She's also in a special program for gifted teenagers at San Jose State. Have you noticed a pattern in the nights I stay late in the office?"

She shook her head. "I only drive by once in a while. But you're there every time. And I've heard people talk about the hours you work."

"The hours I used to work. Some stories never die. Let me tell you what I'm doing. Jessie and I are in the lab, Elizabeth. We've been there three nights a week since the beginning of July, working on her science project. She's writing software for little kids. Computer games. We're doing it together. We have a perfectly normal relationship, except that she's brilliant and I have a hard time keeping up with her. Despite my divorce — which I admit was partly due to the hours I worked back then — Jessie has been the top priority in my life since she was born. Until now."

Elizabeth felt dazed. "You mean —"

"You thought I was at the office night and day? That my quality of life was so bad I had nothing in it but work?"

Put that way, she realized the injustice she had been doing him all these months. "Yes," she admitted.

"So when you knew I wanted you to share that life, it frightened you." She nodded, her forehead against his shirt front. "And now that you know the truth? Does it change the way you feel?"

"I... I hardly know what to think. My feelings are doing somersaults."

He went down on one knee, gripping the folds of the dressing gown wrapped around her thighs. "Elizabeth Forrester, will you marry me?"

"You can't be serious."

"I've never been more serious in my life. This is scarier than a stock market crash."

She didn't smile. "Will you forgive me?"

"What for?" he asked, gazing up at her as though she were the sun rising.

"For not realizing the kind of man you really are," she whispered as a fat tear overflowed and rolled over the bruise on her cheek, leaving a shining trail in the lamplight.

"Oh, God, Elizabeth," he groaned, and clutched her around the waist, pressing his face against her stomach. "I love you so much. Tell me yes before I —"

"Yes. Now and for the rest of my life." Her sweet scent rose to his nostrils, arousal mixed with Chanel No. 5. He tried to control his body's reaction. She couldn't want this, after the violence she'd just survived. "Garrett," she whispered, a breathy little sound, a sound she made when the anticipation was too much.

His sex quivered, stiffened, filled. He nuzzled the terrycloth of the robe that wrapped over her belly, and pulled the tie away. Her fingers moved convulsively in his hair as his lips found her skin. "My love. I love the way you smell." His tongue circled her navel, then traced a path down one bare hip. She gasped as his cheek brushed her curly thatch, and she shifted, spreading her feet to invite further exploration as he kissed the delicate, inner skin of her thigh. "So sweet," he murmured, licking the inside of the other thigh. Her breath hitched, and she whimpered. He tongued the hollow at the apex of her thigh. "I want to eat you."

"Please, Garrett," she begged in an unsteady whisper. "Please. Erase what happened tonight. Love me."

His cock ached with urgent pleasure, throbbed with every beat of his heart. "Take the robe off."

She arched her back, and the robe slid to the floor behind her. He slid his tongue into her wetness, tasting her lovingly, spreading her folds until he found what he wanted. Clasping her slender hips with both hands, he licked the slick, hooded pearl, first with the hard tip of his tongue, then with the flat, kissing and sucking until her legs trembled, and she unconsciously pulled his hair.

"Garrett, oh, oh —"

She shuddered and bucked against his face, but he pulled her relentlessly onto his tongue, holding her in a kiss from which she couldn't escape.

She bit back a scream and came, the wet rush of her orgasm filling him with triumph and joy. Her legs buckled and she slid down onto the carpet in front of him, quivering and gasping.

"I need you," she managed. "Now."

All he could think of was fulfilling her need, as fast as possible. Stripping his trousers, underwear and shoes off in seconds, he pulled her onto him and impaled her, swollen and wet, on his rigid cock. Her hair swung forward and the diamond earrings she still wore bounced madly as she threw back her head and forced him deeper.

He gave her control, loving the way the tight grip of her body clasped and slid the length of his aching sex, loving the full curves of her breasts, the way her luscious nipples teased him. He cupped her breasts as she stroked him, and felt the wild pleasure surging up out of his body, tearing his doubts away in an explosive rush, giving every cell of his being to the woman he loved.

Garrett Hill laid his resignation letter on Alan Stratton's desk with a flourish. "There you are, Al. The official two weeks' notice."

Alan gave him a glare that was so patently fake they both laughed. "You bastard. After all I've done for you."

Garrett grinned. "Don't give me that. You know startups are in my blood. I've rounded up some venture capital and I'm going to diversify a bit. At Elizabeth's suggestion."

Alan's face softened. "Congratulations. You're a lucky man."

"Thanks."

"I'm not going to lose Elizabeth, too, am I?"

"Hell, no. For some reason she likes this place. Both of us can't stay here, so I'm going to be the one to leave. To tell you the truth, I'm excited about the challenge."

"How does Jessie feel about it?"

"The three of us are spending weekends together. Jessie was a little reserved at first, but they seemed to take to each other. There aren't many people who can resist Elizabeth."

"Including you." Alan waved a hand. "Can't understand what she sees in you. Now, get out of here and earn your severance package, dammit. Don't go giving me short-timers' syndrome."

Garrett laughed and strolled back to his corner office, where Elizabeth waited. She laid an urgent hand on his coat sleeve. "Well, what did he say? Did he bite your head off?"

Garrett shook his head and gathered her into his arms, waltzing her in a circle and pulling her down with him onto the leather couch. "I've known Alan a long time. He wants us to be happy. The only guy biting anything around here is..." His voice faded into a muffled murmur of satisfaction as he traced the silk-covered curve of her breast with his cheek.

"Don't you dare! I have a meeting at nine!"

He chuckled and lifted his face for her kiss. "The down side of office romances," he grumped.

"I guess you'll have to make up for it tonight," she whispered, touching his cheek.

They smiled into each other's eyes. "Tonight and for the rest of my life," he said, echoing her own promise, and he kissed her.

About the author:

The shape and texture of words — their sensuality — have fascinated Shannon Hollis since she learned to read. She got her first positive review at the age of eight on a school composition, and completed her first novel at seventeen. Shannon has an Honors BA in Creative Writing from the University of California, and works in a high-tech company in Silicon Valley. The beauty of romance, she believes, is that its focus is on the things that are important to a woman: laughter, learning, friends, family... and a committed relationship with the man of her choice. In romance, no matter what the obstacles she must face, the woman always wins. Like her heroine in "Strictly Business," Shannon fell in love with and married her boss, and they live in the house he built for her after the 1989 earthquake.

Insatiable

by Chevon Gael

To my reader:

I have always been fascinated by the games people play when they fall in love. They go to great lengths to avoid, deny, ignore and even refuse what they feel. Alas, love latches onto you like a bad virus — with a lot of the same symptoms — and never lets go. Love doesn't play fair and lust throws all the rules out the window — as my hero and heroine find out. Enjoy the game!

To the girls of the Golden Horseshoe Chapter, thanks for not censoring me. I love you Mom and Dad for believing in my dream. And for CM in Chicago who woke me from a long, long, sleep!

Chapter 1

Marcus Remmington finished reading the directions on his frozen microwave dinner in time to be startled by several successive rings of the doorbell. He tossed the package into the kitchen sink and shouted, "Hold your horses, I'm coming."

Before he had a chance to wonder who was playing his doorbell like a piano, his gaze fell on the entry his assistant had made in his diary. Daagmar's spidery scrawl was spread across the page as a cue to block out the entire evening. He barely noticed the words, "Ashly-Tate"; then beneath it, *"Bedroom Eyes."*

"Shit," he muttered. The appointment had gone right out of his head after the ugly scene this morning with Yolande Johannsen, his latest runway diva. She'd shown up while he was in the shower, ready to scratch out his eyes. Of course, she'd quit on the spot. Marcus had expected as much so he wasn't terribly disappointed. He also wasn't disappointed at the shots he took yesterday, so Yolande's bailing out wouldn't cost him a job, but she'd never work with him again. Losing her as a bedmate didn't bother him. Losing a model to sit for the gallery opening did. Professional models of his acquaintance weren't interested in working for nothing. Besides, if Marcus was completely honest with himself, he was tired of the single name supermodels with their super-egos and over-inflated breasts or the underfed, wasted-waifs with their heroin-haunted eyes and six figure contracts. They wanted the runways at the end of the rainbow; not the hungry, artistic, pay-me-nothing-but-experience jobs that meant working in rain, snow or triple digit humidity. Just working period.

He no longer had the patience to scour amateur portfolios of thirteen-year-old virgins who offered to let him change their status in exchange for their first job. Nor did he have the cash flow to indulge in big money contracts for temperamental spoiled brats like Yolande. If it wasn't for the extra money coming from his **Bedroom Eyes** work, he couldn't afford his share in the gallery at all. So if his evening appointment was late and he missed out on supper, he didn't mind. He was grateful for every job.

He flipped on the outside porch light and prepared his professional side to flatter some bored housewife. He opened the front door and braced himself. The sight of the petite, dark-haired woman in the red cocktail dress stunned him into silence.

Her slightly glazed, green-gold eyes stared back at him in surprise. The halo of the yellow porch light reflecting in her glasses made her seem like some smoldering angel from wet-dream Heaven. She swayed slightly and shivered.

Instantly, Marcus stood aside to allow her to enter. When she hesitated, Marcus was afraid she might be someone who just had the wrong address. Luck was with him, however, when she finally spoke.

"Is this **Bedroom Eyes**?"

Her voice was soft and uncertain. Marcus felt his groin stir as he breathed in the heady scent of an unfamiliar brand of perfume, mixed with the candy-sweetness of licorice. "Miss Tate?"

His assumption was answered with high, bubbly laughter.

"No, I'm not Lola." She stared down and critically assessed the bodice of her strapless dress. "Definitely not," she confirmed.

Marcus stood there in the open doorway, still not quite certain who had shown up for the appointment. But he didn't object when the woman walked past him into the hallway. Suddenly the heel of her shoe caught the end of the carpet and she toppled off balance. He lunged forward and caught her, his hands grasping her bare shoulders to steady her. Instantly, every nerve in his body was alive with sexual energy. He marvelled at the satiny texture of her skin, smooth and flawless in the dim light. The overwhelming urge to caress the rest of her surprised him. This woman was a stranger, a client.

Instead of turning around to face him, she leaned back against his chest until her head rested beneath his chin. She sighed loudly and tilted her head up to look at him. The corners of her frames poked the side of his jaw, knocking her glasses askew.

"You're tall," she said, one arm slowly reaching up, almost touching him. He held his breath for a heartbeat, hoping she would touch him and was disappointed when she only re-adjusted her glasses and slid them back up her nose.

Marcus gently pushed her away, his body strangely protesting the loss of her warmth against him. "And you're tipsy. Listen, we can do this some other time."

She answered him by removing her strappy sandals and pointing at her polished toes. "We match." She smiled and lifted the hem of her cocktail dress to reveal part of a dimpled knee beneath a slender thigh. Marcus found himself unable to tear his gaze away from her legs. He jiggled his suddenly tight shirt collar. When had it turned so warm?

"We?" He cleared his throat and leaned against the wall in the shade of a potted hibiscus tree, happy to observe this strange elfin creature.

"I forgot," she giggled. "You don't know. I went and had a paint job this afternoon. I wanted everything to match." She held up her hands and splayed her fingers out toward him. "Fingers, toes and dress."

"I know I'll hate myself for asking, but why do you have to match?"

She planted her hands on her slender hips. Again, he found himself following her every move. Was she trying to hypnotize him?

"Because I'm not a blonde," she frowned, her ruby-red lips forming a plump, luscious pout.

Marcus' keen eye feasted on her lips. As a man he found them inviting. As a photographer he was aware that their fullness was refreshingly natural. Yolande would kill to have a mouth like that. Her overzealous surgeon injected too much fatty tissue into her lips. They looked ridiculously large compared to her tiny sculpted nose and the scooped-out hollows of her cheeks. While he was aware of Yolande's flaws, the memory of her face had suddenly vanished. The woman in front of him had overloaded his senses. He forced himself to continue the conversation.

"Since when has not being blonde been a crime?" Marcus wondered what she would do if he took her in his arms and showed her that it wasn't.

She looked at him then, and answered in a tone which made an explanation totally unnecessary. "Greg."

Marcus held his tongue. He wasn't even going to ask. Instead he steered her toward the purpose of her appointment. "Is Greg the one you're doing this for?"

A petulant frown touched her lips. "I'm doing this for me. Greg can go to hell," she snapped.

So, Greg was history. He was strangely relieved to hear that. "Miss…ah," he searched his memory for the notation in his date book. "Ashly, is it? Follow me to the studio."

"Have a seat and I'll be back in five minutes. Here," the man who greeted her at the door handed her a glass of wine. "Relax and think about the kind of look you want." Then he vanished up the stairs and into another part of the house.

Ashlyn sat in a black leather easy chair and surveyed her surroundings. The entire evening since leaving the restaurant was a blur. Only one detail remained perfectly clear, her now ex-boyfriend, Greg, leering at the enlarged chest of his date.

Ashlyn took her mind off the memory by concentrating on the walls of the studio. They were covered in black and white photos of what she guessed to be past clients. Women of various ages and tastes stared back at her. In her present state, their toothy smiles and eyes signalling invitation seemed to be making fun of her. She could almost hear them snickering. *They* probably had boyfriends or husbands who would look at their pictures and appreciate them in the ways that only intimate couples could. She sighed and sipped her wine. Might as well make the best of it now that she was here. Come to think of it, her host — who had introduced himself as Marc somewhere along the way — was making her visit as comfortable as possible.

The man himself was extremely comfortable on the eyes. He reminded her of Brad Pitt. Tall — but then, everyone was tall compared to her, and compactly built. No wasted space anywhere. His dark, wavy hair was lightly peppered with gray. It was a little longer than what she was used to, but she liked the way he pulled it back in a rakish queue. It made him look classical yet exotic at the same time. Not every man could pull off that look.

She watched him take the stairs when he left and was conscious of the way his slacks tightened against his butt each time he took a step. Some men had such flat rear ends. She couldn't decide what shook up her erogenous zones more, his butt or his blue eyes, so blue they were almost silver.

She leaned back completely and sank into the leather chair. She closed her eyes and thought about Marc. No doubt about it, the man was a hunk. Hell, when it came right down to it, the way she was feeling she just might take off her clothes if he asked her to. It was, after all, her birthday present.

"Wake up, beautiful." Marc's voice made a pleasant intrusion on her thoughts. He'd changed into a track suit with some kind of sports logo on the front of the sweatshirt. He flashed her a faintly amused smile.

"Is it time to work?" Ashlyn stretched her arms over her head, unaware that the bodice of the cocktail dress sank down enough to reveal the shadow of a cleavage.

And an impressive cleavage it was, thought Marcus. Her breasts were not overwhelming and most definitely natural. He caught himself wondering how they would photograph. Natural breasts were an erotic road map full of wonderful flaws. One was usually larger than the other; the nipple shapes uneven, areola's differed in shade. Their individual fullness was sensitive to the camera's eye. In his ten years of photographing women, Marcus found that breasts were like snowflakes; no two were exactly the same. In that respect, Miss Ashly would be no different.

"Here," he handed her a red satin bathrobe. "You can change in the corner bathroom over by the hot tub."

When she didn't immediately take the robe, he laid it across her lap. "Whenever you're ready. Want a refill?" She didn't object when he refilled her glass with white wine. Marcus sensed her uncertainty. He thought about offering her the option to back out. Immediately, he discovered there was a war heating up between the fantasies his mind was spinning and the lectures his conscience dragged out.

He damned himself, then half-heartedly offered, "We can do this some other time. It doesn't have to be tonight. The coupon is good any time."

She took a swallow of wine and seemed to be considering his offer. Then she shook her head. "I wouldn't want to disappoint Lola. She's my best friend. She's the one who bought me my makeover this afternoon and these pictures tonight."

Marcus sat down on the ottoman. "Okay, beautiful. You're calling the shots."

She picked at the bathrobe. "Do you have anything else? I mean, what if I don't look good in this?"

Marcus stole a glance at her legs, exposed now by the way the skirt of her dress fell to one side. "You'll look good in anything, Ashly."

She sat forward then until her face was inches from his and he could see his reflection in her glasses. "I like that name," she whispered as if bearing a secret. "It belongs to someone else. Tonight, I want to be someone else. Will you make me someone else, Marc?"

She was dead serious. Marcus read the plea in those luminous eyes, hidden as they were behind the briefcase-and-boardroom style frames. He helped her out of the chair and she slung the robe over one bare shoulder. "That way," he pointed toward the far corner of the studio. "You change and I'll set up the background."

By the time she opened the bathroom door and stepped out, Marcus had finished arranging a neutral beige background behind a sky-blue, satin covered divan. As a force of habit he looked up at the noise. As a force of nature, he looked again.

The robe was short, just barely covering her buttocks. Her shapely, bare legs spoke a language he was all too familiar with. They weren't the longest pair of legs he'd ever seen. God knew, he'd seen his share! And certainly, they weren't perfect. Perhaps it was their imperfection that attracted him to them. Whatever it was, he certainly intended to get his share of those legs, even if it was only on film.

Then, as an afterthought, he loaded the black and white film in another camera and positioned it on a spare tripod. His *Bedroom Eyes* photos were always in colour, but something, an instinct maybe, told him to get some b&w's. Marcus relied on that little "something" that stirred in his gut when he was feeling out a shoot. It told him which shoots were going well and which ones, like Yolande's, were disastrous. His "something" was busy again. It was a signal he couldn't ignore. And, when it came right down to it, this girl — this woman — was sending out signals he couldn't ignore.

An hour later, Marcus wanted to kick his "something" right in the ass. Ashly wasn't working for him. At first she sat rigid on the edge of the divan with her arms folded across her chest. She tugged at the short hem of the robe, trying in vain to cover up those delicious legs of hers. Marcus knew she was no professional but, at least in the past, most of his **Bedroom Eyes** clientele would try and pose. Marcus would joke with them and say racy things like, "Smile and think of your man when he sees this." That usually got rid of some of the tension.

But when he tried it with Ashly, her smile died and a sadness crept into her eyes. She reminded Marcus of his apprenticeship days in the department store baby portrait studio. He almost wished he'd kept that old, stuffed, Sesame Street character. All he had to do was wave it in front of any child and he couldn't get a bad shot if he begged for one. Once again he looked through the camera lens to check the angle.

She cleared her throat. "Could I have another drink of something? I guess I'm just nervous." She shivered and crossed her legs. "And a little cold, too."

The camera lens caught that simple action and channelled it straight into his expert eye. He adjusted the focus in time to pick up her body's reaction to the cold. Her nipples sprouted against the smooth, red satin. Suddenly he needed a drink too. But not before his "something" had crawled out of retirement to kick him in the stomach again.

Marcus could hardly contain himself. The ghost of something exciting revealed itself in that innocent shiver. If only he could get Ashly to loosen up some more. He could chip away at that glint of diamond he saw buried beneath the coal.

He walked over to check her height against the camera angle. She bent forward to retrieve her empty glass. "Okay, I take the hint. Let's take a break. I'll get you something from the bar. In the meantime, why don't you freshen up your lipstick and clean what's left of the old off your teeth. Here," he tossed her a blanket. "Wrap up in this for a few minutes." He picked up her glass and strolled over to the bar. He heard Ashly get up then close the bathroom door behind her. Suddenly, it occurred to him how she could get warm. A second later he was at the hot tub, setting the whirlpool timer and checking the temperature.

He set both their drinks on the ledge, being careful to first transfer them into tall, opaque plastic tumblers. He shed his track suit and slid into the tub before Ashly opened the bathroom door. He motioned for her to join him.

"Ta-da. Instant heat."

Ashly clutched the blanket around her shoulders. "I can't get in there."

"Why not? It's not like you have to know how to swim." He raised his drink and saluted her. "Cheers, beautiful. Now, come and warm up. Then we can get back to work." He followed his argument with more coaxing. "My time is yours tonight, remember. This is your birthday and I haven't had the chance to buy you a drink."

He was charming and irresistible, as were the bubbles that churned around him. She watched their hypnotic patterns swirl against his chest. His words swirled around her ears. *My time is yours tonight...it's your birthday.*

Lola's words at the restaurant crowded her thoughts. *A night to remember...*

The implications of what was happening finally dawned on Ashlyn. What had Lola really bought for her? Glamour photos for her bruised ego, or a fantasy night of passion for her battered heart? Either way, she had to get things straight now while she still had the strength to walk out of here. Her vision was a little out of focus; her brain, fuzzy. Abstract visions of Greg rose to haunt her. His distorted voice taunted.

Daddy's little yes-girl...but you won't say "yes" to me. You're a tease, Ashlyn. You needed Duncan to get you a date.

"Ashly?" Marc's voice burst Greg's ugly bubble. Marc. If it weren't for Lola, she wouldn't have him either. The truth was always ugly. Her ego fought back. She didn't need anyone to get her a man and she wasn't a tease. She was just... careful. And good.

"But I don't want to be good tonight," she whispered, forgetting for a moment that she wasn't alone.

"Huh?" Marc slid over to the edge of the hot tub and examined her, uncertainty crowding his handsome features. And he was handsome. She didn't need all those glasses of champagne to convince her of that.

"I'm sorry, I meant I want to look good, for the camera and the pictures." For you. For me. She knelt down to sit on the side of the hot tub and dared to dip one toe into the churning water. Steam rose up to cloud her glasses and dampen the beautiful satin robe she wore. She should shed it before it became ruined. She found herself slightly embarrassed about revealing her all in front of a strange man. Her mind searched for a way to discreetly suggest that he turn his back.

Marcus found himself staring up at Ashly, a little confused but willing to go along. It hit him then why she was hesitating. And he suddenly realized what being around all those willing young models had done to him. *Marcus, you're an insensitive ass.* He silently tore a strip out of himself. At the same time, he was amazed that her modesty had rescued a scrap or two of moral behaviour. He discreetly turned his back. When he heard her settle into the hot tub, he retrieved her drink from a small utility shelf above him where he noticed she had placed her glasses for safekeeping. He turned to hand Ashly her drink and discovered she was neck deep in bubbles. She lay back, eyes closed. Her feet floated to the surface, just inches from his chest. Marc had the ridiculous urge to reach out and tickle her toes.

"This is wonderful," she purred.

"Don't get too dehydrated," he warned. "Here. There's plenty of juice in this."

Ashly straightened up until her shoulders peeked out of the water. Marc had to fight to keep his gaze from slipping beneath the water line. She took her drink and pressed the icy tumbler against her cheek. He watched intently as cool droplets of condensation slid down the side of the tumbler and splashed into the hot water. Through the churning water he imagined the tell-tale dark shadow between her legs. He knew she sat against two water jets; one massaged her middle back while the other, more strategically placed jet, pulsed between her buttocks no doubt sending hot tongues of water between her legs to lick at her clitoris.

His mouth went dry at the thought of his own tongue taking on the task of her arousal. His graphic musings sent his cock shooting straight up. *Down, boy!* He slid deeper into the water, unsure of what her reaction would be if she knew his thoughts, but not imagining the best case scenario. Marcus knew he had to get his mind back on track — fast!

She moved the edge of the tumbler to her lips and Marc stopped her. "Happy

Birthday." He touched his tumbler against hers in salute.

"Thank you." She took a big gulp — which she instantly regretted. "Wow!" she gasped. "What's in this, rocket fuel?"

"Just a little imported rum," he assured her.

"Imported from where, NASA?"

He chuckled; a low, comfortable rumble that must have started deep in his chest. Ashlyn wasn't immune to that sound. It certainly was much more pleasant than the short bursts of loud guffaws that came from Greg when he watched All Star Wrestling.

Marc didn't seem like the wrestling type. Well, maybe some intimate wrestling perhaps. She stole a covert glance at him over the rim of her tumbler. Could they be any more intimate here in the hot tub, nearly-naked and not even an arm's length between them? She shifted her bottom to relieve the pressure of the water jets. The rushing water created an interesting stimulation; slipping between her outer lips, drumming against the tiny bud of her clitoris, causing it to swell. Not even Greg's faint attempts at manual foreplay had aroused her like this. A few more minutes of this and...

"That's the rum mixing with the sugar in the passion fruit."

"Huh?" Her mind tumbled from her near climax and she felt herself blush. "Passion fruit? I've never had that before." She sidled away from the perilous jet and took another sip, slower this time. "It's good. Well," she presented her drink to him once again. "Here's to passion...fruit."

Marc swallowed the tight knot in his throat. Passion. Right. The temperature of the water was rising. And that wasn't all. His raging hard-on forced him to stay on his own side of the hot tub — at least for a while. His drink and his libido needed some ice.

"Am I being rude if I ask you how old you are today?"

"Not at all. My twenties are officially behind me."

"Ah, I remember when I hit the big three-oh — barely. But that's another story. What I want to know is, why a beautiful, mature —"

"Careful —"

"— woman such as yourself is spending her birthday alone."

"It's not a crime," she defended, her shoulders inching a little higher out of the water. Bubbles danced around the shadow of her cleavage but she seemed not to notice either the rushing cascades or his look of longing as he watched the pattern of those bubbles.

"Like not being a blonde?" he reminded.

"That's different." Her free hand toyed with a cluster of bubbles circling close to her right breast.

Marcus watched her casual water-play and decided he had either died and gone to heaven and was about to be reincarnated into a bubble; or the devil had finally taken him after all and the nagging pressure in his groin was there to stay. He felt droplets of sweat bead across his upper lip. He licked the dampness from his mouth before trying to swallow past the burning hunger building in his chest which he knew had nothing to do with his missing supper.

"He must be crazy."

"Who?" She upended the tumbler and drained the last of her drink.

"The guy who dumped you."

"Oh, him." She reached into her glass and fished out an ice cube. It melted quickly between her fingers and her tongue darted out to catch the falling drops of cold water. She pressed the melting cube against her cheek then casually trailed it down her neck and across the vee of her exposed breasts. Marcus had never wanted to be an ice cube so much in his life.

"Greg's not crazy. He's not too bright, that's all."

Marcus agreed. And it was a good start. Apparently, she was getting over Greg fast. And that was good, at least for her. On the other hand, Marcus knew the warranty on his self-control was about to expire. Time to get on with it, whatever "it" was going to be.

"Do you want to carry on with the shoot?" Nice, safe territory.

"Not yet," she replied, completely oblivious to his predicament.

Okay, kid. Go ahead and torture me. I deserve it for what I'm thinking.

She obliged him. "Just a few more minutes. I feel much better now."

Marcus couldn't decide how he felt. He wanted her in here. He wanted her clothes off. He wanted her relaxed. So far, he'd gotten everything he wanted. So what was the problem? There was an old proverb about getting what you wanted. Whether it was good or bad, Marcus couldn't remember. He didn't care.

"Five more minutes, please Marc."

Marcus, old boy, you're the one who likes it when they beg for more.

"Ashly." His voice was ragged and her name rolled off his tongue like a plea. "Ashly, I'm warning you, I want to —"

"If I tell you what I wished for tonight, will you promise not to laugh?" She was serious.

"Okay, beautiful Ashly. I promise."

"I might not get it because I missed the candle the first time."

"Sure you will." Whatever her wish, Marcus wanted to make it come true.

"I want to have a wildly mad affair. I want to do something crazy and impulsive. I want to lose control completely and not care. That's what I want."

Marcus was stunned into silence, again. *Say something, stupid. Something polite, benign.*

"I… I want to… that is… I hope you get your wish, Ashly." The thought was genuine but the words sounded phoney. Apparently, she didn't notice. Before Marcus could stop her, she slid over to his side of the tub with her back facing him. "Rub my neck, please Marc."

Damn! There it was again. *Please, Marc.* He didn't have any more time to think as she pressed her naked back against him, trapping his erect flesh between them. He felt her stiffen then. A strangled "oh" escaped her lips and floated across the churning water.

At that moment, Marcus realized two things. First, regardless of how many candles she missed, Ashly was going to get her birthday wish. And second, no matter how bad she wanted that wish, she was still wearing her panties.

Chapter 2

Marcus sat in the hot tub, trapped between the hard wall of the spa and the silken back of the woman reclining into his crotch. He knew Ashly was too far gone from the drinks, even if she didn't. To take her now was asking for trouble. Even if she was aware of what she was doing, which he doubted, she would certainly regret it later. She'd feel used, he felt sure of it. And, if he were honest, so would he. Yolande's boot heels were still fresh in his mind. It wasn't fair to Ashly to go to bed with her simply because she was available and he was in need. He had a list of willing fingers ready to scratch such an itch. Besides, no matter how much she might want it now or how sweet or hurt she was, his lack of protection in the water was reason enough not to proceed.

Instead, he slid out from behind her, smoothly climbed over the side and quickly wrapped a towel around himself. "That timer goes off in about 30 seconds," he warned. "I'll duck into the bathroom and change."

As he disappeared through the bathroom door, Ashlyn heard him say, "We better think about getting back to work, if that's what you want."

"Okay," she replied dreamily. But what did she want? The offer was certainly there. He was obviously ready, no doubt sufficiently able and definitely willing. Yet, he hadn't come right out and made a direct pass at her. He seemed to be waiting for her to initiate the action.

Her confusion was lost in Marc's warning about the timer. Instantly the bubbles dispersed and the water became clear and calm. She should get out and dry off while she still had her privacy. She could hear Marc moving around in the bathroom. The muffled sound of the tap water running; the whirring of a hair dryer. She towelled off and slipped the bathrobe back on. Dry satin contacted with wet nylon reminding her that she still wore her panties. She slid them off and wadded them up in the towel.

Now, where to hang them? She would wait for Marc to finish, then lay them over the shower curtain rod to dry. Maybe she could use the hair dryer to get rid of the excess moisture. Whatever she did, she suddenly realized that the short robe left her in a very revealing position. She wrapped the wet towel, sarong style, around her waist in time to hear the bathroom door open. There stood Marc looking very refreshed and very covered in his track suit.

"Hey, beautiful. Ready to continue?" He shook his slightly damp hair which he now wore loose. It fell to just below his neck. Ashlyn wondered what it would be like to touch it; to feel it wild and flowing across her fingertips. His whole nature was so totally removed from the men she usually had to deal with in her life. Duncan, her ultra-conservative father who was so set in his ways or the too-chic and delicate look of Greg who wouldn't be caught dead with a short, mousse-sculpted hair out of place.

Next to the in-bred pedigrees of her acquaintances, Marc was the lovable mutt who begged to have his ears scratched and his belly rubbed. And Ashlyn was a soft touch when it came to strays.

Tonight, when she confessed her wish to Marc, he hadn't laughed or criticized or any of the things she might have expected from Greg. Marc seemed so laid-back and comfortable with his life. He loved his work, as demonstrated by the photos on his wall. To a degree, Ashlyn was envious. Success at Fraser and Associates was measured in quarterly reports; never an encouraging word or gesture from her father.

Good was unacceptable; best was passed over for perfect. Seduce, persuade, brainwash, even lie to the public if it meant increased sales. Just keep the client happy. Keep Duncan happy. Marc didn't seem to care about success yet he came across as being completely satisfied with his lot. Could he teach her his secret, she wondered?

"You can toss the towel in the hamper," he said, motioning to the wicker laundry basket beside the hot tub.

The moment of truth had arrived. And, by God, tonight she was going to play by her rules. *I'm going to be happy.* A self-indulgent smile tugged at the corners of her mouth. She suddenly felt as if she had climbed out of her body and was watching someone else. Slowly, she loosened the towel from around her waist and allowed it to slide to the floor in a heap. The lace of her discarded panties peeped through the folds, offering her one last chance to change her mind. She knelt down, picked up the towel and strode carelessly over to the basket and dropped it on top of Marc's already discarded one. The last of her armor gone, she squared herself and walked over to the divan.

"I'm ready, now." For the first time in months, she really meant it.

Marcus adjusted his lighting, changed the background again and set the tripod to the correct height. He deliberately kept busy until Ashly was sitting comfortably on the divan.

"Slide down to the end," he instructed. "Good. Now, tilt your head up. To the right. Okay. Shift your left shoulder towards me." He issued one instruction after another, all while making corrections through the camera lens. He looked up several times and critically surveyed her from different angles as if trying to convince himself of something. Finally he said, "can you lose the hair?"

"My hair?" Instantly her hands were behind her head to protect her precious French roll. "This hair cost a fortune and you want me to ruin it?"

"Yeah. You know, take those pins out and let it down?" Marcus recognized the feminine defense mechanism. Professional or not, no man crossed into the sacred territory of changing a woman's looks without meeting some form of resistance. But Marcus *was* a professional, and ready for a counter-attack.

"It looks great, but the effect would be far more sensational if you let it down. If only you could see yourself through the camera the way I do, I think you'd agree." Marcus was a master at dealing with difficult subjects.

"Well, if you really think —"

Before she could finish, he was standing in front of her, his fingers gently working on the pins. He tilted her head forward until her forehead rested on his waistband. Too late, he realized the shock of touching her was about to undo all his concentration. He practically wrenched the last pin from her hair, making her wince. "Sorry," he muttered and stepped back.

He studied her for a moment then pointed at the bridge of his nose.

"Off," he ordered.

"Off?" She repeated, confused.

"I know my studio is acoustically perfect. I built it myself. There is no echo." He levelled a stern "me Svengali" look at her.

"Chill," she mouthed and removed her glasses.

"Much better," he assured. "Now, shake your head. That's it. I — Wow." The effect *was* stunning. A hue of reds and browns swirled around her shoulders, picking up the gold in her eyes. The color cast shadows in the hollows of her cheeks. Marcus hadn't seen natural beauty like hers since the Scavullo exhibition at MOMA. She had the air of a classic celluloid diva, a cross between a young Katharine Hepburn and Lauren Bacall.

With barely contained excitement, he realized he'd found what he was looking for. The savior of his exhibition was sitting right in front of him. He tried to imagine what she'd look like silhouetted naked on a nine-foot-high matte of black and white splendor. His expression became dreamy. *Oh, yeah!*

"What are you grinning at?"

Her question brought him back to the studio as she grinned back at him, letting her head fall to one side and sending a cascade of hair across one shoulder. Instinctively, he snapped the photo.

"Hey, no fair. That one doesn't count. I wasn't ready."

"Candid, beautiful. I want you natural. No fake `say cheese' photos for you. Just let yourself go. Pretend I'm not here. Get up close and personal with the camera lens."

"You mean 'intimate' don't you?"

Marcus tried to ignore the teasing tone in her voice. "Exactly. I'll dim the lights a little for you. There, now I'll bet you can hardly see me. Right?" He stepped behind the tripod.

"Actually, I can't see anything without my glasses on. You're just a blur, Marc." She squinted in the direction of where she thought his voice was coming from.

"Well, that's one I've never been called before," he quipped.

"What?"

"Nothing, just lay back. That's it," — click — "Now, lean forward, cross your legs and prop yourself up on one elbow." Another click. "Perfect."

Ashly was aware of low, soft music and she recognized Kenny G playing in the background. Safe sax — her favorite. The generation-aged disco Greg loved grated on her nerves. She'd gone through the 70's and once was enough, thank you. She closed her eyes and allowed the fluid rhythm to guide her movements. Gradually a sense of freedom took over and she began a wonderful journey of erotic self-discovery. A storm of trapped images, whispered sounds and repressed feelings flowed up to vent themselves.

She straddled the divan and purred like a kitten for Marc who urged and coaxed and begged her into impossible positions and instigated her transformation. The role-playing was unfamiliar yet exciting. She was a slave to Marc's masterful commands. She dared the camera with every click, teased out every flash. Marc's encouraging words became a litany.

"You're beautiful. Be sexy. Fantasy time, give me more. Great. Now, tease me. That's right. Pout, close your eyes, big sigh. Terrific."

The music was a turn on. The camera was a turn on. Having Marc tell her what to do and how to do it was a turn on. She felt like a teenager again, exploring the danger zone of the back seat. Daring. Pleasurable. Taboo.

She'd reached into the candy jar, copped the biggest piece and lingered on the decision of whether or not to bite quickly or suck slowly. She decided to bite.

Marcus' resolve, already pushed to the breaking point, foundered completely as Ashly slipped her arms out of the robe and clasped her hands in her lap. She sat cross-legged on the divan, facing him. Her creamy white breasts shone like two luscious pearls under the lights. Their pink tips stood poised before the camera lens. Marcus lifted his head from behind the camera to make sure he was seeing the proper image. The image he saw was anything but proper.

Gone were the inhibitions of the shy, mousy working girl. This woman was a feast for the eyes, *his* eyes. His fingertips stood poised on the flash button. At that moment, she was totally and utterly his. If he depressed the button, she would be his forever, captured in his fantasy to look at whenever he wanted for as long as he wanted. But she also might belong to someone else some day; someone she might be intimate enough with to show the pictures. The thought of sharing his Ashly created an uneasy and unfamiliar feeling that lodged in his gut. He couldn't imagine another man looking at her the way he was and wanting her the way he did. A sudden possessive urge distracted him from his purpose and he flinched to clear it. In one hair-trigger reflex, Ashly became frozen in time forever as he heard the click and saw the flash. A satisfactory blush rose up from her waist and ended at her hairline.

But to his horror, she wasn't through. She bent slightly forward, pressing her arms into her rib-cage and forcing her breasts together to meet in a deep 'v.' It was the act of a woman in the throes of a seduction. A deep, throaty whisper confirmed his suspicion.

"Marc."

It was all the invitation he needed. In seconds he was kneeling beside the divan with Ashly wrapped in his arms. To his surprise, he found himself trembling inside, the thrill of anticipation doubling his pulse. He wasn't sure who started the deep passionate kisses that fed the fire burning inside him, he only knew that she aroused him like no other woman ever had before.

He pressed her warm body against him and cursed the clothes he still wore. Yet, he hesitated to break the kiss. She tasted of sweet wine and citrus. Marcus could feel her lack of experience in the way she kept her mouth closed at first. Then gradually, she became bolder, more secure with the feel of him as he pressed her down on the divan. He broke their passionate embrace long enough to whisper, "Baby, let's come up for air."

But Ashly would have none of it. "Want to drown," she murmured and drew his face back to her own.

"Then at least open your mouth, sweetheart, so I can drown, too."

Ashlyn willingly obeyed and was rewarded with a long, slow, deep kiss, the likes of which would have knocked her socks off, if she'd been wearing any. Never had a man kissed her the way Marc did. He was gentle yet sure of what she wanted. He didn't mash his teeth against her own while carelessly fumbling at her breasts. He took his time. He took *her* time.

The feel of his warm, hard body against her own naked skin excited her. There was something pleasantly erotic about almost wearing someone else's clothes, especially when someone else was still in them. If this was foreplay, she'd take all she could get. This new pleasure prompted her to try a little foreplay of her own.

Ashlyn slid her hands underneath his sweatshirt and trailed her hands up his back. His sudden intake of breath nearly stole her own. He broke away and in one swift motion, peeled off the sweat shirt. He was back on top of her before she missed the heat of his body. For the first time, Ashlyn had the luxury of his skin against her breasts.

His springy chest hair tickled and teased her sensitive nipples. He fed off their arousal. His husky moan encouraged her to continue her exploration. Her fingertips followed the muscle-play of his arms and shoulders as he expertly kneaded and nibbled her breasts. Her breath caught and she heard herself gasp from the sheer pleasure he gave her.

Ashlyn indulged in one of her earlier curiosities and tangled her fingers in his long, dark hair. The silky strands slid across her hand. She toyed and played with it, winding it around her fingers. One by one, she freed each finger being careful not to tug too hard. Gradually she caressed a path down his back before settling in the downy-soft patch of hair at the base of his spine. She ached to go further but waited for a sign of acquiescence. Instead of giving her a sign, he opened the door for her by reaching down and placing her hand on his half-exposed buttocks.

She heard her own soft, surprised sigh at the intimacy of her new discovery. She gave in to the urge to gently knead the hard, muscular cheeks of his ass. She always considered herself an "ass-woman." Most of her girlfriends giggled and speculated about the bulge in a guy's crotch. Ashlyn's fascination had always turned her head to watching men walk by her. It afforded her the pleasure of a long, lingering gaze, instead of having to avert her eyes suddenly or hide an embarrassing flush.

Marc had a great ass! Tight, not too much hair covering his skin, hot to the touch and sensitive! He expelled a sudden growl when she firmly grasped one cheek then the other. His hot breath between her breasts created a tingling inferno of pleasure. She arched up to give his mouth better access to her breasts. She wasn't disappointed.

"Beautiful," he murmured as he took one swollen nipple into his mouth, then the other. "You feel like silk... so natural... all pink and white... warm perfection..." He suckled each breast in turn until the rosy tips became hard and puckered. Then he captured the nub between his teeth and flicked his tongue over the very end in a torturous frenzy.

Yet there was no urgency in his lovemaking. He gloried in scraping at every raw nerve in her body. He began a tortuous rhythm of insinuation as he nestled his crotch against her thighs. Her hips copied the motion and she opened her legs to cradle him. The length of his hard cock prodded her naked mons before sliding between her tender outer lips. She felt her own dewy moisture dampen the cotton fabric of his pants. Marc began to rock back and forth against her swollen clit.

The unfamiliar feel of rough cloth against her sensitive flesh only heightened her pleasure. It was a keen reminder that very little stood between her and the point of no return. She couldn't stop now if she wanted to. And she wouldn't stop Marc from removing the final barrier.

And he was going to. He told her, in searing detail, exactly what would happen.

"I'm going to fill you up, baby doll. Take you, inch by hot, lovely inch. I want to feel those dimpled, little knees strapped tight against my ears while I give you full penetration. Then, I'll turn you over, come in from behind so I can play with your clit at the same time. Would you like that?"

Ashlyn was at a loss for words; mesmerized by the images he described. She could do little but dumbly nod her head.

"I didn't hear you."

"Yes," she managed to whisper.

"Yes, what?" he demanded and reached down between them to explore her thatch of pubic hair.

The feel of his fingers gently probing her outer lips caused her to cry out in frustration and beg for more. He teased her instead.

"Not until you tell me what you want," he gently chastised, then allowed one finger to brush over her swollen bud.

Ashlyn nearly screamed. "Now! I want you inside me now."

"Patience, my love. The first time's going to be hard and fast. Not time enough for both of us to enjoy it. But then we'll do it again... and again... and again."

Ashlyn accepted every word as easy as drawing breath. And her next breath mingled with his as he shared a deep, lingering kiss. Ashlyn was sure he was stealing her soul, but it didn't matter. Nothing mattered now but the man in her arms.

The air filled with his soft growls and her own urgent groans. The louder she groaned, the faster and more forcefully he ground himself against her until she felt her last groan being drawn into a sudden gasp. A rush of sensations erupted into a powerful climax. She wrapped her legs tighter around his waist in an effort to try to force him inside. She wanted him deep, penetrating. She wanted to hear the sharp slap of his balls against her ass. She wanted to come again only this time with him fully imbedded inside her. She wanted to feel the splash of warm come against the sensitive walls of her canal. Was it a dream or did she hear herself emptying her soul of all these secrets to the man who held her?

Marc tore his mouth from hers and kissed a path to her ear. She thought she heard him whisper something coherent and sensible like, "protection." Instead of responding to his question, she gently bit the hollow of his neck.

"Don't go. I want you inside me." He was making magic and she'd be damned if she'd let him break the spell. But break it he did. He struggled to sit up, taking her with him. He held her close and kissed her head. And her eyes. And her nose. Finally, he landed a series of short kisses on her mouth as he spoke.

"I'll... be... right... back," he whispered and climbed off her. He turned and strode across the studio to the door that led into his private living area. In the dim light of the studio, Ashlyn had a perfect view of just how aroused Marc was. His erection created a tent inside the once-loose sweat pants, giving startling evidence that he was generously endowed. Ashlyn couldn't keep her eyes off the site. A thrilling shiver rushed through her thighs and she pressed them together. They tingled with anticipation while the delicate, still sensitive bud of her clitoris quivered, ready to jump back to life. No wonder she'd come off like a rocket! And that had been with his clothes on. She tried to imagine what it would be like once he was inside her buried to the hilt.

As she watched him disappear behind the door, a thought struck her. She was not being invited into his bedroom. A more horrifying thought gripped her. *Oh my*

God, what if he's married?

The champagne, combined with the liqueurs, wine and cocktails made her brain fuzzy. She couldn't remember if he was wearing a ring, not that it was an accurate sign of any permanent attachment. She tried to recall seeing any womanly signs as they walked through the house to the studio. She remembered seeing a picture of someone in a red dress flirting with Marc. The scene drifted by her in slow-motion and became part of a distorted jumble of images. The room spun at a dizzy angle. If she could just lay down for a few minutes, she might feel better.

She closed her eyes against the lights of the studio. They had suddenly become harsh and glaring. Why had he turned up the lights? A thumping noise poked through the haze. She tried to lift her arms to cover her ears but they seemed weighed down. Someone called her name but she couldn't respond. She felt something rough and heavy settle over her body. She relaxed into it's warmth and was eternally grateful when the room became dark. She managed a slurred "thank you" before falling asleep.

She didn't hear the disappointment in the voice that answered.

"You're welcome, beautiful."

Chapter 3

Marcus pushed his way through the crowded streets of Hazelton Lanes toward the gallery. Briefcase gripped tightly in his hand, he was only vaguely aware of knocking it against a woman pedestrian as she walked past him. He disregarded her cheerful smile and only muttered a curt, "excuse me" after the hard, square leather connected with her thigh.

His foul mood, a leftover from the past three weeks, was instigated by his waking up that Sunday morning and finding Ashly gone. Nor could he find any trace of her in the days following her disappearance. He cursed Daagmar a thousand times over for not getting Ashly's telephone number. He badgered her for days about any detail she could remember until finally, Daagmar told him where to go.

"Ashly whats-her-name didn't make the appointment. Somebody-else-Tate did," Daagmar snapped and promptly told him to piss-off.

He wasted no time in developing the film he'd shot. The results fortified him. Ashly was magnificent; the most perfectly proportioned collection of black and white dots he'd seen in a long time. He spent hours examining film negatives through the magnified light box. He enlarged print after print and then faxed her picture to every modelling agency in the city, and a few in L.A. and New York. Each time he got the same answer. No one had her under contract or had even seen her before but, could she be persuaded to sign?

Marcus was less than amused. He was aware of the less than professional remarks being circulated as a result of his queries. She had slipped through the experienced fingers of Marcus Remmington and was now known as "the one that got away." It was purely by accident that Marcus discovered some of the agents he'd sent Ashly's picture to were working behind his back to find her.

He answered a frantic summons from Alexis Tremayne, his partner in *Nirvana*, the up-scale art gallery located in an exclusive shopping section of downtown Toronto. He arrived in time to speak briefly with the construction foreman working on the renovations. Most of the crew had already packed up and were gone. News that the project was on schedule should have pleased him. He suspected that wasn't the only reason Alexis wanted to see him. He wasn't surprised when she raked him over the coals about his behaviour and the entire Ashly incident.

"Marcus, dear boy." Alexis embraced him through the cloud of cigarette smoke that always surrounded her. Marcus constantly harangued her about the habit. She, in turn, bitched incessantly about his long hair, his scruffy but very expensive designer jeans and his fondness for bourbon. It was her right, she argued, and a privilege of her age to decide to commit ritual nicotine-induced suicide, and he could go to hell. Marcus defended his right to breathe and warned her that she would not live to see her next and fifty-third birthday.

Alexis used to own a modelling agency and had learned about Marcus' problem through a mutual contact. She was concerned enough about Marcus to leave several strong warnings on his machine. Alexis represented a lot of money. As his partner, he knew he couldn't afford to rile her. The wisest thing to do was to hear her out and get his "sorry ass" down to the gallery!

"So show me this little piece of tail who's tied a knot in your, ah," she paused and pointed her cigarette holder at his groin, and gave him a teasing smile, "reputation."

"My psyche," he snapped. "She's screwed me up, Alexis." Except for the two of them, the half-renovated gallery was empty. Marcus listened to his words as they echoed off the high ceiling. Admitting them out loud didn't make them any easier to bear. The naked truth was painfully sad and honesty plain out sucked, big time.

Because there were no other chairs besides the one Alexis sat in, Marcus pushed back a corner of the protective tarp and sidled onto her desk. Alexis made a disapproving face and leaned forward, planted one elbow on his pant leg and propped her chin in her free hand. Marcus could feel himself being scrutinized through the wraparound sunglasses she always wore, day or night. He had the urge, but never the courage, to ask if she wore them while entertaining one of her many lovers. In her other hand she clutched her cigarette holder, another permanent fixture. Alexis was eccentric enough to be the kind of person who might conceal a weapon in the tip. Marcus swore that if he met her without her two props, he wouldn't recognize her. She tapped the end of her holder on the oak desk top, drawing his attention back to her.

"I'll lay it on the line for you Marcus, since it seems to be the only way I'll get through to you. *Nirvana* opens in two months — that's 60 days, if you're keeping track. I want to know if, in two weeks, you'll have your exhibition ready. If not, then…well, dammit Marcus, I'm a business woman. Don't sit there and pout like some little boy mooning over his first crush. The only way to get over this is to take out your black book and…"

She stopped when Marcus silently handed her one of Ashly's photographs. Marcus nearly fell off the corner of the desk when Alexis slowly raised her sunglasses while angling the photo into the dim light. The woman had eyes — bloodshot — but they were there and they were scrutinizing his Ashly. And it suddenly occurred to him that he wanted Alexis' approval — badly.

He counted the heartbeats until Alexis slid her sunglasses back into place. He waited for her to toss the photo back at him, as she had with countless other infatuations. When she didn't, he held out his hand and raised his eyebrows to question her hesitation.

"I'll hang on to this, if you don't mind."

He did mind, but she closed any objection by exhaling a large cloud of smoke in his direction. In retaliation, he coughed loudly and fanned the air, using several exaggerated arm gestures, and one not so subtle hand gesture. She answered with a peevish grin and slid the photo into a faded, leather portfolio under her desk. Case closed, as it were.

"If I were you, Marcus, I wouldn't spend too much time on this obsession," she warned.

Marcus rolled his eyes in defence. "I'm not obsessed."

"Some men hang fuzzy dice from their rear view mirrors; others carry a rabbit's foot." She took a long drag off her cigarette and continued. "But not our Marcus. No sir. He carries around women's underwear." She pointed the cigarette end of her holder towards Marcus' open briefcase where a swath of pink silk and ivory lace peeped accusingly from one of the worn leather pockets.

Marcus glared at her while he stuffed the treasure back into the zippered compartment and snapped the lid shut. He cleared his throat against the image that had haunted him ever since that night; the image of Ashly, the fledgling seductress, teasing off her robe to reveal herself naked as the temptation of Eve. He'd discovered the silky swatch while sorting through the laundry hamper. Impulsively, he decided to hang on to it. Just in case.

"Interesting concept you have, Marcus. You know, Prince Charming carried a glass slipper from door to door. What *are* you hoping will fit into those?" Her laughter, meant to embarrass him, only served to fuel his resolve. "I'll find her."

"Where?" she demanded.

"I don't know. Yet," he managed through gritted teeth.

"You have two new competitors following in your footsteps. I'm surprised you haven't noticed them scratching at your heels," Alexis said casually and butted out her spent cigarette.

Marcus scoffed, he knew where this was leading. "If you mean that rich kid, shutterbug wannabe and his latest mattress decoration, I've noticed them. So he got a few shots of daddy's yacht into the Toronto Island Yacht Club Directory. It doesn't mean shit, Alexis."

"Brian and Ellen are very talented. They're eager. They're *hungry*. You remember what that's like, don't you Marcus?"

Marcus was ready for the remember-who's-putting-up-half-the-cash-for-this-venture speech. "You don't scare me, Alexis."

"Wipe that smug look off your face. Yolande's been spreading a lot of crap about you. Word on the street is she wants your blood. And she'll get it if she isn't up on these walls as the star of this exhibition." She waved her empty cigarette holder at the newly finished drywall partitions.

Marcus followed the gesture and stared at the bare walls, the freshly sanded hardwood floors and the gaps in the ceiling where the imported light fixtures would soon hang. He only hoped they had enough money between them to finish the renovations on time. Alexis didn't need to know that his line of credit was almost non-existent or that the money from the Bedsong shoot wouldn't arrive until after Christmas — after the opening. His next job was almost a given. If he could arrange an advance against the job, then he could breathe easier. His next appointment would tell the tale. In the meantime, he would live like he always did, by his wits. He nodded toward Alexis's portfolio. "Yolande can be replaced. She already has."

"If you can find her," Alexis reminded.

"I'll find her."

"Why?" Alexis let out a frustrated growl and slumped back in her chair. "You don't need her. You've worked hard and helped launch the careers of dozens of young girls. Clients want you. Agents want you. So what if this Ashly doesn't want you? You're practically a legend in the industry and after this exhibition you'll be a household name. Your work will be in demand. Art snobs and celebrities will buy up your prints and drive up the price. You'll make money," she paused for emphasis. "*I'll* make money." She grinned wide, displaying two sets of extraordinarily white teeth in contrast to the amount she smoked. "And that will make your bankers very happy." With that, she got up, stretched lazily and yawned. "And you, my darling Marcus, will be a star."

Marcus squirmed when she came around and tried to pinch his cheek. "And all without the help of Ashly whoever." She finished by tugging none-too-gently on his freshly secured pony-tail, causing errant strands to fall out of place.

"Stop that," he admonished and slapped her hand away. "I have a meeting this afternoon with the DiAngelo brothers."

"I heard the pride of Milan was in town pushing their new perfume. I'm surprised you have time for them, what with combing the city for Cinderella," she quipped.

"I'll find her," he promised.

The words haunted him as he made his way to Fraser and Associates later that afternoon. He walked from the gallery in Hazelton Lanes to Fraser's University Avenue address. It gave him time to mull over the problem.

I'll find her. But how? It was one hell of a big city. He was almost ready to admit that Alexis was right. He was obsessed.

I'll find her. If he ever found her again he wasn't sure what he'd do first, lose his temper, or himself.

"You wanted to see me, Dad?" Ashlyn took a seat across from her father and hoped the trepidation in her voice wasn't too obvious. Duncan never called anyone into *the red room*, as Brian once dubbed it, unless there was a lecture involved. Duncan's office was a sea of burgundy leather and antique brass studs. Over the years Ashlyn occupied herself during numerous lectures by counting the brass studs that outlined the huge leather-topped oak desk and two matching wing chairs. She knew exactly how many studs were on each piece of furniture. She hoped Duncan wasn't offering her another chance to refresh her memory.

She watched him briefly flip through, then discard, the portfolio containing the mock-up ads she and Sharon painstakingly put together during the last week. Lines of disapproval crowded his forehead. Any hopes of reprieve were lost in those furrowed brows.

"Did you enjoy your trip to Europe?" she asked, hoping to lighten his mood.

Duncan answered without looking at her. "I met with the DiAngelos in Milan."

"Did you go alone?" The recent wedding was so quick and quiet that Ashlyn didn't want to admit the name of her father's fourth wife had slipped her mind.

"Your stepmother went with me."

"I hardly think that someone who isn't old enough to drink in some states qualifies as my stepmother."

"That's enough, Ashlyn. You don't have to like her."

"Like her? I don't even know her. You'll have to introduce us one of these days."

"Don't be sarcastic. You *were* invited to the wedding.

"Was Brian?"

He ignored her probe and continued. "I left a message on your desk."

"A pink telephone slip does not a wedding invitation make. Come clean, Dad. Why all the secrecy?"

Duncan heaved an impatient sigh. "Her name is Kirsten, or Mrs. Fraser, if you prefer and yes, she went with me to Europe. Are you finished prying?"

Ashlyn rolled her eyes. "My father marries a teenager he's never introduced to his *grown* children and he thinks I'm prying. I have a right to pry."

"You're covered if I die tomorrow. That is what you're worried about, isn't it?"

"If it is, then I have a long wait behind the three ex-Mrs. Frasers. No thanks, Dad. I have no desire to watch them all shop together after you're gone."

"I settled with your mother years ago and the other two remarried," he snapped.

"Yes, Stephanie and Jennifer got smart. Why mother still carries a torch for you is beyond me. What I can't figure out is where Miss Teen Idol fits in. Unless... Oh, my God! She is, isn't she! That's why everything was so hush-hush. I'm going to be a...a sister."

"I would appreciate it if you wouldn't talk about this around here. It's no one's business but mine."

"Oh, I'd say it'll be everyone's business in about six months. Tell me, Dad, are you sure its yours?"

"That's enough. I'm old enough to choose what I want in life."

No, it wasn't enough. Her father was acting like an idiot. His temper be damned. "Did she even give you a choice, or did her parents threaten statutory rape? It must have been some choice, marry me or it's off to court we go, not to mention the newspapers. Did you ever hear of safe sex? By the way, have you been tested for any contagious diseases?"

"Ashlyn! That's enough!" He bellowed loud enough for anyone on the same floor to hear him. Ashlyn shut her eyes against the picture her life would present for the rest of the week; the circumspect glances from her fellow employees, silent pity ringing out from their faces. If he flogged her publicly in the town square, the humiliation couldn't be worse.

Determined to recover what little self-esteem she possessed, she changed the subject. "Can we please get back to discussing some strategy?"

Ashlyn listened to her father's input. With each passing minute, her hopes sank lower and lower. 'My-way-or-the-highway' was what Duncan meant by strategy. The so-called strategy was nothing more than a platform for Duncan to solicit her opinion, discard it, and go with his own. Ashlyn knew the ads were rough by her standards, but they were something to show the client. And she was proud of them, even if Duncan wasn't.

Ashlyn had learned to deal with Duncan's constant criticism by handing him benign, satisfactory answers. Schooled in the art of deception, she no longer blushed or lowered her head when battered with Duncan's public corrections. She would rather die than admit that her own father embarrassed her. Instead she reinforced her resolve by squaring her shoulders and lifting her chin. Duncan often commented on what excellent posture she had, never realizing he was the cause. The only outward sign of her discomfort was her nervous habit of adjusting her glasses. Just as she found herself doing now as she listened to him lecture her.

"This account is very important to the company. It could make up for the business we lost during the recession. I can't afford to have you screw this up."

Ashlyn's answer was designed to cause him no less stress. "I'll be fine." Of that she was sure. She knew better than to commit herself or her ideas. Duncan's lips pressed into a grim, flat line. Ashlyn knew he wanted her to say something else. Something to reassure him that he had produced at least one clone of perfection. *Sorry, dad. The world isn't ready for another Duncan Hardwick Fraser, and the world isn't going to get one, either.*

Ashlyn was relieved when she heard Duncan's name over the paging system. He answered the page from an interoffice phone on the wall. He barked into the receiver. "Yes. I see. Show them in and offer them coffee. We're on our way." He replaced the receiver and snapped his fingers toward the door. "Let's go," he ordered, as if she were one of the half-dozen thoroughbred hunting dogs he owned.

Ashlyn dutifully followed behind. For the first time in her life, she found herself hating her job. She hated herself for not standing up to Duncan. And she hated what's-her-name, the current Mrs. Fraser, for involving her father in such a cheap scandal. Surprisingly, she didn't hate Duncan. She pitied him and the idea that the company he loved more than his family was now running him. She didn't envy the financial responsibility he had to bear. Perhaps it was that pressure that drove him to the bed of a pretty, gold-digging Lolita. Ashlyn thought about her own recent indiscretion and knew she shouldn't be casting stones at her father. She might have ended up in the same situation. That Marc guy must have used some protection, since her period came as regular as clockwork the following week.

The night in question was still a muddle, but it gave her a secret source of pleasure to know that for one moment, a man wanted her because he thought her attractive and not because she was a savvy business opportunity. That knowledge brought a smile to her lips and raised her spirits. It was a revived and confident Ashlyn who entered the boardroom, ready to gamble the future of her father's company on a slender bottle of scented water.

Chapter 4

If Duncan hadn't realized Ashlyn wasn't perfect before now, then he knew it ten minutes into the *Insatiable* presentation. He sat at the back of the room, scowling in the dark as she narrated the merits of each advertising program. As she talked, she kept one eye on the two representatives who chattered in Italian between themselves. Clearly, they were not overwhelmed by what they saw.

"I'd appreciate your comments, gentlemen," she said. Finally they stopped talking.

"The woman," one of them, a man named Giuseppe - Joe, her father had introduced him - made an hourglass shape in the air. "Where is the woman?" he asked in exaggerated English.

"As I mentioned previously, Mr. DiAngelo, every perfume on the market uses a Hollywood personality or a supermodel to endorse their product. Our research department has found that the celebrity's name is remembered first, and then the product. We want your product to be noticed for its unique qualities, not for some actress who has to be replaced every time her contract runs out. That's a lot of money to spend on a short term advertising campaign. You'll find the cost figures on page 14 of the report."

Which lay unopened in front of them, she noted disheartedly. Ashlyn knew she was losing this round. What was worse, she knew Duncan knew it too. And, since he usually sided with the client, he made his displeasure no secret.

"I understand what Mr. DiAngelo is getting at. He's thinking along the lines of what I had in mind all the time."

Thank you, Dad, for the translation and the vote of confidence.

Instantly the reps turned toward Duncan. Ashlyn stood forgotten and had no choice but to sit down and listen to what Duncan had to say.

"If I hear you correctly, Joe, and I think I do —" he gave the men a conspiratorial smile, "in order for us to get the message to women consumers, then it should come from one. After all, these women know how to talk to each other, eh?" The men laughed among themselves and nodded agreeably.

Ashlyn fumed in silence but swallowed her anger and attempted to reason with them. "I thought we were selling perfume, not sex." She didn't miss the look of reprimand from her father, or the lack of interest from the DiAngelos. She tried one more time. "I've been wearing the sample of *Insatiable* and I —"

"Of course we're not selling sex, Ashlyn. We want to get the message across that if you wear the perfume then you feel sexy. And if you feel sexy, then you are sexy. Right?"

Ashlyn thought carefully before answering. *Right, Dad. You know everything about women. Just ask Jennifer or Stephanie or the most recent one whose name escapes me.* Then she remembered her recent conversation with Gerry Dolan, their chief accountant warning her of their unstable financial position. "Of course, gentlemen. If that's what you want we'll certainly work towards putting together a suitable campaign." She redoubled her efforts to smooth things over, not because she agreed but because the interest on the bridge financing was due.

Duncan reinforced the offer. "Yes, of course," and motioned for her to back up his assurance.

"We can get a draft to you by, say, next —"

"By tomorrow," Duncan interjected.

Ashlyn flashed him an incredulous look, which Duncan quelled by marginally narrowing his eyes and ever-so-slightly lowering his head in her direction before he continued. "As a matter of fact, the photographer should be joining us shortly."

"Photographer?" Ashlyn tried to hide her confusion and was losing the battle. She ground her frustration between her back teeth. She felt the heat of anger flame her cheeks. Disappointment stung her eyes.

Duncan stepped in. "I invited Marcus Remmington to join us. Don't you remember, Ashlyn?"

At Remmington's name, the reps responded with favorable "ah's", and made impressive remarks to Duncan. "His work is *molto bene*. How you say, very good. Yes?" Francesco nodded enthusiastically, forcing another benign but polite smile from Ashlyn.

She was aware of Remmington's reputation. He could turn a respectable ad campaign into a peep show before you could say 'market share'. There was nothing like a nude, bronzed butt cheek to catch the eye of the potential perfume consumer. It made perfect sense to her.

"I believe he's just finished shooting the Bedsong account with Yolande." Of course Duncan would keep on top of his own idea. He knew what he wanted all along. All he needed was her own bad handling to slide right in and catch the unwary client. Another demonstration of the golden rule at work. His earlier words took on a menacing double meaning. *Get this account at any cost.* Even if he had to ruin Ashlyn's career in the process. Brilliant strategy. *And you walked right into it, didn't you Ash?*

And Remmington. His ace-in-the-hole. How had he managed that? Remmington had a notoriously strict code of independence. Ashlyn conceded that it was prob-ably another one of those male bonding efforts. A few beers, some chatter about sports, a handshake later and it was done. Who said the old boys club was dead?

Duncan stood. "Now, Francesco, about that tour of the country club I promised you…" As they turned to leave, Duncan tossed her a crumb. "Ashlyn will stay here with Giuseppe to discuss the campaign. When Remmington arrives the three of you can brainstorm some ideas. I'm sure you'll have a draft by the end of the day." The words 'or else' hung unspoken between them.

Francesco bid her, "*Ciao*" and Duncan escorted him out. Giuseppe reseated himself right next to Ashlyn. The overpowering scent of his cologne caused her to wrinkle her nose and cough discreetly. There was nothing discreet in the way Giuseppe leered at her.

"You like work with you papa, no?"

NO! The silent scream echoed in her head. Politeness intervened. "I appreciate the opportunity, but I have to work as hard as anyone else." There was a fine line between truth and contempt.

Giuseppe leaned closer, casually trailing his index finger along the sleeve of her shell pink linen jacket. "We have been to other companies with our product but we think you have much more to offer." He smiled, his gaze drifted from her face down to where her thighs met the hem of her matching linen skirt.

"Th-there are many talented people here at Fraser & Associates. Perhaps you'd like to meet some of them." She started to rise but Giuseppe's hand on her arm stayed her.

"Your papa, he say you not married." Guiseppe's stare raked over her slender figure like a wolf eyeing a plump, innocent rabbit.

An alarm sounded inside her head. Was she being used as bait for *Insatiable*? Did he think Duncan was willing to offer *anything* for a chance at the account? Duncan was devious but she was still his daughter. It was time to draw the line between business and pleasure.

"My father is correct, Mr. DiAngelo. I'm not married, but I have a boyfriend," she added quickly and continued the lie. "It's quite serious." She saw confusion in Giuseppe's face followed by the discreet withdrawal of his hand.

For a moment, she could think of nothing to say to him. She filled the gap with small talk about his home in Milan and his trip to Toronto. At last, the intercom buzzed. Thankful for the distraction, she picked up the receiver. "Thank you, Marie. Show him in." She turned to Giuseppe. "Mr. Remmington is here."

At last, the Fraser receptionist escorted Marcus to the boardroom. He tried to clear his mind and prepared himself to flatter the DiAngelos. It was a common ploy and he used it whenever he expected any resistance from a client. And he always got his own way. He prided himself on it. The Fraser executive would be no trouble. Perhaps the day wouldn't be a total loss.

He acknowledged the familiar form of Giuseppe DiAngelo with a handshake. Giuseppe's thick, broken English was worthy of a *Godfather capo*. He immediately turned toward the account executive and held out his hand.

Then he froze — but only for a second. Suddenly he couldn't breathe. The air was gone. No it wasn't. He'd just forgotten to inhale. And it was hot. So hot he could feel the blood pounding against his temples. He was breathing again but it was hard. It was always hard when your heart was slamming against your chest, trying to break free.

He smiled at her. He shook her hand. He took in the suit, the sensible shoes and the prim topknot of hair. He looked past the plainness, right through the glasses and into Ashly's panic stricken face. His Ashly. At last, he'd found her.

He fought for control and smiled politely. "Pleased to meet you, Miss, ah..."

"F-Fraser. A-Ashly, er, Ashlyn. Ashlyn Fraser."

Her voice was barely a whisper. A slight tremor rocked the hand that took his. He stared down at their clasped hands and felt her tugging from his grasp. He leaned toward her, out of Giuseppe's earshot and whispered, "You left the ball a little early, Cinderella. I have something that fits you." Then, louder, "but *you* Miss Fraser, can call me *Marc*."

The next hour was sheer hell on Earth for Ashlyn. She sat across the boardroom table from Marc, her knees clenched tightly together, her toes curled and sweating inside her flat shoes. The realization of what she had done refused to settle in. Had she really gone to bed with the infamous Marcus Remmington? Could there be two Marcs with the same silvery eyes and seductive smile? Could Marcus Remmington, the arrogant, smirking womanizer, be the same Marc that seduced her into her own wanton split personality?

She concentrated on the wall just above the men's heads, never looking directly at them when she spoke. Her gazed shifted from one side of the room to the other. She talked down at the layout on the table, to the presentation easel, but never once did she raise her eyes to meet Marc's.

Marc, on the other hand, delighted in distracting her. He whistled through his teeth, drummed his fingers on the table, coughed and cleared his throat until Ashlyn was sure he was having some kind of an attack. Through all of the distractions, his eyes never left her.

She summoned all her will to remain professional. Perhaps her indifference would convince him that he wasn't seeing Ashly, that he'd made a mistake. Later she could take him aside and explain that she was often mistaken for other people. She even thought of dropping a slutty twin sister into the picture. Anything, so long as she didn't have to admit to being the wanton creature Marc so hastily seduced in his studio.

Giuseppe was saying something to her. "Excuse me? I'm sorry, would you mind repeating that, *Señor* DiAngelo? Yolande? No, I don't think she's the proper spokesperson for *Insatiable*. Besides, I believe she's contracted to Bedsong." Ashlyn silently applauded her recovery. But it was short lived.Marc snapped open his briefcase and drew out several photos; black and white head shots of assorted models he probably worked with from time to time.

"I believe *Insatiable* deserves a new, fresh face, not some over-exposed glamour girl whose face is in every current magazine, ad nauseam." He paused and stared pointedly at her, his silvery eyes twinkling. "I have another model in mind for the shoot. A new girl, very beautiful, very talented."

"Really?" Ashlyn answered, but heard the word as if it was spoken through a dream.

"Oh, yes," Marc gave an exaggerated nod of approval to Giuseppe. "Trust me, *Señor* DiAngelo, she's perfect."

Ashlyn felt her mouth go dry and swore the pounding of her heart could be heard by everyone around the table. She held her breath while Marc sorted through his pile of photographs. He took the very last photo and pushed it toward Giuseppe. A flash of fire-engine red silk and the spill of mink and gold curls proclaimed her nightmare officially underway.

"There's your girl," Marc announced.

Ashlyn didn't have to look at the photo to know who Giuseppe was ogling. She kept her head lowered and toyed with the frames of her glasses. From the corner of her eye she caught a glimpse of her reflection in the chrome-plated water jug in front of her. Her cheeks were flushed scarlet, her lips drained of color. Through a haze she heard Giuseppe murmuring, *"bella, mille bella"*.

"Now, she's *Insatiable*. Don't you think so, Miss Fraser?" His voice was light and deliberately mocking.

Ashlyn looked up to find Marc's gaze leveled at her. She fought the urge to bolt. Quickly, she recovered herself. "Personally, I find the exploitation of women to be demeaning and bordering on sexual harassment." There, she'd said it. Duncan be damned. And as soon as she'd said it she knew it was the wrong thing to say in front of Giuseppe DiAngelo. She met his disapproving scowl and tried to explain. "Wh…what I mean is, your advertising budget will go a lot further if we don't have to pay an inflated agency fee for a model. I've heard rumors for months that heroin is ravaging the modeling industry. Do you really want to take that chance? Couldn't we just use the floral garden sequence? We don't have to pay flowers to pose or spend endless hours retouching make-up."

Marc clasped his hands behind his head and leaned back in the swivel chair. He idly swayed back and forth drawing out an ear-itching squeak. He stared thoughtfully up at the ceiling. "If memory serves, Miss Fraser, didn't this agency have the True-Taste Banana account a couple of years ago?"

Damn his memory! Ashlyn knew what he was leading up to. Since it was useless to deny it, she nodded.

"And didn't someone here write that obscene banana-eating commercial?"

"For which we won a *Bessie* —" she defended.

"— and which was censored?" Marc lowered his gaze to Ashlyn's face. He raised his eyebrows in declaration of winning their game of one-upmanship.

"I want-a her." Giuseppe tapped his index finger sharply at what Ashlyn could see was her own partially exposed left breast. She fought the urge to cross her arms over her chest to protect herself. She could almost feel the pressure from Giuseppe's poking fingers.

Anger and tears welled up inside her and she fought them down. How dare Marcus Remmington display her body as if it were some table centerpiece. The man had no morals, no ethics. He'd betrayed their professional relationship and violated a personal trust. She would never forgive him.

"You give me this girl and I give you the account." Giuseppe's ultimatum left no room for argument.

She longed to snatch the picture from Giuseppe's hands, tear it up and order them both out. The responsibility of meeting next month's payroll stopped her. She could feel Marc's eyes on her as she weighed her decision. Finally, she relented. "I'll see what I can do, *Señor* DiAngelo. If this is the girl you really want…" her voice trailed off. She knew she was beaten.

"Then I guess it's a done deal," Marc announced and shook hands with Giuseppe. He smiled sweetly at Ashlyn. "Miss Fraser."

Ashlyn glared at him but said nothing. Instead, she shook hands with Giuseppe and walked him to the door.

"*Ciao*, Miss Fraser and congratulations. *Insatiable* is yours."

Chapter 5

Once Giuseppe departed, a pregnant silence was all that remained. Marcus stared at Ashly's rigid back. The language of her stance was unmistakable. The defiant tilt of her head, the aggressive poise of her delicately curved shoulders as she thrust them back in a challenge to anyone who dare cross her, right down to the muscle play of her shapely calves as they flexed in readiness to either charge or retreat. Lady Ashly was ready to do battle — with him. Marcus steeled himself for the onslaught.

"You scum!" Her voice cracked through the air like a whip. "How dare you!"

She turned sharply and advanced on him, ever so slowly. Marcus swivelled the chair from side to side in a lazy rhythm and studied her as she continued to stalk him. The once golden hues of her eyes now burned a glittering shade of topaz. His cavalier attitude threatened to slip when he thought of what all that beautiful anger might become if positively channeled into the right kind of emotion, namely, passion.

For the moment however, he knew he was caged with what might turn out to be a very dangerous animal. He should watch his step. She was ready to draw out his punishment and he eagerly awaited the confrontation. Yet, he wouldn't let her off the hook just yet. His ego was still smarting from her abandonment.

"Relax, babe. He didn't recognize you. I thought he might have for a moment when he first looked at the photo. He was simply a man being struck by a woman." Marcus shrugged his shoulders. "Happens every day."

"I don't know how you have the gall to sit there so casually and just throw my picture out for the entire world to see."

"It looks like the entire world will see it, if Giuseppe has anything to say about it. Would you like to see the rest?" he asked innocently.

"Give me my pictures and get out." Shaking, she pointed to the closed door.

"Not before I give you a business proposition."

"Screw your proposition. I could sue you, Marcus Remmington, and then where will your precious reputation be?"

"And I could pull out of the shoot and then where would your precious account be?" he mimicked.

The point settled on her, briefly. But she was far too angry to consider the consequences. And she thought Duncan had humiliated her. It was a love tap next to the blow Marcus Remmington dealt her. But before she threw him out on his butt, she'd make sure he knew exactly how she felt. "You think you're the only bloody photographer in this city?"

"I'm the only one who photographed you in the buff." There was a meaningful twinkle in his eye. Not a threat, not exactly. It sounded more like he wanted her to know the kind of ammunition he had at his disposal.

"You think this is some terrific joke, don't you. You could have ruined my career."

"Hey, don't look at me like that." He unclasped his hands from behind his head and leaned forward to unlock his briefcase. "Besides, I have something else that belongs to you." He bit his tongue to keep from grinning as he flipped up the top and removed Ashlyn's panties. "Here," he tossed them onto the table. "Your glass slipper, m'lady."

Ashlyn gasped, blushed, then lunged for her underwear. Before she could snatch back her panties, he grabbed them and held them up out of her reach. His large fingers kept a tight grip on the delicate lace trim as teased her. "Not so fast."

"You — you...b-bastard!" She sputtered, balancing on her toes and wildly grabbing at the prize he carelessly dangled just inches from her grasp.

"Uh, uh. Temper, temper, *Ashly*. Or should I call you, *Miss Fraser*. Miss Ashlyn Fraser, all straight and starchy like everyone else does around here."

"Stop it!"

"*Miss Fraser*. With her hair pinned up and her geeky glasses, looking like a refugee from some convent. Where's the mystery woman who walked into my studio? Where — Oh!"

He doubled over from the unexpected force of her punch to his unguarded middle. But even while clutching his stomach, he maintained his grip on her panties.

"Hell of a... a right hook you... you've got there," he managed between breaths.

"Just a man being struck by a woman," she replied smoothly.

Marcus seethed, not because of her retaliation but because she was right. He was lost the moment he walked in and saw her. He winced again. "Geez, I think you broke something."

"I hope so."

He regarded the smug satisfaction on her face and clutched his treasure even tighter.

"Give me my panties," she demanded, "or I'll hit you where I can do some real harm."

"Why?" He baited her but instinctively lowered his hands in front of his groin.

"Because they belong to me." The stubborn press of her lips told him she wasn't ready to give in.

"Why else," he demanded, eager to challenge her; determined to break through the wall she'd hastily erected since he first walked through the door. He saw a glimpse of the real Ashly. The woman who bewitched him in his studio was inside her somewhere. In her determination to recover her lingerie, her hair had slid out of its topknot. The top button of her blouse had come loose and dangled by a single thread. She was red from embarrassment and shaking from spent rage. She'd never looked more beautiful. At that moment Marcus would have sold his soul for a camera, even a cheap disposable. But somehow, he doubted if he would ever forget her like this.

He wanted her, all of her. Right here, right now. To hell with anyone else. But he also knew she'd never give in. So he decided to take the only piece he could get. He shoved his silk and lace trophy back into his briefcase. In one swift movement, he closed and locked it.

Ashly opened her mouth and started to swear at him again but stopped. She looked longingly at the closed briefcase and then back to Marcus. It was then he noticed the glistening betrayal behind her glasses.

"Please," she whispered. "Haven't you shamed me enough?" A solitary tear escaped from behind her dark, square frames and slid down her brightly colored cheek.

Oh God, Ashly. Please don't cry. Marcus reached out and wiped the tear away. He noticed more gathered at the rims of her eyelids like watery little soldiers, ready to assault his conscience. This was all his fault. A lump suddenly lodged in his throat and he tried to deny how it got there. He had a feeling he might be developing a sudden case of the guilts. His stomach churned, and not from the impact of her fist.

He found himself holding her hand. The touch of her petal-soft skin soothed his aching mid-section. The site of her lovely eyes, shimmering with tears, created a new and different kind of pain. He hadn't meant to hurt her, only tease her a little to get back at her for leaving him without a way to find her.

"Truce?"

A tiny nod of her head and he raised her hand and pressed a gentle kiss across her fingers. "I'm sorry, Ash — I...Hey, what do you want me to call you anyway?"

She tilted her head to look at him, regarding him as if considering the question at great length. Finally she answered. "I'd like it if you'd call me Ashly."

Marcus answered her smile with his own. "Okay. Ashly it is. But only between the two of us, okay?" Confident he was back in her good graces, at least temporarily, he folded her into his embrace. He held her gently and she lay her head against his chest. After a few seconds, he tucked the loose strands of her hair back into its lopsided topknot. "There's something I've wanted to do since the moment I walked in here," he murmured.

"Me too," came her muffled reply.

"I mean besides take you here on the boardroom table," he teased.

She tried to struggle away from him but he held her fast. "I'm only kidding," he soothed and she settled back into his arms. He wasn't really kidding, but now that he'd found her, he decided to stick to a conservative strategy. No use scaring her off again. Still, that nice, flat boardroom table was awfully tempting. All they'd have to do was lock the door and privacy would be ensured. Then he'd lift her pretty little bottom onto the table and start kissing each of her stockings — or whatever she was wearing underneath — down her gorgeous legs. *Yeah!* Marcus smiled dreamily at the thought. He'd start at the top of her silky-smooth thighs, all white and pink. Stop and breathe in the tempting scent of her, maybe even plant a tantalizing kiss on her —

"Marc?"

...bite the little creases on the backs of her knees —

"Marc."

...raise her skirt, lay her down and —

"Marcus!"

He winced at the sharp poke to his mid-section. The subject of his fantasy was creating an annoying distraction. He became aware of her body, trapped between his own and the edge of the table. There was an alertness in her eyes and he obligingly nudged himself against her. Her soft gasp confirmed his discomfort. His body was definitely ready to indulge in the fantasy.

"You want me to let you go?" He barely recognized the edge in his voice; the kind of edge that comes with losing something valuable, finding it, only to risk losing it again. He chased the thought away by squeezing her possessively. A strained moan escaped her lips and he loosened his grip on her. But his mind branded her. *Mine, dammit.* He stopped the thought before it reached her ears but the feel of her body against him created an unmistakable sign. For the second time, he found he could not control his reactions. He couldn't summon the objectivity that came so easily with his job. He was used to being around women, stunningly beautiful women wearing less than nothing and sometimes nothing at all. They were business, nothing more. He had catalogues full of assorted feminine body parts. Yet none of them had the effect a fully clothed Ashly brought on. He'd felt himself go stiff as a flagpole the moment he laid eyes on her. It was unnerving and embarrassing, to say the least.

Tension and frustration fueled his erection. He stroked her with a hard, mock thrust. Instead of moving away from him, as he expected her to do, she parted her legs and invited him to settle between them. It was almost too much to bear. Marcus had a vision of coffee cups, pencils and file folders flying off the table.

"Ashly?"

She shook her head mutely and surprised him by hopping up on the table and wrapping her legs around his hips. Spurred on by weeks of unspent desire, he was unable to resist her invitation. He kissed her hard and deep, savoring the taste and feel of her. A groan of satisfaction rumbled from somewhere deep in his throat. The moment his lips touched hers, he knew it hadn't been a fluke. Lightning had struck — again.

The scent and soft heat of her flooded his senses. Her pictures just weren't enough, would never be enough. He had to have her, all of her. His lips became more urgent, more demanding. He explored her body, his lips and hands claiming new yet familiar territory. Her soft moans drove him on. He ground his pelvis into hers, creating a torrid, raging fire in his crotch.

"Ashly, my love. My sweet, sweet, love." He lifted his lips from hers and was pleasantly surprised when she combed her fingers through his hair, directing his face back to her. Her instincts had kicked in. She wanted more. "We have to stop this now," he warned, "or I might not be able to."

"I don't want to," she confessed between kisses.

And she didn't, she realized. Somewhere between losing her temper and losing her dignity she had also lost control. Marc! Marc! her heart sang. He hadn't forgotten her. He carried her in his memory. He carried her pictures with him. Hell, he carried her underwear.

She couldn't recall exactly when her glasses found their way off her face but she knew Marc meant business when he carefully placed them out of harm's way. The last thing they needed was one of them rolling on top of her glasses and breaking the lenses.

"Just a moment, darling," he whispered and his blurred figure darted across the room for a moment. She was about to question him when she heard the sharp click of the deadbolt lock. He was back before the heat of his body left her fevered skin. His thoughtfulness on all accounts amazed her.

There was no champagne-induced dullness for her senses to hide behind this time. And her senses were raging, along with her hormones. The feel of Marc's warm hands fondling her buttocks was to die for. She ached for him to touch her everywhere, just as she was touching him. Suddenly, their clothing became an annoying barrier.

Ashlyn was determined not to let that stop her. She nipped at his lower lip, buried her mouth in the sensitive skin along his neck. His face was rough and stubbly from the day's growth but she welcomed the feel of it scraping her cheek, ached for the same chafing sensation between her thighs. Her mind raced ahead of the game and she imagined his face buried in her mound and kissing her where no man ever had. In a sexual frenzy, she covered his lips, teased open his mouth and treated them both to a deep, soulful kiss. Their tongues danced and lapped at each other. Suddenly she knew where she wanted his mouth. He had crept into her dreams these last weeks. She reveled in the visions of his dark head buried between her thighs, his magic tongue easing the tension, only to awake, finding herself alone and frustrated. This was one time she wouldn't leave frustrated.

She broke the kiss, eager to share her desire with him. "I want you to kiss me," she whispered. "Everywhere... I want you to touch me," she breathed and snuggled into the heat of his embrace. "Touch me in all the secret places I've dreamed of sharing with you."

Marc answered her demand with a throaty growl. "Anything else m'lady wishes?" he asked, giving her a hard nip beneath her earlobe.

"Oh, yes," she sighed, shivering from the electric chills shooting down her neck and pooling deep in the pit of her abdomen. Dare she expose her fantasies to him along with everything else? Her body made the decision for her as Marc's fingers contacted with the front of her blouse and fondled her silk-covered breasts. She gasped sharply, suddenly, and pressed herself into the waiting palms of his hands. She felt the momentary tug of buttons releasing, the rush of cool air against her heated skin, then new waves of acute sensations as Marc slid a hand inside her bra. He gave each breast an intimate caress, pausing to fondle the ridges of each taut peak, before expertly releasing the front clasp of her bra.

"Do you approve?" he murmured before kissing her again.

Approve of his possessive touch as his fingers roamed freely over her naked skin, or the hard press of his groin against her tender inner thighs? Ashlyn couldn't think to answer him. Somehow, she knew she didn't have to. Her body was doing all the talking.

He shifted his weight and leaned into her. The hard surface of the boardroom table groaned beneath her bottom. She rubbed her stockinged feet up and down the back of his thighs. From her position on the table, she couldn't do much more. Certainly, she couldn't do what she wanted which was to dig the balls of her heels into his hard, muscled buttocks. A moment later, she got her wish.

She found herself laying flat on her back on the table, blouse open to the waist, bra loosened and pushed to one side. Marc all but climbed on top of her then and buried his lips into the hollow of her neck before making his way to the valley between her breasts. He captured each swollen tip between his lips, nuzzling and sucking each in turn. Waves of pleasure cascaded over her and she wrapped her legs around his hips, firmly planting her feet across his backside.

Ashlyn coiled her fingers tightly in the long, soft hair shielding his face from her. Sometime during the seductive frenzy, his pony-tail slipped out of the leather thong which had so sleekly secured it. Now it hung in wild tangles across her skin, brushing and teasing her as much as his hands and mouth were. He reminded her of a lusty barbarian; saying little but demanding all. All is what she would give. She knew he would take no less. She lifted her hips slightly off the table and pressed herself against him.

Marc looked at her. In spite of his fever-laden eyes, he asked her, "are you sure, Ashly? Once you say 'yes' there's no going back. I won't stop, even if you beg me." There was something hypnotic in that dark, hooded gaze, something that didn't allow her to hesitate. No wonder he had gotten his way with her so easily that first night. Marc wove a tapestry of sex magic around women. She was no different.

Even before she had a chance to reconsider, he stripped her pantyhose off her legs. And she helped him. What's more, her hands were fumbling with his belt buckle, deliberately passing over the bulge which protruded at an angle from his zipper. Ashlyn hated things that were out of place. She followed her compulsive behavior by tugging down the metal zipper of his pants and reaching inside to grasp his sex through his briefs and lay it flat against his belly. She heard Marc gasp, saw his eyes widen and felt the pulse of his rod quicken at her touch.

"Oh, God! Baby, touch me. Reach inside and put your hands around me. I want to feel you. I've waited so long for you. Don't torture me."

Ashlyn found herself grinning wickedly at his demands. For all that he'd put her through today, she now had him eating out of her hand, begging for the slightest favor. She kneaded the hot length of him, feeling the girth increase slightly with each firm squeeze. How much larger would he get? The tip was already peeping over the top of his briefs. She released him then in favor of grabbing another handful of his hair and urged him to kiss her again. Naked skin met naked skin as Ashlyn felt the round, velvety tip of his rod sear her stomach. A tiny drop of fluid dripped onto her belly, then Marc thrust against her. All the while he breathed love words, sex words, into her ear.

"I'm going to bury it deep in you. Flood you when I come. Brand you forever, like you've branded me. You've cast a spell on me, little witch. I'll never let you go. The way you smell. The way you taste. The way you feel, especially the way you feel."

Through his heavy breaths that mingled with her own, she was vaguely aware of his hands gripping her bare buttocks. She didn't remember taking off her panties, couldn't recall how her skirt had bunched up around her waist. It didn't matter. Nothing mattered but the feel of his fingers slide between her thighs and dip into the well of her sex. Wetness oozed around his finger tips and he rimmed her outer lips with her own moisture.

Marc carefully positioned his cock at her entrance, kissed her once, roughly, and quickly thrust into her. The jolt hit them both. Marc arched his back and gasped suddenly like a swimmer breaking the water's surface after staying under too long. Ashlyn raised her legs higher until her knees bumped his elbows. Full penetration caught her off guard. He was hard and hot and the engorged tip rubbed deep inside her. The friction brought her pleasure unlike anything she had ever experienced, including the night in Marc's studio.

Now she was completely sober, her body alive and absorbing every ounce of passion, every nuance, every raw and primitive urge that Marc awakened inside her. She couldn't lay still. Her inner muscles milked him. She ground her pelvis into his. She raked furrows across his ass with her fingernails. She raised herself off the table to bury her face in his chest, bite the corded muscles in his shoulders and suckle his flat nipples. She felt a demon being unleashed inside of her. The dark side was free at last and she recognized something of the woman she'd discovered in Marc's studio. Wild, untamed, a sexual predator.

Marc thrust against her womb, forcing himself deep inside her. With a sudden toss of his head, he reared up, gritted his teeth and let out a strangled gasp. He shuddered in a series of sudden convulsions. Hot semen flooded against the walls of her womb. Hard and fast, it was over for him. A moment later, he collapsed on top of her.

An eternity passed before she heard him whisper and apology. "I'm sorry," he mumbled against her neck. "You were just too much. Too tight, too hot, too wonderful to bear. Next time I'll wait for you." He moved to one side to adjust his weight on top of her. Ashlyn started to sit up.

"Damn! My purse is in my office. I think there's a hand towel in the coffee cart." She climbed down off the table, trying not to notice how wobbly her legs felt and avoiding the large gilt mirror at the far end of the room. She picked up her panties and hosiery on her way to the wheeled cart. She opened the lower doors and breathed a sigh of relief. Thank goodness, Marie had filled the cart up before the meeting. She pressed the small terry-cloth towel between her legs and began to repair the damage.

Behind her came the sound of Marc smoothing his own rumpled clothing, the muffle of cotton settling over his body, the metal rush of a refastened zipper. She pulled the remaining pins from her hair, shook out her tangled mane and reshaped the mass into the prim knot she'd started out wearing. What other signs would give her away? She cast a sidelong glance into the mirror and was horrified. Her clothes were a mass of wrinkles, her cheeks flushed and her skin red in spots, bearing the imprint of Marc's teeth.

She wiped a trace of lipstick from her chin and stopped. She raised the palms of her hands to her nose and sniffed. Fragrance of a man clung to her; a lingering whiff of male cologne, the tangy odor of expensive shampoo, the musky scent of enraged sex hormones. The potent mix had permeated her clothes and mingled with her own warmth. A sinful smile stole across her lips as she realized she would carry the scent of him around with her the rest of the day. What would her co-workers think when she left the boardroom, clothing rumpled, hair disheveled, and smelling like Marc's aftershave? On second thought, they'd probably applaud.

Marc put his arms around her. She shivered at the sound of his voice next to her ear.

"I woke up and you were gone. That's never happened to me before," he confessed as he kissed a trail between her ear lobe and the nape of her neck. "I was a little put out. I wanted to find you, to find out what I did to scare you off. I thought everything was fine. I," he paused and tilted her head up so he could look at her. "I felt good with you. Things felt... right," he explained.

Ashlyn knew exactly how he felt. They had bonded. The magical force that had found so many of her happily attached friends was suddenly revealed to her in all its splendor. She was a member of the club, part of an ancient society of women who had been both hunter and hunted — often by choice. A primitive longing unleashed itself inside of her. She knew what it was like to be in lust with a man. The awkward experiences of her teen years were clinical, at best. Certainly Greg's sloppy, tongue-twisted attempts never unleashed a raging torrent of desire. When Marc kissed her, the jolt was enough to blow the toes out of her sensible shoes. Was she actually falling in love with him?

The idea frightened and excited her, although neither one had yet to speak the word. Maybe that came later. Right now, she didn't care. Marc brought so many new ideas to tempt her away from her safe, comfortable life. And oh, how he tempted!

"It felt right for me too… after a while. Things just happened so fast. I've never done anything like that before," she murmured lazily, still savoring the thrill of his kisses.

"What," he chuckled. "Fallen asleep on a man's couch?"

Ashlyn opened her eyes and looked up at him. "No, I. — I…" She lowered her eyes and grinned sheepishly. "I mean going to bed with a man on the first date."

Marcus stopped stroking her hair. He looked down into Ashlyn's face. There was no sign of the usual coy tricks or mock innocence. She was dead serious. Her flushed cheeks were all the proof he needed. The realization of what she insinuated hit him like a sledgehammer. No wonder she came at him spitting like a wildcat. She thought he'd taken advantage of her after she passed out. If it had been any other woman in his past, he might have laughed at the situation. Did she really think he was low enough to resort to something like that? He must have made some first impression. Not only his pride was damaged but his integrity as well. He let her go and stood back.

"I know it must have seemed like it was the kind of thing I do all the time," she continued, "but with the wine and everything, I guess I got carried away."

Marcus digested her words. *It. Thing.* Like what they almost shared wasn't worth labeling properly. She considered their aborted lovemaking a trivial experience; an experiment perhaps. He had given those kinds of lessons countless times and to pupils more willing and with far more experience. What kind of euphemism would she use to describe what just happened between them? How would she excuse it this time?

"Happy to be of service," he snapped.

Ashly's smile died. Her expression clouded and her eyes mirrored the hurt in his own soul. But at the moment, he didn't care. After all, why should she be upset? Wasn't she the one who left him?

"You *do* think I do this all the time," she accused. She pushed him away and stalked across the room. She bent down, retrieved a shoe from under the table and jammed it on her foot. Marc fervently hoped she would calm down before leaving the room. She probably didn't realize her pantyhose were strung around her neck, or that her skirt was twisted around backwards. He stepped closer to help her but she froze him with an icy glare.

"What did you think to accomplish by seducing me, Marc? A docile executive who won't cramp your style on the set? Or is it…" she paused then, the anger on her face dissipating into hard realization. Marcus felt a knot growing in his stomach. He knew what was coming, knew what she supposed to be the awful truth. The problem was, she was half right.

"You want *her. Ashly.* You need *her* for this job."

"No! You're wrong. That's not what happened here. Ash —"

"You can't have her. She doesn't exist!" Ashly spat her denial at him, almost challenging him to prove her wrong. His own anger took up the cause.

"Oh Ashly does exist. Maybe not all the time. But she's here. She's hiding behind some spoiled little rich girl who lets her father walk all over her. The real Ashly would have the guts to defend herself and take control like she did in my studio and even now." He stopped and slammed his fist on the table, on the very spot which still bore the damp evidence of their lovemaking. "Unless she only comes out after drunken birthday parties and behind locked doors."

Marcus braced himself for the slap that never came. The silence in the room was louder than any of Yolande's projectile tantrums. He watched Ashly raise herself to her full height. With as much dignity as she could muster, she straightened her glasses, buttoned her blouse and swept back a loose tendril of hair. The purring kitten he held in his arms a moment ago became a spitting tiger. Dammit all anyway, he'd done it again.

Ashlyn glared at him and pressed her love-swollen lips into a thin line. She took a long, slow deep breath and exhaled sharply, expelling the remains of her earlier mood. Her mind worked quickly, searching for some way to show him that she wasn't ready to be used and then tossed aside. She'd had enough male browbeating for one day.

Whether he knew it or not, Marc had just become the cause of an impulsive decision, the second one in her life since she'd met him. He was becoming a bad habit, one she intended to break immediately. She thought of the flurry of consequences she would have to endure because of that decision. *Well screw the consequences!*

She could land the *Insatiable* account without the help of Marcus Remmington. She could find another photographer for the shoot, one who wouldn't try to blackmail her out of her clothes. *I'll get Brian*, she thought quickly. Her own brother was struggling to make a name for himself, why not give him the opportunity? She wouldn't tell Duncan. Let Dad see for himself that Brian had talent. It might even help mend the rift between them. And all without having to endure Marc or the emotional head games that went with him. She could direct the shoot herself and use her own ideas. Of course Duncan would blow a gasket, but he'd get over it. After all, the man had been married four times. It wouldn't be the first time a woman had disappointed him.

Satisfied she had made the right decision, she turned her attention back to Marc who stood beside the chair he had occupied during their meeting. He was a mask of closed emotion as he rifled through his briefcase. His scowling features had eradicated any trace of the passion that filled his eyes only moments before. So much the better. It would make her next task easier to accomplish. She leveled her gaze at him. She thought her voice sounded oddly flat and unemotionally cool as she heard herself say the words.

"You're fired."

Chapter 6

"I can't do this." Ashlyn repeated the phrase over and over again. Even as she sat in Vlad's make-up chair in the portable on-site dressing room, her mind reeled at the idea.

Her world was in turmoil, her plans crushed. How was she to know that Brian was out of town and couldn't be reached? And Marcus hadn't been feeding her a line. She turned the city upside down looking for a reputable commercial photographer, but she couldn't get anyone to fill in on such short notice. Duncan hounded her as the deadline for a draft ad loomed like a threatening, black cloud. At the eleventh hour, when the storm threatened to burst over her head, she had no model, no photographer and no hope of finding a replacement for either one. In the end, she was forced to admit that Marcus was right and that *Ashly* remained her only hope. But even when she'd fired Marcus, she'd known she couldn't model for anyone else.

Daagmar sat across from her, nodding her head each time Vlad asked for approval, although she never took her eyes off the raspberry-colored negligee she was hurriedly altering.

"What's taking so frigging long?" Marcus bellowed from outside the trailer. "If you don't hurry up, I'll miss the sunrise. The day will be shot!"

"I wish someone would shoot him," mumbled Daagmar as she held the cloth up to her mouth and severed a loose thread with her teeth.

"Get in line," Ashlyn murmured as Vlad applied another coat of fresh lipstick. She checked her watch and tried not to yawn. She had been up since three thirty this morning. "The sun won't be up for another hour, what's he worried about?"

"He worries about everything," Vlad snapped. "Now hold still, I have to proportion this blush properly, or Marcus will have a bug up his ass about that, too."

"There." Daagmar stood up and shook out the garment. "I'll just give this a quick press and we'll be ready to go."

A moment later, Daagmar and Vlad eased the gown over Ashlyn's carefully arranged hair. Ashlyn felt shy and embarrassed with Daagmar's intimate fondling as the woman arranged the gown around Ashlyn's body. But Daagmar was all business when she reached between Ashlyn's cleavage and adjusted her breasts. "Perfect," she announced.

Ashlyn turned toward the full-length mirror and gasped in horror. Her breasts spilled over the top and sides of the slender garment like water over Niagara Falls. The front of the gown was cut clear to her navel and the skirt was slit so high up the centre, Ashlyn could see the dark shadow of her own pubic hair. To make matters worse, the bodice of the gown was fitted with a sheer lace fabric while rest was nothing more than a hint of translucent chiffon which left nothing to the imagination. Ashlyn would have felt more covered in a band-aid.

She saw her cheeks flame bright red with shame as she tried to cover herself by crossing her arms over her chest. "I can't go outside like this, I'll freeze. Besides, people will see me. Oh, he can't be serious."

Vlad and Daagmar circled around her like a pair of vultures, poking at this, re-arranging that. "Come now, darling. Try and relax. I'll fix you a double cappuccino supreme if you promise to sip it through a straw. Marcus has photographed hundreds of girls wearing a lot less in front of a lot more people. Ingenues," Vlad clucked and reached for a small lip brush. "I swear they'll be the death of me."

At least Daagmar was sympathetic to her plight. "Here," she tossed Ashlyn a full length chenille bathrobe. "Put this on. At least you can keep warm until the absolute last second Marcus needs the shot."

Ashlyn gratefully accepted the robe and wrapped it around her, securing it with the matching belt. Her skin warmed instantly and she relaxed a little. At least now she could go outside. She left the trailer, careful not to trip over the bathrobe as she descended the narrow metal stairs. A faint glow started to appear on the horizon, adding a soft blue tint to the black sky. The stars were beginning to fade and the quarter moon looked pale and soft in the October sky.

"Okay. Positions, people." Marc shouted instructions and orders to the set assistants. Ashlyn took in all the paraphernalia. Between the spot lights, flash umbrellas and tinted screens, she wondered why Marc didn't simply wait for more daylight.

Then he appeared behind her. "What the hell is this?" he barked and tugged at the belt holding her bathrobe.

Ashlyn turned and faced his disproving frown. A shock of black hair spilled idly across his forehead. He looked more like a petulant schoolboy than a profes-sional photographer. "Daagmar said I should stay warm until you were ready."

Marc planted his hands on his hips. "Well, I'm ready. Off with it. Now."

Ashlyn's anxiety returned at the thought of losing her shield. "I won't. I can't," she cried and then lowered her voice. "At least let me put a pair of panties on."

"Nope. No underwear. It will spoil the silhouette. I don't want a lot of nasty lines I'll have to brush out later. Now get up on that rock and look longingly into the sunrise."

But Ashlyn was determined to argue the point. "I don't get it. I thought the layouts called for upper torso only. The DiAngelo's approved the mock-ups. Nothing was said about a full body layout."

As she spoke, she could see Marc was losing his patience. His frown deepened to a scowl and his brows knitted together in obvious irritation. It was on the tip of her tongue to tell him go straight to hell and cancel everything.

As if he read her thoughts, he leaned and whispered harshly in her ear. "Be-have yourself, darling. We have a bargain, remember?"

She remembered.

"Oh, all right," she grumbled and gave the belt an angry tug. Marc took a half-step forward to help her but she skirted around him and yanked off the bathrobe. She let it lay where it fell to the ground in a fluffy puddle. She turned and stalked over to the outcropping of rock.

Instantly, Marcus felt his mood change from irritation to admiration. He couldn't imagine getting through this without the old Ashly coming to life and sparring with him.

The location he'd chosen was in a northern provincial park, now closed for the season until the following spring. Featuring several rocky outcroppings and sand dunes, it simulated a desert.

The park was fairly remote and deserted this time of year. It was miles to the nearest comfortable accommodation and Marcus had chosen it just for that reason. He planned to stay out here for a few days and try to mix a little pleasure with business, no matter what Ashly said.

And she had said a lot the night she phoned him, humbled and desperate. Perhaps that's why he'd given in so easily. That, and the fact that he knew she didn't have any other choice, no matter how hard she tried to disguise her motives.

"I have some good news for you, Mr. Remmington," her voice on the phone that night sounded cool and condescending. "I've decided to re-hire you to shoot the *Insatiable* campaign."

Marcus bit his tongue to keep from laughing and played along. "That's very generous of you, *Miss Fraser*."

"Generosity has nothing to do with it. I'm only interested in what's best for my client."

"Then your client is going to be disappointed." Marcus counted the seconds before she answered.

"I — I'm afraid I don't understand. The DiAngelos said they... I mean, Giuseppe is expecting you..." Her voice faded and Marcus picked up the erratic change in her tone. It was time to bait his hook.

"Look, Ashly. I know you're in a spot. It's a busy time of year for commercial shoots. Anyone worth their weight in film is already booked up. So why don't you just come out and admit that you need me."

Just as much as I need you. But Marcus bided his time. Her rejection in the Fraser boardroom still stung and he was sure that she knew nothing of the follow-up phone calls he'd received from Duncan himself. That rankled Marcus more than anything. He'd stood in the reception area while he waited for the elevator and tried to reconcile what had just happened between them. His feelings were raw, his emotions high. He was elated and excited beyond belief one minute, angry and vengeful the next. Only a special kind of woman could do that to him. And she was special. But why didn't she believe in herself? Why didn't anyone else?

The answer, of course, was right in front of him.

Although Ashly's tempestuous decision to fire him stung his ego, he couldn't help remembering the way her father all but humiliated her in the boardroom. Duncan didn't treat her like an employee, much less a daughter. It bothered Marcus that Duncan didn't recognize Ashly's talent and intelligence. Ashly had a vision of where she thought the company should go, and it was a good one. Why then did Duncan snub the very woman who could be the key to the company's success? The answer had come in the form of an annoying giggle.

Marcus had turned around to the site of white-haired Duncan Fraser fondling that little piece of tender tail he married. Marcus frowned and shook his head. He quickly stepped into the open elevator door, eager to be out of Duncan's domain. The scene still left a bad taste in his mouth. He'd hoped to God he wouldn't be like that in twenty years.

Why Ashly allowed Duncan to treat her that way was beyond his thinking. He would have given the old man the kiss off long ago and wondered why Ashly hadn't. He thoughts were still with Ashly when the elevator doors slid open and he stepped forward without looking to see if the way was clear. It was then that he ran smack into Miss Tate, to whom he apologized and offered to buy her a coffee. When he realized she was *that* Miss Tate, the best friend who made the original appointment for Ashly, the opportunity to gain some insight into Ashly was too powerful to ignore, so he joined her.

What he learned about Ashlyn Fraser not only surprised him but made him realize that she'd been telling the truth when she believed she had slept with him. He also learned that Fraser & Associates was in dire straights and the fate of the company hung on Ashly's next move with *Insatiable*. When Marcus got home later that day, he had already made up his mind to call her.

But she had beaten him to it. He could barely control the fluttering in his gut when he'd picked up the phone and heard her panicked voice. She came right to the point.

"If you want me to stroke your ego, then fine. Whatever. You artist types are eccentric, so you better tell me in advance what buttons you want me to push."

Marcus laughed softly into the receiver. "In the first place, Ash," he emphasized her name to gain her full attention. "It's not my ego that needs stroking. Secondly, you don't have to push my buttons. It's enough that you've swallowed your pride and called me. I know you're the kind that doesn't swallow." He let the innuendo hang in the air. He expected some kind of terse dressing down, but it never came. She must be doing one hell of a job of holding on to her temper, he thought admirably.

"Then tell me what I have to do to get you back." Her voice sounded sincere and contrite, almost desperate. It was the closest he could expect to an apology, he supposed. But he couldn't afford to lose his chance to bargain with her. He tumbled carelessly onto his bed, rolling onto his back and letting the cordless phone rest lazily against his ear. He sighed loudly into the receiver, knowing he held all the cards.

"This is really going to put a crimp in my schedule. Let's see," he paused and grabbed a newspaper and rattled it noisily. He gaze momentarily fell on one of his favorite color photos of Ashly smiling back at him from behind the glass of a pewter frame. "I could fit you in here…no, no wait. I have something tentatively planned. Hmm. Here? Nope. I'd have to change an appointment —"

"Marcus!"

He ignored her impatient retort and the soft curse that came after it. "I think I can squeeze you in…"

"Next week, Marcus. I'm on a deadline and you know it."

"Next week sounds fine. Does that suit your schedule, Miss Fraser? Think you can squeeze a big guy like me into your tight, little deadline?" Marcus grinned and was sure the phone line was burning in her ear. He'd almost bet if he looked out his front window, he could see the sky reddening in her part of town.

"Fine," she snapped.

"One condition, honey."

"I suppose you want me to sleep with you again."

Marcus grinned from ear to ear, nodded furiously and patted a pillow beside him. His better judgement held him in check. "Aw, gee. Thanks. But if we're going to make the deadline then we won't have time for that sort of thing. I was thinking of something more along the lines of some extra photos. You see, Ash, making room for you will mess up my plans for a very important exhibition near Christmas. In order to accommodate you, I'll have to cancel the sessions I had planned with my models. I'm afraid you'll just have to fill in for them."

This time there was serious silence over the phone. Marcus assumed she was thinking over the proposition. He was willing to let her off the hook if she said no and he would have bet his contract that she would. But once again, she surprised him.

"Fine."

Marcus jumped on her answer. "You mean it, Ashly? No backing out. It's a deal?"

"Deal."

It was the last word he spoke to her until this morning. Their offices traded faxes and contracts and the result was that both of them were here in Sandy Beach Park, with the late Autumn frost covering more than the grass. They hadn't said a civil word to each other. Having Daagmar alter Ashly's gown to his specifications was just the beginning of what Marcus hoped would be an interesting day.

The sun was high in the sky before Marc ordered a break. It was only ten o'clock and already Ashlyn was trembling with fatigue. The temperature was a balmy 45 degrees and she was sure her butt was frozen as hard as the uncomfortable rock he ordered her to lay on. So much for her preconceived notions about the glamour and excitement of modeling. Back in the dressing room trailer, she huddled inside the bathrobe trying to warm her freezing fingers around the cup of cappuccino Vlad had promised her hours ago. Daagmar sat across from her, readying another skimpy costume. Her face mirrored Ashlyn's thoughts.

"This is ridiculous," Daagmar muttered. "You really will catch cold and die if he keeps this up. What's going on anyway? You both act like this is some kind of penance instead of a job. I thought you two had it big time for each other."

Ashlyn blew the steam off her drink before answering. "What we have is a love-hate relationship. We love to hate each other."

"Sounds more like you hate to love each other."

Ashlyn almost choked on her coffee. "I don't think so. Maybe in the beginning it was lust at first sight, but then I found out he was just a macho pig like my ex-fiance."

Daagmar eyed her, apparently unconvinced. "Uh-huh. That's why he's got your photograph on his night stand with your flashy greens staring him in the face twice a day. I think your brain froze out there. Why do you think you're here and not Yolande? When she found out Marcus was shooting *Insatiable* for the DiAngelos, she showed up at the studio crying, begging and pleading to work with him. Marcus threw her out on her surgically altered rear."

Ashlyn listened half-heartedly. "So, how do I know that he won't do the same thing to me someday? What'll happen when the next pretty face comes along?"

Daagmar finished sewing the last sequin on a pair of slippers. "I guess you'll have to stick around and find out, won't you?"

"No, thanks. I only have one heart to break and it's bruised enough already."

"Suit yourself. Just remember, while he's putting you and everybody else through pure hell, he's also going through hell himself. I know. I've watched him the last few weeks and this is more than just infatuation. I don't agree with the shabby way he's treated you today, but I do care that he's putting his own battered heart on the line. If he didn't care about you, Ashly, he would have thrown you to the dogs. Having you around is hard work for a man like Marcus, a man who is used to having his own way, used to being boss, not bossed. Here," she stopped and tossed a slipper in Ashlyn's direction. "Try this on and see how it fits."

Ashlyn shed the robe and stood in front of the mirror while Daagmar helped her change gowns. When they had finished, Daagmar yelled out the door that it was safe for Vlad to come in and touch up Ashlyn's hair and make-up.

"Before you go back out there, Ash, just remember one more thing. Marcus loves to push the envelope with people. You have to stick up for yourself. If you feel he's getting on your nerves, and God knows he's getting on everyone's today, then give him a taste of his own medicine." She stood back and tugged at the gown's seams so that they fell in whispy layers over the curves of Ashlyn's hips.

"You've got power, girl. Use it." She winked slyly at Ashlyn, gathered up her sewing box and left the trailer.

Ashlyn stared at her reflection in the mirror and contemplated Daagmar's words. *You've got power.* She began to pace the trailer. What had she done that first night at the *Bedroom Eyes* studio to make him so anxious to take her photograph? Was it the wine? The music? The hot tub? Memories of that evening crowded into her mind in no particular order yet none of them spurred her consciousness. What she remembered most about that night was the way he talked to her, looked at her in that all too convincing way that made her want to please him. That was the magical ingredient and it was missing.

She heard the trailer door open and saw Vlad peek in to see if it was okay to enter. That was something else. They didn't have an audience that night. Maybe that's what bothered her the most. If she was going to conjure up "Ashly," it would have to be with far less prying eyes. She waved Vlad into the trailer. She caught sight of herself in the mirror once again, her brows firmly etched with the labour of her thoughts. Perhaps there was a way, after all.

She whirled around. "Vlad, when you finish with me, I want you to take Daagmar and those two harassed set people and disappear. Tell Daagmar I said it was okay. She'll understand."

A moment later she watched the foursome climb into Daagmar's station wagon. The doors were barely closed before the car disappeared in a cloud of sandy dust, leaving her alone with Marc.

Chapter 7

A sudden sound startled Marcus and he looked up from his camera in time to see his entire on-site crew speeding away.

"What the hell —"

He tossed the camera aside and ran after the car, yelling and waving his arms. When he reached the spot where the car had been, he found himself looking into a cloud of dust.

"Son of a bitch!" He yelled and kicked at the sand. It was then he spied Ashly, looking innocent, too innocent.

She shrugged. "Maybe they thought it was time for lunch."

Fists clenched in anger, he stalked over to where she stood.

"You put them up to this," he accused. "You... you..." He couldn't get the words out. He stood shaking his finger at her in impotent rage and mute frustration. His bottled emotions had been at the breaking point for hours. His excitement and energy at starting a new project; the sheer joy of seeing her again and above all, his burning desire for her, barely controllable but gnawing inside him. He couldn't wait for the day to be over. He hoped it would never end.

"Tsk, tsk. How unprofessional. I thought we were here to work, not to argue."

Marcus exploded. "How dare you talk about work. So far you've had all the enthusiasm of a snail. I could get more life out of a statue. You're supposed to be selling perfume. You couldn't sell lifeboats to the Titanic."

Through it all Ashly stood there, idly tracing a design in the sand with the toe of her slipper. "You know, you're handsome when you're angry."

He stared, open-mouthed, while she continued. "In the boardroom, remember? You said I was beautiful when I was angry. Well, so are you. Handsome, I mean."

He became aware of shock yielding to understanding. So, that's what this was all about. How could he have been so blind? Turnabout was truly fair play. Ashamed and unsure how to react, he stared down at the ground. His bottom lip twitched when he noticed that she had traced the shape of a heart in the sand, only this heart had a jagged line through it's middle. He scrubbed his hands through his hair and muttered, "They're still in my briefcase. I'll get them for you."

"Get what?" she questioned.

"Your panties. You're still mad because I embarrassed you in front of the DiAngelos and wouldn't give you back your panties. All this is my fault," he sighed. "If I hadn't been so eager to avenge your abandonment of me, we wouldn't even be here. How could I have been so... so..."

"Stupid?" she offered. "Pig-headed. Selfish. Shall I continue?"

Humbled, he stood there staring at her. Yes, he was all those things and more. What had started as a practical joke could cost Ashly her father's company. He'd only meant to tease her with the pictures but the strategy blew up in his face. He was as surprised as she was when Giuseppe DiAngelo decided she was the right girl to represent *Insatiable*. He'd never intended any of this to happen. Of course, he resented her firing him from the project and, for a while, it looked like he might even be out of a job. But then Duncan had gone behind Ashly's back and Marcus had been tactful enough not to mention the altercation.

Between that and witnessing the scene in the reception area with Duncan and his wife, he'd seen enough of Ashly's family to realize they were using her as a doormat. That was the last straw. She didn't deserve the way they treated her. She was smart and beautiful and dedicated. Then, when he learned how desperately she was working to hold her father's nearly bankrupt company together, he decided to help her any way he could. If only his wounded pride hadn't got in the way. Listening to her beg back his services broke his heart rather than soothed his ego. He knew she would die rather than admit she needed his help.

He wanted her to know just how much she had hurt him and decided that making her wear those ridiculous costumes would be just the ticket. Instead of humiliating her, he found it nearly impossible to control his desire for her. The part of him that always demanded control, the part he could always count on to be professional and impartial, had deserted him. *She* was in control, whether he liked it or not and that irked him.

Now he was alone with her. It was a situation he longed for and now feared. He wouldn't blame her now if she wanted to bury him alive in the sand. Hell, his head was as thick as the rock he had forced her to sit on for hours. How could he ever make it up to her?

Tell her how you feel. Tell her what's in your heart. Tell her you love her.

He took a breath, ready to reveal himself to her when her tiny voice quelled his courage.

"I would have said `yes', you know."

Marcus stared in astonishment, unsure of what he heard. "You mean sleep with me?"

"That, too," she blushed and lowered her gaze.

Understanding phased him. "Oh, you mean the pictures."

"Duh! Yes, the pictures. I really resented being forced into them, but now that we're here we might as well do them. I suppose I really wanted a little more time for the idea to settle in. I'm not exactly a professional."

Marcus grinned at her choice of words and almost laughed at the face she made when she realized her mistake.

"Don't we have some work to do?" she snapped.

She turned her back to him and slithered out of the bathrobe. She left it lying in a heap in the sand, on top of the jagged heart. She practically strutted over to where he had changed the set, leaving him no choice but to follow. It was as if she had slipped an invisible leash around him. The thought of having her in control sent a thrill of excitement through him and he felt himself grow hard. His crew was gone at least for the remainder of the day. The trailer held all the comforts of home, including a bed. But first, they had work to do.

"Maybe the DiAngelos will like the pictures you took this morning. It may buy us a little time to get the gallery photos done," she said as she started to climb back up on the rock. Then she stopped. "Wait a minute." She jumped off the ladder, picked up the hem of the red satin negligee and ran through the sand over to where the unused equipment was sitting. She retrieved a portable CD stereo along with a handful of CD's and ran back to the rock. He watched her set the stereo down and ponder over which selection to play. Then she popped in a disc and turned the volume up loud.

The deserted set suddenly came alive with the sound of *Legs* by ZZ Top. Marcus watched her climb up the ladder, each foot taking a step in cadence, her bottom swaying to the rhythm of the music. Now she stood on the rock, towering some six feet above him. Her entire body started to move with the beat. She raised her arms up to the sky and threw back her head, totally destroying her carefully arranged hair. Then she whipped herself forward, bending at the waist and hung there limp. A second later, she reared up and kicked off her slippers.

Marcus watched, fascinated, as she undulated from side to side, teasing him, using the center slit to expose each of her slender legs in turn. He stood there, awstruck. Ashly, *his* Ashly had returned. He knew he should be taking pictures but his arms refused to move. Only one part of his body was seeing any action. It too, pulsed to its own beat.

"Well, don't just stand there. Take some pictures." When he didn't move, she danced to the edge of the rock and dropped down on all fours so her breasts could take the full force of gravity. The effect teased all of Marcus' senses and he staggered forward for a better look. It was then that Ashly changed the game completely. She shook her shoulders slightly and let the micro-thin satin straps slide down her arms. What little protection the lace cups offered slithered downward as she shed the straps, leaving her magnificently naked from the waist up. Her rosy nipples reacted to the cool air immediately and the areolas blushed a deep pink.

Marcus felt his mouth go dry. There was plenty of bottled water on the set but he knew only one thing could quench his thirst and that was to bury his face between her breasts and start licking.

She sat back on her heels and crossed her arms. "Well, I'm waiting. Better get to work before it gets too cold. Ashly might get bored and run away again."

Her threat spurred him into action. "No, you don't. Don't you ever go away again. Understand?" Instead of using the small step-ladder, he took a run, lunged at the side of the rock and scrambled up onto the flat surface where Ashly sat waiting.

"You forgot the camera." She sounded mildly annoyed.

He sat down and wrapped his arms around her. "Screw the camera," he growled softly before he kissed her. She responded immediately, opening her carefully painted lips so Marcus could deepen the kiss. She was an intoxicating mix of honey and silk. She affected him like one of the high-priced drugs he knew were abundant in Alexis' crowd, although he had never been tempted to alter his own reality. Nothing could compare to the high of holding Ashly's warm, soft body in his arms. This was the only reality that mattered to him.

He felt her slip a hand up the back of his neck and tug at the cord that held his neat pony tail. With a sudden jerk, the black leather thong became part of the scenery. His hair fell forward in an unruly fashion but he hardly noticed. In fact, he barely felt Ashly grab a handful as she started to pull them down on the rock's flat surface. The stone felt warm from the sun and it occurred to Marcus that he had told one of the set assistants to spread a tan-colored blanket across the surface to shield out the glare from bright specks in the granite. He located the still folded blanket and quickly shook it out. Then he eased her down onto the blanket as if she was a precious, fragile treasure.

He kissed her again, letting his tongue slide through her generous, wet lips. He felt the contact of her smooth teeth and wondered if she would allow herself the luxury of experimenting in a bit of oral sex. He groaned into her mouth at the thought of the hard tips of her teeth grating up and down the length of his fully erect cock. He would, of course, return the favor.

As if his own fantasy had wandered into her thoughts, he felt her teeth gently close around his tongue. He allowed her to suck and stroke him before breaking off the kiss. When she protested, he reassured her.

"You know, there are ways of asking for something if you don't feel comfortable using the words. Am I correct in assuming you just asked?"

She looked away from him and nodded. Marc smiled and caressed her cheek, coaxing her back to him. "Look at me, Ash. I won't make jokes about this. Have you ever done this before?"

She shook her head, answering him in silence again.

"It's okay. If you don't want to, you don't have to. But if you do, I'll guide you through it. You can stop anytime you want. And," he trailed a finger across her forehead and down to the end of her nose. "I promise to reciprocate."

Her wicked smile returned and he kissed her again. "That's my girl. Care to help me off with these?" He started to unzip his jeans when she stopped him.

"I think I can manage this without any help."

And Marcus lay back, allowing her to finish undressing him. He only helped her by lifting his hips off the ground so she could slide his jeans down his legs. A cool breeze brushed his nearly naked body. It was cold! And to think he had put her through this and she'd performed with few complaints. Marcus was surprised he hadn't ended up with one of her slippers up his arse by now.

But then he felt her hands slip under the top of his white briefs and the chill he suffered dissolved into a slow-burning fire. He closed his eyes and gave himself up to the pleasure she created. And when her hands closed around his erect shaft, every muscle in his body sounded out a three-alarm blaze. Maybe he wouldn't make it through her first lesson.

"Now what?"

He opened his eyes to meet her questioning gaze. He licked his lips and swallowed before answering. "Sweetheart, this is oral sex. Just do what comes naturally."

Easy for him to say, thought Ashlyn. His organ throbbed between her palms and the full, round head made a wet stain against the white cotton. These, she decided, would have to go. As she did with the jeans, she slid the garment over his hips and down his legs.

Now he lay naked before her. His rigid organ sprang straight and proud from his groin. The tip was wet and shiny in the sun. Tiny blue and purple veins pulsed beneath the skin. Ashlyn began to wonder what that great pulsing member would feel like against her skin. She didn't run from the urge to taste him, to find out how he would react to her kiss.

She knelt down until she was face to face with his massive erection. Her mouth quivered with anticipation.

"Go ahead," he urged in a shaky voice. "Take me in your mouth."

She licked her lips and placed them gently over the smooth tip. She delighted in hearing Marcus gasp loudly. She placed her hands under his buttocks, fearful that he might pull away. She loved the muscular feel of his round butt and she dug her fingers into his flesh. They contracted under her touch and his penis pulsed double-quick in her mouth. She moved her tongue experimentally along the length of him, licking him slowly, exploring every rigid contour. The taste of him was slightly salty but not unpleasant.

She noticed how he especially liked it when she ran her tongue around the head. His breathing quickened, becoming almost ragged. His body trembled and his head thrashed from side to side. For a moment, Ashlyn thought he was in agony, that she had inadvertently nipped something that caused him pain. When she paused to question him, he pleaded with her.

"Don't stop. Oh, God. You don't know how good you feel."

Ashlyn giggled wickedly. "Not yet, but I will." She continued her ministrations, alternately licking the head and kissing his shaft. During this process it seemed to her that he actually grew larger. Soon she would have him deep inside her. A tremor passed through her and she responded by applying more pressure on him with her teeth. After a moment, he placed his hands on her cheeks and urged her off of him.

She looked up at him in question. "Just a precaution," he chuckled softly. "Don't want things to end too soon." She kissed the glistening tip one more time and impulsively buried her nose into the velvety soft sac where his balls hung. He smelled clean and musky and she took an intimate, womanly delight when the small globes swelled slightly when she nuzzled them.

"Do all men grin then when they get touched like that?"

"Just the ones in heaven, honey. Just the ones in heaven." A moment later he joined her on the blanket. He wrapped his arms around her, kissing her while easing her down to the blanket.

"My turn," he whispered.

Ashlyn was quick to understand when he kissed a trail down her neck, between her breasts and across her belly to the nest of soft, dark curls and the swollen outer lips just beneath. A cool breeze brushed the hood of her aroused clitoris where it peeked anxiously through the moist lips and she shivered. As if sensing her discomfort, Marcus bent his head into her lush thatch and nuzzled her mons. Low, growling sounds came from him and she soon joined in the music, free to cry out her pleasure in the security of their isolation.

And Marcus gave her a lot to cry about. What began as a hesitant, kittenish sigh soon gave way to an exotic howl of supreme delight. Her blood rushed faster, her heart pounded a fierce echo. It seemed that the harder she cried, the more effort he put into torturing her sex, as if he were taking vicarious pleasure in her heightened state. Ashly realized then that he was enjoying this as much as she was.

He nudged and teased her clit with his tongue. The sensation caused her belly to tighten and her toes to curl. He nipped and nuzzled the little bud until it swelled larger with anticipation. It was as if every sense, every nerve had flowed to that one tender little spot beneath her bush. At that moment, the man whose head was buried between her thighs owned her soul.

Yet he proved himself a considerate lover, plying her supple breasts as if it were possible to entice more pleasure from her already overwrought body. He reached up with one arm and stroked each one in turn and tweaked the nipples as they hardened under his palm.

Ashlyn groaned out loud as his tongue dipped into her inner flesh while his other hand teased the entrance to her body. She gasped as one strong finger slipped into her. Her pelvis automatically tilted toward him as if it had a life of its own. Marcus was playing her like a fine instrument, strumming, stroking until he got the right pitch from her. Right now, her pitch was near a frenzy. She moaned softly and bit her lip.

"More," she begged.

Suddenly he stopped and eyed her thoughtfully. "More?" he questioned. "Are you sure?"

"Oh, yes. Yes!"

"Say, `please', my hot little witch."

The delicate grasp she had on her control slipped dangerously. She was going over the edge. Fast. And she wanted to. She deserved to. For the first time, she let go.

"P-please. Please don't stop."

"That's what I want to hear," he soothed and kept his promise by slipping another finger deep inside her. He forced open her outer lips once again and nibbled in earnest. His tongue flicked over the sensitive bud again and again. Each pass drew a ragged groan from her. Pressure built.

Her whole body writhed uncontrollably. Arching her back, she tilted her pelvis up and offered him a sexual feast. He noisily devoured her, making low slurping and sucking sounds deep in his throat. He was a many-tongued fire licking flames of need throughout her body. She heard her own voice, shrill and demanding as she begged for more. Seconds later, the pressure broke and a blissful release flooded her. She cried out his name over and over again.

Minutes later she became aware of his dark head resting across her belly. With shaky fingers, she reached down to play with the silky strands of his hair. He turned his face toward her and nuzzled her hand with his chin, then proceeded to gently suck each one of her fingers.

"Ouch!" she cried when he bit a little too hard on her thumb. She gave him a playful swat.

"I think you should change your name from Miss Fraser to Miss Roman Candle," he teased.

Ashlyn laughed nervously. "More like Miss Nuclear Explosion. What the hell was that, anyway?"

Marc rolled over on his stomach, inched up beside her and kissed her. "I believe *that* was an orgasm." He stroked her hair lovingly. "What's the matter, Ash, no man ever take the time with you before?"

Ashly closed her eyes, giving in to the magical shivers his fingers through her hair created. She sighed. "Let's just say my last lover couldn't spell foreplay, let alone acquire any finesse. Greg should have been named, `old two-stroke'. He barely got the condom on in time before his world came to an end."

"Ah, so that's the Greg whose neglect drove you to my arms." Marcus chuckled softly and shook his head. "I must thank him if I ever see him, although I don't feel the least bit sorry for him about what he threw away. Some men wouldn't recognize the ideal woman if she were surgically attached to him."

Ashlyn moved to lay on her side to face him. "And you would?"

Marc looked taken aback. "Look at the trouble I went to just to get you here."

He swept his hand around the site. "Not to mention the fact that I hounded you, coerced you, bargained and finally blackmailed you. What else am I supposed to do? For God's sake tell me because I've run out of ideas. Please, I'm begging you. What moves Ashlyn Fraser?"

What indeed, thought Ashlyn, as she stared up at the cloudless sky then back to the scenery past Marc's shoulder. What part of herself did she give up to be here, naked in the middle of nowhere with the most perfect specimen of masculinity she had ever known? Sure, Marc was a sexy looking guy, a savvy business man, an artist in his craft. But how did one get to know the man inside? She was certain that under the silk shirts and camera equipment lurked an ordinary person who wore dirty socks and never put the toilet seat down.

Being honest with one's own self was painful but necessary, if she were to grow beyond the sacred walls of her father's company. She had already taken the first step, she had found a man who believed in her. Now it was time to believe in him.

She took a deep cleansing breath before answering him. She turned her head so that their eyes met and locked. She saw honesty in his rugged face and expectation in his gaze. And there was something else, something she had seen in herself. One half of a raw emotion reaching out to find its mate, to become whole. And she accepted the fact that she was in love with this man, realized that it was possible he felt the same way. But now was not the time or the place for either of them to confess their love.

So, what moved her? She knew he was waiting for her answer. She reached up and gently brushed a stray lock of hair from his face. She smiled then, knowing she held the secret in her arms.

"Just be yourself, Marc."

Chapter 8

Without any further discussion, he did just that. He helped her up off the blanket and enfolded her into a deep embrace. He surprised her by kissing her tenderly at first. Then he became anxious and impatient. His lips parted to allow his tongue to intrude forcefully into her mouth. He growled softly and crushed her against his body. Soon she discovered the reason for the change in his mood.

He wanted her. Now. She knew this time would be for him. He made bold thrusts against her inner thighs, silently expecting to be admitted. Ashlyn gave a mute response by parting her legs. Her permission spurred him into action and he broke the kiss. "C'mon. Let's get back to the trailer. It's cold out here."

He snatched up the tan blanket, shook it out and placed it around her shoulders. He stopped to don his briefs before helping her down the ladder. They strode hand-in-hand across the sand back to the trailer.

"The benches in the kitchenette fold down into a bed," he explained while they walked. He paused to pick up a couple of cameras, some lenses and to shut down the lights. Ashlyn had a feeling they wouldn't be working any more today, at least outside.

She started up the metal stairs when Marc stopped her. "Uh, uh." He shook his head. "We're doing this properly." With that, he swung her up off her feet and into his arms. He ascended the three steps, paused to fumble with the door handle and then they were across the threshold. Inside, as well as outside on the set, Marc issued instructions.

"Lock the door while I make up the bed. There's some champagne in the bar fridge and glasses in the cupboard."

Ashlyn searched the cupboard, barely aware of the sounds of Marc readying their love nest; the creak of the middle table being stowed and benches being lowered, the muffled flap of sheets being spread across the foam mattress, the fluttering of her heart and quickening of her pulse. When Marc finished, he stripped off his briefs and climbed in. He leaned back against the pillows and held out his hand, silently beckoning her to join him.

Ashlyn padded toward the bed, weighed down with the cold bottle and two fluted goblets. Her legs still felt a bit wobbly, as if she were walking the deck of an unsteady ship. Outside on the rock Marc had played her body like an instrument of Eros using only his hands and mouth and her insides still hummed to his intimate tune. She almost hesitated to think what he would do with her now that he intended to use the rest of his body. And his intent was obvious by the way his stiff rod poked against the white satin sheet like a sleeping volcano ready to erupt under a mountain of snow. The large mass quivered slightly under the sheet. A tiny dark stain emerged where the tip pressed against the cover, proof that he was more than ready for her.

Ashlyn was aware that she was staring at his arousal. For the first time, she didn't feel the least bit embarrassed by her bold curiosity. She was relieved that he wasn't making fun of her. In fact, he seemed to be enjoying her silent perusal. She looked away, slowly, her gaze travelling up and across his bare, muscular chest with its springy dark curls. Finally she had the courage to look at him directly. What she saw more than pleased her.

His eyes seemed to darken under her intense gaze. His lips parted slightly and he swallowed. There was only the sound of their breathing broken by the occasional loud hum of the refrigerator. The calm before the storm.

Ashlyn broke the spell by setting the glasses down on the ledge above the bed. When she came near, Marc greedily nibbled at one of her breasts through the bodice of her gown. With her breast trapped between Marc's teeth, she had no choice but to sit beside him. He nuzzled the teat with his mouth and tongue, dampening the thin material. Her tiny, round nipples hardened under the assault. Satisfied by the response, Marc rubbed his nose across the silk-covered bud, teasing her even more.

Enjoyable as they were, his playful actions made an impossible task of unwrapping the gold-colored foil from around the neck of the champagne bottle. Frustrated, Ashlyn finally ripped it off. Then she worked on the wire holding the cork in place. Her efforts were hampered by his hands which had suddenly found their way to her shoulders and were deftly sliding the thin silk straps down her arms. Ashlyn tried to ignore him as she untwisted the wire cradle and pressed her thumbs against the stubborn cork. All at once, the bottle released its plug with a fierce "pop". The force sent her toppling back against Marc. At the same time, her breasts slipped out of their restraints and into his waiting hands.

Ashlyn tried to right herself, ever mindful of the open bottle in her tenuous grasp. But Marc's fingers were busy massaging her bare breasts while his lips played with the sensitive area below her ear. A thrilling shiver shot through her and she sighed, full of soft, warm pleasure. "If you don't stop, I'll spill something."

"So will I," he muttered, burying his face into the hollow of her neck.

Ashlyn gave a shaky laugh and forced herself to move away from him. Marc pouted but relented while she filled each of the glasses in turn. She handed him his drink and snuggled in beside him.

"What shall we drink to?" she asked once she was settled.

A twitch of his lips played into a wide wolfish smile.

"What, Marc?"

"I was just thinking about the last time you and I shared a drink together. It was your birthday and you were wearing far less than you are now. Honey, you have no idea how close I came to taking you right there."

"You mean all that steam didn't come just from the water?"

"Hah! Your innocence is wasted on me. My love, you are a sadist. You tortured me mercilessly and all I did was find you irresistible. Just like now. Let's toast to you taking off the rest of that dress," he grinned over the rim of his glass.

Ashlyn trailed a finger across his chest. "I thought I'd let you do that. A reward for your, um, torture."

"Ah! I get to be in control, is that it? About time." The smirk on his face told her he was only kidding.

"I thought you liked being in control," she teased.

The eyes behind his smile were serious. "Honey, I haven't been in control of Jack Shit since you walked into my life. Not my assignments, my staff, and especially my libido." He gave his protruding member a hardy pat in emphasis.

Ashlyn was taken aback by his confession. It was the closest he had come to admitting that they shared an attachment on an emotional level. And she thought *she* was the only one whose life was in turmoil. Marc was revealing himself in more ways than one. Still it wouldn't hurt to remind him of his part in the *Insatiable* conspiracy.

"Oh, yeah?" She raised her glass menacingly over his dark head. "And just how did I come to be out here in the first place? Talk about a control freak. Who picked the middle of nowhere, not to mention my skimpy wardrobe? My buns are just starting to thaw out. I'll probably die of pneumonia."

Marc slid down under the sheet, trying to evade a possible champagne bath. "Okay," he cried, his voice laced with mock defeat. "I surrender. I give. Guilty. Now stop that or you'll drown us both. Besides, your buns look cute in that shade of blue."

They laughed together as Marc righted himself again and picked up his glass from the ledge. "I have a better idea," he said, tipping his glass towards hers. "Here's to the successful mix of business and pleasure, emphasis on pleasure."

Marc's heated stare locked with her own as their glasses touched. A clear "ping" sealed the bargain. To Ashlyn, it was like the sound of a boxer's bell intoning the end of a round. Right now it looked as if they had both won. But the day was young.

The afternoon sun had positioned itself right above their window and Marc reached up to draw the curtain. "No need to corrupt any wildlife," he said with a sly wink. "There now. All nice and cozy. Lots of privacy. I don't want any prying eyes or big ears listening in."

Ashlyn slowly sipped her champagne. "And what would anyone hear if they were listening?" It was a leading question but she was becoming quite fond of Marc's verbal foreplay.

Marc drained his glass. After topping up hers and refilling his own, he set the half empty bottle on the floor. Then he wrapped his arms around her and placed his warm mouth next to her ear. His breathing tickled a stray lock of hair around her earlobe and she allowed him to tuck her hair back out of the way. The feel of his hands made so common an action feel like the most intimate caress in the world and she shivered with delight.

"First we're going to finish this glass. That will make you relax a little. Then, I'm going to play with your nipples, like this," he paused to illustrate his meaning. His warm fingers closed around her bare breasts. Then he moved his callused palms across the soft, sensitive tips in a circling motion. He sighed deeply against her ear when he received the anticipated response. He captured the taut peaks between his thumb and forefinger, gently, but firmly kneading them. Ashlyn could see the deliberate rise and fall of her chest, stronger and a little faster than it had been just a few moments ago.

"Then what," she managed to breathe.

"Well, now that the twins are hot and bothered, I'll move on to nuzzling your neck. But I won't do that yet. Slowly. I want to move slowly with you. Shall I continue?"

Ashlyn could do no more than nod her head weakly.

"Good. Now, just a reminder. Who's in control?"

Ashlyn sighed. His hands wove a magic spell around her that started in her nipples and travelled directly to her anxious pelvis. She could feel herself getting wet. She should do something about getting undressed soon or the garment would be ruined. She was less worried that her reputation would suffer the same fate. She tried to wiggle out of Marc's grasp but he tightened his hold on her until she winced from the pleasure-pain of her pinched nipples. His silky voice threatened her. "Did I tell you to go anywhere, slave? I asked you who is in control and you didn't answer me. Do I have to ask again?"

She vigorously shook her head. She could get into this game. Maybe he had a little bondage in mind. Who knew what lurked in Marc's lascivious imagination? She wanted to find out so she decided to play along. "Y-you are," she stammered, trying to sound sufficiently meek and subdued.

"I am what, little pussywitch?" he hissed into her ear and bit down softly on the fleshy part of her earlobe. Ashlyn vaguely recognized the sound of an earring hitting the floor before she answered.

"You are…" quickly she searched her ragged senses for something that would please them both. "You are… master. My hot, dominating master. Teach me to please you. Show me what I need to know."

"You learn fast." He sounded pleased. But no more than she was. She was unbelievably wet. Her inner flesh tensed and twitched, impatient to be pleasured. The game was incredibly exciting. How did he know she would like it?

She felt the tension on her nipples ease. "Now, when I let you go, what are you going to do?" Ashlyn hesitated before answering, unsure of which phrase to use.

"Nothing until you tell me to."

"I would have also accepted, `anything you want' but I'll take your first choice. And if I tell you to suck my cock, will you do it?"

She nodded.

"And if I say, `peel off that rag, I want to lick your pussy' would you do it?"

Again she nodded.

"Then do it. Get rid of that dress." He released her and she got out of bed to stand in front of him. So, he wanted the dress off. The possibilities presented themselves to Ashlyn. What would he like? Another sexy dance? A striptease? With her mind engaged, she didn't notice the bottle until she almost kicked it over. She bent down and righted it before the game had to be called on account of broken glass.

"Ahem." The master called, his empty glass balanced between two fingers. He tipped it up and over and back again, eager to demonstrate what it was he wanted. Ashlyn was instantly on her knees, kow-towing like a harem slave. Then she picked up the bottle and refilled his glass. He smiled a thank you before leaning back against the pillows. He gestured impatiently for her to get on with his wishes. Ashlyn stuck her tongue out at him and decided to give him what he asked for. If he wanted a show, then he was going to get it.

She stood up. With her legs planted shoulder width apart, she grasped the skirt of the dress where it hugged her hips. Slowly she inched the material up her legs; first sliding the hem across her ankles, then brushing up her calves, skimming the dimples and curves of her knees. When the bottom of the dress finally met the shadowy 'v' between her thighs, she stopped, leaving only a teasing glimpse of glistening curls. Then she turned her back to him so that he could see her bottom was still covered. She ran her hands over her buttocks, flipping up the hem once in a while to give him a flash of round, naked flesh. Her butt cheeks might no longer be blue but her own cheeks felt flushed. She widened her stance and began to bend at the knees, plié style while she swished her bottom from side to side in what she thought was a hypnotic motion.

Just for variety, she bent over every once in a while, a quick, thrusting movement that exposed her pubic curls to his view. She longed to see his face and what kind of reaction she was getting. Her gaze slid to the full-length dressing mirror. Bingo! He might have a front row seat but so did she. She kept her head moving from side to side so he wouldn't notice her own voyeurism. Somehow, she doubted if anything could pry his attention from her.

He lay spellbound, his untouched glass gripped by fingers that were nearly white at the knuckles. His head was tilted slightly so he could see her when she bent down. His hips under the sheet partnered her every move and she knew his cock must be pulsing madly. She smiled and increased her momentum. Now for the finish.

The dress stayed bunched up around her waist as she slid both hands between her legs and bent over straight-kneed. She looked like an upside-down V in the mirror. She saw Marc inch closer to the edge of the bed for a better look. He licked his lips several times before he seemed to remember the drink in his hand. He downed the entire contents of his glass in one swallow. Ashlyn grinned wickedly and let her fingers do the walking around the back entrance of her swollen outer lips. She carefully parted them as if to reveal a sacred treasure. She rimmed the entrance to her vagina, forcing her sex juices out where she could best display what she had to offer. She stroked her clitoris until it felt wet and creamy. The little bud swelled with her effort and it was all she could do to avoid lingering there until she climaxed.

Suddenly, as if reading her mind, Marc left the bed and was behind her on his knees. His warm, wet tongue licked and probed, driving her to an unbearable frenzy. His lips nibbled her clit to her first orgasm and she yelled as her wobbly legs nearly collapsed underneath her. But he didn't stop there, his tongue invaded her slick opening and he suckled noisily. Then there was a moment when his tongue left her and she felt herself being pulled toward the bed. Then something bigger, harder, forced its way between her lips and into her body. With one quick thrust he slid inside her. Marc had sat on the edge of the bed and taken her with him. Now she was sitting on top of him, but with her back to him. At last she had the feel of his hot flesh inside her. It took only a moment for her to become accustomed to the stinging stretch his presence caused. The intense pressure of him prodding the neck of her womb was unlike anything she had ever known.

He tugged at her hair until her head was tilted up. She realized he was watching them both in the mirror. *He knew! Damn him, he'd known all along.* His voice became an echo somewhere in her mind.

"So, the little pussywitch likes to watch. Don't hide from it, babe. Watch me. Watch your lover take you. Can you feel me deep inside you, stroking you? Can you see me buried to the hilt?"

She could. He lifted her off him slightly so she could see his cock, all shiny and slick with her juices. He played with her clitoris and once again, the sweet, tense pain boiled in her belly. She gave herself up to Marc's ministrations and

once again she slipped over the edge, along with Marc who yelled sharply behind her and buried his face in her wildly tangled hair.

After a few moments they crawled back into the bed. Ashlyn lay locked in
Marc's embrace. Both their bodies were slightly damp from their efforts but neither minded. They could shower later, together, even. Ashlyn closed her eyes and
gave herself up to the languid afterglow. Soon she began to drift off. She heard
Marc stir and she heard the sound of him quenching his thirst with the last of the
champagne. She felt she should say something but her mind was empty. Finally
she murmured, "nice game."

Marc set his empty glass on the floor and hugged her to him. "Yeah, especially when *some* people play by the rules. And speaking of rules, don't forget
about the gallery. We still have a lot of film to shoot. I've got less than a month to
prepare." His voice was lazy and heavy with fatigue.

She yawned and buried her face in the pillow. "Sleep first."

He snuggled against her. "While you can."

Ashlyn smiled, drowsy against his warmth. "This is lovely," she breathed.

Marc wrapped his arms around her and settled in beside her. "No, Ashly. This
is love."

She cautiously opened one eye. "You mean love making."

"No," he whispered. "I mean, I love you." Then he kissed her, as if to seal the bond.

Ashly kissed him back, ecstatic at the revelation yet too exhausted to do more
than wiggle her bottom against his groin. She managed one final thought before
allowing fatigue to claim her. "With all the arguing and trying to outmaneuver
each other, how did we ever manage to find time to fall in love?"

He sighed and his hard, warm breath tickled her ear. "I think falling in love
was the game."

"Then who won that round?"

"You did," he murmured against her hair.

"Cheater," she whispered. "You'll want revenge."

"Later," he mumbled and minutes later, Ashlyn discovered she was a lone
audience to his light snore. Later, indeed. Tonight, tomorrow. It didn't matter.
She'd always be ready for him. She closed her eyes to wait for sleep, satisfied that
this time, they had both won.

About the author:

Chevon lives in a small town east of Toronto along with two dogs, a cat and ten thousand books. Her animals are the perfect audience for her work — they don't blush when she reads out loud! When not writing, Chevon passes the long Canadian winters on the ski slopes.

Beneath Two Moons

by Sandy Fraser

To my reader:
Change time and place, past to future, city to desert, Earth to the stars. One constant endures: the fiery passion of a man and a woman. Lose yourself in the fantasy.

Chapter 1

The shuttle from the Tarquin set down in a cloud of fine red grit, and Dr. Eva Kelsey peered through the shield for signs of life. Nothing moved except a lone dust devil.

"See anything, Leon?"

"Looks like the Texas Badlands," the pilot said. He hunched over the console. "No welcoming committee. But I got the right coordinates and time. How long do we wait?"

A hideous roar split the low hum of the shuttlecraft, and Eva started. An immense splay-footed beast, a brown lizardy nightmare masquerading as a horse, shuffled from a sand canyon. The animal was saddled and bridled. And in the saddle sat a huge man.

He urged the creature close to the shield. The lizard rolled its eyes and stamped its feet, but it obeyed.

Confident, relaxed, the rider leaned forward and his penetrating stare burned Eva, as if he'd crisped her neosuit to explore the possibilities beneath. She fought an urge to cover her breasts with both hands, to protect herself from the attack of his eyes.

"Conor." Eva caught her breath, her mouth tightened. Low in her belly a hot memory woke.

He held his seat on the nightmare nonchalantly, reins loose in his lap. Always in control, Conor, even when he looked sleepy-eyed and careless. That's when he was most dangerous. His steel-grey eyes never shifted from Eva's face, and unsettled, she smoothed her hair in its confining Baradian twist, and tucked in a stray curl.

Damn! She knew better than to signal that he'd unnerved her, but it was too late. A smile flickered across Conor's lips, a smile that implied she'd come off-world to re-ignite an old fire.

He was more man than most women could handle. Except Eva. Conor's aura of intense maleness presented no danger to her. She'd had the experience, like some exotic disease, and she was immune. Her self-control had intensified in the last two years, and he wielded no power over her.

"Is that *the* Conor? The legend in the flesh?" Leon adjusted a stabilizer and chuckled. "Hey, Doc. I'm impressed."

"Then you're a chump for personality cults." Eva patted his back and rose abruptly. As Conor backed his creature into the shadows of a dune, Eva touched the pilot's shoulder. "Thanks for the ride, Leon. You can take off after I unload. I've only got the two cases."

Minutes later, ankle-deep in the planet's sand, she was assaulted by the thirsty air, and heat shimmered over the arid earth. Every breath scorched her lungs, and tiny beads of sweat collected on her upper lip and evaporated in an instant.

Leon shot her one last wave and the shuttle slipped away, shrinking in an instant to a silver dot of light and then vanishing, separating her from the Tarquin, leaving her on Feldon-9 for months. For the first time, she couldn't suppress fears that accepting the assignment had been a bad idea, a risk. But assignment refusals alerted the Psych Board, and files were pulled, notes were made.

And she'd had enough notes to last her a lifetime, all the same complaints. Diminished objectivity, personal involvement. There would be no more notes to call the Board's attention to her loss of self-control.

Delaying the inevitable, Eva fiddled with the neck of her white neosuit, and raised one hand to her eyes. Red dunes and flats and the total absence of green, the stark landscape imposed itself on her, brutal and unforgiving. This was a man's planet.

Conor's planet.

Suddenly, she was in shadow, a giant, broad-shouldered shadow. As always, Conor invaded her space, radiating his own special brand of heat. His presence coiled around her, weakening her knees and emptying her mind of cool reason.

"Dr. Kelsey. Welcome to Laredo." Resonating, deep, like a primitive drum, his voice rumbled, vibrating a string between her navel and her core. In her very depths, in her soul, the voice, criminally compelling, like a sexual command, echoed and rippled, and her breath came shallow.

"Dr. Kelsey?"

Eva closed her eyes, straightened her shoulders, and masked her nervous trembling. The trick, she knew, lay in avoiding locked stares. She forced a friendly smile, a textbook picture of the objective colonial investigator, and turned to Conor.

He reached out one hand, almost daring her to take it. As if staring at his hand would buffer her from the necessity of meeting his eyes, she focused on the hand. Like his body, enormous, tanned and rough, these callused fingers had tugged her nipples into stiff peaks, had cupped her wet flesh, had elicited her helpless moans. Caught in the memory, her nipples hardened. But her skin-tight neosuit hid no secrets, and, blushing, she sneaked a quick upward glance to check Conor's reaction.

Conor was looking down at her breasts. He licked his lips, and met her eyes. Stark hunger rode across his face.

"Eva." His voice roused need in her belly as his hands once had roused her body.

Eva swallowed her memories to study his hand again. It was just a hand. And Conor, he was just a man. Simply a man like any other. Not a legend, not a fever dream from long ago. And while she was here on official business, she'd prove it to herself. And him. But her guts twisted and she clung to the lie even as it disintegrated.

Conor was not a man. Conor was a hunter, a demon whose mere presence excited the prey, hypnotized them into his arms.

Eva flicked her gaze everywhere but his eyes. He'd pulled back his long sable hair and tied it with a leather thong. And curiously, he wore buckskins, shades of the old trackers and explorers she'd seen in compuvids.

His face was hard planes and angles, even the nose, as if chiseled from granite, strong-jawed, the lips cruelly masculine. Except when, hot and electric and dev-ilishly practiced, they had ravaged her breasts, captured her mouth. Softened in the flame of contact, they'd curved and swelled as he'd slanted them over her protesting lips.

"How very nice of you to meet me." Summoning her reserves of professional self control, Eva took his hand, and tilting her head, met his gaze. Her fingers quivered, lost in his grip.

"My pleasure, ma'am." Conor checked his smile and his hunger. Eva Kelsey could pretend till the end, the final surrender, the final scalding fusion, no matter how coolly she stared him down now, lying to her body that she didn't want him. But if it took the rest of her stay, he'd have her, wet and begging and frantic.

He ran a hunter's swift inventory. Had she changed? No. Still creamy-skinned, hair like gold silk, almond-shaped blue eyes whose ice he'd melted into hot liquid compliance, the full rosy mouth he wanted to bite. Tight-assed as usual, she'd followed the rules and poured herself into the crisp white uniform that proclaimed her scientific status even while it hugged every soft curve.

Gorgeous high breasts and legs that ended in heaven, a heaven he'd never forget. He pried his attention off the hint of that sweet cleft he'd caressed until she'd spread her legs and whimpered.

"Let's get to town. Mayor's nervous as a long-tailed cat in a roomful of rockin' chairs." He hoisted her cases and led her to the beast. "Cayuses, we call them here on Laredo." He whistled and from around a sandhill slithered another of the critters, apparently an elephant-sized baby version of the colossal cayuse.

"He's darling. Is this my mount?" Eva took a tentative step toward the monster.

Mount. Beneath the snug buckskin, Conor's erection strained the tanned hide of his breeches, heavy and hot. By God, one suggestive word out of her mouth was all it took to make him hard. After two years, one look, one touch, and he wanted to drop her in the red sand, peel off her neosuit, expose her like a ripe fruit. Tease her, suck her breasts and drive into her till she came and came, screaming his name.

"What's this little guy's name?" She stroked the cayuse. It gurgled, closing its eyes, sappy at her touch.

Like Conor himself.

"Hondo," Conor grated, the craving for her now a throbbing ache in his groin. "But he's too young to ride. Just a pack animal for now." He positioned the cases in the rope slings, and patted Hondo's leathery hide.

"But where do I ride?"

"On Sweetheart." He gave her a wicked grin. "With me."

"With you? Up there?" Eva blinked and tipped her head back to measure the saddle on the giant cayuse.

Sweetheart flattened her floppy ears, eyed Eva, and squealed. Casually, Conor gave the beast an elbow to her tree trunk of a front leg. Sweetheart snuffled at his neck, begging until he stretched to pat the thick hairless chest.

"Just jealous. A female." He shrugged and bent, lacing his hands. "Up on board, ma'am. Sit behind me. You can hang on."

Eva anchored her foot and Conor lifted her slowly, inhaling as her feminine mound grazed his nose. His nostrils flared, and through the neosuit, he detected her wet heat.

Conor held, stroked one long leg as Eva ascended the rope ladder onto Sweetheart's back. With practiced moves Conor climbed into the saddle and took the reins, grateful for the dry, faintly acrid reek of the cayuse that overpowered Eva's wildflower scent.

Straddling the huge beast, Eva squirmed to make herself comfortable. Her thighs clasped Conor's firm rump and molded the hard muscles of his legs. Humiliated at the intimacy, she stuggled to gain distance between them.

"Arms around my waist, unless you want to fall thirty feet. Crack your head on a rock, and I have me a carcass to haul into town," Conor growled.

Eva glared at Conor's thick neck, the cluster of black hair, and tried to hang on by grasping the buckskin shirt. Impossible. Obviously, the man must've worn a size too small to show off the taut carving of his frame.

"Around my waist," he roared.

Eva laid her cheek on the steel of his back, and wrapped her arms tightly. No matter how she flexed and strained, she couldn't encircle him. Her breasts mashed into his solid torso, and her areolas puckered. The softness between her legs ground into him, an electric friction.

The rise and fall of the animal's gait, the gentle rocking and swaying, produced a fine irritation, then warm pleasant pain, wetness. Her woman flesh felt swollen and yielding. Eva gritted her teeth and closed her eyes. This could not be happening. Unlike animals and wild people like Conor, she was so civilized, she had been selected to judge the civility of the colonists.

She controlled her body, fed it intelligently, exercised it, limited its desires and needs. And she neither desired nor needed the persuasive rubbing of her clit against Conor's spine, against his buttocks.

She squirmed a few inches away, holding herself at an angle to escape the contact until her back ached and Conor roared again. "Damnit, woman. I said, hang on."

At first the cayuse strolled among the barren dunes, but as the land rolled flat, Conor clucked and Sweetheart picked up a surprising speed. The sway increased, the jiggling too, and Eva held her breath. Conor's iron velvet massaged her sensitive breasts, and tingling heat raced up her legs. She was pilloried on his unyielding body. Tension built almost to the bursting point.

"Please," she gasped. She jerked at Conor's arm. "My legs are killing me. Is there some other way I can ride, Conor?"

He glanced over his shoulder. "Yeah. But I'm only going to stop once. If you choose it, you're stuck with it."

For a second Eva read a quirk of his lips, but she gave a mental shrug. Anything was better than being brought to orgasm by the mere touch of Conor's backside.

"Anything," Eva agreed.

"That's my baby. Slow down, darling, and I'll give you what you want," Conor murmured, his voice low and seductive, and Eva's cheeks flamed.

"If you think you can take advantage of this situation," she began, gearing up to set limits to this barbarian.

"I was talking to my cayuse. Jealous?" A mocking laugh lay under his words, and Eva clamped her mouth shut. A smart reply would only spur him on.

Obediently, Sweetheart slowed, stopped, and twisted her neck for a stalk of dried vegetable treat Conor offered from a brown saddlebag. "Is that good, baby?" Conor crooned.

While Sweetheart munched and worshipped with her yellow eyes, Conor extended both brawny arms over his head. He reached back. "Grab on and stand up, Doc. I'll haul you over my right shoulder. C'mon. One leg at a time."

Eva rose gingerly, her muscles quivering with the hour of rigorous stretching. She found her footing, and clung to his hands for balance.

"I won't let you fall." Utterly the master, Conor gripped her left hand and levered her until she straddled his shoulder. She had a sudden image of Conor taking advantage of her precarious position to nuzzle the moistness between her thighs.

And she was horrified that she was so aroused she imagined jutting herself toward his face, impatient for his tongue like all his bed partners, inviting him to taste the evidence of her desire, to rub his face into her.

"Other leg now," he ordered, the perfect gentleman. He slid her down into his lap over buckskin so tight he might as well have been naked.

"Sidesaddle for ladies." Conor adjusted her in his lap. "You can sleep. Better?"

For the first few moments, she held herself stiff and aloof, but Conor pressed her head against the slabs of his massive chest and forced her to lean into him. Then he bent toward her, and his beard stubble grazed her cheek.

"Look at me, Eva." His frown, dark and compelling, was the equivalent of his elbow in the cayuse's leg. "Is this better?"

"Better," she whispered, ashamed that she thirsted for Conor to cuddle her. And as if he read her mind, he cradled her in his arms, picked up the reins, and Sweetheart galumphed into the silent sands.

Silence. Flailing herself for her weak will, Eva searched for a reason to provoke his disturbing voice, to measure her strength against him. Tentatively, she placed her hand where his buckskin shirt revealed the outline of the flat male nipple over his heart. Conor sucked in a great breath, and beneath her hand, his heart thudded.

"Is the colony scratching so hard for survival they can spare only one man to pick me up?" Unobtrusively, she studied the tension in his jaw muscles for the telltale signs of a lie. "I told the mayor I'd get you." He pierced her with a single look.

"You *told* him?"

"Surprised? Why? You saw pack leader/top dog syndrome in my psych-form when you knocked me out of the program. What clever heading did you paste on it, my pretty professor? Alpha-male behavior?"

"I classified you under *prefers to work alone*," she said defensively.

"And almost cost me the opportunity to colonize Laredo." His laughter rumbled under her hand. "But despite your damndest, I got here." He tugged the reins and Sweetheart veered left. Little Hondo gave a squeal and rushed out in front, wagging his long lizard tail. Conor grinned. "Smells the lake from miles away."

Conor shifted and faced the horizon bounded by a blue-green sky. He swayed from side to side on the leather pad, and made a low sound in his throat. His shaft swelled against the soft flesh on the underside of her thighs. Her face flamed.

She cursed herself. Why hadn't she bitten her lips and endured the painful ride on the too-broad rump of the cayuse? How could she have missed the implications of nestling in his groin?

"My cramps are gone," she said cheerily. "Look." She pointed her toes and stretched her legs. "If you don't mind, I'll take my original seat now."

Sandy Fraser

"Oh, but I do mind." His hard hand clamped down about three inches below her knees, and he killed her stretch. "I told you, I'd only stop once." Slowly, he exhaled and rocked her in his lap, forcing her to feel the steadily increasing thickness of his erection. "Besides, Dr. Kelsey, I like you exactly where you are."

His lips had lost his arrogant smile, and he closed his eyes, but his dominant maleness enveloped Eva as surely as if he'd staked her out and covered her with his body.

She shuddered and remembered the first time Conor had bruised her with that voice, burned her with his heat, the first time he'd manhandled her.

Against her will, she remembered every detail of her first meeting with Conor.

Chapter 2

"Dr. Kelsey, Dr. Kelsey." Judy had scurried around her receptionist's desk. She'd pointed at Eva's seclusion room. "He's in there, your first appointment. He, I mean Mr. Conor, got here early and you're five minutes late."

"Thank you, Judy." Eva raised one eyebrow. "And you let him into seclusion unattended?"

Judy failed to control a scarlet blush. "He asked, and somehow — well, I just couldn't say no."

"Really? You've never broken the rule before. Quite persuasive, this Mr. Conor." Eva patted Judy's arm and smiled. "Now stop the hand-wringing. What's done is done."

Putting on her professional face, Eva swung her porta-bag and waited a second for the slider to recognize her, to part and welcome its owner.

Suddenly she understood Judy's fluttering. Conor's presence overwhelmed the sim-walls, the soft brown rug, and almost overwhelmed her. Physically, he was a giant, sprawled in a chair that for the first time had stretched its flexible limits to accommodate him.

Casually he rose, towering over her, deep-set, steel-gray eyes appraising her from under dark, heavy eyebrows. A mane of black hair fell to the shoulders of his black jacket. His firm lips opened to reveal perfect white teeth. Animal vitality filled the room. Eva swallowed. Hard.

A successful predator flashed across Eva's consciousness. She pictured his powerful legs pumping, running down his hapless prey, the brawny arms seizing the struggling creature, rendering her helpless and compliant, the sharp teeth biting her neck. My God. *Her?* Had she lost her mind? Eva resisted an impulse to shake her head to roust the picture. *Get a grip, Kelsey. He's just a man. An immense man, the kind of man who diminished other men, but just a man.* She'd evaluated hundreds of these guys.

"Mr. Conor." She extended her hand, and, with a hint of a smile, he covered it in his enormous grip. A galvanizing jolt of sheer sexual power coursed from his hot touch up her arm, shot through her body, and raced down to tell her knees to buckle, to tell her to fall on her back and spread her thighs.

Eva battled her desire. She had too much at stake. The instant attraction would skew her analysis of the man. If she lost control, she'd color the interview, and invite another file note from the Psych Board.

She dragged her hand out of his grip, and scuttled behind her desk. "Please," she murmured. "Please."

"Please what?" His voice resonated and sounded even when his words ended.

"Please… make yourself comfortable," she croaked. She perched in her chair, hid her hands under the desk, and pinched the tender skin between her thumb and index finger. The pain restored her common sense, and she folded her hands. "Let's get started, shall we?"

Conor was standing before her. He'd left her two choices. Either stare at the hefty bulge straining his pants, or tilt her head to meet his penetrating eyes. She closed her eyes and waved, praying he'd resume his seat.

"Oh, lady, I'd like to get started," he rumbled and folded himself into the lounge. He smiled again, a quirk of his lips that signalled some dark question she wouldn't acknowledge. He crossed his ankle over the opposite knee.

Eva clasped her hands on the desk. "I have all the records. Physical, psychological profiles, and work and personal history, Mr. Conor."

"Conor. Just Conor." It was a command.

"*Mister* Conor," Eva insisted. She had to take control. "You know all the paperwork and what it entailed. But we need to get the feel of you." The heat of a wild blush surged up her neck and into her cheeks. Conor grinned.

"I mean, the emotional nuances that compsychs and paperwork won't divulge."

"Take your best shot," he invited.

"What's your dream, Conor? Mister Conor," she corrected hastily. "Is it colonizing Feldon-9?"

"My dream," he repeated, locking his hands behind his head, and contemplating the ceiling. He straightened, uncrossed his legs, and riveted her with those piercing eyes. "To be free and open and big on a world that's like me."

"Free?"

"Of all the bowing and scraping a man has to do to be honest and open."

"Ah, you'd prefer a place without laws and manners?" She tried to restate him, incriminate him. "A lawless, loose, primitive world?"

"C'mon, Dr. Kelsey." He cupped his hands over his knees and arched one brow. "We both know what I mean. You know my past, safari guide, mercenary, bodyguard. Hauling people out of tight spots. I need adrenaline rushes. I need to ride to where the boundaries have vanished."

"Very poetic, Conor. But the need for adrenaline rushes, in your case, have included — how can I put this delicately — avidly searching for boundaries in the beds of other men's wives." She displayed a list printed on the pink sexual history sheet.

"I told you I ride to where the boundaries vanish. And I've given some of those stifled women the best rides of their lives."

His infuriating grin enraged Eva.

"This list," she flapped it at him "fairly shouts of incredible breaches of respectable behavior, besides being quite clearly against moral law." Her heart was pounding. "Explain yourself, Conor."

"Ah, may I?" Smoothly, he leaned foward and snatched the paper from her hand. He perused it for a second. "What's the point of compiling a list like this? More evidence of government prying." With contempt, he tossed it back, defiling the perfectly organised surface of her desk. "Lonely women, sad women, some desperate for a change in their lives. Some just wanted to play, to taste a little tabasco on their meat."

Eva pursed her lips. "Although I disapprove of your behavior, it is not punishable by law. But you are a time bomb, an ember waiting to inflame and torch a colony. A disruptive, macho influence and a threat to family harmony."

"That's me, Doc. One powerful, reckless bastard."

"Did you know, Mister Conor, not one of these women stayed with her husband? Not one! I can see from your expression that comes as news. And what do you think that means?"

"Hell, Doc. What do *you* think that means?"

Eva adopted her frostiest tone. "I assume a man of your type doesn't hold himself accountable."

"And what type would that be, Doc?"

"The rutting stallion type, Mister Conor, the bull, the dominant kagalon inseminator of Pastor-12." She leaned back and steepled her fingers to allow herself a satisfied smirk. "Have you any questions?"

"Yeah, How come it's *Mister* Conor again? And how come my little flings seem to annoy you?"

"They do not annoy me," Eva blurted in a huff. "I don't care how many beds you gallop through like a stallion who's caught a whiff of a ready mare. Be my guest. Have at it. What is it they used to say? Men like you are limited only by opportunity and stamina."

"I get the distinct feeling you don't like me, Dr. Kelsey."

"I do not, Mister Conor." Eva rose. "And because I play no games, I will give you my evaluation now. I cannot recommend you for colonizing Feldon-9."

"Because I've fucked too many women?" He came out of the chair like a steel spring. "Or because I haven't fucked you?"

"Get out of my office." Eva trembled. Her hand shook as she pointed to the door. "Before I — " She groped for the security button and missed.

"Before you what?" He reached and pulled her across the desk, one hand an iron band around her waist, the other tipping up her face. She thrashed her head from side to side, but Conor stilled her, gripping her chin and pressing her back against the holo-desk.

"Look at me, Dr. Kelsey. We're in seclusion, so save your breath. Unless you want to scream with pleasure when I do this." He brushed his mouth across hers. Fiercely she bit his lower lip. She tasted his salt blood. In an act of defiance, she spat in his face.

"Now you have to pay." He slanted his mouth over hers in a punishing kiss that forced her mouth open and tore a whimper from her throat. Like some strange drug, Conor's touch paralyzed her into submission, sapping her will, making her an accomplice in her own seduction.

"I hate you," she got out, but she couldn't even convince herself. Her lashes swept her cheeks, her eyes half-closing in lust, but she made one more effort. Eva struck his face, a thin, anemic blow. She had no strength against him. Conor chuckled, and her fists opened, palms flat against the wall of his chest.

"Such little fists," he whispered. "Is that the best you can do?" He held her closer, kissed her softly, hushing her like he'd calm a frightened doe.

Conor tapped the catch of her neosuit, and swallowed her weak protest in another kiss. He yanked the snow-white suit down to her waist, immobilizing her arms in her own clothes, rendering her helpless.

His eyes, gray as a winter storm, scanned her breasts. "God, you make me hard.

I want to rip this suit off, throw your legs over my shoulders, and ride you like a bull." His voice was strained and rasping. "Tell me you want it."

She licked her dry lips and moaned. He was worse than an animal at stud. All those women, panting and wailing under him. Eva's cry of protest died in her throat.

"You're very beautiful. Do you know that? Feel what you do to me." He nudged her legs apart and rubbed the rigid bow of his erection on her cleft.

Then he weighed her breast, his big hand cupping the undercurve while he thumbed the taut nipple. He kissed her and rolled her sensitive peaks between his thumb and forefinger.

Slowly, he took his lips from hers and his eyes were dark as smoke. "I'm going to kiss your breasts now, Eva, suck you until you want me to do more." He bent his head, biting her neck, gliding a provocative string of kisses lower and lower.

Battling even as her will drained out of her, Eva moaned and arched into his hand, instinctively offering her breast with its pebbled areola. He closed his teeth on the hard nub while she whimpered. His tongue twirled and lapped, and Eva strained to thrust more and more of her breast into his mouth.

He flicked his tongue wickedly, paused to blow on the moist skin, then plucked at her nipple while he licked and nibbled her other breast.

She squirmed beneath him, and Conor slid his fingers into the curly nest between her thighs. "You're beautiful here, too. So hot and wet." His fingers worked in and out and his thumb rubbed her clit, faster and deeper, and Eva tensed and moaned, wanting and afraid to want as the currents of desire pulled her far from herself into a blinding place where everything spiraled down to Conor's enormous hand boring into her swollen vulva, and his steely eyes boring into her soul.

On the edge, the split second before she fell over the brink into an electric oblivion, Conor stopped.

He withdrew fingers wet with her essence, and wiped them in the curls on her mound.

In an agony of lust, she swiveled her hips shamelessly. "Finish. Finish me."

But Conor raised her and slipped the suit up till it fastened around her neck. He swung her into his arms as if she weighed less than the pink sheet of his harem, and carried her into her private bathroom. He set her before the mirror, and held her braced against his massive torso.

"Look, Dr. Eva Kelsey."

Eyes glazed, Eva stared into the mirror at her fragile feminity, her pale gold melded to Conor's dark maleness. She reached back and clasped his muscular thighs to support herself. The mouth of the woman in the mirror had lips swollen with his kisses, wet and smeared with lust. Her skin glowed, dewy with the heat of passion.

Her turgid nipples marred the smooth skin of the suit, and even as she stared at the flare of her hips, Conor took possession of her mound. He cupped her, the hard heel of his big hand rocking, rubbing her distended flesh, again dragging her closer to orgasm. She shook and trembled, poised on the brink.

He stopped again, bent to suck the lobe of her ear, and flashed a cruel smile.

"Why? Why are you doing this to me?" Eva heard the begging note in her voice, the pleading, and she didn't give a damn. She was desperate, needed him to complete her anyway he could.

On tiptoe, she thrust into his retreating hand, fighting to maintain the sweet pressure.

"I dreamed about the colony, pretty Dr. Kelsey, lived for the dream, and I've passed every test. But yours." He released her and stepped away. Eva clutched at the cold sink and still his eyes held her gaze.

"I wanted you to know how much you can want something and have it taken away at the last second." He clenched his fist and a muscle twitched in his strong jaw.

"Wait, wait, Conor." Her own voice was strange, pitiful in her ears.

"It's been a treat, Dr. Kelsey." He mocked her with a bitter smile and a salute. "And thanks for all the fun."

Barely able to stand, Eva heard the sliders whoosh, and she was in seclusion again. Alone. She pulled in great gulps of air, and her pulse raced. She averted her concentration from the mirror and counted the green glass tiles. When she reached ninety, her pulse still thundered, her respiration was shallow and too fast. She gave it up as a bad job and took a long, calming breath.

"What do we tell patients? Look yourself in the eye and deal with the truth." Still shaking with the need Conor had waked in her, she lifted her head and stared into the mirror. Hair disheveled, lips branded with his kisses, Dr. Eva Kelsey had confusion written all over her face.

"But I know, I *know* who I am," she declared, "and a ten-minute lust bout with a bed-hopping hunk can't change me.

"Logic and reason. Logic and reason." She repeated her mantra until her cracked and whispery words made her desolate, made her cry. Eva touched her throat. She bit her swollen lips, and she hated herself as she watched fear replace confusion. Who was she if Conor so easily destroyed her civilized, analytical philosophy?

As tears coursed down her cheeks, Eva forced herself to ignore a heavy ache of frustration, of emptiness. And what had it meant to him? Another almost-conquest? The Conors of the world, men who oozed hormones and charisma, took great pride in reducing women like herself to mindless females, pliant, eager for sex.

Not that Eva hadn't had sexual encounters, the sophisticated trysts recommended by the professional guilds. Her partners had always been other pros anxious to fulfill their own guild requirements. Dr. Eva Kelsey knew her duty and had referenced her sexual activities in her guild file to prove she was fully experienced. The Psych Guild insisted their members be competent to minister to patients with mating dysfunctions. Conor escaped that category. Conor had his own category.

Tentatively, Eva fingered her mouth, remembering his mind-drugging kisses. She had endured the mechanical efforts of partners determined to practice the maneuvers of sexual athletes on the compuvid's Kama Sutra channel. When the man was through, she'd clock the minimum three minutes of afterplay and give a sigh of relief. She'd dress and scurry to have the institute's door robot verify her visit with the pink seal. Sex never had meant anything to her before, nothing except animalistic stimulus and response, sweaty wrestling.

Until today. Until Conor.

He had shockingly skilled hands and lips. But it was more than his natural gifts. Eva had felt truly safe, protected in his arms, free to be a different Eva. With his knowing caresses he had released the passionate woman terrified of intimacy, the woman who struggled to present a picture of a cool and collected psych doctor. A woman above reproach, above challenge from her peers and the Psych Board, a woman who slept in her lonely bed, detached, aloof from desire, untouched and invulnerable.

Logic reminded her Conor was a man with an erotically charged past, a man looking forward to a blazing future. Reason warned her that chaos lay in her wild response to him.

"Logic and reason," she said and splashed her face with cold water. "Logic and reason," she said as she completed her neat Baradian twist, every hair in place.

The simple act of smoothing her neosuit made her close her eyes and imagine Conor's hands cupping her hips and drawing her into his arousal. Her eyes flew open. No. His effect on her had been an aberration, a weak, needy momentary lapse on her part.

Again she heard his husky voice. "Save your breath, unless you want to scream with pleasure when I do this."

Eva covered her lips. She'd solve the problem of Conor by relegating him to a mental limbo where she isolated disturbing events. And as for seeing him again, she had few worries. No doubt he'd find a slot as a squad leader in Mercenary, Inc. She could see Conor in the jungle, or a desert's edge where, her official inquiries noted, he was respected and liked by his men.

Eva's belly tightened. The reports praised him as a fierce, intelligent, relentless fighting machine whose special gift was an uncanny ability to sense danger. And then to fix it with whatever it took. What an asset for Feldon-9's civilian colonists!

What an asset she'd thrown away on the basis of the pink sexual history sheet. Eva checked her suit's power tab and met her eyes in the mirror. Guilt flickered across her face.

And then the tough Dr. Eva Kelsey jerked the controls from this new, soft Eva.

Dr. Kelsey mocked her reflection. "Grow up. You followed your best professional judgment. He's a menace to peaceful settlement. In a few hours, we'll do emotional housecleaning and toss out Conor."

"Lord help me," Eva whispered. "Make it so I never see him again."

Chapter 3

Though a week had passed since Conor had shamed her, and cold logic demanded she hate him for exploiting her weakness, Eva's traitorous body still hungered for his probing hands, his plundering tongue.

During lunch with a friend or a run in the park, in the middle of a seclusion session, the memory of Conor suckling her breasts surfaced, a flush reddened her cheeks, her nipples erected into stiff, tingling buds, and a creamy dew slicked her private flesh.

Sometimes a friend, or her secretary, or an evaluatee asked, "Something wrong, Dr. Kelsey?" And glibly she lied, and poured water from a carafe.

But of course something was wrong when she opened a folder and the glassy surface of the holodesk lay cool under her hands. And like the stab of a sharp knife, the memory rose of Conor. How he'd lifted her, spread her out, shivering on the glass, a half-naked sacrifice to his revenge.

And now, forced to sit politely, professionally in the setting where he'd played with her body like a living toy, Eva squirmed. If Conor aroused her, a woman he'd just met, to a fever pitch to punish her, what did those others feel? Those women he flirted with, seduced for his pleasure? Had he kissed them until they wept, tongued and fingered them until, crazy with lust, they begged him to bury his engorged arousal deep in their wetness?

Desperately, she tried to erase a kaleidoscope of Conor with willing women, Conor masterfully changing their positions, driving into them, bringing them repeatedly to climax, until they lay limp in his arms.

"He's an animal without conscience," Eva shouted in the dark quiet of her air sedan. And she hated him for showing her what was missing in her life, the cost of her detachment.

She heard again his mocking questions. "Do you hate me because I've fucked too many women? Or because I haven't fucked you?"

On the verge of a decision about Conor, she snapped awake. Her sleek Austin slid around the last curve, pulled to a smooth stop before the gates, and announced, "We have arrived at our destination, Miss Kelsey, the estate of Roger J. Kelsey, your loving father who would like a grandchild before he's too old to take the kid on sarafi."

"Thank you, Austin," she said. She sighed. Her father insisted on his staff maintaining her vehicle, and no matter how often she'd erased Austin's reminders, the mechanics carefully reprogrammed him at her father's directions.

Wearing a huge smile, Randall, the gateman, stuck his head in her window.

"Go round back, Miss Eva. Your papa's invited damn near half the city."

Eva saluted, and Austin glided onto a sideroad, and into the estate's garage. While Austin exchanged greetings with the other vehicles, Eva set off on the wandering path toward the house.

"Some house. I really grew up in a giant theme park." She lingered in the Shakespeare garden and the herbarium her mother had loved. In the cool damp of the fern forest, she heard faint music escaping from the house, the perfection of a world-famous string quartet.

The music grew in volume as she entered the house by the solarium door. In the main salon, she navigated clusters of movers and shakers, nodding and smiling until she found her father, tall and distinguished and used to imposing his will. A kiss and a hug, and he resumed talking.

Eva circulated and joined a group of laughing friends. The knots of sophisticated guests swirled, formed and reformed. Eva, in an instant becoming aware she was the target of an intense stare, struggled to sustain social chatter. She glanced over the rim of her wine glass. Suddenly the crowds parted. And *he* was there, leaning with one elbow on the Carrera marble mantelpiece.

Conor, as jarringly out of place as a panther in a farmyard. From twenty feet away, she read the challenging smile on those lips she'd bitten, read the dare in eyes that knew her secrets. "Go on," he seemed to be saying. "Tell Daddy and have my ass kicked."

Despite her drink, Eva's mouth went dry, and the wine quivered in the champagne flute. Conor in her family home. Another violation, almost as personal and ruthless as his penetration of her seclusion room. *And herself.*

"Excuse me. Excuse me," she said, automatically planning her route through the guests to her father. Then she'd have her real revenge when Conor got dragged off the estate. And how would Conor maintain the slavish admiring gaze of the silly females he'd drawn like filings to an erotic magnet?

She'd managed to get halfway across the parquet floor when a massive hand captured her elbow. The scent of woods and jungles and wild places, the scent of the untamed animal. Conor. Her nostrils flared, and she stiffened. Around him the temperature rose. Conor radiated extraordinary heat, the hunter's heat.

But she was no one's prey. Not Conor's, not any man's. Though the top of her simple coiffure barely reached his heart, she inclined her head and shot him a venomous glare.

"How dare you touch me in a public place?" Her voice shook with indignation, even as her knees weakened.

"I'd like to touch you in a private place."

"My father will have you castrated when I tell him what you did."

"Ah. You haven't told him yet?" Far from hanging back, Conor ran interference through the throngs.

"I *had* no intention of upsetting him," Eva said. She put an edge on her voice even as Conor's touch unleashed desire in her belly. "Until you intruded here. My father is a hard man who doesn't take kindly to men who manhandle women. But now I see my silence has done nothing but encourage you."

"Guess I'll have to pay the price, Dr. Kelsey." He smiled, hugely satisfied, and Eva burned with the urge to slap his face.

He brought her in front of her father.

"Daddy, this man — "

"You've found Conor, I see." Her father patted her cheek. "Good show. Fences mended after the evaluation problem?" He tapped the ice cube in his scotch and raised one bushy eyebrow.

"Problem?" An ominous chill raced down Eva's spine.

Casually, Conor draped his arm over her shoulders. "I haven't told her yet, Roger."

"You call my father Roger?" She blurted, her voice brittle with astonishment.

"On safari, I called him *bwana.*" Both men laughed and exchanged fake punches.

"My dear, you are as precise in the colony selection process, they tell me, as a surgeon with a scalpel. The teams you qualify reek with success." Her father considered his drink, looked up quickly, and his gaze bored into hers. "But Conor has been exempted from your approval."

"Exempted? You went over my head?"

"He's a rare man, Eva. Feldon 9 needs his rare qualities."

"I see. The propensity for bedding every female between eighteen and eighty? Is that sleazy trait among his so-called special qualities?" Her eyes flashed, and she dislodged Conor's arm violently as if repulsing a snake.

Eva stormed out, slowing only when she reached the private family terrace, and clung to a giant oak. The frivolous music mocked her. Furious tears wet her cheeks, and she fought to maintain her self-control. How dare her father interfere? How dare he use his influence to shove Conor down her throat?

Conor down her throat. The innocent words changed, the common saying developing in her imagination like a vidscreen show. Eva kneeling between his legs, weighing his heavy sac in one hand, holding his enormous cock to her lips, his fingers tangled in her loose hair. Her own flesh slick and heated by the act of pleasing him, by the promise of the intense pleasure he'd give her after her lips and teeth and tongue had brought him to the edge.

"No," she moaned. She pressed her face into the bark, hurting, welcoming the harshness. From the house a reggae band off Luna cranked up the volume, and the guests shouted and danced. She heard not a single footfall until Conor was upon her, smooth and deadly silent as a panther under the cover of darkness.

Easily he gripped her wrists in one hand and stretched her arms over her head. His muscled torso and iron thighs, as efficient as a vise, held her against the tree.

"Get your hands off me," she directed, cold and determined to show him no weakness, no willingness.

"Going to scream, Doc?" He rolled the heavy arc of his erection into the hollow of her back.

"I won't give you the satisfaction."

"Oh, but you will."

He nudged her legs farther apart, absorbing the ineffective kicks she aimed with her heels. There was more than one way to shrivel the ego of a beast in human clothing.

"You amuse me, Conor," Eva said. "I've had a chuckle or two over the years from you and your ilk, a pitiful dying breed of testosterone-maddened males. If you're expecting — "

"Expecting this?" He lessened the pressure, leaned down and jerked up her silk skirt, and tore off her lace panties. With a fever-hot hand, he explored her buttocks, caressing the firm cheeks. "If a man could be maddened by testosterone," he whispered, "the sight of you would drive him crazy."

Eva flinched as his big demanding hand worked its way between her and the tree, briefly toyed with her breasts, followed the curve of her belly and ruffled her pubic hair. She was drenched, slippery, and with one blunt finger he massaged her erect clit, delved into her swollen vulva.

He rested his tongue on her throat where her pulse fluttered like a snared bird, bit the curve of her shoulder, and whispered into her ear. "Unless you've been playing with yourself and thinking about some other guy, you're wet and creamy and ready for me."

"Is this your answer to everything, Conor? Sex? Is this how you defeat women?" Her voice grew faint, she slumped, her knees buckled. "Sex whether they want it or not?"

"You want. You've wanted me from the first time I walked into your office." Conor loosed his belt, tapped the catch and his arousal sprang out. "And God, I've never wanted a woman as much as you." He groaned and shivered as the sensitive tip slid between the cheeks of her buttocks and found her sweet heat.

He inserted just an inch and stroked her clit, her labia, pressing her against his engorged tip.

"I'll scream if you don't stop." In spite of herself, Eva jutted her hips into his erection to give his hand free access.

Conor grazed her nape with his teeth. He bit his lip and clamped his eyes shut. No woman, not any, from the very first when he was fourteen to the Australian model he'd fucked a week before seeing Eva, had inflamed him like this woman.

Cool and pale and restrained, she was everything Conor was not. So sophisticated, looking down her patrician nose at "the animal" as she called him, yet like an inferno under an ice cap, she simmered.

Now he battled the desperate urge to spin her around and bury himself between her dripping petals, but he held off. She flung her head back, panting, resisting, in the throes of the most intense sexual temptation she'd ever felt. Her golden hair escaped from its taut coils.

Inhaling the provocative scent of her mane, Conor danced his fingers in her heat and growled, "This means nothing?" "Nothing," Eva gasped. Her thighs loosened. "*You're* nothing but a sex machine."

"Want some more?" He gave her another two inches and tormented her with his callused thumb. Eva shuddered, and he thrust half his cock in. She was shimmering on the brink. He read it in the trembling of her legs.

"I hate you," she got out between ragged breaths. "And you — you can't force me — to experience sexual satisfaction. If I don't want to."

"You can't help yourself." He tried to produce a mocking laugh, but he had started to shake, and the muscles of his legs quivered. Conor pushed the remaining four inches, at last fully lodged, and held himself motionless in her velvet sheath. A series of tiny spasms, constricting ripples, squeezed him. He gritted his teeth. He broke out in a sweat, fighting for control.

"Conor," she moaned. "Let me go."

"I can't," he said, no longer capable of remaining still.

"I've got to have you, Eva. If I roast in hell, I'm taking you."

In a heartbeat, her protests melted into soft, mewling cries. "Conor. Conor." She arched her back to give him total access.

Instantly, he withdrew, spun her around, and a low sound was ripped out of his guts as her shaking hands inserted him. He buried himself up to the hilt, lifted her till her legs encircled his waist. With a bruising kiss, he swallowed her scream of pleasure-pain. Rhythmically, his tongue plunged into the sweet wine of her mouth in tandem with his thrusts.

Her hips rocked into his, slapping into his hard pelvis, and his enormous hardness stretched her beyond thought, beyond reason, beyond all but total sensation. She sucked his tongue, then broke the kiss, and concentrated, shrinking her world to the juncture between her legs where Conor's length burned.

"Give it to me, baby," he groaned, and pumped. His strokes grew shorter, and the dense curls surrounding his shaft brushed her clit until, like a firestorm, she blazed.

"Now, Eva, now," he demanded.

And Eva froze in a paralysis of sensory overload, and climaxed, a furious, heart-stopping orgasm, with blood pounding in her ears, deaf to anything but Conor's roar of completion matching her own howl. Hot sperm jetted and met the pulsing contractions of her fevered core.

Eva shuddered and wept and forced her pelvis into his groin. Only Conor's powerful legs kept her from collapsing. He cupped her buttocks, and gently continued his strokes into her wetness, into her sweet aftershocks.

"Let's go someplace," he rumbled into her hair. He thrust again and she whimpered. "Someplace close."

"Garage." Savagely, she rained bites on his throat, his cheek, his lower lip. "No. Please, Conor. Stay inside me, don't put me down." She lowered her voice to a soft murmur. "I don't think I can walk, darling beast, my darling animal."

"What if somebody wanders out of the party, finds their way into this garden?" Conor tested her need, found her mouth. Her kiss spoke a desperate, rising hunger.

"Let them." She was limp in his arms. And in the silver moonlight, she traced the strength of his jaw, threaded her fingers through his midnight hair.

"Does it excite you, knowing we could be seen?"

"*You* excite me." Eva fastened her mouth to his, and he carried her, speared on his throbbing flesh, down the winding walk. Eva moaned and sobbed. She shrieked softly, and around his shaft, she pulsed and contracted. Her sharp nails raked his neck.

"You're coming again, without waiting for me," he teased. And imbedded in her body, he felt more masculine, more the master, more the protector than he'd ever felt in his life. This was the one. This was Conor's woman.

Wordlessly, she nodded and clung to him, her perfumed breath in his ear making him harder, more swollen than he could endure.

At the end of the path, she gave an order to the garage, and the slider opened.

"Hello, Miss Kelsey. Did you have a pleasant time?"

"Lovely, Austin." She unwrapped her arm from Conor's neck long enough to point at the chauffeur's bedroom door. "In there. Quick." She nipped Conor's ear.

He navigated the door, kicked it shut, and with a sharp intake of breath let her slide off his penis onto the bed. Wanton, her eyes shuttered, Eva slid her silk skirt up to her waist. Conor shucked off his clothes and in the dim light of a small bedside lamp, took in her beauty.

Her nipples, thick as cherries, peaked, pointing through the thin mauve silk. And Eva ran her hands down her sides, let them linger on her thighs. She spread her legs, and Conor stared greedily at the tiny wet curls of wheaten hair on her mons, at the pink fleshy folds. Her nub seemed to ripen as he feasted his eyes on her.

"God, you're beautiful," he rasped.

"Touch me. Come deep inside me. Do everything." Her words were strangled. "I've never felt like this." The tip of her tongue wet her lips, and she raised her long nails to her breasts, lightly scratching her nipples. "Do everything, Conor. Please." Eyes bright with desire, she thrust her hips higher, offering herself to his mouth.

His arousal knocked against his belly, and he stroked himself, his hand gliding over the creamy residue she'd left, the gift of her depths. He bent over the bed, and ran a finger over her. Eva whimpered and writhed beneath the slow touch.

"Open yourself," Conor said, his voice aching with need. She parted her core, and he held his breath as her mauve fingernails glistened against the wet pink petals. Conor slipped his finger in and out, and held it to her lips.

"Suck on it," he said softly, "the taste of your sex and mine." Her gaze locked on his, and she nursed his finger between her tongue and the roof of her mouth.

Impatient, Conor pushed her hands away, and tore open the silk dress. She lay completely exposed and vulnerable and wanting him desperately.

"Eva." He groaned. "I want to fuck you. But not yet."

"Do me. Do me now," Eva begged.

He cupped her mound, juicy with his come and her own heated gushing. He let his fingers wander over her ripe, distended vulva. Conor gently took one nipple between his teeth and suckled, then the other as she arched and writhed into his hand. He thrust two fingers deep inside.

Eva imagined his erection probing her again, stretching her, her core magically accommodating his impossible thickness, his incredible length.

"Conor, Conor." Her nails dug at his shoulders. "Come inside me. I need you now."

Conor glanced up from his suckling, and smiled a lazy smile.

"Not until your nipples are raw, and you show me you're ready to come. I want you to come, Eva. Can you come for me? Still holding back? Come for me." He brought her on until she screamed and bucked, and her tight sex gripped his fingers, and milked them with waves of muscular contractions.

In the throes of orgasm, Eva clutched his head. When her moans of pleasure died away, subsided into croons of after-pleasure, she smiled up at him and raised herself for a kiss.

"No one has ever made me feel this way, Conor. No one but you." Light kisses, butterfly kisses, and she sank against the bolster.

"What way? Talk to me." He massaged her mons, played with the wet curls.

"Fishing for compliments?" Eva reached for the rails of the headboard. "Ah, Conor, I'm naked and soft and melting, and totally at your mercy. And you're not even in bed with me yet." Her voice dropped, low, seductive. "Do you like playing with me? Hmmm? Or do you like this?"

With an eager sigh, she reached for his shaft and thumbed the smooth head. With her sharp fingernails, she traced the thick veins, and Conor hissed through his teeth.

"I want you in my mouth," Eva whispered, replaying her fantasy.

"And I want my mouth on you."

Conor flung himself on the bed, lifted her like a cougar might grip a rabbit, and turned her till her head rested on his thigh. "Spread your legs."

Straddling his chest, she licked the tip of his cock just as his tongue found her clit and lightning shot through her.

"You taste like wild honey," he breathed into her wetness, and she shuddered. "Take me, Eva. Take all of me."

Eva weighed his heavy sac in one hand, and thrust him into her mouth. She flicked the pulsating vein on the underside, explored the crevice where the plushy head divided, and withdrew the huge organ. She moved her hand up and down his smooth length until his massive sex jerked involuntarily and jumped with a life of its own, and Conor's hips came off the bed.

Eva engulfed it again and bobbed her head, her own body shaking under the delicious titillation of Conor's tongue, finding herself mirroring on him each stroke he laved on her vulva. And when he plunged his tongue rapidly, she whimpered and squirmed, and he gripped her buttocks, forcing her mons down onto his mouth.

Frantically, she scraped her teeth on his flesh, and he responded by nibbling her inflamed clit. Eva rotated her hips wildly over his skillful lips, sobbing for release.

"Finish me," she wept, "Oh, God, please finish me."

Conor bucked up until he gushed into her mouth, and she screamed while her own juices trickled onto his mouth and jaw.

Instantly, he pulled her under him and, still iron hard, lunged while the frenzy rocked her. In a haze of mindless pleasure she clung to him, savoring his salty tang on her tongue, the bruised tingling of her nipples as they brushed the pelt on his chest.

A second wave of electricity shot through her, and she dug fiercely into Conor's shoulders. His black hair a curtain over her face, he plunged like a stallion on a mare. Eva opened her mouth to shout a mindless prayer, but pleasure overwhelmed her, sent her flying high into a midnight place where only she and Conor existed, locked together, and finally fell to earth, mute with exhaustion.

His sex beat inside her, the throbs gradually slowing until he rolled over, maintaining the connection, banding Eva to him.

"Stay with me, Conor," she had murmured. "Sleep with me, my wonderful animal."

❧⟨✦⟩❧

The cayuse thundered along at high speed and jolted her out of the memory, the unforgettable memory of making love with Conor. And in the here and now, Eva lay nestling into Conor's chest, nestling into the smell of woodsmoke and the smell of a heat that had no name but Conor.

She yawned and half-raised her lashes. Tiny hairs on her skin prickled, and an ominous dry wind weighed on her.

"Conor, what's changing?"

"You should live on Laredo, lady. You've got the fine tuning to survive." He raised one arm and extended his finger. "North. See the dark cloud moving this way?"

"Aren't we at the lake yet?"

"Not close enough to beat the storm. But there's a canyon cave just ahead. I keep the outer caves stocked." Sweetheart stretched her long neck and raced toward a looming mesa.

At the mouth of the cavern, Conor swung Eva down, pulled her inside, and thumped the cayuses's leg twice. Sweetheart gave a complaining squeal, and sank to her knees. The giant creature folded herself. Her bulk barricaded the jagged opening of the cave.

They'd barely unpacked blankets and water when the storm hammered them. Amid the dizzying effects of changing air pressures, Eva paced the confines of the small cavern and twisted her hands nervously.

"The animals, Conor. Sweetheart and Hondo. How can they survive out there?"

"The wild ones live on the desert, and ride out storms like this every week." Conor grinned and started a fire. "See? Old Sweet Thing tucked herself up like a camel and closed her eyes. She'll snooze, and so will the baby."

Shaking her hair loose, Eva sighed, accepted a cup of herb tea, and settled into the downy blankets.

He caught her studying him over the rim of the cup, the ice-blue eyes reflecting the flames near her white boots.

Conor hunkered next to the fire and filled his mug. Through the hour of the ride, Eva's nearness had tortured him, and he'd had visions of the past, fragments, quick scenes of Eva under him, and under his control.

Eva, the cool professional, her shell destroyed under his busy hands, moaning for satisfaction he'd withheld to teach her a hard lesson about frustration.

Eva trapped against the tree on the estate while he caressed her sensitive breasts, her wet flesh until she welcomed his penetration.

Eva impaled on his erection while they recklessly hunted for a private place to continue. Then the dark hours of frantic pleasuring until they both lay exhausted, awash in the strange sweet sadness of completion.

All of it, every scene replayed during the cayuse ride, with Eva molded to his thighs, his torso, cherished in his lap. Yeah, he'd replayed every scene but the last, the one so painful and perplexing, Conor usually cut it from his erotic reveries. The last time he'd been with Eva.

Conor, wary as an animal, had wakened with Eva in his arms hours later, listening for footfalls, for voices. Out in the garage, the cars traded gossip and endless recountings of their repairs.

He grinned. After the night's sensuous bouts, *he* needed repairs. He feasted his eyes on Eva, melded to him in the narrow cot. She cradled her head on his bicep, one hand trying and failing to encircle it. Delicate and white, her other hand lay on his chest. His heart swelled. Her tiny hand lying in the valley of his pecs made him feel ten feet tall.

Conor pressed a kiss on her disheveled blond hair and tightened his arm around her. His woman. Eva. This was his woman. A wave of protectiveness surged over him. Pink and gold Eva, so strong yet so vulnerable and yielding in his hands. He would kill to keep a stone from her path. He would never let her go.

In her sleep she murmured and snuggled closer to him, her breasts swollen, the peaks and areolas soft and relaxed, silk. Her long mauve nails hid like exotic creatures in the forest of his thick pelt. A tiny tremor, a shiver, coursed over her, and Conor grabbed the quilt from the floor and spread it over them. The night light barely illuminated her face. He smoothed her lips, lips bruised and ripe with his savage kisses. Beneath her eyes lay the evidence of hours of love-making, lavender-blue smudges whose weariness he kissed reverently.

He tucked his arm under his head and wondered at himself. In all the encounters, all the women, all the warm and sex-scented beds, Conor was notorious for escaping, for slipping away. No excuses, no apologies. A final kiss and he was gone.

But in this small bed he cuddled a woman, and the thought of letting her go, dressing and returning to the concrete canyons and crowds of the domed city, those thoughts failed to get a toe-hold in his mind. He wanted to hold her against his length all night, wake up to her in the morning. Keep her.

Eva squirmed into his warmth and opened her eyes. "Conor," she breathed. "For a second, I wondered if this was real." She laughed unsteadily and sat up, tossing the wild fall of her hair behind her shoulders. "Conor." A lilt of amazement tinged her voice. "We really happened."

"Want us to happen again?" Conor gripped her waist and trailed his hand up her ribs to her breast. Instantly, her nipple sprang erect, and her eyes went smoky.

With a little moan, Eva bent over him and kissed the tip of his nose. She smelled of sex, the rich, heady smell of sex. "I'd love to darling, but I really can't stay." She swung her long legs over the side of the narrow cot, and stretched luxuriously on the braided rug like a golden cat.

Stung, and covering his disappointment, Conor leaned against the headboard, his balls tense, his cock lengthening, a fierce ache developing in his groin. "Going out there naked?" He dangled the ruins of her silk dress before her.

"Come prepared is the Kelsey motto." Mischievously, she put her fingers to her mouth and gave a two-note whistle. Out in the garage an engine thrummed to life. When Eva opened the slider, there Austin was waiting, his trunk open.

With a small case and a duplicate of the dress she'd worn, Eva popped into the bathroom and when she emerged, she was clean and fresh, the perfect replica of what Conor'd seen hours earlier at the start of the party. Not a hair out of place.

"I'd love to kiss you good-bye, Conor, " she closed the clasp of her case, "but I think you have other things in mind. And I know better now than to get within range." She laughed, a soft tinkling laugh like a sweet weapon. "See you later."

Conor had lain stunned, staring at the closed door, the perfumed musk of sex billowing around him, his body sticky with dried sweat and smeared with both their juices.

No woman walked away from him. Then why should the one he desperately wanted to stay saunter off, as if she'd discarded him like a used toy?

⁕᪥⧉☙⁕

In the garage, Eva leaned against the slider and let the tears come. Conor left the women he pleasured. Was she the first to walk away? The first to avoid the agony of losing him by running?

Eva set Austin to travel backroads. She trusted the air car to navigate the traffic, but she couldn't trust herself to drive, not with eyes blurred with tears, and an ache in her throat. Worst of all, logic and reason reminded her she was suffering the pain of loss for a passionate melding that would never happen again.

Despite her shower, Conor's scent had imbedded itself in her skin. Conor's touch still tingled on her nipples, Conor's lips still pressured her mouth. Eva drew a shuddering breath. The intense pleasure of their joining — how could she ever forget wildly indulging herself to the limits? How could she forget the magic of being covered by Conor's hard body, hearing his dark promises?

"Conor," she said. His name sounded stony and final. If only he'd go away. If only he'd spend the month till boarding for Feldon-9 doing what his files showed that he did best. He'd escorted refugees through battle zones, slipped behind enemy lines to sneak POWs out of prison and nuns out of jail.

He was an enigma, a savior, a rescuer, and at the same time a charismatic seducer. What lay in his heart? Surely, not commitment to a true relationship. She was just another mark on his score sheet. She closed her eyes, utterly miserable, and a fresh flood of tears rolled down her cheeks.

Was Conor really through with her? Had he relished her capitulation, her eager surrender, melting her resistance? Had he paid her back enough for cutting him from the colony list? If he decided to extract another payment to salve his ego, could she escape with her resolve never to see him again intact?

And what would she do if he came to her, coaxed her with his rough, knowing hands, his lips whose touch drained her of the power to fight?

"Please, Conor," she whispered aloud. "Let me go. Help me. I can't see you again. Ever."

"Why?" Austin inquired.

"Be quiet. I'm not talking to you."

"This Conor, was he the specimen lying on the chauffeur's bed?" Austin deliberately reduced speed and dawdled. "I heard the two of you, you know, the shrieks, the loud moans." Austin's voice carried a tinge of curiosity. "We *all* heard."

"Stop it, or I'll override." Eva paused with her finger on the control panel. "Who heard?"

"Well, Mrs. Pinchot's Silver Cloud Rolls Royce almost boiled over. The old girl has led a sheltered life. Then Rodney Lee's Instigator said — but its response was predictably coarse. So, why don't you want to see this Conor again? Has he hurt you in some way?"

"No. Yes." Telling Austin was like telling a mechanical friend, a robot ear who'd make sympathetic noises until she had shed her burden. Eva dabbed her eyes with a tissue. "How can I stay objective when this man, with a single look, can make me forget my status, my dedication to my job? Conor made me love sex for the first time in my life."

"Is this not a good thing?" Austin sounded perplexed.

"Yes. No." She clasped her hands and sighed. "Good sex should enhance an individual's life. But some people, Austin, maybe some people find it too disturbing, too invasive. Hormones instead of logic."

"Like a mechanic tampering with my turbo-carbs with a cold tension probe?" Austin was trying.

"More like a car-doc fooling with your original program."

"Changing the real me?" Austin's voice rang with shock.

"Exactly. Action, that's Conor's appeal. Oh, Austin, he's got a month to come after me. I can't face him."

"In that case, you need a long vacation, Dr. Kelsey. How about the polar resort, The Ice Queen? Would he track you there?"

"Ah, brilliant, Austin." Eva felt a ray of hope. "The guest list confidential, no unauthorized landings. By the time Conor tracks me down, he'd be AWOL from the project. He won't sacrifice his berth on the ship anymore than I would my psych rating."

Austin chuckled and slid into the slow lane of the skyway to Metro from where Eva would escape to the icy north. She'd never again see Conor, never again hear the deep compelling voice.

Chapter 4

"So quiet, Conor." In the cave, Eva made a simple statement that he knew was really a test.

He used both hands on the cup, and stared into the ashy film dulling the randoo branches. Spurts of flame escaped from the nexus where sticks crossed. Idly, Conor sipped his tea and poked at the fire.

He'd planned to sandbag her, wait her out, spoil the revelation she'd extract from him through an innocent remark. But sly Dr. Kelsey was good at waiting too, and that damned perfume, like musk camouflaged with roses, coiled a sinuous finger around his neck, turning him to face her. Conor stalled for another minute.

"Can't hear the storm through tons of cayuse flesh, Doc."

"I meant *you*, Conor. *You're* so quiet." In the echo of the cave her voice seemed stifled, unnatural. Tense?

Conor stretched out, propped on his elbows and ran a slow inspection of her from toes to teeth. He was gratified when she fussed with the tap closure at the collar of her suit, and he hid a grin.

"Dr. Eva Kelsey." He paused and studied her from shuttered lids. "Seems to me if I'd answered your question with a remark about how I was daydreaming or thinking, you'd have laughed and said you meant the storm. Isn't that the way of it, ma'am?" He sucked the cinnamon crust off a randoo twig. "Keep a man off-balance? Geld him with the sharp comment like you'd castrate a steer?"

Eva's voice dropped thirty degrees. Into the ice zone.

"When you finish parading around as Old Texas Billy Bob, I'd like a straight-forward answer."

"You mean, you want to get something straight between us? Doc, we did that a couple of times." Conor lightly fingered his crotch. "Damn, lady, my straight thing memorized you chapter and verse. As we'd say here on Laredo, almost wore hisself to a frazzle, pore feller."

Eva's eyes glittered, her lips tightened, and her calmness seemed to take great effort. "Of course. How had I forgotten? Everything must be on the very lowest level or you're unable to deal with it. Deal with it? You're not able to give it a second's room in your head."

With a swing of his cup, Conor dowsed the fire. One small branch gave light, and flickering shadows decorated the rough walls.

Conor heard her gasp of surprise, the rattle of her gourd cup as it bounced off a rock. In the dancing light she was struggling to maintain her equilibrium, but she was in shock. And that was enough, all it took to open her up. One abrupt act, one act close to the edge, and despite her starched control, her professional demeanor, Eva lost her ability to sit perfectly at ease with folded hands and prim lips.

He'd needed another signal, a sign that their night together had imprinted itself as deeply on her heart and mind as it had branded itself on his consciousness. Every cell was marshalling his body to move, to follow the surprise with a kiss, an embrace, a melding of bodies to induce her open-mouthed, open-thighed surrender.

"Now," he began, trying for a reasonable tone, "you ask me why I'm so quiet. You know. But you want to hear me make a fool of myself, hang myself up as your target."

Eva struggled to her feet and flung back the riot of hair that had escaped from the Baradian twist. "I don't know what you're talking about, Mr. Conor."

"Damn, you're good! That *Mr. Conor*, now, that sure put me in my place." He chuckled. "But we're not tip-toeing around Metro City. We're not pretending. We're not civilized anymore, Doc. See, I rode out to get you. Alone. I have you locked in a cave in a storm miles from the settlement in an uninhabitable desert."

Fighting to rein in her tone, Eva said, "What I see is that once again, my assessment of you was uncannily accurate. Conor. An anachronism, a throw-back to primitive ancestors who had their way with club and force. You are as unsuitable, as dysfunctional here as you were on Earth, except for the occasional bizarre job niches you occupied to satisfy the unspeakable needs of similarly deranged employers."

Conor threw back his head and loosed a roar of laughter. "Ah, you give yourself away, lady. The more hifalutin' you get, the more you've lost a handle on the situation. Eva, Eva, you can't even admit I was the reason you opted for this assignment."

"Of all the egomaniacal — "

He was across the cave in two strides, bent slightly, and swung her into his arms. She weighed nothing, and felt like everything he'd hunted for his whole life.

"I want you under me, close to the fire. I want to see your eyes open wide, and then close when you take me inside." His throat constricted with need, and in that moment in the light of the savage, primitive scene, her fire-burnished hair cascading over his arm, Conor craved her like the caveman of ancient times lusted for a mate. "Kiss me, Eva. Kiss me like you mean it."

She felt his uneven breathing warm her cheek, the ragged rise and drop of the great pectorals as he lost the regular rhythm to wild panting. He crushed her to his brawny torso, and her sensitive flesh, tormented by his hard nearness during the long ride, shrieked for her to find his lips and plunge her tongue into the alien cinnamon scent of his mouth. Shrieked for her to strip herself, let her breasts revel in the harsh brush of his beard stubble, wrap her arms around his neck and force her nipples into that devilishly knowing mouth.

With a soft moan she met his lips and began to slip away into his hunter's heat and the lure of the kisses she had spent two years aching for. She gave herself up to the drugging kisses, turned in his arms to press her swollen breasts into him, to meet more of his flesh and bone.

Like a panther, he growled into her mouth. "You're what I've waited for, burned for. You burned for me, too, my pretty lady." He took her lips in another bruising kiss. And when she had to break the kiss to gasp for air, he tightened his hold. "Tell me how bad you've wanted me, Eva."

His words penetrated, and shocked awake, Dr. Eva Kelsey, champion of cold logic and utter objectivity, swam to the surface Conor had clouded. Mentally, she listed his heroic acts, his bravery, his larger-than-life exploits.

The diagnostician woke and evaluated his request to admit she needed him. His overwhelming, granite arrogance was revealed in that simple command. How badly *she* had wanted *him*? Dr. Eva Kelsey should've laughed in sheer, stunned astonishment.

For in the end, Conor was Conor was Conor. His heat had reduced her to a whimpering female offering her genitals to sate his animal needs, tearing away her rational surface and exposing an emotionally unstrung bitch animal with a pink cleft made wet and hungry by his masculinity and his strength.

And did Conor have a kind of scoreboard here, too? A coterie of slavish females and a peanut gallery of admiring males to cheer him on? "The legendary Conor," Leon the pilot had said.

Gathering her willpower, Eva attempted to free herself from the bonds of Conor's raw sexuality. She thrashed, eluding his bids to still her mouth with his kisses, trying to find the cave's floor.

"Conor. No. Not now." She shuddered, her reactions too swift, too violent to convince him to wait. "Put me down, Conor, please... please."

"Let me, Eva. Just a little." Conor possessed her mouth, his tongue following the seam of her lips, coaxing her to yield despite her determination to withstand him.

He went to his knees in the soft sand, still anchoring her to the wild thudding of his heart, and her pulse skittered, an erratic crazy dance that sent hot blood to pool in her loins. Deep inside, her resistance shattered like flawed glass. And she sent Eva Kelsey, Ph.D, mute and enraged, back to some quiet place within her mind.

Eva closed her eyes to shut out the shadows playing on the stalactites, to shut out the strangeness of the cave. Behind her lids, there was only the image of Conor. Conor, all man, who made her all woman.

Whimpering, she hoarded her energy, directed it like a tight laserino to pinpoint the fevered flesh at her center. She moved her hips restlessly, and Conor slipped his hands between her loosened thighs and thumbed the hint of her clitoris through her neosuit.

He fastened his teeth on the rise of her nipples through the suit, and the rub of the fabric like a second skin over her wildly sensitive flesh jolted her.

"Conor, Conor." She clutched his clubbed black mane and fumbled with shaking fingers to untie the leather thong.

Then he stopped, lifting his head, his gaze dark and penetrating under his thick eyebrows. From the depths of his deep-set storm-colored eyes, his stare, like a scalpel, excised the shreds of her self-control.

Lightly, he brushed her lips, and weakened his hold on her. And though she felt the stiffness of his massive shaft, he only traced the curve of her cheek and brushed her hair from her face.

"Conor?"

"From now on, Dr. Kelsey, the guy you call animal will be tame as a pussycat." His grin should've reassured her, but underneath the gleam of white teeth and loaded promise, Eva sensed a darker purpose. With a final gentle kiss, he deposited her on the warm sand beside the feeble fire.

He knelt beside her, and raised his hands above his head, the enormous tanned hands that had forced her to his sexual will, confining and restraining her until he'd elicited an outpouring of desire.

Eva's hands trailed down the powerful muscles under the taut buckskin shirt. She fondled his swollen erection and watched the muscles tighten in his jaw.

"Tame? Is this tame?" Eva teased him, her voice throaty and low.

"From now on, you show *me* how much you want me."

"What kind of game is this, Conor?"

"You spell out everything you want me to do. Teach me, poor untrained bastard that I am. After all, what can you expect of — what was it you called me — bizarre? dysfunctional critter? A throwback to the times when men dragged screaming, but secretly delighted, women back to their caves by the hair." Conor folded his arms, biceps bulging.

"I said those things." Eva licked her lips and hooded her eyes, letting her fingers slide to his iron thigh. Defiantly, then, even as the urge to engulf his thick penis in her willing flesh tortured her, she added, "And I see no evidence to change my opinion."

"Exactly. I'm Laredo mud in your hands, Doc. Won't make a move without orders from the all-knowing Dr. Kelsey."

She reined in an outburst of temper. "You're giving me total control of your body and mind?"

"Only way I can give you evidence I'm — " he coughed into his fist, "civilized."

Her pouting labia lay slick against the crotch of her neosuit, and she squirmed as unobtrusively as possible, needing the relief Conor held just out of reach.

"You make no move, say no word unless I command it?"

Conor nodded and dropped his hands to his sides.

A collage of luscious possibilities raced through Eva's imagination. She sat back, crossed her legs Indian-style, and tested him.

"Stand up, Conor."

He rose without so much as a quick breath and looked down on her.

"Strip. That shirt. And boots, too." Eva put her hands behind her, bracing herself while Conor caught her stare and slowly, oh so slowly, gripped the hem of his tunic and inch by inch raised it.

Eva's mouth went dry. He exposed the black tip of hair that pointed to the huge treasure below his belt, and widened into a matted pyramid as he pulled the shirt higher. The pelt swirled around his flat male nipples, and Eva remembered her tongue on the pebbled surfaces.

Conor dropped the shirt and kicked off his moccasins. He waited, bronzed in the pale firelight, a perfectly chiseled archetype of virility.

"The pants," Eva got out after a long hesitation, determined to best him at his own game.

As if to call attention to what she should look at, he brushed his groin briefly, and Eva felt a tide of warmth creeping up from her collar and glanced away, only to be drawn back.

Without a grain of self-consciousness, Conor untied the leather strings at his waist and slid the trousers down, revealing the thick patch of black curls at the apex of his legs.

He paused for a few seconds with gritted teeth to stretch the pants over his jutting penis. Freed from the constraints of the skins, it sprang free.

With one hand, Conor brushed the angry swelling erection.

"I didn't order you to touch yourself," Eva snapped.

A quick duck of his head in agreement, and Conor shucked off the pants and threw them aside. He stood before her, heart-stoppingly male, every taut muscle, every articulation of bone and ripple of tendon and sinew releasing a flow of creaminess from her core.

"Fix the bed, I mean, the blankets," she stuttered and he bent to spread the feathery quilts, his strong toes digging into the soft dirt. At the sight of his testicles, furred and high and tight, Eva's fingers curled involuntarily.

When he turned to her, his great erection knocked against his belly and she shivered imagining his thickness pushing, stretching, thrusting into her dripping vagina.

She'd planned on directing Conor to undress her slowly, to kiss her breasts, to suck her clit until he was half-maddened with lust. She'd planned to make him wait before he emptied those heavy balls in her body.

His eyes, gleaming with sexual excitement, measured her fierce readiness. She met his gaze and tried to play the ice queen but it was a joke. She was shaking with need for him. Waiting be damned. Teasing be damned.

With one trembling finger she indicated the tap-catch on her collar. Huskily, she pleaded, "Open me, Conor."

He undid the lock and stepped back.

"No. Get it off me. Make me naked." She could barely hold back the urge to scream at him to hurry.

Conor stripped her of the suit as neatly and quickly as peeling a glove off her hand. And stopped.

"No," she moaned, reaching for him. "Carry me to the bed. Lie next to me." Conor swooped her up and held her high on his chest, keeping her well away from the throbbing she wanted to feel skimming her buttocks.

He laid her close to the wall and stretched out beside her. He laced his fingers as primly as a solo singer and stared at the ceiling, pretending to be oblivious to his mighty penis with its enlarged veins and head.

Eva bit her lip. Hot and aroused and furious with need, she wanted Conor to take charge. Though she'd initiated the game, Conor knew all the right moves to drive her insane. But she could still win. After all, how long could a man like Conor keep his hunger in check?

Should she play with him, the way she had in the estate's garage room? Flicking his sex with her tongue, teasing with her fingernails?

Or should she drive *him* mad with instructions to play with her body? And at the last minute, command him to stop? This wasn't, after all, really about lust and satisfaction. This was about revenge, the payback for Conor's smooth dismissal of her power and importance, his treating her like an inconsequential cog in the bureaucratic machine.

From somewhere in her mind, the eminent Dr. Eva Kelsey sneered and mocked. "Revenge? This assignment was all about pursuing a man you couldn't forget." Then she went silent.

"Lick me, Conor," Eva whispered. "All over." Half-closing her eyes, she raised her hands over her head and sifted the sand through her fingers.

She expected him to start with her face, but Conor rolled over and, bracing himself on the other side of her waist, he nuzzled into the delicate skin under her arm. His warm tongue, wide and wet, laved her repeatedly. She moved slightly, urging him without words to her swelling breasts, to suck her nipples.

But Conor by-passed her breasts and licked down her ribcage.

When he plied his tongue in the crevice between her thigh and torso, Eva moaned and fought to keep her hips still. He would soon bury that wonderful tongue deep inside, lap up the cream that had been flowing since her first sight of him, since he'd ridden out of the canyon. Dominant, devilish, all-controlling Conor.

He knew what she wanted, damn him, and was not giving it to her without a fight, without her croaking nonsensical commands. Squirming, she turned her mound into his face, feeling the accidental, heavenly grain of his beard stubble scratch her clit.

She shuddered, but Conor's knowing tongue skipped over the aching nub and slid down her leg.

"No, Conor. Eat me." She spread her legs, embarrassed to say the words, but too desperate to care. "Or fuck me. Or do anything you want. The game's over," she groaned. "I want you so bad I hurt."

"Don't you want me domesticated, tame?" he said. "Tell me, Eva. What's it going to be? The real me or the civilized, sanitized version?"

"You. Oh, you, Conor." She choked with craving for him, her breath shallow. "Please. The game's finished."

Smoky-eyed, Conor shifted, placed a heavily muscled forearm over her belly to hold her in place, and, with his rough fingers veed to keep her open, worked his mouth over her distended flesh. Finally, her jouncing against his mouth became so violent, he immobilized her with both hands on her hips in an iron grip.

Then he stopped, and whispered into her wet, heated core. He spoke soft, dark words, words she could guess, love words from the Cygnus system, from Mars, sounds from the rustling feathers of mating pteradrakes. He blew tiny gusts into her until she cried for the feel of his mouth again.

At her cry, Conor loosed her hips, and sucked on her clit while his hands massaged her breasts, and plucked her painfully erect nipples.

Just as she arched her back for relief from the impossible tension, Conor freed her, lifted her shaking legs over his shoulders and had barely penetrated when she shrieked and reached to claw at his shoulders.

"So wet and creamy, so ready for me, but so tight." He pulled out except for the tip and raised one eyebrow. "Too tight. Why? Tell me, Eva."

"No." She rocked her head back and forth on the feathery blankets. "Come in me. I won't scream."

"How far? This far?" He shoved in an inch and she tensed her vaginal muscles. "No more, my pretty lady, until you answer."

She touched his face, closed her eyes and turned her head to the wall. "Conor," she breathed raggedly. "There've been no other men since that night."

Then she realized she'd said the perfect words. Across his face she saw flickers of wonder and tenderness and delight. His immense penis swelled even larger, and he pushed its stiffness in slowly.

"I don't want to hurt you, lover," he said, his voice rough with shock and happiness and restraint.

"If that's the only way to have you, hurt me," she whispered, and suddenly she surged upward and engulfed all of him. Her whisper built into a long, painful scream that rang in the cave. But she would not let him withdraw.

After endless moments of Conor between her thighs, suckling her breasts, and kissing her deeply, he began to test her with slow, measured thrusts. Eva felt herself adjust to his massiveness, his fullness stretching her body's limits, and she lifted her hips to meet his hard pelvis in a magic, ancient rhythm.

Chapter 5

Eva's trembling gradually ceased, and she clung to Conor, imprinting tender kisses on his flesh, tasting the beads of sweat.

"I'm too heavy," Conor whispered, and loosed her arms from around his neck. He kissed the tip of her nose and grinned. "Pay attention now. When we get to town, we have to set some limits, Doc, or we'll both be dead, exhausted." He bent and lazily licked her nipples. He tried for a light tone, but he missed and hoped she'd see his gaze was serious and penetrating.

"Limits?" Eva stretched like a cat beneath him and ran her fingernails through his hair. "What limits do you mean, lover? One position fits all?" She laughed, a sleepy, teasing laugh, but her eyes clouded as if she knew what he was asking.

He braced himself on his forearms, and let his thumbs play where her breasts softly grew from her ribs. "If you ever tell anybody I said this, I'll swear on my cayuses's head that you're a liar." Conor drew a deep breath. "Eva, you're the only woman I've ever had who sucks the stamina, that animal energy out of me. You even block my sixth sense, my female-sensor, and who needs other women, darling, when I've got you?"

"Why, Conor, I do think that's a compliment." She bit his lower lip, and his guts boiled in a spasm of need. He clenched his jaw. Without withdrawing, he got hard again.

"So we need limits. Limits as in, how often we see each other like this." He moved in her, and elicited a moan. "Answer me, Doc. What's it going to be? Maybe three nights a week? And the weekends?"

Eva massaged his shoulders, and palmed his chest. Her voice was a whisper and all the lightness had vanished. "Let me sit up, Conor. I can't think about anything when you're deep in me, except — "

She slid away from under him, pulling him from the dripping velvet of her sheath, and he gritted his teeth against the pain in his groin. Eva tossed back her mane of wheaten hair, while a very small smile played on her lips. "If I did sexual calisthenics like these five days a week, Conor, I'd be as limp as a Venusian gel-eel, and twice as useless."

"That's how I like you, woman. Limp and wet," he growled, "but only afterward when we've dowsed all our fire." He lay on his back, brawny arms and torso glistening in the dimness, his hands stacked behind his head.

Eva felt for her suit, conscious of his hot inspection, conscious of the picture she made, her breasts, full and ripe, weighed by gravity, within Conor's reach, aching for his touch and his mouth.

But he was right, and she blushed with shame that she, a professional, had been forced to think of her obligations by a colonist.

She slipped into the suit and collared up, locking the tab. Swiftly and efficiently, she coiled her hair, fished a stay-pin from her suit, and was once more, on the surface at least, the respectable cold fish, Dr. Eva Kelsey, Colonial Selection Specialist, Investigator.

She cocked her head and listened to a diminishing roar. "Has the storm blown over?"

Conor rose and dressed quickly. "You've got the ears for this place." He tied his hair in its leather thong. "Like I said before, Doc, you were born for Laredo. Should've tested and settled here yourself."

At the cavern door, Sweetheart grumbled and shifted, lowered her rhubarb-eared snaky head and peered in with a squeal of delight. In the brilliant shafts of light allowed into the dark by the cayuse's movement, Eva folded blankets while Conor kicked the rantoon sticks apart.

"Quit dodging the question, Doc. How many nights?" Hands on hips, Conor stood with his legs apart, planted like a stone monument, with no intention of going anywhere until she answered.

Eva had a flash of herself with Conor constantly on her mind. The renowned Dr. Kelsey, approaching every problem, every evaluation, every test, with the silky false perceptions of the truly satisfied woman. She could almost hear the rushed interviews, larded with omissions because all she'd want was the damned things to be over, for Conor to bed her, recklessly, with total mastery, reducing her to compliant sexual slavery. Like all the women he'd seduced and abandoned, made mindless and wanting.

How long before the Psych Board found out? And they always did. She could see the five old gentlemen, Freudian-trained and Tatroset-depth sharpened, impassively reviewing her files. The quintet shaking their venerable heads, sighing as they added another note, another accusation of personal involvement.

She'd shown some spunk, that time on the estate, when she'd walked out on him to repay him for humiliating her at her office, his easy manipulating of her father to bypass Eva's judgement. But the truth was simpler than revenge. She had been terrified of wanting Conor. Loving Conor.

And now, he'd reduced her to an emotional, quivering jelly.

Was this Conor turning the tables, laughing at her under the guise of sincerity, pretending to be on the verge of declaring love? Conor getting even? Conor jeopardizing her standing?

The down blankets held protectively over her breasts, Eva said, "We hardly know each other. I really am at quite a loss to explain any of this." She nodded toward the depressions in the sand next to the wall where they'd lain, where he'd brought her to one stunning climax after another.

"Quite a loss, you say?" Conor's grin was devoid of amusement. "You're so full of doubletalk, your suit must be straining at the molecular level." His laugh chilled her. "The damn thing should explode and leave you naked."

"Ah, there it is, what I was waiting for, the old Conor, the beast so near and dear to all our hearts." She snapped out her words like the crack of a whip. "I will not be seeing you three nights per week, or the weekends, or anytime during my visit. I am not here for your pleasure, but to improve my file, do my job."

Conor grabbed the saddleback of utensils. "Nothing surprises me about you,

Doc. What surprises me is that, after all my hunting experience, I let you ambush me twice."

"What are you talking about?" Eva's stomach somersaulted, as if the planet spun and Conor had floated out of range.

"The garage. You let me know I was scum when you dressed and ran home." He strode toward the opening, and turned back. "And today you put me in my place again."

Flustered and furious, Eva stamped after him and shouted, "You're delusional with obvious tinges of paranoia. How dare you equate my professional concerns with your bizarre notions that somehow I'm wreaking revenge on you?"

"Yup, that's me. Crazy Conor. I'm a sick bastard. But don't offer me free treatments, good doctor. Your methods only make things worse." He threw down the pack, snatched the blankets from her and lifted her onto the ladder as impersonally as he'd hoist an elderly man.

"Get aboard. Sit still, and for God's sake, keep one of those blankets between you and me. I've had plenty of women — "

"Hundreds!" Eva shrieked. "Thousands!"

"— but I never had one who got off rubbing herself on my butt while calling *me* an animal."

When he climbed up and stowed the pack, Eva shrank away and obediently stuffed the blanket between them, the fence, the barricade, the wall to keep them apart. "Happy now, Conor?" she said evenly.

He didn't bother to answer, just clucked to Sweetheart, whistled for Hondo, and guided them across the flatlands to the lake.

⁂

"Laredo City. Population 400," the weathered sign proclaimed. The sun was casting angular shadows when they rode into the settlement by the lake. Shards of light, broken by a brisk breeze, danced on the water. Eva licked her lips. The sight and cool smell of the blue-green water made her even more thirsty.

Twice Conor had offered her his canteen, and she'd refused. *Stupid*, she chided herself. *Stupid to ride for hours craving a drink just for the satisfaction of saying no to him.* But she brushed aside her self-accusations, and studied the efforts of the colonists.

Fastform buildings imitated the raw structures of a western ghost town and lined the main street. On boardwalks, men in blue trousers and cowboy hats mingled with women wearing sunbonnets and calico dresses. Was that the right word, calico?

Where were the efficient neosuits with their bright colors and occupational designations?

Almost as if reading her mind, Conor spoke. "These clothes work best in the climate. The women patterned one of the fabricators, and pretty soon they had us all gussied up. Gussied up," he repeated, "means dressed nicely."

"Thanks. I've been reading a dictionary of western old-speak." Eva could've kicked herself. Obviously, Conor was making gestures, almost apologizing for his attitude, and she'd rebuffed him. A few miles before town, she'd let the blanket slide down, then draped it across her shoulders like a cloak in the cooling air.

Conor had seemed not to notice the press of her breasts. His posture, his breathing, his position in the saddle, nothing changed. She smiled and scanned the clumps of welcoming folk and couples at the roadside, but the ones who stood out, frantically waving, were women. And the bonneted ladies were not wasting their waves on her.

How many of them had he taken? How many had been drawn into his enveloping, musky heat? How many had eagerly spread their thighs, opened themselves to his ravages?

When Conor raised one hand over his head, the crowd cheered. These people knew the real Conor, the one who led and hunted, and protected, the one she'd penalized in Metro City with her biases. She'd made a mistake. Untamed, he mirrored the rawness of Laredo. The perfect world for him and his power and his arrogance.

Eva gave a polite wave or two, quickly returning her free hand to Conor's waist. Nodding at a cluster of older men in quaint suits, she wondered how many of them would be cheering Conor astride his cayuse if they knew Conor had also been astride their wives.

At the tug of Conor's reins, Sweetheart halted. A gang of little boys, grubby from play, shouted Conor's name and rushed to greet him. He waved, swung out of the saddle, and urged Eva to climb down the ladder.

Men unloaded Hondo, and stacked Eva's cases next to the general store. But no one came forward to help with Sweetheart who froze, rigid, her immense ears flattened against her neck.

"Dr. Kelsey, welcome to Laredo." The mayor doffed his hat, and bent to kiss her hand, the remnant of sunlight splashing on his bald head. He jammed his hat on, and took her arm. "I'm Mayor Tim Ballard, and this here is Noah Rain, our young sheriff."

"Pleasure, ma'am." Noah touched the brim of his hat, tilted rakishly on blond curls. His file raced past in her memory. Only twenty-three, killer good looks, great body. If anyone on Laredo could give Conor a run for his money, it was the young sheriff.

And, if she had appraised him, he was returning the favor. His bright blue eyes took her in from teeth to toenails. No secret, he liked what he saw.

Take that, Mr. Conor, she gloated.

But a shrill squeal ended her flirtation, and sent her into Noah's arms. When she jerked around, Conor, head high, hadn't paid the slightest bit of attention to the sheriff and herself measuring each other for a jump in the sack. Instead, he'd climbed aloft, signalled, and he and Sweetheart had begun trudging down the middle of Main Street.

"Conor and that damned critter," the mayor apologized.

"I'd think the men would have helped him with her," Eva said.

Around her the group chuckled. "Ah, she don't take kindly to anybody touching her but Conor," the sheriff informed her.

"What's more, she don't take kindly to anybody touching *Conor* but herself."

"Fair warning, hey?" The mayor offered his arm. They deposited her work cases in the office which he shared with the sheriff, and he escorted her to Mrs. Donovan's boarding house.

The plump and apple-cheeked Mrs. Donovan must've drawn herself off a compuvid landlady of 1950's horse operas. She made a wonderful fuss over Eva and got her settled in a room at the front of the house. The settlers had decorated the walls with a rose-bouquet paper, and the theme was repeated in a white hob-nailed vase of newly-cut cabbage roses.

"Now, after your shower, missy, put on these. I ran the fabricator myself. Gingham." Proudly, she displayed a blue print dress and a bonnet hanging on the back of the door. "Here's your little leather slippers." She lowered her voice. "Now we don't wear underclothes here, my dear. Too hot."

"This is extraordinarily kind, Mrs. Donovan, but for professional reasons, my suit — "

"Oh." The landlady's face fell, she put her hand in her apron pocket, and suddenly smiled. "Well, landsakes! How foolish of me. 'Course you must wear your neosuit. Now, you freshen up and come down for dinner." She bustled down the stairs, leaving Eva to contemplate the dress and her silly feelings of guilt at hurting the kindly woman's feelings.

Eva sat on the thick mattress and stared at the toes of her suit. Mrs. Donovan must've known that the suit had a cleansing mode, and that Eva really didn't need a shower. Watching her eyes grow smoky in the shadowy mirror atop the dressing table, she stroked the warmth between her legs.

On the ride in with Conor, she'd tabbed in the hygiene program, with special limits. The suit, per instructions, sanitized her, but had avoided her most private place. On the chenille bedspread, Eva squirmed, and her delicate woman parts, swollen and slippery, slid wetly against each other, closing the ripe crease Conor had fingered and pierced and licked.

Eva shuddered in a small orgasm, unable to fight off the memories of Conor, his dark head moving between her legs, his mouth searing her, tasting her, thrusting his tongue deep, nibbling and sucking her clit until she'd screamed and tore at his hair in her wildness.

"Stop this. Right now. Stop this," she hissed at her image.

Eva skinned off the suit and popped into the bathroom. Under the warm spray, she scrubbed off all evidence of Conor's musky, male scent, Conor's savage love-making. She closed her eyes and her traitorous body remembered his teeth grazing her hard nipples, her buttocks, the sensitive skin on her throat.

Her eyes flew open. Her throat. Eva leaped from the shower and lifted her chin. Huge love-bites, Conor's brands, stood out like purple blooms in a kind of sex-necklace.

Eva panted with fury. Who had seen the damned things? The mayor, she'd bet, and that sharp-eyed young sheriff. Eva clapped her hands to her face, and felt the blood beating in her cheeks.

And, of course, dear Mrs. Donovan must've got a good look.

Wrapping herself in the fluffy towel, Eva dried herself. She slid into the neosuit. But the mirror showed her that the collar was too low, and the bruised skin flashed like ion-signs above the whiteness of her uniform.

Close to tears of rage, she tore it off, flung it on the rag rug, and pulled the gingham dress from its hanger. But even the high neck's sweet frilly finish wasn't enough. Eva had to leave her hair down, too soft and girlish, trailing over her ears, and down her breasts. Mrs. Donovan had left her no petticoat, no underwear, just the long dress whose tiny blue bows winked down the bodice. For all the length of the skirt, Eva felt more naked than she'd ever felt in her life.

Who could take her seriously during her investigations, decked out, "gussied up" like some pioneer adolescent advertising for a husband?

"Damn Conor to hell for this." Remembering Austin's cry of disbelief about a man who changed the original self into a new creature, Eva snarled into the mirror. "I let him change *me* because I wanted him. I let him do this. I hate myself." She dashed tears from her eyes, and tried to decend the stairs with the dignity befitting her official status.

In the foyer, she tugged at her skirt, arranged the cascade of hair over the fitted bodice, and arranged a smile on her face. As she entered the formal dining room, she parted her lips to greet the diners, but her eyes widened, her mouth stayed open, and the greetings locked in her throat.

Framed before the filmy batiste curtains at the enormous, lace-covered table sat Conor, as out of place as a cougar in a rabbit hutch.

Chapter 6

Conor rose, dwarfing the two normal-sized men and a middle-aged woman. His eyes glittered, reminding Eva of their shared sensual secrets, and the shock of seeing him was so acute, Eva felt the blood drain from her face, then return in a flood of heat and embarrassment.

Mrs. Donovan rushed in from the kitchen, cooed welcoming cries and introductions, and seated Eva directly across from Conor. Eva bit the inside of her mouth, draped the nakin on her lap, and addressed chunks of squash in a steamy broth.

At first, she was grateful to whatever fates had plunked her on the opposite side of the table from Conor. Next to a balding chemist who hardly seemed to generate enough thermal units to warm himself, she smugly congratulated herself at avoiding Conor's fire.

But as Mrs. Donovan cleared the soup plates, Eva felt something brushing her ankle, something encased in soft buckskin moccasins. She glanced up at Conor. With a corner of his napkin he was dabbing those demanding lips that had forced screams of ecstasy from her throat.

He wore a perfectly straight face, features that were a model, an example of self-control, even under torture, all except for his eyes taking in her nipples, erect, frictionized by the sturdy cotton.

By the time Mrs. Donovan arrived with the platter of roast gilk, Conor was well-satisfied that Eva could not face him without the picture of their terrific fuck fueling the flames. Leisurely he moved his foot higher, intruding under the protection of her dress.

Eva glared at him, and tried to back away, but where was there to go? What could she do? Excuse herself and run from the table? He knew it wouldn't happen. She'd do it verbally. That was her style.

"What a curious name. Gilk. Whatever does it mean?" Eva poked a thick slice swimming in the gravy on her plate.

"Why it's a meat creature from the forest, Dr. Kelsey," the chemist explained. "Gilk. That's the cry it makes as it expires. Or so we townfolk are told."

"And you don't believe that story? A wise skepticism, if you've never actually killed one yourself." Eva smiled, and took a bite. "Delicious. My kudos to the hunter and the cook. I know the cook. Do you trust the hunter?" Laughter around the table punctuated her question.

Conor used the distraction to slide his foot back and forth over her knee. He put food in his mouth. It was tasteless, and he was aware that the fever of wanting

Eva had shut down anything extraneous to his goal of having her again. It was like being on the hunt, when he was numb to heat, insect stings, and he zeroed in on the prey.

His erection stirred, and he shifted. He was in pain, but not enough to abandon tormenting himself, touching her with his toes through the thin buckskin. God, he wanted to clear the table with one sweep of his arm, throw that damned dress over her breasts, and pump till she begged for mercy.

"Everybody trusts Conor. This guy hunts and stocks the caves. That was his idea, stocking the caves in case somebody got caught in a storm." The chemist buttered a scoop of potato-like starch. "He rides the perimeter every day."

"And don't forget catching the wild cayuses," Mrs. Donovan added. "And all his exploring. My, my. Did you see how even the little boys admire him?"

"Oh, yes. He's quite remarkable, a regular pillar of the community. And a real catch." Eva wore a small proud smile.

Mrs. Donovan snorted. "He says he's got no time for women."

Conor forced his foot between Eva's closed thighs, and caressed the soft skin with gentle urgency. He watched for any sign of desire on her face, but like a marble statue he'd once seen titled "Purity Assaulted," Eva ignored him and pretended to be taking part in the dull conversations.

She coughed genteely, her napkin to her mouth, her gaze burning him over the white hem. She clamped her thighs on his foot, but it was too late. Conor was on target, the tip of his moccasin wet with her juice, rubbing her nakedness, moving in slow circles on her mons, in the downy triangle, on the stiffening nub that loved his attention though Eva's manner denied it. Her body made a liar out of her.

She fidgeted, chatting up the chemist, playing with her silverware. She sipped water, inched the salt cellar away from the pepper mill, asked for the vegetables to be passed, and surreptitiously read her time band. The boarders discussed the weekend.

And Eva chimed in, as if she cared. "What a challenge, trying to re-calibrate my circadian rhythm to a ten-day week."

"You have been sadly misinformed," the chemist said. "We have only five days in a week."

"But Conor, Conor said — " she tried to go on, but stuttered to a halt and fixed her eyes at a point just over his left shoulder.

Now she realized his wanting her three days plus the weekend meant wanting her *all* the time. The way he wanted her now, to come in polite company with only his hidden manipulation.

Her nipples looked immense, and, as he imagined rolling them in his mouth like sweet, hard candies, Conor's penis thickened, and he hovered on the brink of explosion just by looking at her, feeling her. Damn, that was a kid weakness he'd put behind him when he was fifteen.

Eva's breathing quickened, and she dropped her napkin on her plate. "A lovely dinner. And so nice to meet everyone." Her eyes were glazed, unfocussed, and her breathing rapid and shallow.

Come, Eva. Come. Imagine my tongue lapping all that hot pink flesh while you let go. Imagine my cock stretching you. Come for me, baby. Conor gave silent commands and smilingly agreed to a statement he hadn't heard from the maiden lady.

"Nonsense, Doctor. You shall have some perciple pie," Mrs. Donovan insisted. From the sideboard, she transferred a gigantic ceramic pastry dish, and placed a wedge of flaky crust bursting with syrupy yellow fruit on a dessert plate. "It's our favorite, peachy and crisp. Now you sit still and take as much as you want."

Conor licked his dry lips. "That's right, Dr. Kelsey. Sit still and take as much as you want."

Eva turned crimson, and despite herself, opened fully and rotated her pelvis. Conor worked with more speed, finally centering on her clit and teasing mercilessly.

Suddenly, her fork clattered on her plate, and she gasped, eyes tightly shut. She gripped the table edge, white-knuckled, and froze in a spasm. "Ooh, ooh, my God." She shuddered and slumped forward.

"Lord, she's had some sort of allergic fit," cried Mrs. Donovan. "It was the pie! I'll never forgive myself."

Before the boarders could move, Conor strode around the table, lifted Eva, and cradled her in his arms. "Finish your supper. I'll carry her to her room."

Mrs. Donovan rushed before them, and had a damp cloth waiting for Eva's brow. "Yes, put her atop the coverlet, Conor."

"Do you think I should call the medic?"

"No medic," Eva whispered. "Just a little rest. Go back to your guests. I'm so sorry to have been a bother."

"I shall not leave you here alone," Mrs. Donovan said firmly.

"I'll stay. You should be with the roomers." Conor's voice brooked no argument, and he sat beside Eva, turning the washcloth to its cooler side.

"Dear, dear. It never rains but it pours. Look here. You've spilled something on your moccasin, Conor."

"Some juice," he said. "I'll fix it later."

As soon as the sound of Mrs. Donovan's footsteps ended in the foyer, Eva opened her eyes. Conor was practically on top of her, and her response to him left her weak, out of control. Again.

The submerged Dr. Eva Kelsey rode to the rescue, protected Eva's vulnerability, barricaded her from the urge to throw herself into his arms. She jerked the cloth from his hand and struck him across the face. Dr. Kelsey put words in her mouth.

"If you knew how much I detest your vulgarity, you would wither and dry up," Eva ground out between her teeth.

Conor cupped her mons through the gingham skirt. "No fear of that happening down here," he said, his voice low and husky. "You're like an oasis, all nectar and cream, and I'm dying to drink. But tonight I'll have to settle for this. Making love in your office, in the cave, seems like a hundred years ago. Seems you're burned into me. Eva, don't you feel it, too? I'm complete for the first time in my life."

He squeezed her rhythmically. Eva jolted into a series of aftershocks, staring into his eyes, clutching his wrist. Conor stayed his hand till the last tiny crisis passed. When he rose, his fingers were as wet as her dress.

He ran his tongue over them, savoring her essence. "Second-hand. But better than nothing, my beautiful Dr. Eva."

"Enjoy the moment because after tonight, that's what you'll get. Nothing." Her eyes were bright with self-anger and shame.

"Nothing? Not even when I've saved this for you for two years?" He captured her hand and pressed it to the bulge pulsing and struggling to escape his breeches.

"There's been no one. Damn it, woman, you know it. I love you, Eva."

Eva wrenched away. Her thoughts whirled in a stupid jumble, all mixed up, the attraction to his domineering maleness, her compulsion to touch him, to tremble at his hungry look, to melt in surrender. The now and needy high tides of lust inspired by Conor's nearness had colored her habits of careful deduction and analysis. Worse, the most heinous Psych Board sin, involvement.

She stifled a moan and tried to sharpen her voice. "I have professional responsibilities, Conor, that take precedence over personal feelings. Besides, I don't intend to join your list of discarded women. I can't see you again."

"But you will." He straightened her skirt, brushed his mouth on hers, and headed for the stairs.

꧁ৡ৻(ꗞ)৴ৡ꧂

The next morning, the Mayor waved her into his office. It smelled of dust and disuse, and she made a mental note to chart that under the column entitled "Community Energy." Dust motes floated in beams creeping through the smeared windows. The lone jail cell was empty.

Swelling with pride, Ballard pointed at his desk. "The Sheriff and me, we put your cases here. And allow me to add, ma'am, you're sure fetchin' in that sundress and bonnet. Same blue as your eyes." He drew a heart in the dust on a ledger.

"So, Dr. Kelsey, not askin' you to commit yourself to anything, whaddya think? A general impression of our little village?"

Eva perched on the edge of the chair. "On the basis of limited observation, Mayor, I've never seen happier citizens. All smiles, grins, hugs and kisses. Is it in the air?"

"So some say, so some say." Their chuckles blended.

Eva gathered scattered pencils to clear a workspace. "I'm all set, and thanks for your efforts, Mayor."

"Now don't get too involved in paperwork today, Doc. You got months, and, after all, you better know the landscape, the plants and critters. So I made arrangements for you to get the grand tour."

"The grand tour? Oh, I'll do that later," she said hastily. "I really must begin interviews." Suddenly, the windows rattled, and the floor quaked under Eva's feet.

"All the time in the world," he insisted, ignoring the earth-shattering thumps. "Yup, I asked Noah to take you round — "

"Ah, the Sheriff." Eva breathed a sigh of relief.

"— but that young scamp, he's caught up today. So I asked — by gum, speak of the devil. Here's your guide, pullin' up to the old hitchin' post this minute."

Eva leaped up. Through the dirty glass, Sweetheart's yellow eye discovered her. The cayuse opened her fearful mouth and uttered a screech. She vented her bad humor by darting a bite at a second cayuse standing quietly in the middle of the street.

And then Conor performed the empty ritual of draping the monster's reins over the log. What a joke. Nothing could hold back that creature if she wanted to stampede.

"I know it's important for your records to check the lay of the land, so to speak. I'll leave you in Conor's capable hands for now. Me and the Missus, we got some..., well, let's call 'em chores." He winked and slammed the door behind him.

Eva frowned. He couldn't have possibly meant what the wink implied, could he? Of course not. A man of his age and his position would have strong notions of propriety, the rigorous requirements of his status. And damn his stupid plans. She reseated herself and punched a few file buttons.

Tight-lipped, she bent to her bio-com, wearing an expression of professional interest. True, it was necessary to visit the outlying environs, but there was no way she'd get dragged out of this office by Conor.

※※(◯◯)※※

"That's better, Doc. Sidesaddle good? Just the thing for ladies who don't wear britches." Conor grinned. "Now don't get testy and saw at the reins."

"What I'd like to saw is your skull from your neck," she said. She labored overtime to steel herself against his charm. "Did you or did you not hear me say we couldn't see each other anymore?" Summoning all her self-control, she waved at the Sheriff lounging across the street with his gaggle of girls.

Conor completely ignored her reminder and instead nodded at the cayuse's wiggling ears. "I notice Hercules likes you. And Sweetheart approves." The male ducked his neck, crooned, and bathed Eva in a bashful stare. He had very long eyelashes. "Poor guy, he can't help himself."

"Then he's ridiculous," Eva said, secretly pleased at her conquest. Conor wasn't the only one with a devoted beast. She scratched Herc's neck, and he rumbled a thank-you. The cayuses lumbered down a wide path where the town met the sparse woods. Eva inhaled the freshest, most fragrant air she'd ever tasted, air permeated with the faint scent of cinnamon and lavender.

Some of the trees twisted and displayed a peculiar variety of barks, and one, a brilliant green from root to branch stunned her with deep-lobed purple flowers. On its trunk a dead fox-like creature hung as if he'd been glued.

"Conor, what's that?" Eva leaned forward in the saddle and pointed.

"Gripper tree," he said. "Anything that strolls too close gets invited to stay... permanently." He exhaled. "No matter how beautiful a planet or a person, there's always a dark side. But who'd know better than you?"

Eva struggled for composure. Her trips into the wild, anywhere, were rare. Later she'd confide in Conor that this was only her second off-Earth colonization report. "Of course, of course," she said abruptly, and, despite the aura of security he exuded, she dug for a question to conceal her nervousness. "But it's so horrible. Have these trees any practical value to the colony other than snaring small animals?"

Conor raised one knee and planted his foot on the saddle as casually as if he sat in his living room. "I don't want to tell tales out of school, Doc, knowing how you're collecting data about us and all. Some couples like to take walks out here, use the gripper trees for fun and games. Shameful, hey?"

Swallowing a laugh, Eva clucked at Hercules and, over her shoulder yelled, "Is there anything, absolutely anything that doesn't remind you of sex?"

"Nothing, when I'm with you," he shouted, brimming with sheer wickedness. "And when I catch up with you..." He roared, his bigger-than-life, bold laugh.

But Hercules poured it on, skirting the dense forest and carrying her out into a meadow of blue-green grasses where orange and yellow birds flitted. The flatlands stretched out in a forever vista, out to the horizon. A tug at the reins, and the cayuse stopped and munched on a clump of grass.

Eva strained to listen. No voices, no thrum of machinery, no mechanical attention from robots or talking cars. A twitter from a flock of the tiny birds, the sweet whisper of a soft, scented breeze enveloped her. The sound of joy.

From deep inside, Dr. Eva Kelsey imperiously delivered curt jabs of iron self-control, interview schedules, and a wealth of complicated social diagrams, a planetary caseload of reports.

But the soothing aromas, the hypnotic undulations of the grassy fields, stilled Eva.

Astride an ugly creature whose tonnage she couldn't guess, on the outskirts of a small town sprung from myths three hundred years old, all the shields and restraints began to crack, and a great peace descended on her.

Conor rode up and signalled with a jerk of his head. "We'll ride around the lake, if you like," he said, his deep-timbered voice disconcertingly muted.

This is a first. Conor asking instead of telling. But his gentleness disarmed her. She tapped her skills as a psychologist to search for causation. Maybe the combination of the liquid air and fragrances and Conor's deference to her wishes had melted the rest of her shell. And, shockingly, forbidden illogical thoughts whirled through her brain.

Who gave a damn about her proper behavior? Who cared? Did she care? No. Not any more.

"Thank you, Conor. That would be lovely." Her tone surprised her, feminine, compliant. From the depths of her soul, the crisp Dr. Eva Kelsey gave a despairing shriek and vanished. And suddenly the safe world of repressing her desires, subjecting her ideas to relentless analysis and criticism seemed very far away. The Psych Board could fill her file with condemnatory notes, if only her man could fill her emptiness.

Conor's smile was inscrutable. In the lead, Sweetheart found a wide trail at the edge of the woods, and Hercules hurried to walk beside her.

"So beautiful, so peaceful, so… so kind." Eva almost sang the words. "I love this place. And I feel wonderful." Overflowing with exuberance, she flung her hands over her head. "Oh, Conor, all of you, free of the crowds, the noise, are incredibly lucky. And you're just being yourselves."

"You could be lucky, too. Stay here with us, Eva." Conor reined Sweetheart closer, and his eagerness infected her. "Do your report. It should be easy now that you've got a feel for Laredo. What have you got to go back to?"

Eva felt the pull of her icy professionalism, and for a moment, all her obligations and training battled the temptation of genuine freedom. Her hand flew to cover her mouth. "I couldn't. I have — "

"Another man?"

"Oh, Conor." His face darkened when she laughed. "Since the first time I saw you, there's been no room in my life, in my bed for anyone but you. I've analyzed the situation, and decided on a course of action."

"And?"

"And there's simply nothing to do but this." Eva lifted the gingham skirt. The capricious wind played, and she gave herself to the sensation of coolness. She riveted her gaze on Conor while she slid a finger into her mouth and sucked.

Conor's breathing grew ragged, and when she dipped her other hand into her nest of curls, he swung out of the saddle, and climbed halfway down the rope ladder. Then, wild with haste, he pushed off and plummeted to the ground.

"Come to me, lover," Eva breathed.

"Come to *me*," Conor countered and stretched his arms toward her.

Without a second's hesitation, she leaped, her skirt billowing around her like a crazy parachute, and fell into his embrace.

Chapter 7

The two moons, pale and lopsided, had risen, and the townsfolk had gone to bed, but Eva sat at the mayor's desk, idly twisting her hair.

A month, twenty days, the happiest in her life, had flowed by, one into the other like the movements of a graceful ballet, seamless and rich. The bio-com had recorded all the interviews, and she'd replayed them endlessly, struck by the curious lack of edge in her questioning, amazed at laughter she'd shared with her subjects. The good-natured, friendly colonists.

Happy. That was this place's secret. They were all happy.

She was happy. Obscenely happy. She, stiffly correct Dr. Eva Kelsey, Colonial Selection Specialist and Investigator, deliciously liberated and intensely sexualized, hungry for Conor. Always ready for Conor.

Was there something wrong with this picture? She sighed, and pushed her fingers through her hair, unbound, untethered, undisciplined. Like herself. She examined her hands. Her nails had resumed their natural pinkness. Mauve seemed cruelly artificial, out of place on Laredo.

Her lips had changed, she knew, had grown fuller, poutier, riper, suffused with her blood's redness instead of gloss. Her very flesh and skin shone with vitality and, there it was again, a kind of sensual readiness.

"Ready?" Conor had whispered not two hours earlier, buried to the hilt in her, teasing, withdrawing until her legs vised his waist, and she shook with lust. "Ready to come?" he'd asked, the teasing tone fading into a low growl revealing his own violent hunger, his need.

But she had been on fire, ablaze, and her silent answer had been the sudden contraction that grasped him tightly and repeated, narrowing her passage in a chain of palpitations.

And she didn't care who heard her cries of passion as intellect and reason abandoned her, and Conor spurted his seed, and bruised her lips with his kisses and filled the emptiness of Eva's heart with love.

"Conor," she announced to the deserted office. Her voice rang with determination and decisions forged. "Do you hear me, gentlemen of the guild? Write the note and write me off." Her anxiety, her eagerness to rise in the Federation of professionals dissolved. Thousands of light years from Earth, she'd have no opportunity to practice colony selection. But she could return to her first love, counseling. And she could stay.

"It begins and ends with Conor. I want him. I want him enough to stay."

Her simple declaration melted the last shards of Dr. Kelsey's icy restraint, and

Eva sprang to her feet and spun, dancing the joy that bubbled in her laugh, in her heart, and finally she was fully alive.

❦⟨✠⟩❦

"I have to what?" Eva squeaked. She let Mrs. Donovan's screen door slam, and stamped out onto the front walk. The noon sun beat down, she was sweating, and her three hours of sleep had left blue circles under her eyes and the grit of Earthside temper in her craw. And the girls lingering beside the garden gate to flirt with the handsome sheriff added nothing to her thorny disposition.

"Sorry, ma'am." Noah tilted his Stetson and dangled a straw between his lips. "That's what Mayor Ballard said, to come fetch you for a fitness evaluation by the town council."

"This is an outrage," Eva sniffed. "*I* am the person who qualifies candidates for colonization teams. *I* have the training and expertise to select skilled, compatible individuals. I am professionally objective enough to verify my competence and emotional stability."

"You sure can talk, once you set your mind to it," Noah remarked admiringly. "Think you could teach me to talk like that? We'd best stroll right quick, ma'am. The Council don't like to work too long. And that Conor, he purely hates squatting indoors."

"Conor? What has Conor to do with this? Some kind of character witness?" Ah, blessed relief. They all adored Conor. Her problems were solved. Her beloved Conor would make it right.

"Oh, no, ma'am. Conor, he's the one suggested it. Says you ought to get a taste of your own whip." He whistled "Buffalo Gals," and lengthened his strides.

Eva's throat hurt from quelling a shriek. She pressed her hands to her diaphragm and breathed deeply. "Well, well. Conor. Imagine that. What a clever fellow, supposedly on a hunting and exploring trip, and still finding time to attend a hearing. Sheriff, what are we waiting for?"

Eva practically ran down Main Street, her skirt flapping behind her like a pangabark's sails. Swallowing her chagrin, she paused long enough to tuck her hair behind her ears, realized the sweet bruises of Conor's teeth on her throat would be on display, and yanked her hair forward again.

She straightened her shoulders and entered the meeting house, the perfect lady. It was hot, and a rivulet of perspiration slid down her side.

At two long tables sat the mayor and his five councilmen. She recognized them all, remembered grilling three and marking their applications questionable.

She had sweated them during their qualifying interviews, and her stomach churned with anxiety.

They removed their hats and mopped their brows. On a stand in the corner, a rotating fan treated them to occasional blasts of air.

Fancying herself a modern Joan of Arc at the Inquisition, she curtsied and asked humbly, "Gentlemen, how may I help you?"

"Good-day, Dr. Kelsey. I s'pose you wonder what the heck we're about, eh?" The mayor's chuckle dwindled under Eva's frown.

"Not at all. I understand perfectly." She turned a venemous gaze on Conor, decked out in his hunting clothes, who straddled a chair in the first row. Despite major efforts at self-control, just the sight of him, the thick biceps that flexed when he positioned her, the enormous hands that stroked her breasts and her aching wet folds, opened floodgates of desire, and dew slicked her sex.

"Seems like you're the applicant here, asking to stay on Laredo. Is that the gist of it?"

Eva nodded, torn by conflicting emotions, and not trusting herself to speak.

"Shucks, ma'am. We know a bit about you, your hifalutin titles and all, and that's right as perciple pie. But, well, the main thing is… the main thing is… damn, what is the main thing, Conor?"

Conor shifted and hung one meaty arm over the chairback as if he roasted professionals every day. He grinned, evilly. "The main thing, Dr. Kelsey, is your lack of sexual experience."

"My lack of — ?"

"The folks of Laredo have had two years to shed the old repressions, to know themselves, and enjoy their bodies. We've got our priorities straight. What've you been doing for the last two years?"

The council members leaned forward, all ears and moustaches.

"Answer the question, missy."

Her mouth went dry, and she blinked with bafflement. It was a simple question. She could answer it.

"I worked, worked hard, for the welfare of… of off-world teams," she stumbled over her thoughts. "I exercised. I read." And her mind went momentarily blank. "Oh, I was active in Federation professional societies."

One councilman scribbled on a pad. Another contemplated the ceiling.

"What about sex?" Conor demanded.

"I was really very busy," she croaked. "Time. The time."

"Are you saying here in front of the council and everybody," the mayor sputtered, "that for two years you slept alone?" They buzzed and whispered and shook their heads.

Eva looked down at the plank floor. "Yes. Yes, I slept alone. I had no sex, but it wasn't my fault."

"And whose fault was it, Dr. Kelsey?" Conor rested both arms on the toprail of the spindle-backed chair.

"Yours, Conor," she shouted. "How could I ever, ever forget you? And how could I ever let another man touch me?"

The councilmen grinned and nudged each other and talked. Dimly, through the roar of her own blood in her ears, she heard their comments.

"Well, 'course, after Conor, what would you expect?"

"She got gumption to speak out."

"Good enough for me. He can catch her up."

"Two years' worth? Hell, that's a piece o'cake for Conor."

A chair crashed, and Conor was striding down the aisle, crushing her in his embrace, savaging her mouth. He swung her up into his arms, and spun to face the cheering council. Eva hid her blush in Conor's buckskin shirt.

"How say you, gentlemen?" the mayor hollered.

The room rang with ayes, and Conor whispered, "I love you."

He didn't have to kick the door open. Noah tipped his hat and obliged.

"Where are you taking me, Conor?" Eva murmured. She kissed his bronzed skin, inhaled his man-smell. "No. Don't tell me. I don't care."

Night fell, and in complex, shifting shadows fragmented by moonlight, Eva strolled hand-in-hand with Conor under the trees.

"Eva." He took her around her waist, sheltered her under his massive arm, and massaged her breast until the nipple begged for him. But she slipped out of his hold, stepped away.

"Even in the dark, I know what your eyes are revealing."

"And is that wrong, wanting you again?"

"My darling, this —" she touched the apex of her legs through her skirt "— this is raw and hot and sensitive. And full of you." She closed her eyes and concentrated on the creamy residue of their love. The lubrication, the blend of her female moisture and his come at once soothed her and stimulated her, made her want him again. Desperately. But not until...

"If you need a rest from me, don't talk like that," Conor teased. "Don't you know a man gets hard when a woman says she's raw and hot?" He sidled up and kissed her cheek. "Now, how was that for pure innocence?"

"Oh, Conor, look," Eva said breathily, "the ferns at night, so cool and beautiful." She brushed the fonds and stepped off the path. In the dappled moonglow, she exposed her mons and lured him. "I need to be kissed."

"Eva, baby." Conor came toward her, and she launched herself into his arms. He laughed, a great masculine bark, caught her, and, slightly off-balance, he staggered backward. Eva twisted and maneuvered him into the gripper tree. She skittered left, and stood just out of reach.

"Now, mister give-her-a taste-of-her-own-whip Conor, I've got you just where I want you." Triumphantly, she paraded around the tree.

"And where would that be?" Conor inquired.

"Helpless and at my mercy." She rubbed her hands together and tried not to gloat. "Now, if you have a hope of me setting you loose, raise your arms overhead, that's right, so all of you is stuck fast."

He made rocking motions, muscles bunching under his tunic. Finally, he leaned back, still. "So you've got me. What of it?" Conor's voice was cool and studied.

Eva detected a hint of a smile, his teeth white in the darkness. She tapped her chin and examined the captive. "Thought you were cute, did you, forcing me to admit I had no sex for two whole years because of you, how you turned me into a lust-crazed female. Oh, don't lie. I know you loved it, loved hearing me give a testimonial to your cocksmanship."

"I wish I could shrug my shoulders, Doc, but I can't, so I'll have to say it without the gesture. If you got it, flaunt it." He seemed oddly comfortable, and she couldn't tolerate it.

"Then flaunt this." Eva untied the flap over his groin, and gently lifted out his genitals.

"Don't, Eva." Conor tried for a conversational tone, but he delivered her name with a distinct note of pleasure.

"Of course, Conor. Anything you say, Conor." Busying both hands, she weighed his sac and smoothed the ridges of his fast-hardening cock. Slowly she played, ringing her thumb and index finger around it, announcing with fake surprise,

"Look, Conor. I can't make them meet. Will I have to tell that at the town meeting, too?" And then she knelt and lipped the thick round head.

Eva glanced up. Conor's jaw was clenched, and she couldn't see the dappled moonlight reflected in his eyes because he'd closed them.

He sucked air between his teeth and groaned. "Pull me free. Now, Eva."

Eva, her own flesh overheating, rose. On tip-toe, she lifted her skirt and brushed her nakedness on his nodding erection.

"So big, so hard. Do you wish you could drive it up me? Push it into me to the hilt and take me here under the moons?"

Her voice cracked with need, and her composure hovered on the verge of shattering, but Eva was determined to wring this last bit of revenge out of him. Then, when he was totally aroused, she'd work him loose from the gripper tree's clutches. If she could hold out that long herself.

"I think you'd like me to drop you here on the forest floor, on your hands and knees, lodge myself good and tight." From low in his guts, a tormented groan escaped, and he said, "Admit you're praying for me to take you from behind, reach around under your belly and tickle that bud you're dancing against me." He was panting. "Keep you bent over, speared on my cock, massage your breasts, drive you crazy. Would you like that, Eva?"

Frantic, her need boiling inside her, she clawed at his hide shirt. "I can't, I can't get you loose. Oh, Conor. Please."

"It's easy. See? I just walk away." And he did, laughing at her confusion, capturing her.

"But you were stuck. I saw you struggle," she managed between kisses. She arched into him and moaned.

Against her lips, he whispered, "You were having such a good time getting even, I didn't have the heart to disappoint you. But a gripper tree hangs onto things too weak to struggle. Are you listening? I love you Eva. Marry me." Masterfully, he kissed her until she gasped in an agony of wanting him, and her knees weakened.

"Don't lecture, Conor. Do me. I want you so bad I'm hurting. I need you deep in me."

Conor stripped her and himself, and they collapsed to the leafy forest floor. Eva, trembling with desire, rolled onto her hands and knees, and jutted her buttocks.

He licked and kneaded the firm globes, and teased her swollen vulva with the tip of his cock.

"Are you too weak to struggle, Eva?" he whispered before he was engulfed. In the silence, he mounted her and, losing all control, made the first thrust hard and deep like a stallion on a mare in heat.

Whimpering, Eva lowered herself onto her elbows, and rocked with his pounding surges. In her core, heated honey flowed, and taut nerves collected their energies for a colossal outburst. She began to moan his name in rhythm to his strokes, and when his blunt fingers pinched her clitoris, and she felt his juices spurt, she spasmed, and the only sound in the world was Conor's exultant shout.

Shivering in the aftermath, they lay together on the perfumed leaves. In the safe haven of his love, snuggled in his arms, she sighed contently. Conor slid a possessive hand over her breasts, her belly, and sleepily drew circles in her wet curls.

"I'll never get enough of you, sweet Eva," he confessed, "and like a human gripper tree, I'm damned glad you're too weak to struggle. Aren't you?"

Beneath two moons, the fragrance of alien trees washed over them, and a nightbird sang.

Eva, open and free and uninhibited, writhed under Conor's fingers. Just before she surrendered herself to his delicious attentions, before she became mindless with greedy lust, she imagined the shuttle from the Tarquin returning in a few months. The boarding door would open, and Leon would stick his head out.

And there she'd be, Eva Conor, handing over the cases, happily wearing a bonnet and a calico dress. Eva, minus breast cups and panties, the hot desert wind sneaking under her skirt, the tiny gusts fondling her, making her yearn for Conor's caress.

"About that question a while ago, Conor." She nuzzled at his throat, kissed a strand of his hair, and explored the ridges of his lean belly.

"I'm not too weak to struggle, darling. I'm too smart."

About the Author:

Sandy Fraser lives in Southern California where she grows old roses and new stories. Published in book-length women's fiction, she loves the opportunity to push the sensuality envelope and to tell the forbidden in **Secrets**.

Dear Reader,

We appreciate you taking the time out of your full and busy schedule to answer this questionnaire.

1. Rate the stories in **Secrets Volume 5** (1-10 Scale: 1=Worst, 10=Best)

	Alias Smith and Jones	Strictly Business	Insatiable	Beneath Two Moons
Rating				
Story Overall				
Sexual Intensity				
Sensuality				
Characters				
Setting				
Writing Skill				

2. What did you like *best* about **Secrets**? What did you like *least* about **Secrets**?

3. Would you buy other volumes?

4. In future **Secrets,** tell us how you would like your *heroine* and your *hero* to be. One or two words each are okay.

5. What is your idea of the ***perfect sensual romantic story***? Use more paper if you wish to add more than this space allows.

Thank you for taking the time to answer this questionnaire. We want to bring you the sensual stories you desire.

Sincerely,
Alexandria Kendall
Publisher

Mail to: Red Sage Publishing, Inc.
P.O. Box 4844
Seminole, FL 33775

If you enjoyed Secrets Volume 5 but haven't read other volumes, you should see what you're missing!

Volume 1:

In *A Lady's Quest*, author Bonnie Hamre brings you a London historical where Lady Antonia Blair-Sutworth searches for a lover in a most shocking and pleasing way.

Alice Gaines' *The Spinner's Dream* weaves a seductive fantasy that will leave every woman wishing for her own private love slave, desparate and running for his life.

Ivy Landon takes you for a wild ride. *The Proposal* will taunt you, tease you, even shock you. A contemporary erotica for the adventurous woman ultimate fantasy.

With *The Gift* by Jeanie LeGendre, you're immersed in the historic tale of exoctic seduction and bondage. Read about a concubine's delicious surrender to her Sultan.

Volume 2:

Surrogate Lover, by Doreen DeSalvo, is a contemporary tale of lust and love in the 90's. A surrogate sex therapist thought he had all the answers until he met Sarah.

Bonnie Hamre's regency tale *Snowbound* delights as the Earl of Howden is teased and tortured by his own desires—finally a woman who equals his overpowering sensuality.

In *Roarke's Prisoner*, by Angela Knight, starship captain Elise remembers the eager animal submission she'd known before at her captor's hands and refuses to be his toy again.

Susan Paul's *Savage Garden* tells the story of Raine's capture by a mysterious revolutionary in Mexico. She quickly finds lush erotic nights in her captor's arms.

Volume 3:

In Jeanie Cesarini's *The Spy Who Loved Me*, FBI agents Paige Ellison and Christopher Sharp discover excitement and passion in some unusual undercover work.

Warning: This story is only for the most adventurous of readers. Ann Jacobs tells the story of *The Barbarian*. Giles has a sexual aresenal designed to break down proud Lady Brianna's defenses — erotic pleasures learned in a harem.

Wild, sexual hunger is unleashed in this futuristic vampire tale with a twist. In Angela Knight's *Blood and Kisses*, find out just who is seducing who?

B.J. McCall takes you into the erotic world of strip joints in *Love Undercover*. On assignment, Lt. Amada Forbes and Det. "Cowboy" Cooper find temptation hard to resist.

Volume 4:

An Act of Love is Jeanie Cesarini's sequel. Shelby's terrified of sex. Film star Jason Gage must coach her in the ways of love. He wants her to feel true passion in his arms.

The Love Slave, by Emma Holly, is a woman's ultimate fantasy. For one year, Princess Lily will be attended to by three delicious men. She delights in playing with the first two, but it's the reluctant Grae that stirs her desires.

Lady Crystal is in turmoil in *Enslaved*, by Desirée Lindsey. Lord Nicholas' dark passions and irresistible charm have brought her long-hidden desires to the surface.

Betsy Morgan and Susan Paul bring you Kaki York's story in *The Bodyguard*. Watching the wild, erotic romps of her client's sexual conquests on the security cameras is getting to her — and her partner, the ruggedly handsome James Kulick.

Volume 6:

Sandy Fraser is back with *Flint's Fuse*. Dana Madison's father has her "kidnapped" for her own safety. Flint, the tall, dark and dangerousmercenary, is hired for the job. But just which one is the prisoner — Dana will try *anything* to get away.

In *Love's Prisoner*, by MaryJanice Davidson, Jeannie Lawrence experienced unwilling rapture at Michael Windham's hands. She never expected the devilishly handsome man to show back up in her life — or turn out to be a werewolf!

Alice Gaines' *The Education of Miss Felicity Wells* finds a pupil needing to learn how to satisfy her soon-to-be husband. Dr. Marcus Slade, an experienced lover, agrees to take her on as a student, but can he stop short of taking her completely?

Angela Knight tells another spicy tale. On the trail of a story, reporter Dana Ivory stumbles onto a secret—a sexy, secret agent who happens to be a vampire.She wants her story but Gabriel Archer believes she's *A Candidate for the Kiss*.

Volume 7:

In *Amelia's Innocence* by Julia Welles, Amelia didn't know her father bet her in a card game with Captain Quentin Hawke, so honor demands a compromise — three days of erotic foreplay, leaving her virginity and future intact.

Jade Lawless brings *The Woman of His Dreams* to life. Artist Gray Avonaco moved in next door to Joanna Morgan and now is plagued by provocative dreams. Is it unrequited lust or Gray's chance to be with the woman he loves?

Surrender by Kathryn Anne Dubois tells of Free-spirited Lady Johanna. She wants no part of the binding strictures of marriage to the powerful Duke. But she doesn't realize the Duke wants sensual adventure, and sexual satisfaction.

Volume 8:

Jeanie Cesarini tells the story of Kathryn Roman. She inherits a legal brothel but refuses to trade her high-powered career in Manhattan for a life in the wild, wild west. Little does this city girl know the town of Love, Nevada wants her to be their new madam so theyíve charged Trey Holliday, one very dominant cowboy, with *Taming Kate*.

In *Jaredís Wolf*, by MaryJanice Davidson, Jared Rocke will do anything avenge his sisterís death, even believe in werewolves. What he doesnít believe is that heís attracted to Moira Wolfbauer, the she-wolf sworn to protect her pack. Two enemies must join forces to stop a killer while learning that love defies all boundaries — even those between species.

My Champion, My Love, by Alice Gaines, tells the tale of Celeste Broder, a woman committed for a sexy appetite that is tolerated in the men, but not the women of her time. She desperately needs a champion, and finds one in mayor Robert Albright. *If* she can convince him her freedom will mean a chance to indulge their appetites together.

Liz Maverick debuts in **Secrets** with *Kiss or Kill*. In this post apocalyptic world, Camille Kazinskyís military career rides on her ability to make a choice—whether the robo called Meat should live or die. Meat's future depends on proving heís human enough to live, *man* enough... What should Camille do with this man/machine that makes her feel like a woman?

Men you've been dreaming about!

Secrets

Satisfy your desire for more.

*F*eel the wild adventure, fierce passion and the power of love in every **Secrets** Collection story. Red Sage Publishing's romance authors create richly crafted, sexy, sensual, novella-length stories. Each one is just the right length for reading after a long and hectic day.

Each volume in the **Secrets** Collection has four diverse, ultra-sexy, romantic novellas brimming with adventure, passion and love. More adventurous tales for the adventurous reader. The **Secrets** Collection are a glorious mix of romance genre; numerous historical settings, contemporary, paranormal, science fiction and suspense. We are always looking for new adventures.

Reader response to the **Secrets** volumes has been great! Here's just a small sample:

"I loved the variety of settings. Four completely wonderful time periods, give you four completely wonderful reads."

"Each story was a page-turning tale I hated to put down."

*"I love **Secrets**! When is the next volume coming out? This one was Hot! Loved the heroes!"*

Secrets have won raves and awards. We could go on, but why don't you find out for yourself — order your set of **Secrets** today! See the back for details.

Secrets, Volume 1

Listen to what reviewers say:

"These stories take you beyond romance into the realm of erotica. I found *Secrets* absolutely delicious."

—Virginia Henley,
New York Times Best Selling Author

"*Secrets* is a collection of novellas for the daring, adventurous woman who's not afraid to give her fantasies free reign."

—Kathe Robin, *Romantic Times* Magazine

"...In fact, the men featured in all the stories are terrific, they all want to please and pleasure their women. If you like erotic romance you will love *Secrets*."

—*Romantic Readers* Review

In *Secrets, Volume 1* you'll find:

A Lady's Quest by Bonnie Hamre

Widowed Lady Antonia Blair-Sutworth searches for a lover to save her from the handsome Duke of Sutherland. The "auditions" may be shocking but utterly tantalizing.

The Spinner's Dream by Alice Gaines

A seductive fantasy that leaves every woman wishing for her own private love slave, desperate and running for his life.

The Proposal by Ivy Landon

This tale is a walk on the wild side of love. *The Proposal* will taunt you, tease you, and shock you. A contemporary erotica for the adventurous woman.

The Gift by Jeanie LeGendre

Immerse yourself in this historic tale of exotic seduction, bondage and of a concubine's surrender to the Sultan's desire. Can Alessandra live the life and give the gift the Sultan demands of her?

Secrets, Volume 2

Listen to what reviewers say:

"*Secrets* offer four novellas of sensual delight; each beautifully written with intense feeling and dedication to character development. For those seeking stories with heightened intimacy, look no further."

—Kathee Card, *Romancing the Web*

"Such a welcome diversity in styles and genres. Rich characterization in sensual tales. An exciting read that's sure to titillate the senses."

—Cheryl Ann Porter

"*Secrets 2* left me breathless. Sensual satisfaction guaranteed…times four!"

—Virginia Henley, *New York Times* Best Selling Author

In *Secrets, Volume 2* you'll find:

Surrogate Lover by Doreen DeSalvo
Adrian Ross is a surrogate sex therapist who has all the answers and control. He thought he'd seen and done it all, but he'd never met Sarah.

Snowbound by Bonnie Hamre
A delicious, sensuous regency tale. The marriage-shy Earl of Howden is teased and tortured by his own desires and finds there is a woman who can equal his overpowering sensuality.

Roarke's Prisoner by Angela Knight
Elise, a starship captain, remembers the eager animal submission she'd known before at her captor's hands and refuses to become his toy again. However, she has no idea of the delights he's planned for her this time.

Savage Garden by Susan Paul
Raine's been captured by a mysterious and dangerous revolutionary leader in Mexico. At first her only concern is survival, but she quickly finds lush erotic nights in her captor's arms.

Winner of the Fallot Literary Award for Fiction!

Secrets, Volume 3

Listen to what reviewers say:

"*Secrets, Volume 3* leaves the reader breathless. A delicious confection of sensuous treats awaits the reader on each turn of the page!"
— Kathee Card, *Romancing the Web*

"From the FBI to Police Dectective to Vampires to a Medieval Warlord home from the Crusade — *Secrets 3* is simply the best!"
— Susan Paul, award winning author

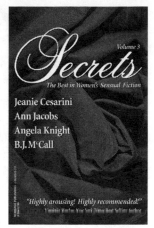

"An unabashed celebration of sex. Highly arousing! Highly recommended!"
—Virginia Henley, *New York Times* Best Selling Author

In *Secrets, Volume 3* you'll find:

The Spy Who Loved Me by Jeanie Cesarini
Undercover FBI agent Paige Ellison's sexual appetites rise to new levels when she works with leading man Christopher Sharp, the cunning agent who uses all his training to capture her body and heart.

The Barbarian by Ann Jacobs
Lady Brianna vows not to surrender to the barbaric Giles, Earl of Harrow. He must use sexual arts learned in the infidels' harem to conquer his bride. A word of caution — this is not for the faint of heart.

Blood and Kisses by Angela Knight
A vampire assassin is after Beryl St. Cloud. Her only hope lies with Decker, another vampire and ex-mercenary. Broke, she offers herself as payment for his services. Will his seductive powers take her very soul?

Love Undercover by B.J. McCall
Amanda Forbes is the bait in a strip joint sting operation. While she performs, fellow detective "Cowboy" Cooper gets to watch. Though he excites her, she must fight the temptation to surrender to the passion.

Winner of the 1997 Under the Covers Readers Favorite Award

Secrets, Volume 4

Listen to what reviewers say:

"Provocative…seductive…a must read!"
— *Romantic Times* Magazine

"These are the kind of stories that romance readers that 'want a little more' have been looking for all their lives…."
— *Affaire de Coeur* Magazine

"*Secrets, Volume 4* has something to satisfy every erotic fantasy… simply sexational!"
—Virginia Henley, *New York Times* Best Selling Author

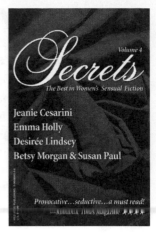

In *Secrets, Volume 4* you'll find:

An Act of Love by Jeanie Cesarini
Shelby Moran's past left her terrified of sex. International film star Jason Gage must gently coach the young starlet in the ways of love. He wants more than an act — he wants Shelby to feel true passion in his arms.

Enslaved by Desirée Lindsey
Lord Nicholas Summer's air of danger, dark passions, and irresistible charm have brought Lady Crystal's long-hidden desires to the surface. Will he be able to give her the one thing she desires before it's too late?

The Bodyguard by Betsy Morgan and Susan Paul
Kaki York is a bodyguard, but watching the wild, erotic romps of her client's sexual conquests on the security cameras is getting to her — and her partner, the ruggedly handsome James Kulick. Can she resist his insistent desire to have her?

The Love Slave by Emma Holly
A woman's ultimate fantasy. For one year, Princess Lily will be attended to by three delicious men of her choice. While she delights in playing with the first two, it's the reluctant Grae, with his powerful chest, black eyes and hair, that stirs her desires.

Secrets, Volume 5

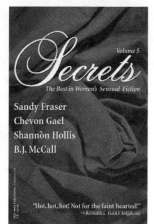

Listen to what reviewers say:

"Hot, hot, hot! Not for the faint-hearted!"
— *Romantic Times* Magazine

"As you make your way through the stories, you will find yourself becoming hotter and hotter. *Secrets* just keeps getting better and better."
— *Affaire de Coeur* Magazine

"*Secrets 5* is a collage of lucious sensuality. Any woman who reads *Secrets* is in for an awakening!"
—Virginia Henley, *New York Times* Best Selling Author

In *Secrets, Volume 5* you'll find:

Beneath Two Moons by Sandy Fraser
Ready for a very wild romp? Step into the future and find Conor, rough and masculine like frontiermen of old, on the prowl for a new conquest. In his sights, Dr. Eva Kelsey. She got away once before, but this time Conor makes sure she begs for more.

Insatiable by Chevon Gael
Marcus Remington photographs beautiful models for a living, but it's Ashlyn Fraser, a young corporate exec having some glamour shots done, who has stolen his heart. It's up to Marcus to help her discover her inner sexual self.

Strictly Business by Shannon Hollis
Elizabeth Forrester knows it's tough enough for a woman to make it to the top in the corporate world. Garrett Hill, the most beautiful man in Silicon Valley, has to come along to stir up her wildest fantasies. Dare she give in to both their desires?

Alias Smith and Jones by B.J. McCall
Meredith Collins finds herself stranded overnight at the airport. A handsome stranger by the name of Smith offers her sanctuaty for the evening and she finds those mesmerizing, green-flecked eyes hard to resist. Are they to be just two ships passing in the night?

Secrets, Volume 6

Listen to what reviewers say:

"Red Sage was the first and remains the leader of Women's Erotic Romance Fiction Collections!"

— *Romantic Times* Magazine

"*Secrets Volume 6* is the best of *Secrets* yet. ...four of the most erotic stories in one volume than this reader has yet to see anywhere else ...These stories are full of erotica at its best and you'll definitely want to keep it handy for lots of re-reading!"

— *Affaire de Coeur* Magazine

"*Secrets 6* satisfies every female fantasy: the Bodyguard, the Tutor, the Werewolf, and the Vampire. I give it Six Stars!"

—Virginia Henley, *New York Times* Best Selling Author

In *Secrets, Volume 6* you'll find:

Flint's Fuse by Sandy Fraser

Dana Madison's father has her "kidnapped" for her own safety. Flint, the tall, dark and dangerous mercenary, is hired for the job. But just which one is the prisoner — Dana will try *anything* to get away.

Love's Prisoner by MaryJanice Davidson

Trapped in an elevator, Jeannie Lawrence experienced unwilling rapture at Michael Windham's hands. She never expected the devilishly handsome man to show back up in her life — or turn out to be a werewolf!

The Education of Miss Felicity Wells by Alice Gaines

Felicity Wells wants to be sure she'll satisfy her soon-to-be husband but she needs a teacher. Dr. Marcus Slade, an experienced lover, agrees to take her on as a student, but can he stop short of taking her completely?

A Candidate for the Kiss by Angela Knight

Working on a story, reporter Dana Ivory stumbles onto a more amazing one — a sexy, secret agent who happens to be a vampire.She wants her story but Gabriel Archer wants more from her than just sex and blood.

Secrets, Volume 7

Listen to what reviewers say:

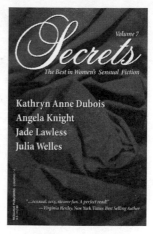

"Get out your asbestos gloves — *Secrets Volume 7* is...extremely hot, true erotic romance...passionate and titillating. There's nothing quite like baring your secrets!"
— *Romantic Times* Magazine

"...sensual, sexy, steamy fun. A perfect read!"
—Virginia Henley,
New York Times Best Selling Author

"Intensely provocative and disarmingly romantic, **Secrets Volume 7** is a romance reader's paradise that will take you beyond your wildest dreams!"
— Ballston Book House Review

In **Secrets, Volume 7** you'll find:

Amelia's Innocence by Julia Welles
Amelia didn't know her father bet her in a card game with Captain Quentin Hawke, so honor demands a compromise — three days of erotic foreplay, leaving her virginity and future intact.

The Woman of His Dreams by Jade Lawless
From the day artist Gray Avonaco moves in next door, Joanna Morgan is plagued by provocative dreams. But what she believes is unrequited lust, Gray sees as another chance to be with the woman he loves. He must persuade her that even death can't stop true love.

Surrender by Kathryn Anne Dubois
Free-spirited Lady Johanna wants no part of the binding strictures society imposes with her marriage to the powerful Duke. She doesn't know the dark Duke wants sensual adventure, and sexual satisfaction.

Kissing the Hunter by Angela Knight
Navy Seal Logan McLean hunts the vampires who murdered his wife. Virginia Hart is a sexy vampire searching for her lost soul-mate only to find him in a man determined to kill her. She must convince him all vampires aren't created equally.

Secrets, Volume 8

Listen to what reviewers say:

"*Secrets Volume 8* is an amazing compilation of sexy stories covering a wide range of subjects, all designed to titillate the senses. …you'll find something for everybody in this latest version of *Secrets*."

— *Affaire de Coeur* Magazine

"These delectable stories will have you turning the pages long into the night. Passionate, provocative and perfect for setting the mood…."

Escape to Romance Reviews

"*Secrets Volume 8*, is simply sensational!"

—Virginia Henley, *New York Times* Best Selling Author

In *Secrets, Volume 8* you'll find:

Taming Kate by Jeanie Cesarini
Kathryn Roman inherits a legal brothel. Little does this city girl know the town of Love, Nevada wants her to be their new madam so they've charged Trey Holliday, one very dominant cowboy, with taming her.

Jared's Wolf by MaryJanice Davidson
Jared Rocke will do anything avenge his sister's death, but ends up attracted to Moira Wolfbauer, the she-wolf sworn to protect her pack. Joining forces to stop a killer, they learn love defies all boundaries.

My Champion, My Lover by Alice Gaines
Celeste Broder is a woman committed for having a sexy appetite. Mayor Robert Albright may be her champion—if she can convince him her freedom will mean a chance to indulge their appetites together.

Kiss or Kill by Liz Maverick
In this post-apocalyptic world, Camille Kazinsky's military career rides on her ability to make a choice—whether the robo called Meat should live or die. Meat's future depends on proving he's human enough to live, man enough…to makes her feel like a woman.

It's not just reviewers raving about *Secrets*. See what readers have to say:

"When are you coming out with a new Volume? I want a new one next month!" via email from a reader.

"I loved the hot, wet sex without vulgar words being used to make it exciting." after *Volume 1*

"I loved the blend of sensuality and sexual intensity — HOT!" after *Volume 2*

"The best thing about *Secrets* is they're hot and brief! The least thing is you do not have enough of them!" after *Volume 3*

"I have been extreamly satisfied with *Secrets*, keep up the good writing." after *Volume 4*

"I love the sensuality and sex that is not normally written about or explored in a really romantic context" after *Volume 4*

"Loved it all!!!" after *Volume 5*

"I love the tastful, hot way that *Secrets* pushes the edge. The genre mix is cool, too." after *Volume 5*

"Stories have plot and characters to support the erotica. They would be good strong stories without the heat." after *Volume 5*

"*Secrets* really knows how to push the envelop better than anyone else." after *Volume 6*

"*Secrets*, there is nothing not to like. This is the top banana, so to speak." after *Volume 6*

"'Would you buy *Volume 7*?' YES!!! Inform me ASAP and I am so there!!" after *Volume 6*

"Can I please, please, please pre-order *Volume 7*? I want to be the first to get it of my friends. They don't have email so they can't write you! I can!" after *Volume 6*

Finally, the men you've been dreaming about!

Give the Gift of Spicy Romantic Fiction

Don't want to wait? You can place a retail price ($12.99) order for any of the *Secrets* volumes from the following:

① **Waldenbooks Stores**

② **Amazon.com** or **BarnesandNoble.com**

③ **Book Clearinghouse (800-431-1579)**

④ **Romantic Times Magazine**
Books by Mail (718-237-1097)

⑤ Special order at other bookstores.
Bookstores: Please contact Baker & Taylor Distributors or Red Sage Publishing for bookstore sales.

Order by title or ISBN #:

Vol. 1: 0-9648942-0-3

Vol. 2: 0-9648942-1-1

Vol. 3: 0-9648942-2-X

Vol. 4: 0-9648942-4-6

Vol. 5: 0-9648942-5-4

Vol. 6: 0-9648942-6-2

Vol. 7: 0-9648942-7-0

Vol. 8: 0-9648942-8-9

Secrets Mail Order Form:

(Orders shipped in two to three days of receipt.)

	Quantity	Mail Order Price	Total
Secrets Volume 1 *(Retail $12.99)*	_____	$ 8.99	_____
Secrets Volume 2 *(Retail $12.99)*	_____	$ 8.99	_____
Secrets Volume 3 *(Retail $12.99)*	_____	$ 8.99	_____
Secrets Volume 4 *(Retail $12.99)*	_____	$ 8.99	_____
Secrets Volume 5 *(Retail $12.99)*	_____	$ 8.99	_____
Secrets Volume 6 *(Retail $12.99)*	_____	$ 8.99	_____
Secrets Volume 7 *(Retail $12.99)*	_____	$ 8.99	_____
Secrets Volume 8 *(Retail $12.99)*	_____	$ 8.99	_____

Shipping & handling (in the U.S.)

US Priority Mail
1–2 books .... $ 5.50
3–5 books .... $ 8.50
6–8 books .... $11.50   _____   _____

UPS insured
1–4 books $15.00
5–8 books .... $22.00   _____   _____

SUBTOTAL   _____

Florida 6% sales tax (if delivered in FL)   _____

TOTAL AMOUNT ENCLOSED   _____

Name: (please print) _____

Address: (no P.O. Boxes) _____

City/State/Zip: _____

Phone or email: (only regarding order if necessary) _____

Please make check payable to **Red Sage Publishing**. Check must be drawn on a U.S. bank in U.S. dollars. Mail your check and order form to:

Red Sage Publishing, Inc.   Department S8   P.O. Box 4844   Seminole, FL 33775

Or use the order form on our website: www.redsagepub.com